'Ann Aguirre proves h[...]
and altogether wonde[...]
delicious. I can't wait to see w[...]
New York Times bestselling author Patricia Biggs

'An authentic Southwestern-flavored feast, filled with magic,
revenge, and romance, spiced with memorable characters
and page-turning action. *¡Muy caliente!*'
New York Times bestselling author Rachel Caine

'Rising star Aguirre moves from outer space to the Southwest
in this new first-person series. Corine Solomon peers into a
dark world filled with ghosts, demons and sorcerers. With
murder, magic and romance, this is an enticingly dangerous
journey. Don't miss out!'
Romantic Times

'Corine has a great narrative voice – snappy and full of
interesting observations on everything around her . . .
Blue Diablo is fast-paced and entertaining'
Charles de Lint, *Fantasy and Science Fiction*

'Ms. Aguirre plunges readers into a fast-paced tale where
her human characters are enhanced by their extraordinary
gifts. *Blue Diablo* delivers a strong start to the series with a
well-defined heroine, intriguing paranormal elements,
and an emotion-filled romance'
Darque Reviews

A CORINE SOLOMON NOVEL

Blue Diablo

Ann Aguirre

The right of Ann Aguirre to be identified as the author of this work
has been asserted by her in accordance with the
Copyright, Designs and Patents Act 1988.

First published in Great Britain in 2010 by
Gollancz
An imprint of the Orion Publishing Group
Orion House, 5 Upper St Martin's Lane, London WC2H 9EA
An Hachette UK Company

1 3 5 7 9 10 8 6 4 2

A CIP catalogue record for this book is available
from the British Library

ISBN 978 0 575 09397 3

Printed in Great Britain by Clays Ltd, St Ives plc

www.annaguirre.com
www.orionbooks.co.uk

The Orion Publishing Group's policy is to use papers that are
natural, renewable and recyclable products and made from wood
grown in sustainable forests. The logging and manufacturing
processes are expected to conform to the environmental regulations
of the country of origin.

For Ivette, who is seven flavors of awesome cake . . .
with sprinkles.
I'm lucky to have a friend like you.
(Andres said this dedication is totally cool with him.)

Chance Met

Right now, I'm a redhead.

I've been blond and brunette as the situation requires, though an unscheduled color change usually means I need to relocate in the middle of the night or face people burning crosses on my lawn. I've set a new record, going on eighteen months in the same city. No consequences, no demonstrations, and for the last year, I've been a respectable business owner to boot. Maybe I should knock wood.

So I do.

But right now, a redhead. I tell myself it goes with the blue eyes, even if my skin is a little too olive for the carpet to match the drapes. And sure, I get a few looks because it's a true red, Garnier Nutrisse 46R to be exact, not the plum that most women here favor, but I may as well please myself because I will never, ever blend in entirely. The best I can do is to make sure nobody reckons me any crazier than anyone else.

Around here they call me *la Americana loca*, but I figure it's affectionate, as it doesn't stop them from coming to my shop. Unlike many of the open-air *tiendas*, I have a front door and a bell that chimes softly when anyone enters my domain, a dim and shady store piled high with junk or treasure, depending on your definition.

I have handmade pots and broken radios, alleged religious artifacts and rare books in sixteen languages.

A ceiling fan stirs sluggishly overhead, but it never gets hot inside. The buildings are heavy, solid rock covered with plaster, so it's cool and shady when the mercury rises and even the lizards are too lazy to move. Sometimes people step in, wanting a break from the sun or to get out of the deluge during rainy season, but they never leave without buying something. That's part of my unique gift (and why I always work in retail). At one point I sold furniture on commission but it just wasn't fair—fish in a barrel.

Ostensibly, I run a pawn shop marked by a simple red and white sign that reads CASA DE EMPEÑO, but anyone who lives in Los Remedios along the road to Atizapán will tell you it's more. They'll also offer you a fuchsia candy tortilla at the stoplight just before you come to my store; it's the intersection where a man with a mime's face juggles fire and a monkeyless organ-grinder plies his trade dispiritedly (how he lost the monkey is another story). Don't eat the tortilla, don't tip more than twenty pesos, and make a left turn. You'll find me, if you really need to.

I'm an expert at staying hidden. More than once, it's been the difference between life and death, so I live lean and keep my head down. So far as I know, I'm doing well here. Nobody knows what I'm running from.

And I'd like to keep it that way.

Unfortunately, our pasts have a way of coming back, time and again, just like our shadows. Oh, there are ways to sever your shadow, and I know a guy who did, but it was a really bad idea. He took sick afterward, died the slow death of a consumptive, and last I heard, his shadow was making a killing in Atlantic City. Literally.

These are dark times, and I just want a quiet place to ride them out.

Unfortunately, things never seem to work out the way I want them to.

My first inkling that I hadn't covered my tracks completely came on a sunny Monday afternoon. I was sitting behind the glass case in my shop, eyeballing a pair of hand-painted porcelain miniatures I'd bought for two hundred pesos maybe twenty minutes before. Nice, they looked Dutch, and some tourist would buy them by next Friday.

Foretelling isn't really my thing—well, only as an adjunct to my real gift and only as relates to the object I'm handling. When I touch something, I know what's happened to an item, who's owned it, and to a lesser extent, what will happen to it in the future, although that's less sure, as any diviner could tell you. Such prediction isn't much use, unless you're breathless with wondering about the fate of hand-painted Dutch miniatures. Most people aren't.

History, though . . . yeah, therein lies the magick. And the reason folks never stop trying to find me. *If this could talk*, people say dreamily, peering at a piece of antique jewelry. In truth it's generally pretty boring; the item gets worn, and then it goes in a box. Repeat. But once in a while, once in a while an item passes across my palms with a real story to tell.

And that's where the trouble starts.

Trouble smells like singed horsehair. I'll never get past that. When I was ten, my pony died when our barn was burned down, and I'll never forget the way Sugar screamed. That was my first look at an angry mob, but not my last. If you think they don't burn witches anymore, you never lived in Kilmer, Georgia.

And that's the damnedest thing; those same folks will come creeping after dark to your back door, one by one, begging for the moon, but get them together, talking, and they start lighting torches. Not the whole town, of course, but a select few who come in midnight's dark to do their devil's work. They said it was for the greater good, but I saw their eyes before I ran.

To this day, when life is about to get rocky, I smell the burning all over again, one of two legacies my mama left me. And on that Monday, the shop stunk to high heaven as someone pushed through the door, jingling the bell. I put down the miniatures, already braced to make a break for the door off the alley.

But I didn't want to leave, dammit. Thanks to the second gift my mama gave me, I made a good living here and sometimes I even went out on Saturday nights. Nobody brought me tiny pierced earrings from dead babies or soiled mittens from missing children. Nobody expected me to do anything at all, and that was exactly how I liked it.

I don't know my ex's real name. He first introduced himself as Chance; he claims he came by the tag from the silver coin he likes to toy with, rolling it across his knuckles, tossing it for a hundred and coming up tails every time. I'd pumped his mother for information, more than once, but she had a way of changing the subject that was downright uncanny. The most I ever got out of her was, "It would be dangerous if you knew his true name, Corine."

Regardless, his presence in my humble shop in Los Remedios, two thousand miles from where I'd seen him last, could mean nothing good.

"You're a hard woman to find," he said, leaning up on my counter as if he thought I'd be glad to see him. "I could almost be hurt by that, Corine."

Well, I couldn't really argue, as I'd left him sleeping in my bed when I took flight. "What're you doing here?"

"I need you to handle something for me, just one job. I wouldn't have come if it wasn't important." Pleading, he fixed striated amber eyes on me, knowing I was a sucker for that look.

Or I used to be. I wasn't anymore.

Chance wasn't my manager any longer. Or my lover, for that matter. I didn't want to handle charged objects, didn't want to tell people their loved one had been stran-gled while wearing that sweater. I didn't want to *do* that anymore.

We had a hell of a run, him and me. For as many be-reaved families as we helped, we encountered neo-pagan witches, truck-driving mediums, guys who sold genuine lucky charms out of the trunks of their cars, and folks who simply defied description with what they could do and why they did it. Sometimes I felt like we might've even brushed up against angels and demons, slipping by beneath the hot velvet of a summer night.

Chance had a way of ferreting out the weird and the improbable as if his inner compass focused on such things, quivered with unseen divinations. And he looked beautiful while doing it.

My heart gave a little kick. After all this time, he still had the power to make my pulse skip. Some genius ge-netics had gone into Chance's making: long and lean, a chiseled face with a vaguely Asian look, capped by un-canny tiger eyes and a mouth that could tempt a holy sister to sin. I wondered if he'd felt the last kiss I brushed against that mouth, eighteen months ago. I wondered whether he'd missed me or just the revenue.

To make matters worse, he knew how to dress, and today he wore Kenneth Cole extremely well: crinkle-washed shirt in Italian cotton, jet with a muted silver stripe, dusty black button-fly jeans, polished shoes, and a black velvet blazer. I didn't need his sartorial elegance to remind me I'd gone native, a sheer gauze blouse with crimson embroidery around the neck and a parti-colored skirt. I was even wearing flip-flops. They had a big red silk hibiscus on each toe, but were flip-flops nonetheless. It was amazing he could look at me with a straight face.

But then, he'd been raised well. His mom, Yi Min-chin, was a nice lady who made great kimchi, but he'd never say who his daddy was, claiming such knowledge granted too much power over him. And his mother went along with it. I figured it was just more of his bullshit, but with Chance, you never could be sure. He had the devil's own luck, and I wouldn't be a bit surprised if Lucifer himself someday came to claim him.

"It's never just one job with you," I said with a trace of bitterness. "I'm a show pony to you, and you never get tired of putting me through my paces. I am *out* of the life now. Retired. Get it? Now get out, and if you ever felt anything for me, don't tell anybody where I am." I hated the way my tone turned pleading at the end.

I'd built this life. I didn't want to have to parlay to keep it.

Without a word, he flattened his palm on the top of the glass case that housed my rare treasures. When he lifted his hand, I expected to see his coin because the item glinted silver. But as I leaned in, I saw something that sent snakes disco dancing in my belly.

Because it meant I had to help him.

The Pewter Buddha

Hard to believe such a small item could cause me so much trouble.

I stared at it for a long moment, willing it to disappear, but like Chance, it wouldn't. Not until I handled it and followed the trail to its source. The last time I saw this little pewter pocket Buddha, it had been cupped in Yi Min-chin's hand.

It wasn't valuable—such things sold for around two bucks—but his mother rubbed it for luck or when she was nervous, and it had never been out of her possession before to the best of my knowledge. The fact that it lay on my counter . . .

Well, I understood Chance's expression a whole lot better now.

"Tell me what you know." I still didn't touch it, but he knew my acquiescence was a foregone conclusion. Over the course of our benighted relationship, I came to love his mom more than I ever loved him.

Sometimes I missed him; sometimes I hated him. I hadn't thought I'd see him again. My life tends to run by chapters, and when I close one, there are no recurring characters, mainly because they lie beneath six feet of cold dirt. So I suppose Chance did well enough with me; he was still breathing when I left him.

While he seemed to gather his thoughts, I knelt and fished from the minifridge a couple of old-fashioned Cokes, the kind that come in bottles that remind you of a sexy woman's figure. Because I was shaken, the Cokes managed to feed me glimpses of the manufacturing plant and the truck that carried them to the store, the sweaty man with a comb-over who stocked them on the cooler shelf before I bought them.

Focusing my will, I shut it down, a TV show nobody's watching. I have to choose to read something, or I'd be bombarded with images all day long; it takes pure focus born of necessity and habit to keep my gift in check. The more traumatic of a charge an item holds, the worse it is. I had a feeling that whatever his mother's Buddha held would be bad.

As if even my soda pop felt nervous about my situation, the glass bottle immediately began to sweat. I set the drinks down and found a bottle opener.

"I was tracking you." His voice carried a bare-bones quality, like it was all he could do to keep from showing me how deep he was cut.

"How'd you find me?" I thought I'd been so careful, honest to God.

His smile flickered in time to the tumble of his silver coin along the knuckles of his right hand. Fully ambidextrous, he could do it with his left as well, but I wasn't interested in his parlor tricks. At one time or another I'd seen them all, and I missed only the wicked thing he did with his tongue.

"Luck," he said, as if it could've been anything else. "I showed your picture, and a car rental agent in Shreveport remembered you. She looked up where you dropped the car off for me."

Well, naturally she did. She'd probably have volunteered a kidney and her firstborn if he'd only thought to ask. I hadn't used my real name or any of the aliases

Chance knew, but that clearly hadn't slowed him down much.

"So you knew I returned the car in Laredo."

He nodded, eyes fixed on the pewter icon still lying untouched on my counter. "Didn't take too much to figure you must've made the border crossing. Then I just had to figure out where you went from Monterrey."

And that would've been child's play, based on how well he knew me. I fought down the dead man's hand creeping up my back, trying to consider the question with a cool head. If he found me, could someone else? Someone who meant more harm than Chance?

Right now I couldn't let myself think about that.

"How does your mom figure into this?" Wow, I sounded remote.

"She went missing in Laredo," he answered, his tone dull like the pewter of her pocket Buddha. "The police have no leads and I . . . I swear to God, Corine, before this happened, I had no intention of looking you up. I just . . . I wanted closure. I wanted to know where you were, wanted to be sure you were okay."

Oddly, I believed him. He hated uncertainty, hated not being in control, so my taking off must have ruffled him some. So he needed to find me. If he chose not to see me thereafter, that was his call. To Chance's mind, having power and not exercising it was far different than being left in the dark. Frankly, it surprised me that it took him this long to give in to the urge to search.

Maybe, just maybe, once upon a time, I had been disappointed not to find him hot on my heels. Sometimes a woman runs because she wants to be chased. But I was over all that. And him. Right now, I just wanted to find the fastest way to make him disappear.

One thing puzzled me. "What was she doing in Texas?"

"She came out to meet me. Closed up the store in

Tampa and called it a vacation." I heard the guilt lacing his voice like strychnine tea, smooth on top but razors going down, and I felt mildly disgusted with myself for wanting to comfort him.

To distract myself from disastrous impulses, I cracked open the two drinks. The Coke bottles sat in water rings that I smeared idly with a fingertip. He took his and drained half the soda in one go. My hormones clamored; why couldn't I stop watching his brown throat work as he swallowed?

"Is this going to be bad?" I looked at the pewter Buddha like it was a coiled rattler.

He exhaled, the sound of someone letting the air out of a tire real slow. "Maybe. I'm as afraid of what you'll find as you are."

That made sense. Nobody wants to receive bad news any more than I want to deliver it. Goddammit, I thought I was done with this for good. Bracing myself, I reached for the token before I could think better of it. It burned a little before it kicked in and I felt the pain on my palm where the metal blistered my skin.

You see, my gift springs from my mother's sacrifice, dying for me in the fire, and every use of it carries me back to that night. But I didn't let go. I accepted the price and let the vision come.

Fear subsumed me, bolstered by the resolve of a woman who made the better of two bad choices, a woman walking with a lesser devil. She definitely went of her own free will, though. No force, no physical coercion. But there's no sound track; I can't hear what's been said; I just feel what they feel, see what they see.

Details were fuzzy, like I was looking through a dirty lens, but beyond the door, I saw a white truck parked. On the side it read Something Sanitation or maybe Salvation. My head throbbed, almost overwhelming the pain in my palm. Holding on, I watched while the pewter Buddha slipped from her fingers, bounced twice, where it lay until Chance found it.

Done.

The token clattered to the glass countertop as I let go and wrapped my wounded hand around my Coke bottle. It took a minute before the nausea subsided enough for me to speak, but I got it out in fits and starts, knees threatening to give and let me fall to the floor. Not the most horrific handling, but the mystery of Yi Min-chin reminded me of trees that grow in bayou country, miles of root hidden by dead green water.

I couldn't figure why she'd left her luck. Did she think it was tapped out? She wouldn't need it anymore? Well, if she'd known Chance was looking for me, she might have left it as a record. She'd seen me handle, and she knew the scars on my palms didn't come from a self-mutilation fetish. So maybe that was why. Or maybe it was a map; maybe something I'd seen could help us find her.

Chance had probably been turning over similar thoughts. Without a word, though, he reached into his pocket and withdrew a tiny green tin. I felt a spurt of annoyance he'd been that sure of me, but at the same time I appreciated his forethought. His mom had made it for me: honey, aloe, and papaya—she is (or was) a certified homeopathy practitioner.

"Let me have your hand." Delicate as butterfly kisses, he smoothed salve over my skin where scars crisscrossed until you couldn't tell where one stopped and others began. The unguent soothed immediately, numbing the worst of the trauma. After all this time, I didn't let myself consider it might be his touch; he'd always been able to make the top of my head tingle with just a fingertip.

"Thanks."

I prefer handling textiles, where I feel like the item is afire in my hand but it never actually catches, and I don't wear new marks afterward. But over the years I've been offered a lot of metal: rings burning in concentric circles, bracelets leaving welts, and larger items doing damage that it took a doctor to treat.

Why had I done it for so long?

Clients never did understand why I wouldn't handle multiple objects the same day, why they had to pay for a second consultation. I have a pretty high threshold for pain, but that's just beyond me, by and large. On occasion, I've pushed myself to two and effectively crippled both hands.

I won't do that unless it's dire; the last time it was to try to find an eight-year-old girl yanked out of her own yard. The swing was still moving when her mama missed her. They found her alive because of Chance and me. We did some good, back in the day, and it helps offset what came later.

Once upon a time, he fed me soup and ice cream after we saved the kid. We'd watched *Breakfast at Tiffany's* in bed. He had a weakness for Audrey Hepburn, for polished, elegant women, and I never knew what he saw in me. He used to act like he could read my future in my ruined lifeline. I wondered what he saw now, bent over my palm.

At length he raised his head and folded my fingers back. My heart remembered how he used to pretend he was sealing up a kiss for me to save for later. It hadn't all been bad or I wouldn't have stayed so long.

We stared at each other, more than the expanse of a glass case between us.

The Devil Makes a Deal

"You're going to help me, aren't you?" Chance, vulnerable—that was something I'd seen only a handful of times in the three years we were together. This time, it might actually be genuine, and to cover my uncertainty, I took a sip of my Coke.

"I thought I just did." I felt surprised I could sound so cold, particularly where his mother was concerned.

My burned palm tingled in anticipation of what he would ultimately ask me to do. Sure, he'd hem and haw, try to charm his way around asking outright, but the fact of the matter was, he intended to use me to follow her trail. I'm not a human bloodhound, so it's stupid and awkward, but we've done it successfully four times before, including the salvation of that little girl, and the need had never been this personal.

"Not what I meant." He tried on the old smile with a cock of his head, and I found it no longer rendered me witless.

"I know." My answering smile felt touched with melancholy as I moved from behind the counter to flip the sign on the door to CERRADO. I surprised a mustachioed man on his way in, and Señor Alvarez offered an apologetic look, clutching a red plastic bag. He was a slight man of indeterminate age, always clad in tan pants and a white undershirt.

His murmured accent sounded strange, the singsong Spanish native to Monterrey. The peddler hadn't been in Mexico City much longer than me, and he glanced at Chance curiously from heterochromatic eyes. "*Lo siento*, Señorita Solomon. *Usted está generalmente abierta a esta hora.*"

Chance probably wouldn't know Alvarez was just observing that I'm usually open at this hour. I knew a flicker of satisfaction while I conducted business in functional Spanish. I'll never be a poet in this language, but I was capable of making an offer for whatever Señor Alvarez had in the sack. It'd be good too. In the eleven months he'd been bringing odds and ends to my shop, I'd noticed he had a knack for finding things I wanted.

Today he'd brought me a pair of gorgeous silver candlesticks crafted in Taxco. When I recognized the artisan's mark, I knew they'd fetch two thousand pesos in an antiques auction, not that they'd ever see such a thing. Unless I was grievously wrong, they'd wind up gracing the dining room of an elderly lady from New Hampshire, who would reckon them a steal next week at a thousand pesos and rightly so.

We haggled a little because he had some idea of their worth, but in the end, he took four hundred and an ice-cold Coke. "Thank you for your time and again, I am sorry for the interruption," Señor Alvarez said in his schoolmaster's Spanish, letting himself out.

I followed, turning the bolt behind him as a precaution. The peddler was already too curious about Chance, who stood quiet during the negotiations, but I could tell he didn't like being out of the loop. Without speaking, I snagged my drink and passed through an arch that led to my private staircase at the back of the building.

I have a small apartment that occupies the second and third stories above my shop. Sometimes it looks as if my junk is overflowing from downstairs because I don't respect the fire safety code and I store stuff in the stairwell, line the walls with opened crates and stacked paintings. Some of it I've acquired on my own and some I inherited from the old woman who sold me the Casa de Empeño for less than it was worth. Mostly she just wanted to join her sister in Barra de Navidad and get out of the capital before the election. Since the protesters closed down Reforma Avenue this summer, I couldn't blame her.

Chance followed me, touching this and that with feigned curiosity. He wasn't interested in the oddments of the new life I'd built from the wreckage of the old. I'm sure it looked shabby to him, the crumbling white plaster, steps covered in a black vinyl runner. The second story housed my living room, a dining alcove, a half bath, my kitchen, and a small balcony complete with flower box. When I first saw it, I thought it charming, like the boudoir of a working girl in some old Western. Like the store, the bi-level apartment was cool and dim, the windows barred with black iron.

On the third floor, I had a surprisingly luxurious bathroom with an old-fashioned claw foot tub and two bedrooms, the second of which I used as an office. It had a single bed, but right then it was buried beneath a shipment of good pottery, as I hadn't decided what I'd sell and what to give the woman next door for her Tuesday market stall.

I decorated the place in handmade rugs and wall hangings in bright colors and Aztec patterns, although the traditional shrine and painting of the holy mother was conspicuously absent. The only holy mother I acknowledge gave her life for me when I was twelve; her name was Cherie Solomon. You might say I've been at war with God ever since.

It's funny. While she was alive, I never acknowledged that we were different. I don't reckon I knew.

Other kids in my school had daddies that went missing; it wasn't that rare. But other families in Kilmer didn't observe Beltane by jumping a bonfire or putting out food for the dead on All Hallows' Eve. Other girls didn't read the *ABC Book of Shadows* while their mamas made candles that could bring back an old love.

From the beginning, she made sure I knew there were bad things out there, scary things, things that shouldn't exist. She cautioned me. Warned me. But I never questioned that Mama weighed in on the light side. Maybe she had some inkling of what was to come; I don't know.

And I never will. At this point I wouldn't believe it if somebody told me they'd gotten a hold of her, or that she had a message for me from beyond the grave. Because I suspect she gave everything she had, everything she was, in her final working. I think Mama meant to imbue me with all her magick, but somehow it only ever manifests in one way: the Touch. Maybe that's all my limited mind can manage.

But I'll never know whether that's right either.

"Great place," Chance said finally.

I dropped down into the fancifully carved armchair, serpents and feathered gods at my feet. Done in turquoise and crimson, its upholstery didn't match anything else in the room, but that was sort of the point. He struck the only somber note, a dark scar against the otherwise cheerfully raucous decor.

And hadn't that always been the case? We'd always been the raven and the peacock, possibly with all inherent mythological connotations. He sat as he did everything, carefully, not disarranging the satiny profusion of couch cushions I'd thrown in a fit of artistic glee.

In this light, he looked weary. He probably was if he'd come straight from Monterrey, a ten-hour haul for me, nine if you drove like Chance. I didn't like the tug that made me want to push back the crow-wing hair that tumbled over his forehead.

I ignored his comment about my apartment. That was mere filler, as he waited for me to cut through the bull-shit. That too was typical.

"I know what you want from me." I sat forward, el-bows on my knees. "The question is, what can you offer me in return?"

"You can't be so cold," he bit out. "This is my mother we're talking about. She loved . . . *loves* you."

"True. But you're asking me to return to a life that was killing me," I told him as gently as I could manage. "Maybe this is hard to grasp, but I'm *happy*, Chance. Sweeten the pot—make me an offer I can't refuse."

Maybe it made me a coward, but in all honesty, I didn't want him to. I wanted a reason to send him away; his problems weren't mine anymore. I didn't want to be the solution. I'd wanted out eighteen months ago, bad enough to sneak away in the dark.

His eyes turned hard as amber with something old frozen in their depths. "Who the hell are you? You're not the woman I loved."

I smiled then. "Back in the day, I half killed myself trying to please you—and nearly did, that last time. And all you cared about was the next payday. You never once suggested I stop, that it was hurting me—"

"If I didn't love you," he said tightly, "I wouldn't have let you go. I was awake when you kissed me good-bye, Corine. So don't tell me what I felt or why I did the things I did." He broke off, his jaw set.

That rocked me. The past rearranged itself in my mind's eye like a jigsaw puzzle I'd put together wrong. Remembering the intensity, which I ascribed to the rush of completing a job, I realized he'd known it was the last time. I saw our bodies straining, our skin like rayed satin. Saw his back arch, his mouth coming down to mine. He'd kissed me as he rarely did during sex, hot and open, like he wanted to suck all the taste from my mouth.

Afterward, I saw him lying in the rumpled bed, arm draped over his forehead. Feigning sleep so I could go. He lay there, silent, hearing the sounds that meant I was leaving him forever. He lay there, quiet, accepting my Judas kiss.

Did I hurt him? For the first time, I wondered, marveling I might have the power. I'd decided that to him, I was nothing more than the goose that laid the golden egg—with benefits. Or maybe this was just more of his bullshit, wrapped around the fact that he was awake when I left. I tried to steel myself, but I'd already convinced him I was iron.

"Fine," he said. "Revenge is what I offer. You want the people who did your mother. You know why I refused to look before." His smile flashed, bright and unwelcome as a paparazzi camera. "But if I turn my luck to it, we'll find them. And then you can make them pay however you choose."

Chance had always insisted bad things would come if he turned his luck down dark ways. The years we were together, he never gambled for the same reasons I didn't work on commission. But with him, you never knew what was real, what was smoke and mirrors.

This was an old crime, more than fifteen years gone. The mob that converged in Kilmer had long since changed jobs, wed, divorced, and begat children, but he could help me find the answers I craved. Maybe I should have let it go long before now, forgotten the sounds and smells, but letting things go wasn't part of my makeup. I still wanted justice. They should pay for what they'd done.

It wasn't right they'd gotten away with murder and changed me from a nice, normal girl who wanted nothing more than to ride her pony.

My mouth suddenly felt dry. "You can deliver that? You'll turn your luck to it?"

West of Normal

He looked momentarily disgusted with me, as well he might. Forget diamonds; promises are forever. A select few realize that, and that's why Chance always tried to wheedle his way out of giving his word, always tried to leave himself a back door.

"I swear," he said deliberately. "I can and will. But we find my mother first."

That was fair. Justice had waited fifteen years. It would wait a little longer, like the thing that sleeps beneath the Hudson Bridge.

With a sigh, I gave in. Chance was back in my life for a while and I had to live with it, at least until we found Yi Min-chin.

"Hungry?" I asked, like it had been a couple of days, not a year and a half.

"I could eat."

We both smiled because he always could. I went into the kitchen and he trailed close on my heels, leaning on the counter while I buttered the pan for some quesadillas. The right recipe for them includes homemade tortillas (which I buy at the corner *comedor* along with my rice and beans) and good Oaxaca cheese. I heated the former and then I served the food on mismatched ceramic plates with a bowl of fresh salsa.

There's certain fluidity to it as a condiment; you can add pepper, cilantro, and onion according to taste, chop everything fine or leave it chunky. I've sometimes thought you might be able to read a person's mood according to how they make it and wondered what mine said about me as he scooped it neatly onto his tortilla. After one bite, he augmented his quesadilla with a spoon of rice and beans. Noting his appetite, I decided he was worthy of guacamole, so I fetched the container from the fridge.

The sun had gone while we talked before, and it set over the rooftops in a gentle pink haze as we ate. Some women put a clothesline on the roof, but I have a small garden, something I never dared before. I was afraid of putting down roots, afraid of committing to anything I couldn't pack on ten minutes' notice. The plants made this place home.

"How long do you suppose we'll be gone?" I asked eventually.

Chance shrugged. He'd always been able to pack more meaning into that gesture than most college professors could in a thousand-word essay. I'd once found it charming.

After inhaling five quesadillas, he pushed his plate back. I saw him looking everywhere but at me, taking in the whimsical, hand-painted marble iguana tiles inset along the plaster. I thought they were marvelous; he'd probably call them tacky.

"Remember the day we met?"

I nodded. "I was working at the dry cleaners and you forgot your keys."

"You knew they were mine," he said with remembered wonder. "I took two days getting back there, and you didn't even wait on me the first time, but before I said a word, you handed them over."

"And you knew I was somewhere west of normal."

"Special," he corrected in that voice, giving me that look.

My spine tried to turn to oatmeal and I felt like I
needed to get a continent between us. "Don't. Don't do
that. I already agreed to help. Just . . . don't ruin my life.
Please."

Being Chance, he made the predictable leap. "Are
you seeing someone?"

I had to laugh. "If I refuse to sleep with you, there
must be someone else? Don't you ever get tired of lug-
ging that ego around?"

"I bought a wheelbarrow."

"Not a little red wagon?"

"It wouldn't take my weight," he said, prim as a
vicar.

I wanted to laugh, the sheer pleasurable audacity of
him washing over me. For a moment, I considered the
furtive encounters over the last year, men who didn't
want to know my real name or what I thought about.
Then I realized he might take that for validation—if I
wasn't seeing someone, it had to be because I couldn't
find anyone to fill his shoes. That was irritatingly true;
his only flaws were that he was too ambitious (that one
nearly killed me) and he took himself too seriously.

Now, as he joked with me, it seemed I wasn't the
only one who'd changed, but I was afraid to believe in
him. Chance could spin anything, and I didn't want to be
gullible. Not when I'd walked away and made it stick. I
didn't want to be a woman who went back to the man
who hurt her.

I stood then and started clearing the table. When I
bent to collect his plate, he flinched from me. Gawking,
I hovered until he waved me back, but his tiger's eyes
blazed in his brown face, stripes of verdigris and amber
gilded by the setting sun.

He sounded hoarse. Raw. Not polished, not perfect.
"You're still wearing it."

I was. But then, he'd always possessed a sharper than
average sense of smell. This morning I daubed on Fran-

gipani Absolute after my shower, just a whisper at throat and wrists, because my supply was running low, and I didn't look likely to take a trip to London to replenish anytime soon.

In his eyes I saw his memory of that vacation. I was blond then and we'd run across Old Bond Street in Mayfair, laughing in the rain. Well, *I* laughed; he was annoyed at ruining a perfectly good overcoat. But he was beautiful with the droplets beading on his skin. I'd wanted to lick them up, one by one. Still did, really, but I'd learned Chance wasn't good for me, like too many sweets.

Of course that didn't stop me from eating a box of doughnuts when the craving struck.

The idea of tasting Chance made me shudder from head to toe.

I hadn't wanted to go into the perfumery, where even the shop girls looked posh. I swore they'd see the red Georgia dirt ground into my skin. Though I felt gauche and out of place, he wanted something to commemorate the occasion and bought me a ridiculously expensive scent that made him close his eyes in bliss.

When he opened them, he'd said simply, "It smells like you."

Of *course* I was still wearing it.

My tongue felt thick as I tried to work out what to say. I finally settled on: "Yes."

What he would have said, I'll never know because his cell rang. Looking apologetic, he answered (he'd once taken a call while receiving a particularly artful blow job). That too was vintage Chance, and I scurried like a nervous gerbil back to the kitchen, where I occupied myself washing up the few dishes I'd dirtied.

A few minutes later, I felt him standing behind me. Not close enough to touch. That would raise goose bumps on my skin.

"That was the investigating officer in Laredo," he said

in a tone so neutral I heard the pain bleed through. "They found my mom's purse."

His stillness made me want to go to him. Right now, he wasn't even rolling the coin, and I knew what that cost him. Just five feet, the distance from the white enamel sink to the arch leading to the parlor, but it was too far. I couldn't take the steps that would put me within arm's reach; I didn't trust him, and more important, I didn't trust myself.

"Will they let me handle it?"

That was a touchy subject. Cops always want to put everything in clear plastic bags with neat labels. Once it's been sent to a lab, personal items often sit on shelves collecting dust. As a general rule, they don't let weirdos like me near their stuff.

"If I have to, I can bribe the evidence room clerk." He didn't sound concerned.

I hung the dish towel up to dry, taking a last look at my cozy little kitchen before I clicked off the light. "So we're going to Laredo tomorrow?"

Expressionless, he nodded. "I'd leave tonight, but I honestly don't think I could handle the drive."

Since it was full dark and the four hundred plus miles of highway stretching between Mexico City and Monterrey spanned some pretty desolate country, that made sense, but he never admitted weakness in the old days. He could've proposed we catch a flight out, but I'm sure he knew I didn't have a valid passport. The irony of living in Mexico as an illegal alien doesn't escape me.

"I'll make some calls."

First I needed someone to watch my business. I expected a couple of relatively big sales in the next few weeks and it was crucial the shop was open. I didn't want to come back to find my life in tatters because I'd left it unattended.

I dialed Señor Alvarez up; I'd given him a cheap BenQ phone on the prepaid plan so we could stay in touch easier. His success ratio was so good, I'd taken him on as a freelance buyer, more or less. He rummaged the side streets and flea markets so I didn't have to, and rang in on his cell phone to consult with me about job lots of merchandise.

"*Bueno,*" he said as I connected.

That was an interesting thing. *Bueno* means good or well, and people answer the phone that way here. I'd demonstrated my gabacha-ness by saying *hola* until I figured it out. I'm still not sure why we answer the phone like this, but there you have it.

I explained my proposition. I needed to take a business trip, but I'd offer him two hundred pesos a day and thirty percent commission on anything he sold while minding the store for me. Yes, of course I trusted him, and he was honored by the opportunity. We stroked each other verbally for a few more minutes, a practice I deplore, before we sealed the deal. Could he turn up in an hour to receive the key?

When I disconnected, I found Chance watching me. "You picked up Spanish fast."

It was my turn to shrug. "I have a gift for languages—who knew? I'll get the spare bedroom made up for you."

"Can we not do that?" he asked quietly. "I don't even know if my mother is alive, and I don't want to lie across the hall all night, listening to you breathe."

By then, I had clean linens in my hands. My heart slowed, and then tried to make up the extra beats all at once. "What are you asking for, Chance?"

If Wishes Were Candy

He sucked in a breath like he had a hole in his chest. "Something I haven't known in a long time, Corine. A little peace." Then he seemed to read my misgivings because he sighed. "Not sex. I'll even sleep in my socks."

An inside joke—and I heard him laughing all over again at *Coupling*, a British sitcom we used to watch together: *No self-respecting woman would ever let a naked man in socks do the squelchy with her.* I ached suddenly, missing that shared context. God, I was bad at people coming back into my life. But I wanted it again with someone. Someday.

How that was possible when I lived as I did, I had no idea. I couldn't see myself doing PTA meetings and car pools, cheering at soccer games. What would I talk about at a book club? I imagined myself inadvertently searing my palm over tea while handling a charged object. Maybe my only chance (no pun intended) lay with him or someone like him. Someone who existed on the fringes, who defied probability and made normal folk a bit skittish. Well, I was all over that.

I remembered something he said, years ago. "Sometimes when you meet someone, there's a click. I don't believe in love at first sight but I believe in that click.

Recognition." He'd kissed me then and whispered: "Click."

His answer was supposed to make me feel less alone, grouping us together, but I'd had my fill of the us-and-them mentality, even if it contained a grain of truth. Recalling that moment, though, I softened toward him. Perhaps fatally.

"Okay," I said, dropping the sheets onto the couch. "You can sleep in my bed."

Once the words were out, I felt like the blonde in every horror movie who hears a noise in the basement and goes to investigate alone. Sometimes you smell the stupid all around you, but you step in it anyway. This was one of those occasions.

"Thank you." He held my look a beat too long, but that was all. No suggestion in it.

I don't know what I'd have done if he gloated or used a pet name. I like to think something appropriately horrible, like handling his underpants and advising him he'd soon be castrated in a gardening accident. To give myself a little distance, I sent him upstairs to rinse off some of the road dirt. I joked about not wanting his grubby butt in my bed, but we both knew it was pretense.

Chance could be made of Teflon for all I know; he never looks less than perfect. While I waited for Señor Alvarez, I puttered around the apartment and tried not to imagine the man lounging in my bathtub. "What kind of place doesn't have a shower?" he shouted.

I glared, though he couldn't see me. "Mine."

If nothing else, Alvarez was prompt. An hour on Mexican time could mean anywhere from sixty minutes to six days. "*Buenas noches*," he murmured, accepting the key.

"I appreciate this," I said in Spanish. More verbal stroking as I explained the basic bookkeeping system, and we did business in flattery. I came away slippery with it.

If I didn't trust him, though, I'd have no other recourse. The life I've built here doesn't offer backup plans. I have no fail-safe because I didn't expect to leave. I bought gewgaws, for God's sake.

Before he left, I paid him a week's wages in advance, a thousand pesos. Sounds like a lot, but in the exchange it averages to about a hundred bucks: he'd make a decent amount in commission. I hated losing even thirty percent of the big sales, but it was better than missing them entirely with a closed shop. Alvarez was a salesman, as well as my buyer, so he'd take good care of the place.

We exchanged pleasantries and I asked him to water my garden on the roof. He said he didn't mind, didn't ask how long I would be gone, and excused himself with the queer formality I found endearing. I supposed from his perspective, it didn't matter if I came back. If I didn't, he inherited the shop, as possession is nine-tenths of the law, so maybe he was hoping for natural disasters as he departed; it was beyond me to interpret the thoughts swimming behind his eyes.

His face held a certain impassivity; you see it in all waiters and valets. They might want to jam a knife through your left eye socket, but you'd never know it from their expression. Working retail, I've acquired a similar look myself.

Then there was nothing left for me to do but climb the two flights of stairs to my aerie and face Chance again. I reflected on my idiocy while I did so, unable to believe he'd maneuvered me into letting him sleep in my bed. Part of me tingled and refused to stop; my body didn't believe the business about the socks.

"Down, girl," I muttered as I headed for the bedroom.

It wasn't late, but if I knew him, we'd make a start at first light. So I scrubbed my face, moisturized with Olay (hey, it's a classic for a reason), and then brushed my teeth. Hesitating for just a moment, I changed into a seldom worn nightgown. The nights are warm here, and I generally sleep alone. You do the math.

Maybe it was cruel, but as my final act in preparing for bed, I touched up the frangipani on my throat.

I found him sitting on the edge of my bed, wearing striped boxers, a white T-shirt, and, yes, his socks. The sight made me smile, though not as much as seeing him in my boudoir. What a wonderful word. My room definitely rose to the challenge, done in rose, lavender, and handmade lace. It bordered on brothel burlesque, especially with the balcony overlooking the street where I might show my bosoms to prospective clients.

"All set?"

Nodding, I threw some clothes in a bag while fighting off the memory of other occasions where I'd done exactly that. Chance told me we were leaving and I began to pack, no questions asked. Right up until the last, I would have followed him through fire. In the end, I did that too—and that was why I had to leave him.

Is that love? It seems like a pale word, too easily tossed about by people who don't know the meaning of it, who twist it for their own ends. I'm afraid of it now, right up there with clowns, close spaces, and open flames. On our second date, I had a panic attack when Chance ordered cherries jubilee. After that, I felt sure I'd never see him again.

Shows what I know.

As I came around the bed, he shivered visibly. Oh, I knew he was scent-sensitive. An aroma carries him back in time, makes him relive the associated memories, feel the emotion of that moment. The way it affects him, I'd call it a weakness, but how could I pass up the opportunity to torment him a little? How heady that I still have the power; I wouldn't have guessed he was the steadfast sort.

I mean, just look at him. I noticed the glances we attracted when we were together. I'm well aware I'm not sleek and long-limbed like Chance. If I try to wear capri pants, I grow cankles, and there's always a bit of kitsch about me, no matter how hard I try.

In the last year and a half, I gave up on elegance and worked on developing my own style. It generally involves gypsy skirts that show off my rather cute feet and peasant blouses. Luckily these things are readily available here.

He inhaled deeply as I got in bed, his eyes fixed on the décolletage of my undeniably demure gown. I swear I felt the heat of his look tracing the satin trim along my breasts. "You grew a mean streak, Corine."

I recognized his tone. The perfume had been a bad idea, because we were both remembering the last time we'd been together. Christ, the sex was good that night. Looking at his mouth, I began to forget all the reasons why I shouldn't get naked and roll around with him. Determined not to give in, I lay down and pulled the sheet up to my chin.

As if he knew, Chance touched my hair where it spread on the pillow beside him. "Red looks good on you."

"Thanks."

I'd never been a redhead while we were together, and for him, my changing hair acted as a quiet kink. He said it was like making love to a different woman every time. And why was I thinking about that now? Rolling onto my side, I killed the lamp and the room gained the soft luminance of distant streetlights. City noises came to us, cars and too-loud conversation.

"Giving me your back?"

"I'm not giving you anything," I said, glancing over my shoulder.

Mistake. In the half-light, he looked as sad as I've ever seen him.

"Not anymore," he agreed softly.

"Christ. What do you want from me?"

Propped up against the headboard, he smiled then and I saw the silver glimmer of his coin, rolling along his knuckles. "Only what I always wanted. Everything."

Southern Comfort

The words sent a shudder through me. "You can't have that, Chance. Not when you aren't willing to give it back."

For a moment, I heard nothing but silence from his side of the bed. He knew I spoke the truth because while he said the right things, showed affection where appropriate, he always maintained a certain amount of disengagement. Since I'm backward at relationships, I didn't notice at first, but it came to me during sex one night. I looked up into his face and . . . the distance in his expression, combined with his pure technical proficiency, well, he might have been mentally running actuarial tables while making love to me.

I guess I have a certain amount of ego because I needed him to be lost in me; I wanted more than he could give. Somehow I doubt anyone will ever get past that little door in his head. He's afraid of investing himself utterly, so he preserves the distance in case the relationship breaks down; it's a sad, self-fulfilling prophecy because it inevitably does.

"I'd forgotten how you do that," he said at last.

"Do what?"

"Eviscerate me with a few well chosen words."

Irritated, I turned to face him. "Will you lie down and

go to sleep already? We never talked about our relation-ship in bed, and now that we don't *have* a relationship to discuss, it seems a poor time to break with tradition."

His tone was mild as he slid down. "We do, actually. Or do you deny that we're friends? Maybe you'd let just anyone sleep in your bed."

Well, that hurt, and I couldn't control my flinch. "Of course we're friends," I said tightly, ignoring his second remark. I didn't doubt I was hurting him too, although it was beyond me to judge how much.

"That's fucking great." He stared up at my textured plaster ceiling.

I glimpsed then the way we would slice each other up with our broken edges over the next week or so. Christ. It couldn't have been easy to ask me for help. I'd left him, and as a rule, he didn't do recurring roles either. The heart of a Sicilian mafia don lurked inside him; he adopted a "you are dead to me" attitude toward those who walked away, and none of this mattered anyway. It was about Yi Min-chin, whom we both loved. I could put the past aside long enough to find her or learn her fate.

Inhaling, I braced myself and scooted close enough to put my hand on his arm. "I'm sorry. I thought this was some kind of trick at first, but . . . you must be so wor-ried." I felt like kicking myself for refusing to offer a little sympathy before now. "I'm sorry," I said again, like that would fix it.

"I'm terrified out of my mind." He sounded so bleak. "She makes healing salves and scented candles in Tampa now. What would anyone want with her?"

Why does it go down like this? Women who try to heal the world's ills, women who practice patience and tolerance . . . well, the world doesn't deal kindly with them, as if it's possessed by sentient malevolence that doesn't want such endeavors to succeed. But maybe, like everyone, Min had some secrets.

Nobody knew better than I that the past casts a long shadow, but this didn't seem like the time to say so. Instead I shrugged, hoping I wasn't about to make another mistake. But then my life is one long list of them, so what's one more between friends?

"Put your coin on the night table," I ordered.

To my surprise, he complied, but then he'd all but admitted to exhaustion. I wiggled sideways until my knees touched his. This close I could smell the faint citrus of his Burberry Touch cologne, and I felt the same pleasurable shock he must've experienced at discovering the frangipani on my skin. I'd bought it for him, that same trip to London. Touch wasn't as expensive as some of his others; he liked Higher Dior and Dolce & Gabbana's By, but he stopped wearing them. A year and a half later, he was still wearing Touch because I'd liked the way it warmed up on his skin.

Swallowing trepidation, I put an arm around him and he nestled into me as he always had. I was supposed to be comforting him but my face wound up in the curve of his neck. His arms came around me so hard it hurt, and with my hands on his back, I felt the tension coiling him like a spring. He probably hadn't slept in days, not since his mom vanished. With all my heart, I wished he'd come because he needed *me*, not my gift.

But then, if that had ever been true, I might have stayed.

"This is what I was asking for." My hair muffled his voice, along with the unprecedented admission. "This. Don't let go tonight, Corine. Please."

I didn't.

My eyes burned with tears I refused to weep, and I swam through memories all night, long after I soothed him to sleep with finger-walking on his spine. In the morning, my right arm felt numb and my ribs were sore from lying in one position, but he looked a little better. I didn't speak as I went to wash up.

Quickly I scrambled some eggs and we ate those with the last of my tortillas and salsa. I scraped the leftover rice and beans into the trash and then bundled it up in a tiny plastic shopping bag. Chance raised a brow at me but I didn't explain. He caught on when I dropped it in a white decorative basket outside the shop, hung high to deter the dogs.

He grabbed his backpack and I shouldered my overnight bag, stuffed with five changes of clothing. If we stayed longer I'd need to find a Laundromat, but I no longer fretted about such things. Once I worried about wearing the same outfit twice in a week, but living here had persuaded me nobody gave a rat's ass what covered mine.

"Where are you parked?"

"There." Indicating a black Suburban maybe a block down, he set off.

I followed, fighting the odd sensation that someone was watching us. I paused, glancing down the street both ways, but I saw nothing out of place. Nothing to convince me it wasn't paranoia. But if Chance had found me, so could someone else, and there were a number of people who would like to see me dead. Some were even crazy enough to do it themselves.

In morning light, Calle Jacarandas looked a little shabby. Doubtless it would look worse to someone accustomed to sanitized American cities. In addition to all the bars and grates, the adobe and stucco buildings held grime, though people fought it with flamboyant paint. On my street alone, you saw azure, mandarin, goldenrod, sienna, violet, and rose hued houses.

But there were more trees and flowers here too. Mexico City was one of the greenest urban sprawls I'd ever seen. My neighbor had a garden I envied: a huge *noche buena* tree with big glorious red flowers, native frangipani, rosebushes, hydrangea, and a wall full of bougainvillea. As we walked, I tried to see my life through

Chance's eyes and eventually gave up as I clambered into the SUV.

We were quiet as we drove. I guess he was thinking about what waited for us in Laredo, but to my surprise, he didn't need directions to find the *periférico* or to get back on the federal highway that led north to Monterrey. I brought my map, just in case, because I hadn't explored the city much beyond the barrio where I wound up.

He shrugged, correctly interpreting my astonishment. "I drove around here a bit, looking for you."

I didn't ask how he'd found me. Using his gift, he'd have stumbled on someone who knew about my shop. That was how it worked . . . and why he didn't use it lightly. An unscrupulous person would turn such strange luck to any number of bad ends, but Chance had always used his power over coincidence with great care. I felt a flicker of remorse that I intended to warp it in pursuit of my mama's killers, but not enough to change my course.

Chance bitched beneath his breath at the other drivers while we got out of the city. Maybe I should've warned him people here considered a red light a suggestion and that they thought nothing of turning left from the far right lane. Still, the Suburban meant he had a lot of weight to back up his vehicular threats and most folks gave way.

The demarcation from city to country came sharply, and the wide open spaces carried a remoteness you find nowhere in the U.S. Even the likes of Montana and Wyoming don't compare to the vast empty stretches on the way to Monterrey, which sits on the southwestern Texas border. Laredo is about two more hours away from Monterrey, and I hoped he didn't intend to try to do it all in one day. My ass protested the thought.

The mountains are starkly beautiful, but you can go a hundred miles between gas stations with a grazing goat as the only sign of life. Tequila farms lay here and there

along the highway, and far off the road, I imagined I saw
smoke rising from a distant chimney.

Driving from Mexico state to Nuevo León on the *car-
retera nacional* covered a lot of territory. Earlier this
year, I read how a dispute between two Tzótzil Indian
families over a pothole escalated into a full-blown shoot-
out, resulting in four fatalities. It isn't rare for guns to
settle arguments, particularly in poorly policed indige-
nous areas; the modern world with a deputy parked behind every road sign to catch you speeding doesn't exist
out here.

"It's a little scary, isn't it?"

I exhaled, remembering making this drive by myself.
Even so, I'd been glad to leave the border towns. "Yeah.
Anything could happen out here."

Though I didn't say so, anything could happen when
we reached Laredo as well. Adjoining Nuevo Laredo via
International Bridge, the town is a shithole, and I wished
Chance hadn't let Min join him there. Then again, he
probably didn't know about the warring cartels turning
the place into a charnel house. Thanks to their private
war over the I-35 route, which exploded at the intersection of Paseo Colón and Avenida Reforma, the murder
rates there rivaled those in DC.

It took the intervention of the Mexican army to break
up that fight, but I doubted this was common knowledge
for the average American. I knew of it only because an
overly informative U-Haul agent offered the news when
I passed through, along with a warning to get my ass out
of town. And *this* was where his mother disappeared.

I smelled something burning.

On the Road Again

For once, it wasn't merely my nose for trouble.

After Chance pulled off to the side of the road to investigate the reason for the dashboard light coming on, I climbed out to stretch my legs. I wandered around while he tried to figure out how to open the hood. As far as the eye could see, there was nothing but trees and mountains narrowly cut by the well-kept highway. Hard to believe we were only an hour out of the city. For about a minute, I managed to hold my tongue and then my sense of humor got the best of me.

"Let me guess. You didn't check the fluids before we left?"

His head jerked up, his outraged look priceless. Chance did not see to such things. He *paid* people to see to such things, but he would've had a hard time making himself understood at a service station, so I popped the hood myself. Some steam billowed out, verifying there was a problem, but damned if I knew what it was.

The radiator looked intact, and it was beyond me to examine anything else. If we were just low on water, I could walk to one of the roadside spigots, but if the truck needed replacement parts, we were in a world of trouble. I didn't bother checking my cell; the mountains fucked with reception out here and who would I call anyway?

We'd be lucky if a truck driver picked us up within a couple hours.

"Don't turn off the engine," I told him. "Let it cool off while it idles. I'll walk back a ways and get some water. You stay with the Suburban and check the back to see if you have any spare coolant."

"You want me to make you a sandwich too?"

"Turkey on rye," I said over my shoulder. "Lettuce and tomato, no onion."

I found an empty container and set off, grateful we hadn't gone too far past the last water stop. Highly ill advised to drink from the highway taps, but for a vehicle in trouble, they were a godsend. Chance startled me by laughing, audible a hundred feet away. I turned and gave him a quizzical look.

"You're so great," he said. "I'd forgotten that too."

What could I say? I just kept walking. I sweated, the sun beating down on my head as I reflected how blue the sky is so far from civilization. Later I tried to refill the engine's water reservoir. Let's just say Chance didn't think I was so great when I cracked the engine block.

To his credit, he didn't rant, just pulled his backpack out of the truck. I had the good sense not to say anything since I'd teased him about not checking the vehicle. It seemed like we were even on catastrophes. So we leaned against the Suburban in silence, tired and thirsty, waiting for a ride, as we'd done for the last two hours.

Finally, someone stopped for us, but his cab was crowded and I rode for several hours on Chance's lap. If he'd made a comment about his legs going numb, I would've clubbed him with my straw handbag. The trucker took us as far as San Luis Potosí, where we arranged for the rental company to reclaim the Suburban. I didn't want to bitch, but we'd wasted an astonishing amount of time, and we were only around halfway to Monterrey.

So a few hours on the road, a few hours beside the

road, and another few hours on Chance's lap. It was well into the afternoon by the time we sorted out another ride. This time Chance got a Toyota with precious few amenities, looking pained as he slid his credit card across the counter. Mostly, I hoped the vehicle was reliable.

Before departing, we ate at the Holiday Inn there, a nice Brazilian-style place where they laid side dishes in a buffet and then brought to the table skewered cuts of meat for us to choose from. I had the beer-braised chicken and a nice cucumber salad. While he enjoyed a cup of excellent coffee and I pondered having some flan, I heard a familiar voice.

"Chance, is that you?"

There it was again—his luck. If we hadn't broken down, we'd never have stopped here. What earthly reason could Tanya have to be in San Luis? Yet here she was. He waved her over, smiling. She was one of *his* acquaintances, and I'd never liked her, rich and useless to say the least. Of course, I might have liked her better if she didn't seize every possible opportunity to remind me I didn't belong with him.

When she reached our table, she stared at me as if I were something she'd found sticking to the sole of her shoe. In the end, she decided not to dignify my existence with a comment. Maybe she hoped I'd disappear if she clicked her ruby slippers together (though they were bisque and bronze) and wished hard enough.

"I tried to get in touch with you before I left the country," she said to him. "But nobody seemed to know where you'd gone. I have your money. Daddy finally coughed up my allowance because I'm doing something useful these days. I'm a patron of native crafts and culture." Her tone disparaged the art she purported to patronize, but Tanya chattered on, oblivious to our silence. "So odd we'd run into each other here of all places, but then it *is* the only decent restaurant in town. We'd probably die of dysentery if we chanced one of those *tavernas* or taco stands."

I steamed quietly, as I'd eaten in my share of those places and never suffered any ill effects. Chance made an effort to be civil, though I could tell his patience was stretched to the breaking point. We'd be lucky to get there by midnight at this rate, and I'd give myself a lobotomy if he invited Tanya along.

With precise motions, he wiped his mouth on the blue linen napkin and then laid it across his coffee cup. "I wish I could spend more time catching up, but we need to go. If you want to give me a check while we're here, though, that will be fine."

Her expression as she got out her checkbook said he'd been rude. I think she had expected to make some social headway with him but I could have warned her that Chance never fucked anyone who borrowed money from him. He was fastidious in that regard; he mingled, wore the right clothes to intrigue twats like Tanya, but he'd never be one of them.

Though he wasn't a shark with a goon squad that broke legs for him, Chance often made high interest, short term loans to privileged idiots who overspent their trust funds, and *I* was how he'd earned the capital to do so. Still, the number of zeroes on the check she made out to him in U.S. dollars made my eyes widen.

"Good luck with your art show," I said to her in saccharine tones.

As we waited for the valet to bring our car around (in Mexico even Burger King has valet parking), he murmured, "That came at a good time." He paused, as if weighing whether to tell me more. "Things were running a bit lean, and we're going to need that money before we're through."

I rolled my eyes. "Tell me again why you don't play the lottery."

"It would be wrong." Giving me an inscrutable look,

he tipped the man holding his door and got into the piss
yellow Camry.

"Right," I said. "We're the good guys."

Occupied with heading back toward the highway, he
didn't respond. I grinned as he stopped at a PEMEX and
had the fluids topped off; we were taking no chances
with the Toyota. We bought bottles of water there as
well, just to be safe. However, studying him once we got
under way, I decided something beneath his impeccable
tailoring suggested a hero keeping dark forces at bay.

The sun was setting by that point, blazing fire over
the Sierra Madre. Slate and charcoal clouds gathered
over the mountains in the distance. The highway uncoiled before us like a dark, patient snake. We had another four hours to go, and most of the driving would be
after dark. I considered offering to spell him, but he'd
just sigh and shift in the passenger seat. Chance didn't
like being driven—another control issue.

The vastness between towns had a way of making me
feel small, like nobody would notice anything that went
down out here except to hose off the road. Headlights
shining in the rearview mirror made me feel uneasy. The
feeling passed, but the car never did. It kept pace with us
for miles.

I tried to dismiss it as paranoia, but I still remembered
the way Kel Ferguson had stared at me as the bailiffs led
him away. Unlike other cons, he hadn't sworn vengeance or screamed that he knew people on the outside.
His eyes did all the talking, and what they said still woke
me up at night.

"Do you ever think about them?" I asked after the silence started to get to me.

"About who?" He didn't look at me.

I traced a protective symbol against the car window,
like that would help. "The guys we put away."

"I'm glad they're off the street," he said. "And no, I
don't worry about them getting out. We have enough

law abiding citizens after us to make me wary of borrowed trouble."

We'd run afoul of lawmen more than once. In Terre
Haute, they'd all but run us out of town on a rail. I
sighed. "You got that right."

After that, we didn't talk much as we headed north
along 57. If we were so inclined, we could follow the
highway all the way to Piedras Negras, Coahuila, but
our business took us onto 40 instead, marking the last
miles to Monterrey. Over nine hours in the car so far, not
counting the time we spent waiting for rescue.

Since November ranged toward the end of rainy season, the sky didn't open up until well after full dark. The
rain splattered on the windshield as if by the bucket, and
Chance leaned forward, slowing to a crawl as we approached the lights of Monterrey. After replaying what
he'd said about needing money, it occurred to me then
that maybe he knew more than he'd told me, but I wasn't
dumb enough to pick a fight in the middle of a storm.

He had to be tense, worrying about his mother, and
this marked our tenth hour in a car. More like fourteen
since we left my apartment this morning, so it was a
wonder we hadn't killed each other yet. Unerringly, I
found the spot at the base of his skull with my thumb
and forefinger, pressed so that he let out a moan.

"Christ, that's good. Stop while I'm driving, though. I
don't want to run off the road."

Funny how he had the power to take me back in time
with a handful of words. In my mind's eye, I saw all the
other occasions where he'd tipped his head back in bliss
beneath my hand. My chest felt tight; I didn't want to
remember the good times. I'd blocked them because it's
next to impossible to leave someone you really like.

"Head for Diego Rivera," I said as we came into the
city. The buildings took some force out of the rain,
though the other cars made driving difficult. Here, the
streets flooded easily, and some wiseass in a taxi tried to

splash standing water through my cracked window. "It's in the financial district."

So maybe I wanted to show off. I'd spent one night at the gorgeous Quinta Real, a colonial hotel of marble sandstone that looked like a palace. Inside it was more of the same, impossibly sumptuous with a staff that knew service. No pool, but the in-room Jacuzzi more than made up for it—and Tanya's check said he could afford a grand class suite. I sighed, remembering that I'd stayed there alone. Still, a room that contained fine tapestries and sculptures, beautiful paintings with lavish gilt frames, decorative inlaid marble in the baths, and an imperial bed with golden columns could make anyone feel like royalty for a night. There were advantages to knowing a man's weaknesses.

I was desperate to avoid driving farther tonight.

Chasing Geese

I'd like to claim that Chance took one look at the hotel
and fell upon his knees, declaring his undying devotion.
I'd like to say he apologized for everything that went
wrong between us and promised he'd spend the rest of
his life making it up to me. But if I did, you probably
wouldn't believe another word I said, especially with
regard to Chance.

Instead he offered a smoldering look. "Trying to
tempt me?"

"Absolutely. The weather is rotten and we won't be able
to see anyone about the purse until morning anyway."

He sighed and tapped the steering wheel. His answer
came when he swung into the well-manicured drive and
gave the keys over to the valet attendant. We stepped out
of the driving rain and into another world, one filled
with lavish service and utter opulence. Assessing the
foyer in a glance, he said softly, "It's like one of the
grand old hotels in Europe. Can I get a masseuse in
the room?"

"I expect so. You can get just about anything here, as
long as you can pay for it. They'll even do your shopping,
although the mall across the street is closed right now."

He nodded like that was good to know, and I helped
him with check-in. I've noticed most service people

speak enough English to do business in major commercial cities, but they think better of you if you speak
enough Spanish to do it that way; it's an almost intangi-
ble shift, a near smile and a lightening in the eyes.

Once upstairs, I left Chance in the hands of a masseuse who looked as though she wouldn't mind relaxing
him in ways that were only permitted in the *zona de tol-
erancia* in Nuevo Laredo. He was sound asleep when I
finally crawled out of the sunken marble tub, pink and
wrinkled like a newborn. I stood for a moment, wrapped
in my plush hotel bathrobe, and watched him sleep.
Somehow he always looked innocent in repose, a ridiculous premise if you knew him at all.

As I turned, I heard him whisper, "No, don't go."

I didn't hesitate because he wasn't alive in the moment with me but remembering in dreams, perhaps remembering someone else as well. In a remote corner of
my mind, I wondered whether he had spoken those
words aloud as the door closed behind me. Could I believe he'd loved me once?

I couldn't answer that as I lay down on the couch,
wrapping myself up in spare blankets. However, I did
know it would be a bad idea to sleep with Chance again,
even to lay in the same bed, because I had a history of
finding it hard to tell him no. I didn't want to repeat old
mistakes, just get through the search with as much grace
as possible.

We breakfasted en suite, fruit and yogurt for him,
chilaquiles for me. This morning, he looked remote and
well-tailored in dove gray trousers paired with a mist
and mauve striped button-down. To look at him, you'd
almost swear he was gay, too pretty to like girls.

I put on a long skirt and a peasant blouse and kept a
green cardigan out just in case it turned cool, one of
those long retro sweaters with a belt. All told, I possessed a delightful hippie chic, and I took pleasure in the
way Chance squinched up his eyes.

Three hours later, after a painless border crossing, we arrived in Laredo. I had left the U.S. before they changed passport requirements, but they don't look too hard at red-haired women at the border. Chance called the cop in charge from the car, who agreed to make himself available at ten a.m. I wasn't looking forward to it because cops typically got that look when Chance said a victim's family wanted me to examine the personal effects. I preferred private consultations, as life hadn't left me any love for local law enforcement.

By the time we parked outside the station house, I'd worked up a nice set of nerves. "Is he going to give me a hard time?"

"I don't think so. He's not your typical asshole."

As we walked into police headquarters, a sandstone municipal building that could have doubled as a mental institution, I rubbed my fingertips back and forth over the new scabs on my palm. In response, he brushed his hand across my shoulder, the sort of thing he'd done eighteen months ago. I used to take heart from his touch. Now I merely hunched my shoulders, glad I didn't have to deal with Laredo in summer. I thought we'd have to wade through a lot of bureaucratic bullshit, but a detective stood waiting for us at the desk.

"Thanks for making time." Chance shook hands with him, and they exchanged polite words.

My hormones gave a little skip as I gave him the once-over: an intriguing mix of long, tall Texan in battered boots, touched with Latin heat. He had legs that stretched forever in jeans faded almost to white, not the kind bought with designer "wear" but Levi's washed till the seams and creases got thin. He'd clipped his badge to his belt in plain sight.

As I checked out the rest of him, I admired shoulders showcased by a rumpled white shirt and a forest green blazer. He had a striped tie stuffed in his right jacket pocket, probably to satisfy the letter of the dress code. Nice face, I decided, if scruffy and unshaven. Frosting the hunk cake was a tousled mess of tawny, sun streaked hair.

The beauty of being short was that guys didn't usually notice me eating them with my eyes. Of course, most often, their disregard never changed unless they saw me handle. Still, apart from Chance, I tended to attract Lone Gunman types. They appeared to sense there was something different about me, more than the retro-funky exterior, and if I permitted it, they'd commit me to their lifelong quest to prove the existence of the paranormal.

The joke was on them; I *was* the paranormal.

I concluded my visual inventory of the cop's assets. *Out of my league,* I thought with a mental sigh, *and a lawman to boot. Crying shame.* But as I raised my eyes, I saw the guy regarding me out of bitter chocolate eyes.

"See something you like?" His smile said he knew I had.

Shit. Caught me. I'd figured he'd be talking with Chance for at least five minutes before they got around to me.

"Just window-shopping." I shoved my hands in my sweater pockets.

"Thinking about a purchase down the line?"

Despite feeling like an ass, I grinned. "Now, that'd be illegal, unless we were in the *zona,* wouldn't it? Otherwise I'd ask for rates."

He extended a hand. "Jesse Saldana. I'm an investigator with the Capers unit."

I was familiar enough with the jargon to know he meant the Crimes Against Persons unit, whose purview ranged from terrorist threats to homicide to missing persons. "Corine Solomon."

I imagined spelling it out for him. *C-O-R-I-N-E, rhymes with Doreen. You want to write it down? And here's my cell number.*

That would never happen, of course. I lacked the chutzpah to pull off such a maneuver. Plus, I was pretty sure it would be bad form to try to pick up a guy right in front of my ex.

After a moment's hesitation, I gave him my right hand. We shook; I felt an odd shock, as if we'd sparked static off each other. I almost sighed in relief when he let go. I still don't like touching strangers. Though I know it doesn't work that way, I can't quite rid myself of the fear that I'll suddenly start reading people like I do objects, and I can't imagine anything more objectionable or invasive.

Chance stepped in then. "You said we could look at my mother's purse?"

Nobody else would've noticed, but his mouth had pulled tight. If nothing else, I'd succeeded in pissing him off. Maybe I'd flirt a little more. The good detective didn't seem to take it wrong.

"Well," Saldana said. "Let's take a walk to my office and talk about that."

Uh-oh. That sounded like we were about to get played. Chance didn't look happy.

He led us down a long hallway painted in the bile green reserved for government buildings. The floors were shiny, though, as the whole building looked pretty new. Saldana shared an office with another investigator, it seemed. At least there was another desk, laden with empty coffee cups and McDonald's wrappers, but the other guy wasn't around. After he shut the door, he invited us to sit, which we did, and offered us coffee, which we declined. I felt vaguely disappointed because I hadn't seen a single doughnut box. *What a gyp.*

"Here's the thing," he began, and I felt Chance tense beside me. "The lab has it right now, testing for forensic evidence, and afterward, my lieutenant will kick my ass if I let you compromise whatever they find." He hadn't cleared it, I guess, when they talked on the phone. No surprise there; nobody in authority ever wants me to handle.

I forestalled Chance's eruption. "Where did you find it?"

Saldana smiled at me, probably relieved one of us was going to be reasonable. Man, he was cute. "Behind some crates in a warehouse. A security guard saw it and called it in." *Over a lost purse? I don't think so.* He hesitated, eyes on Chance. "There was some blood, signs of a scuffle. We're waiting to see what the lab turns up."

The silence hurt me because I knew how Chance must feel, and I didn't want to be here with him. Not now.

Finally he said, "She's A-positive. St. Joseph's in Tampa ran some tests for her, maybe five years ago. They should have her file." It was just something to say, of course. Something to fill the silence while we all thought about a delicate Korean woman beaten until her blood stained a cement floor.

Saldana nodded, standing to pour himself a cup of coffee. I think he just wanted something to do with his hands. So he doctored it with powdered creamer and Splenda. He drank it light like me, I noted. "Thanks for the heads-up."

The guy had to be ready to evict us from his office, but he radiated unruffled patience. I was willing to bet he was the good cop, every time. Probably his partner was some burly Russian-looking dude with a buzz cut and a bad attitude.

"How long will the purse be at the lab?" Chance's fingers curled around the metal arms of his chair, and I half expected to see it melt between his fingers, but his knuckles just turned white.

"A couple of days, maybe. I'll stay on them," the investigator answered in a neutral tone.

I'm sure Saldana knew we didn't mean to take no for an answer; he just wanted his ass covered when we went behind his back.

Chance stood. "We'll be in touch then."

Great. We had time to kill in Laredo.

Just Like You

Investigating officer Jesse Saldana walked us out.

As Chance headed for the parking lot, the cop caught me by the shoulder, and I felt that soft little static shock again where we connected. I gazed at his hand pointedly and he lifted it with an apologetic look.

"I wanted to speak to you alone a minute."

Gay, I decided with a touch of disappointment, not that I'd ever had a shot with Saldana except in my own fantasies. He probably wanted to know whether Chance swung that way, and it wouldn't be the first time I'd been queried. It was a little unprofessional, but I'd give him the benefit of the doubt and assume he intended to wait until the case was resolved before making a move.

"What's this about?" My shriveled ego gave a half-hearted thump. Maybe he had a thing for faux redheads.

His half smile reflected a patient amusement I couldn't interpret. "You don't know?"

Concluding his interest wasn't sexual and delightfully inappropriate, I lifted a brow. "What I don't know would fill a set of encyclopedias. Care to be more specific?"

He touched me then, just a brush of his fingertips against mine, and for the third time, static sparked between us. Because I was looking down, I saw the soft blue discharge. "What the hell, are you wearing special shoes or something?"

Saldana shook his head, seeming incredulous. "You really *don't* know."

"Know what?"

I felt myself becoming impatient, and waiting for me outside, his fingers drumming on the Camry's roof, Chance had no doubt passed that point. Maybe it was small of me, but I enjoyed provoking him. I'd spent years waiting for some kind of emotional display, proof Chance wasn't as icy as he seemed. The consummate businessman, the ultimate broker—nothing rattled him. At least, it hadn't. His emotions skated a lot closer to the surface these days.

Saldana spared a glance for the desk officer who pretended he wasn't listening. "Perhaps we'd better return to my office." At my hesitation, he added, "I'll be brief. Promise."

"What the hell." It wouldn't hurt Chance to stew a bit, and being annoyed with me would distract him from worrying about his mother.

"Usually your parents would advise you," he explained once we reached his office and he closed the door behind us. "I guess it falls to me. That little flare of static is how we recognize each other, although sometimes it comes from someone with a latent ability."

I didn't sit down because he had. My intention was to preserve the height advantage in the encounter, but standing before his desk left me feeling as though I'd been summoned to the principal's office, so I sank into the chair opposite.

For a moment I considered feigning ignorance. *Ability? What ability?* But I was sure he knew I was different somehow and that I'd lose points for pretending. Why his opinion mattered, I don't know, but I didn't want him to consider me an idiot.

"You're saying every static shock I've received came

from someone else who has some ability, whether they're aware of it or not?" My tone sounded skeptical.

He shook his head. "No, there's regular static and then there's what we do. You'll only see the blue spark when two talents react on each other. It's quite different, but I guess you wouldn't know that if you haven't been educated. To the uninitiated, it's rather like tasting the difference between types of honey."

"There are different types of honey?" I settled back to listen.

Christ, Chance is going to kill me.

"Yeah. For now I just wanted to find out whether you have an excellent poker face or if you didn't know I'm like you."

That sounded like a line. He was like me only in that we were both bipedal in nature. "Uh-huh."

"You're doubtful, a little sad. Conflicted about being here. Worried about Chance."

I sat forward then, gripping the edge of his desk. "How did you—" Shit, did he know I'd been picturing him naked earlier? Was he going to start bending spoons?

"And now," he continued with a grin, "you're feverishly embarrassed. I'm curious to know why, actually."

"Emotions," I realized aloud. "You're an empath."

"Yeah. It helps in my line of work. Cops work hunches all the time, and what I do doesn't deviate too far from that." His dark eyes flickered to my hands, and I knew he must have registered the scars when we shook. "You're a handler? You can't come by it naturally, or it wouldn't come with such a steep price."

A reasonable assumption under the circumstances— psychometry is the most tactile gift—but I still felt mild astonishment that a cop, a bastion of law and order, could accept what I did. Could make the mental leap without scorn or fear of the unholy. In that moment, Jesse Saldana became something more than hot.

"Yeah," I said. "You're right."

He acknowledged that with a nod and a knowing look that said he probably understood more than I did about certain things. "For now, I'll be brief. There's an underground," he said softly. "When you ID someone this way, proceed with caution. They may think they're alone, as you did, and you never know how they're going to react."

I thought about that. "You took a risk in speaking to me."

"Somewhat. I won't go into everything now. Your boyfriend feels like a nuclear warhead in the parking lot."

"He's not my boyfriend," I corrected.

Great, that sounded like I wanted him to know I was available when all I wanted from Jesse Saldana was some answers.

"Used to be?" A spark of interest flared to life in his eyes, quickly quelled. "Never mind. Where are you staying? I'll take you to dinner tomorrow and tell you everything."

"I'm not sure. We came straight from Monterrey." I knew a flash of longing for the luxurious hotel we'd left behind. Unlikely we would ever find anything like that here.

"I'll also do everything I can to get you a look at that purse, although I can't go through channels." Saldana gave an apologetic shrug. "But I understand how important it is now." He regarded me for a moment before adding, "One last thing. Since I found you, that makes me your mentor. If you object, say so and we'll call it."

Found me. That made me sound like a lost dog.

I shrugged. "I don't know you well enough to mind. I don't even know what this entails, so give me your card, and we'll rectify that. I'll call when we're settled."

His smile flashed, white teeth in his scruffy sun-bronzed face. "Sure you will, Corine. That wouldn't be the first time a woman brushed me off like that."

"Yes, it would," I said with no little disgust.

With a boyish shrug, he admitted to the bullshit, which was better than false modesty. "Here you go. Better head out there before you get left, sugar."

By the time I got to the car, Chance looked like he could happily blow things up. Because I was curious I touched him on the arm as I came around to the passenger side. Nothing. No shock. Huh. Whatever Chance did, he did it differently than the rest of us. His power must somehow fall outside the range of "ordinary" human gifted. But then, I'd always sensed something special about Chance, a preternatural polish and grace.

I wasn't sure how I felt about what I'd learned inside the station. Well, assuming Saldana wasn't a nut job. And maybe he was; a badge didn't make him trustworthy. Sometimes it just focused the crazy.

"Have a nice chat?" Chance asked, turning the key in the ignition like he wanted to break it off.

Purposefully I gazed out the window. I hated Laredo. When I'd left the first time, I promised myself I'd never come back and yet here I was. Overall, I wasn't much fonder of the rest of Texas, although I didn't mind Texarkana. When I passed through in July of last year, it was still lush and green, reminding me more of the Smoky Mountains where I'd spent a few summers camping, before my mama died.

She hadn't told me anything about people being gifted or not gifted, or little blue sparks to set them apart. I don't know if all practitioners react to each other this way or only those with limited talents. I'm also not sure if she didn't know about all this, or whether she never got the chance to clue me in. But then, she worked her magick through ritual, focus, and dreamy soft chants that sounded like low, husky lullabies.

If I closed my eyes, I could hear her, even now. Singing.

It never occurred to me to question her about whether

her powers were real or if I should listen to the kids at school who made *Bewitched* jokes. I guess all little girls secretly think their mamas are magical, and mine gave me more proof than most. My mother taught me everything I know about love. She gave me life, and twelve years later, she died for me. What more is there?

I didn't let my thoughts continue to roam that way, but my voice sounded more clipped than I wanted when I finally replied. "Yep."

"Are you planning to tell me what that was about?"

Flicking the card between my fingers, I decided to tell the literal truth. "He wants to take me to dinner while we're in town."

Yeah, I made it sound personal. Sue me. Chance owed me for a lot of bad moments over the years, wondering whether he wanted me or just my gift. Wondering whether he slept with me to keep me biddable.

His hands tightened on the wheel, incredulity and . . . jealousy? . . . warring in his voice. "You made a date with him?"

"Tentatively."

"My mother is God knows where," he bit out, "and you're thinking with your crotch."

Such language wasn't like him. He never lost control, never slipped that way, and I felt savage satisfaction at having goaded him to that point.

I shrugged. "Why shouldn't I? I'm pretty good in bed. Maybe I can win some influence with him. Get him to break some rules. How's that different from the way you pimped me?"

He cut me a daggered look as we turned into the parking lot of a shitty La Quinta Inn. "Were you always such a bitch?"

"Yeah."

"Why didn't I notice?"

Because I cared desperately what you thought of me then.

I shrugged. "Why didn't you notice a lot of things?"

"I have no idea," he said, sounding dazed. "But it turns me on something wicked."

I peeked at his lap as he parked the car and decided he wasn't kidding.

Killing Time

With a snicker, I left him to wait the problem out.

The Chance I remembered didn't suffer from inconvenient erections, nor did he get horny at inappropriate times. He planned lovemaking, all details in place for a perfect, civilized seduction, everything in its place, everything orchestrated. Me, I like a good bit of cloth ripping, panties on the lampshade, and some shouting before it's over. He'd never gotten there with me, and I'd figured it was somehow my fault.

But I was done with that mentality.

I handled check-in while he unloaded the bags. Just as well because the woman's Spanish was better than her English, even in Laredo. Chance came up to the counter just as I concluded the deal, and I passed him his keycard, taking a certain petty pleasure in his annoyance that I'd booked separate rooms. His jaw clenched when I blithely told him how much he owed but he forked over the money.

"Why are we here?" I asked as we walked. Reading his look, I clarified, "This motel. It doesn't look like you, so there has to be a reason."

It was a peeling pink stucco building, set amid an industrial area. The only other open business was the Denny's next door. Everything else had shut down, installing gates and bars to keep kids from breaking in.

"You act like I'm an elitist snob or something. Maybe I'm being frugal."

"You *are* an elitist snob. Why are we here?"

Chance sighed. "I caught a peek at the file in Saldana's office and I saw the address of the warehouse."

That made sense. "So we have a reason for being in this neighborhood."

He'd never have stayed here otherwise, and certainly not with his mom. Wherever they'd stayed, the room was long cleaned by now, and I couldn't reasonably be expected to find anything. At the warehouse, though— well, they'd have probably taped it off as a crime scene, better safe than sorry. Blood made people twitchy.

I stepped into my room without enthusiasm. What they called a queen bed looked no more than full to me, and the mattress felt hard as brick. The room was decorated in vintage motel with a cheap orange spread and muddy paintings on the wall. Gazing at the pasteboard furniture, I felt a touch claustrophobic and hoped I wouldn't have to spend much time here. Worse, it felt damp inside, so I flicked on the air con. In response, water immediately began to drip somewhere from the bathroom ceiling.

My backpack bounced on the bed where I tossed it, and I sank down beside it, unzipping the front pocket to delve beneath blouses and hair ties until I found what I was looking for. Cradling it in my hands, I studied the black pillow, no more than six inches wide and embroidered with white characters I couldn't read. I traced them with a fingertip, remembering.

"I know what being with Chance can be like," she'd said with a half smile. "So I'm giving you some luck of your own."

She had, in a small way, stood in for my own mother,

although Min always respected the half-step difference. She'd taught me to make the noodle soup Chance liked and she had a great laugh, really loud and infectious for such a small woman. Oh, Christ, and she was—

Neither of us held much hope we'd find her alive.

I clutched the pillow to my chest, finally letting loss sweep over me. Over the past day, I'd been keeping it at bay with various defenses, first focusing on him and then the trip. But now there was nothing but me and the stupid drip from the bathroom ceiling. My eyes welled up, and I felt the hot trickle down my cheeks. I wept silently, as I did the night I watched my mother burn.

"They're coming," she'd whispered, pushing me toward the back door. "You run to the black oak in the woods and stay there until morning, you hear me? Don't you come back until the sun's come up."

I'd fought her. I wanted to stay. Even then, I thought I could make a difference. Maybe that's why I've lived my life the way I have.

"If you love me, Corine, you go."

I went.

Behind me, she'd begun a chant, the last one she'd ever speak. In the distance, I saw the scattered lights marching toward our house like a wicked firefly army. I don't know if I knew what would happen then, but my whole world went up in flames.

No more would the hurdy-gurdy man come to supper at our house. Mama used to say his music was magical, and I think it surely was because none since then has sounded so sweet or lifted my spirits the way his harmonica did back then. We had a constant parade of visitors, some more amazing than others; Cherie Solomon never met a stranger.

I sat and rocked, fifteen years removed from that night, weighing it against this fresh loss. In the movies, Chance would have sensed my pain, come to offer me comfort, and everything in my world would've been made right. He would have held me as I did him the night I didn't want him in my bed. In reality, I cried myself out alone and fell into a sleep that left me sticky and thick when I woke.

The room swam with shadows cut with light from the streetlamps and guttering neon from defunct businesses nearby. At first I wasn't sure what had roused me, and then the knock came again. I felt wrinkles from the cheap bedspread imprinted on my cheek, and a glimmer of reflection from the window told me my hair was smashed flat on one side. I answered the door anyway.

"Get your stuff," Chance said, low. "We can't stay here."

"What's wrong?"

His tone alarmed me. "Just come on. Now."

Acting on a type of trust I'd thought shattered forever, I grabbed my backpack and stuffed the handmade pillow inside. As I slid my shoes on and headed for the door, the streetlight sputtered and winked out. Chills rolled along my skin as I watched bulbs flicker and die all along the street. We stepped onto the dark lot, which suddenly seemed to me a cemetery of cars, so much dead, heavy metal.

We left the Toyota parked, his hand on my arm as he hurried me along. I knew the clammy sensation of dread on my skin, and the last time I'd felt this way I nearly died. Though I wanted to ask for answers, I was too frightened to do more than scuttle behind him. The dark buildings seemed sinister, unfriendly eyes peering from broken windows.

"Chance." I didn't dig in my heels as I spoke, kept moving. "What's going on?"

"Did you call the cop?" he asked instead of answering me. "After we arrived. Did you tell him where we were?"

Watching the slow roil of darkness over this particular street, I shook my head. "No. I accidentally took a nap."

"Then he's not our problem." He sounded almost disappointed.

"But we do have one." It suddenly felt about ten degrees colder outside and that was more than just the sun going down.

"Yeah," he said grimly. He laced his fingers through mine, not a romantic gesture but as if in preparation for a blizzard where we'd need a nonvisual link to make it across the street. "No matter what happens inside, don't let go of me, Corine."

My mouth felt dry. I wished I *had* called Saldana. "I won't. I promise."

We stopped behind a warehouse, the reason he'd chosen this neighborhood in the first place. It was a hulking structure with blank windows, no signs of life. There should have been a night watchman on duty, but at the moment it felt as though we were the only two human beings left in the world. The wind kicked up, sending trash skittering across the dead-quiet street. Something besides cloud cover blotted out the stars, and the air felt heavy as lead when I brought it to my lungs.

Stooping for a moment, Chance finessed the padlock on the back door, another skill set I had never examined too closely. The door squealed like a piglet being slaughtered as we pushed past into cloying, copper-scented darkness. His hand felt reassuringly warm against mine; this place had me shivering before we'd gone two feet from the door. I'd never read a building before, but as what my mama called dead man's hands ran down my spine, I knew bad things had happened here. Normal folks ignored that creeping chill, as if it sprang from an overactive imagination, but they probably had a latent gift if they felt the ghostly touch crawling on their skin.

His penlight clicked on, a tiny isle of light surrounded by the shadows that surged with purpose around us. Boxes and crates took on their own identities, sinister shapes crouched in wait. He ignored them and led us deeper into the labyrinth.

"Here," he whispered as we spotted the crime scene tape. "They found her purse here."

I knelt, running my free hand over the cement. It was too big for me to read, but I might get impressions. It sparked a little, the same blue shock I'd received from Jesse Saldana.

Blood. Pain. Death.

If I had anything in my stomach, I would have tossed it up. Something died here; there was no mistaking the necrotic tinge smeared over the floor like rancid butter. But I couldn't quit. If Min had left the Buddha for Chance to find, knowing he'd bring it to me, then she might have left us another clue.

"I need something smaller, something I can hold."

Closing my eyes, I ran my fingers over the floor. I imagined I could feel the tackiness of dried blood texturing the stained cement. I explored the corners of crates nearby and cracks where something interesting might sink. In one of those fissures I found a small round object with beveled edges. It singed my fingers just in picking it up; oh, yes, it held an active charge, secrets to share. I slid it into the narrow beam of Chance's penlight.

"A button," he said with sharp, wicked delight.

"I shouldn't handle it here." Though I couldn't have explained my certainty, I knew it was beyond dangerous for us to linger.

"We need to get out of this part of Laredo entirely." Chance pulled me to my feet in a neat motion that reminded me how strong he was, stronger than he looked for such a lean frame. "Try to lose them before—"

His words died in a nightmare of imploding glass as they found us.

It's No Sacrifice

Needles skated along my spine, and then Chance threw himself against me, pinning me to a crate. His body curved as he sheltered me, curling his arms over my head. I felt a few stinging cuts blossom, though he took the worst of it. The place sounded as though Christmas ornaments shattered all around us, such a delicate tinkling sound for something that could slice us to shreds. Then it settled, as if the air inside the warehouse had equalized to the pressure outside.

And something came in.

Through broken windows, I heard the rush, like wind through dry leaves, before I smelled the sulfur. "It's a sending," I said through suddenly numb lips.

My mama told me about such spells, years ago. But she cautioned me as I sat with a grimoire balanced on my knee. "Only a wicked witch would do such a thing," she'd told me, stirring a pot full of steeping herbs for some potion. "Our first tenet is 'do no harm.'"

My whole body wanted to freeze, but Chance pulled me along as we made our way along the blunt crate edges. "Yeah. It's going to get ugly, Corine. Can you handle it?"

For a brief, panicked moment, I thought of Señor Alvarez, my Dutch miniatures, and my quiet, comfortable life. Then I set my jaw. For Min I could. Damn right.

"I'm behind you. Let's go."

A sending could take many different forms, depending on the materials used in the summoning, though it always smells of sulfur. I wasn't sure what we were dealing with yet, but some sendings are worse than others.

I read about them after Mama died. I'm not sure why. It wasn't like my foster families would let me practice, but I snuck my books out from their hiding place beneath my mattress when nobody was watching. Ironically, nothing from the house but her grimoires survived the fire, as Mama had stored them in a fireproof safe.

Sometimes I stole out to the woods and tried my hand at it, but my heart wasn't in it. Maybe too much sorrow weighed the spirit down, unbalancing the chakras or preventing me from tapping my potential. Whatever the reason, I couldn't make magick like she did. I just had the one soul-sucking trick.

Chance and I had faced off against a few bad apples in our time, practitioners used to getting their own way and not caring how they went about it. We survived a particularly nasty cockroach sending in Reno. *Hope to God it's not insects.*

It wasn't.

When we broke away from the crates and headed toward the door, it zeroed in on us: a wailing presence made of violent wind, dust, and dry leaves that had blown in through the broken windows. Like a sandstorm, the sending stung my skin, determined to force its way into my nose and throat. I'd once seen the remains of someone who choked to death in one of these, and it wasn't pretty.

That was one of the cases Chance and I took pro bono. When a woman came to us and said, eyes downcast, "Somebody's killing people on my block, and the police don't care," I just couldn't refuse. One of those rogue practitioners had turned the projects into his personal hunting ground, testing new spells without giving a shit who got in the way.

I tracked him. Found him. Chance left him chained to a guardrail on an overpass, wrapped up with a bow for the cops to find. Oddly, law enforcement didn't appear thankful. They called us vigilantes.

We had been, among other things, once upon a time. But I was out of practice.

I don't want to go out like this.

My hair whipped around my face as the called storm fought to push into my nose and mouth. I should've put it up, braided it or something—long hair was a weakness out in the field. I saw sparks from holding my breath, but inhaling would be worse.

The winds buffeted, and I fought to keep my feet, but the gale sent me sailing. As my hand tore from his, Chance shouted, "Corine!" though it was madness to speak.

I landed hard, slamming into first a crate and then the wall. Dazed, I lay while the wind howled around me, more dust rising in a malignant manifestation of the summoner's will. The leaves scraping my skin felt as though they were made of salt and ground glass, so I covered my face with my hands.

How do you fight a force of nature? If I stayed low it'd burn itself out, if I didn't choke to death first. No practitioner possessed the power to rage like this indefinitely.

His head down, Chance came to me, crawling. Once I would have given anything to see him like this, but it lacked poetry now. I registered a surge of joy that he'd come for me. His fingers wrapped around mine.

"I thought I told you not to let go," he yelled.

I almost laughed. He held on to me as we forced our way through, blind but determined. It became almost impossible to breathe, and I started to feel faint, afraid to inhale, afraid the demon dust would find purchase in my lungs and strangle me from the inside out. Worse—it might take root, giving the summoner a hold over me.

By the time we staggered outside, our clothes hanging in tatters, I heard sirens in the distance. Leaning down, hands on my knees, I took deep, gulping breaths, willing the black dots to leave my field of vision. We had to get out of here. It wouldn't go well if they took us in officially. I had a history of being near crime scenes, though it was hard to tell what local law enforcement would make of *all* the windows being broken.

"Can you travel?" When he turned without waiting for my reply, I saw that his back was a nightmare of ruined flesh. If he didn't receive immediate medical attention, it would scar. Hell, it might scar anyway.

"Yeah," I told his bloody back, and limped after him.

A guy in a black hooded sweatshirt slid out from between two buildings. I caught the movement out of the corner of my eye and increased my pace to a quick trot. Most likely he was just a vagrant who slept in a box out back, but I didn't take any chances. If the cops questioned him, he might be able to finger us. We needed to get gone.

Because fate isn't always a capricious bitch, the Toyota started on the first try. As we left the La Quinta parking lot, I saw the glimmered reflection of red and blue lights in the rearview mirror. They'd have a hell of a mess to clean up.

I couldn't think about the way Chance had put my safety first back there, how he'd thrown himself on top of me to shield me from flying glass. It controverted everything I knew—or thought I knew—about him. I certainly couldn't think about the way he'd crawled through demon dust and howling winds for me.

Luckily, something else occurred to me. "Where was the night watchman?"

He cut me a grim look, taking his eyes off the road

for only a second. "I hope he's home watching TV. Nothing got out of that place alive, except us."

I hoped he was right. It wouldn't do any good to worry, though. "Where we going?"

"I know a safe house." His voice bordered on curt because the pain had to be staggering. He'd taken the brunt of the glass, maybe had slivers embedded in his skin too. I noticed how stiff he sat as he drove, and my conscience cringed.

Chance made a quick call on his cell, but I couldn't tell whom he was talking to. If the plan involved Tanya, I'd seriously think about going home, even if it meant abandoning Min to whatever fate had befallen her and breaking my word. Forfeiting my shot at IDing the bastards who had led long, happy lives after murdering my mother.

So maybe not. I'd stick.

Twenty minutes later, after Chance told me the plan, I gazed at him in disbelief. "Chuch? You're entrusting our lives to Chuch?"

"Don't underestimate him," he said briefly. "His grandmother was a very gifted *curandera*, and he knows things."

Curandera. Magickal healing woman.

Well, in my eighteen months in Mexico, I've gotten to know a few of those. The occult is a staple of everyday life there, and oddly enough, it blends seamlessly with pervasive Catholicism. People believe in curses that can make you sick, go blind, or lose all your luck. At the plaza near my house, there's a shop where you can find a *curandera.*

Tia gives aura readings, does spiritual cleansings, reads palms, and makes charms, amulets, and potions— that sort of thing. She's sweet as a bowl of figs. But I'm not sure being descended from someone like Tia qualified Chuch to help us out in this situation.

Don't get me wrong; Chuch is a great guy. Funny.

The last time we got together, he'd said, "You call me if you ever need body work done. I totally redid this guy's Mustang, so cherry it was stolen a week after I worked on it."

His full name was Jesus Maria Ortiz Obregón, but he told us, "I'm Chucho, but everyone calls me Chuch," when we met at the Forever Wicker store in Lutz, Florida. Don't ask what a custom car restoration artist was doing in a furniture shop on his vacation, but Chance always seemed to know what random encounters were meaningful, or maybe he just saved every contact we made, just in case. You never know when you'll need your ride tricked out.

Whichever, he kept a Rolodex of business cards he put to use under the most unlikely circumstances. So I guessed it wasn't too surprising that we'd turned up here, bags in hand. Chuch lived in a decent sized stone ranch house on the outskirts of town, and he had three cars in his drive, all in varying stages of renewal. I was still wondering about what Chance had said about not underestimating Chuch, when the door swung open.

I immediately revised my opinion of the mechanic. Salt lined the threshold, subtle but solid, and he had charms on the walls masquerading as art. Whatever he did in addition to restoring classic cars, he was a player. I waited for my invitation to enter.

Medium height and brawny, Chuch greeted us with a wave and a subdued smile. "Get inside, you two." As we came into the light, he winced. "You need a doc, *primo*. Maybe you too, *prima*."

Chance shook his head. "Not tonight, not before the sun comes up."

"So it's like that, huh? Right. You guys want tamales?"

That sounded good, but we needed to clean up first. "Do you have some old towels, maybe some peroxide? I want to take a look at his back."

"I'll set you up in the bathroom." Chuch headed off to collect his first aid kit, leaving me to reflect that if two people turned up at my door in such a state, I doubt I'd be so laconic in my acceptance.

In this light, Chance looked ashen, his face taut with pain he refused to acknowledge. "Tell me you still have the button."

Holy shit. I'd forgotten all about it. If I'd lost it, we might as well not have risked checking the warehouse. I felt a little sick as I thrust my hand into the deep pocket of my very abused sweater. Jumped when my fingers brushed beveled plastic and I felt the same spark I'd received from touching Jesse Saldana.

"I have it." I didn't pull it out, though, as I didn't want to handle it right then.

"Bless that sweater," he breathed. "I'll never say a word about it again."

"Sure you won't." I smiled only because I was meant to.

Chuch returned and beckoned us down the hall and to the left into a green and white tiled bathroom. I thought there must be a woman in his life because it was clean and guest towels hung on the rack in addition to the old ones piled on the counter. He had a thing for frogs too because cute little ceramic statuettes sat all over the room.

"They're good luck," he explained, apparently reading my look. "I'll be in the kitchen. Join me whenever you're ready."

Shoulder against the wall, Chance watched me set out gauze, peroxide, and tweezers. I washed my hands, putting off the moment of truth. After about thirty seconds of lathering, I decided it wasn't fair to prolong his misery.

"Let's do this," I said. "Take your shirt off, please."

He managed a slightly roguish smile. "You don't know how long I've been waiting to hear you say that."

Knowing Things

"Cute," I said as he literally peeled the shirt from his back. Oh, shit. I wasn't a nurse. There was no way I could handle this.

"How bad is it?" he asked through gritted teeth.

"It'll take a while." I kept my voice noncommittal, but he knew. Chance sucked in a breath as I started blotting. A shudder ran through me at seeing his red, red blood on my hands. "Maybe you should get in the shower and I'll run some cool water over you so I can see what I'm doing."

"You just want to get my pants off." He shucked his trousers in one movement. The careless air cost him, though; he blanched as he stepped into the tub.

As the blood washed away, I saw the damage done to him on my behalf. I tried not to flinch as I directed the spray. Pink rivulets trickled down his brown back, staining the water at his feet. I continued until it ran clear.

A few of the wounds probably needed stitches, but I didn't say anything, just supported him as he climbed out and stood shivering in wet boxers on Chuch's fuzzy green rug. For a mere moment, I clung, enjoying the heat we generated. Chance leaned on me, damp forehead against mine. When I put the toilet lid down, he collapsed gratefully, turning his knees toward the shower so I could work.

My hands trembled as I took up the tweezers, probing the first wound. Chance let out a sob of breath that made me feel as though I were torturing him intentionally. I took back all my wishes for him to suffer, but it was too late.

There's probably a lesson in that.

Because it seemed to help, I tried to keep my motions mechanical: retrieve a sliver of glass, blot the wound, repeat.

"I'm sorry." I spoke in a low litany, hating that I had to hurt him.

By the time I finished, I felt sick and he looked worse. He shook from head to toe, his fingers white where they gripped his knees. "Done?" His voice sounded raw, I imagined from the screams he'd swallowed.

"All but the disinfectant."

Chance didn't argue. Though normally doctors recommend simple cleansing with water in case of irritation, we couldn't take the chance with demon dust. It had to be flushed out. Otherwise not only would the wounds fester; whoever wanted us dead could eventually work Chance like a puppet before he died.

This stuff was the worst of the worst, something I'd only heard about before that night in Reno. My mother had mentioned it in passing, but now I knew you had to kill a demon's corporeal form and burn it to ash, and then use it in the ritual in order to wind up with a sending like this. Really wicked shit.

I hated that his welfare rested in my hands, but he wouldn't go to a hospital, never had as long as I'd known him. I watched as the peroxide boiled out the cuts, seeing the telltale shadow in the pink discharge. Yep, this was undoubtedly the right decision.

"Smear my mother's salve on the worst ones. I put it in your backpack."

"Good idea."

Though she'd formulated it for burns, it would promote healing in cuts as well and anesthetize some of the pain. I went to get it but had to spend a moment leaning against the wall before I could return to the bathroom. Hurting him damaged me in ways I didn't care to contemplate right now.

"Almost done," I said, stepping back into sight. "I brought you a change of clothes too."

I painted the ointment down his lean, wounded back. I didn't just hit the worst; I covered all of them and then began the tedious process of taping cotton and gauze in place. I wasn't looking forward to changing the dressings, but I owed him.

"That's a lot better," he murmured, looking almost human again. "Why don't you rinse off too? I'll get changed and then we can talk."

I let myself enjoy a spurt of irritation, like I wouldn't know to shower without his instruction. Instead I got a pair of shorts and a T-shirt and exhibited exceptional common sense by not arguing. I made it quick, though, soaping everything in less than five minutes. My skin felt tender, as if I'd had a powerful exfoliating treatment.

When I joined the guys, they were already eating what looked like excellent homemade tamales, and I have some experience in that area. Chuch stood up when I entered; Chance didn't. He ate with silent economy that told me he knew he needed the fuel more than he wanted the food. Our host waved a hand vaguely around his rather retro kitchen. I took in the burnt sienna countertops and avocado appliances.

"I got *frijoles y queso*, *pollo verde*, and *dulce*. What kind do you want?"

To my mind, tamales should never be sweet. "I'll have the first two, please."

Chuch quirked a brow. "How many?"

"One of each."

I let him wait on me, feeling new aches spring up as I settled onto the chair. When I hit the warehouse wall, I'd banged my knee pretty good and I felt it now, a slow throb like a toothache. Chuch laid in front of me a green pottery plate, two tamales, a little cream, and some crumbled cheese. Then he seasoned them with a dash of salsa. My mouth watered.

The mechanic joined us at the table, attending his own food. It felt like forever since we'd eaten in Monterrey. I dug in, content to let Chance explain the situation, but he was in no hurry. I couldn't honestly blame him.

"So why'd you two turn up at my door looking like this?" Done eating, Chuch folded his arms, leaning back with an expectant expression. "And is it gonna follow you to my house?"

"It might." Chance shrugged. "But your wards are solid, right?"

"Never had nothing get in." Seeming worried, Chuch searched Chance's face with his gaze, a hard, penetrating look. "But there's always the first time. Don't hold back on me, *mano*. I got to know what I'm dealing with."

"A sending rolled us over on the west side," I told him around a mouthful of tamale. I ignored the look Chance shot me. "Nasty piece of work. Demon dust and a howler wind."

Chuch flinched. "Shit. You don't call that up on your first try. You two pissed off somebody powerful."

I'd been testing him in case the salt was a fluke, but it seemed the mechanic knew his way around more than an engine. His grandmother must've taught him well. The rest of the world, full of normal people, lived in blissful unawareness about things that went bump in the night. But a filmy veil of unwanted knowledge and bitter experience would always separate folks like Chuch, Chance, and me from those lucky, ignorant mugs.

Blotting his mouth on a paper napkin dotted with

green frogs, Chance regarded us somberly before he spoke. "We did, but I don't have a choice. They have my mother."

"Who's 'they'?" After glancing between us, Chuch settled on me as most likely to answer his questions. I wished I *had* the answers.

"At this point, we're not sure." I didn't look at Chance as I filled Chuch in with as much as I knew, anyway. Which didn't amount to a whole lot. He seemed surprised to hear I'd been living in Mexico City.

Chuch said, "I'll tell you straight. The only players in this area who could afford a sending like that are the *narcotraficantes*. Could be two or three different cartels, though." My expression must have reflected disbelief, because he added, "What, you think the cartels don't pay for hexes? It's not like Hollywood, *prima*, all automatic weapons and shady dudes with oily mustaches. You live in Mexico; why don't you know this?"

"Sorry." I conceded the point with a nod, glad I hadn't offended him.

"Anyway, hard telling who your mama crossed, no? What was—" Chuch caught himself, but I didn't want to see Chance's reaction to the slip. "Er, what *is* your mom like?"

"She has nothing to do with drug dealers," Chance said savagely. He laid down his fork as if he wanted to stab someone with it. "She owns a homeopathy store in Tampa."

The other man's dark eyes gleamed flat and hard under the kitchen lights. "So she knows things, uses her skill to heal the sick. A *curandera*: that's what she is now, *primo*. But what was she before?"

To my amazement, Chance had no answer for that.

I cleared my throat. "I think we'd better find out. I'm as ready as I'm going to be. So it's showtime."

Both men swung their heads my way as I brought the button out of my shorts' pocket. Since I had scabs atop old scars on my left palm, I used my right hand. Closing my fingers and my eyes, I let the pain come. It washed over me in waves, flames licking down my nerve endings.

Pain unlocked the door.

A dim and murky scene boiled up, obscured as if by smoke. Candlelight. I focused on the images. Four men in dark clothing stood around a circle drawn in colored chalk. At the center stood a woman, and my heart clenched. Yi Min-chin. I saw her lips moving as she led the ritual. Silver glinted as she raised a knife high.

Chicken blood. The cement was stained with chicken blood.

Sacrifice complete, the men knelt to her and she painted arcane symbols on each brow in turn. The spell had the look of a covenant to me, as if his mother had made a deal that night, a compact signed in blood.

I watched as she plucked a button from her blouse and flicked it toward the crates. She was definitely leaving a trail for me to follow. I just didn't know whether I wanted to find her after what I'd just seen.

Feeling the tamales rise, I opened my eyes, letting the button clatter onto the table. It was useless now, like a dead battery. My right hand stung but plastic didn't sear like metal. No new marks. Though I didn't want to, I shared what I'd seen.

The mechanic shook his head, eyes wide. "You got that kind of *hudu*? Could tell that from a button? But you acted like you couldn't believe the cartels use magick when they'll do *anything* to control their territory? I think you were bustin' my balls."

I didn't bother to say what I did wasn't magick. Besides, Chance was already gearing up to argue, sparing me the need to explain. He gripped the edge of the table, quietly livid. "That . . . that's wrong. They must've faked it somehow, planted it for us to find. She isn't— she doesn't know about—"

Very gently Chuch asked him, "You sure, *primo*?"

I don't say my visions are always right. Sometimes the sound track makes all the difference; sometimes I interpret what I see incorrectly. It happens. But I don't know what other spin I could put on this. Yi Min-chin led that ritual with expert precision. She knew the meaning of those symbols. I couldn't blame him for fighting the idea that his mom wasn't perfect. In this world, sometimes a mother represents the only glimpse we ever get of pure generosity, someone who puts our welfare before her own.

Mine wore attar of roses and sang "All the Pretty Horses" to me before I slept. She'd also practiced her craft openly and unwisely in Kilmer, Georgia, believing in the tolerance of her neighbors. When that mistake caught up to her, she gave her life for me.

I've been suffering ever since. It weighs on me because I feel like I need to live twice as worthy a life in order to make up for her sacrifice. And I'm so tired.

For a long moment Chance glared at us both, as if we were to blame for his shattered illusions. Then he dropped his head into his hands. I'd never seen him like this, broken and unsure. I ached because I no longer had the right to comfort him, no longer felt sure he'd welcome my hands in his damp black hair.

"It doesn't matter," he said finally. "If she's in trouble, I have to help her."

Blood never stops calling for blood.

Rock and a Hard Place

"I get that," Chuch said, nodding. "I'd do the same. But you'll get yourselves killed if you don't start playing smart. This is out of your weight class."

"With all due respect," I returned. "You don't know what I weigh."

The mechanic sized me up with a glance. "One forty-two," he decided. "If you're being literal." His accuracy left me blinking as he went on. "If not, then you need to fill me in."

"I'm retaining water," I mumbled. *And doughnuts.* Neither guy was stupid enough to say it aloud if they thought it. "I'll let Chance do the honors. I have to make a call."

Chance glared at me, but he already knew Saldana wasn't our problem, so there wasn't much he could say. He could've played the jealous ex, but he wouldn't want to show that side in front of Chuch. Plus they really did have stuff to discuss.

For added privacy, I went into the other room, decorated in plaid furniture and protective charms. First I needed to get my phone working, though. With reasonable deftness, I popped it open and switched the SIM card.

My cell doesn't have roaming on it, you see. That's for people who want to register for an account and put it on a credit card, leaving an electronic trail a mile wide. I go prepaid all the way, so I slotted the U.S. SIM into my phone and watched it search until it found a signal.

Bingo.

Backtracking to the front door, I located my purse and dug out Saldana's card. Ridiculous the way my heart thumped as I dialed. You'd think I believed the bullshit I'd spun for Chance about the guy wanting to take me out for personal reasons.

On the fourth ring, he barked, "Saldana!" at me, almost making me disconnect.

I had to clear my throat before I could speak. "Uhm. Yeah. This is Corine Solomon. You said something about getting dinner tomorrow night."

Relief colored his buttery drawl, which I liked quite a lot. "Glad you called, sugar. Just a minute." I heard hoots in the background, so I guessed I'd caught him at a bad time. Movement, and then a rough whisper: "I don't suppose you know anything 'bout the mess down at this warehouse? You all right?"

I made unconvincing static noises, though he sounded genuinely concerned. "Huh? You're cutting out."

Luckily he possessed a sense of humor. "Uh-huh. Logan's Roadhouse, seven tomorrow night. It's on San Dario, near the mall. Can you make it?"

"I'll be there." *Whether Chance liked it or not.*

"Oh, *that* you heard." But I could sense his smile.

When I returned to the kitchen, the guys were eating a second plate of tamales, looking like they'd said everything important. Chuch glanced up and then indicated the seat opposite him. As I sat, I saw he'd laid out colored pencils and paper.

"I need you to sketch the symbols," he said without preamble. "That'll gimme a clue who might have some info. Most of the players in town work in Santería or straight *hudu*, but I know people online who can help with more exotic traditions."

I blinked. *Chuch is a regular Lone Gunman. Who knew? Chance did*, I decided, watching him eat. *That's why he kept his card.*

"That's a remarkably logical idea. I've never done this before, though, and I'm not much of an artist. But I'll try."

As they ate, I tried to remember. In the end, I found it easier to re-create the whole thing, starting with the circles. I couldn't draw the people so I represented them with Xs and then took my best shot at the symbols Yi Min-chin had drawn.

When I handed him the page, Chuch studied it for a minute and then shrugged. "Looks like a summoning circle." Which I'd already guessed. "I'll send it to a homie who's into the hermetic stuff. Maybe he can hook us up."

I studied him for a moment, unable to figure him out. "Why are you helping us? You know it's dangerous."

Chuch flashed a slightly gap-toothed grin. "My old lady took off and I don't have anything better to do." I held his look, and eventually he sighed, looking sheepish. "Plus I owe him money." He jerked his head toward Chance. "I expanded my garage but business has been slow. Lot of people leaving Laredo. It's a scary place to be lately."

That made as much sense as anything. Muttering something about scanning my drawing, Chuch headed toward his home office. I didn't like how quiet Chance was. He hadn't said a single word since I came back into the room, not even when I took his plate to the sink for him.

If the silence held, I was going to say something stupid like *Are you okay?* when I knew he wasn't. Finally I settled on "What's on your mind?" Like I didn't know.

"I keep turning it over," he said, staring at his hands. "I wanted to think they must have some hold over her. But I keep coming back to the fact that she knew the spell, and there's a lot I don't know about her. You ever have that feeling? Like you've known someone your whole life but you don't know them at all."

I reached for his hand. No matter the ugly history between us, I was still his friend. I didn't think I had it in me for it to be otherwise. Our fingers intertwined, his long and elegant, mine short and scarred. That was one good thing about the gift, I supposed. My fingerprints never seemed to come out right.

"No," I said finally. "I never have that feeling. Because I don't have anyone I've known my whole life." The words came out starker than I intended, maybe because his sorrow cut through me like a knife.

If he'd been thinking, he would have remembered. Chance knew my history, at least the bare bones of it. He knew I'd spent my adolescence in foster homes. They deteriorated as the years went on because nobody wanted to take me. The first time it happened, I was handling a jeweled hair clip. It singed my fingers and I said without thinking, "This belonged to your great-aunt Cecilia. She was wearing it when she died."

The gentle Methodist lady almost had a heart attack. She'd gazed at me, face pinched and gray, before snatching the hair clip away and fussing over burns she couldn't figure out how I'd gotten. A retired schoolteacher, Miss Minnie was actually the nicest about my weirdness, but she didn't want me around after that.

That night, she called the social workers and said she wasn't equipped to deal with "a child like me." It got worse. I'll just say, I can't play at bondage during sex or watch the *Exorcist*, though it isn't demons that drive my powers. There's no enjoying such things when you've been tied to a bed for real.

I'll leave it at that.

At first, the state of Georgia accused the host families of burning my hands to punish me. Ruined some lives, I guess. It didn't matter what I said about it, although by

the end, they had psychiatrists asking me why I felt the
need to hurt myself. At eighteen, they cut me loose and I
was glad to go. I sure left my mark, even then; left enemies behind me.

Shit, now I felt almost as low as Chance. I didn't usually let it get to me. Done was done, and unless it was a
slight you could avenge right then, it did no good to
dwell on it.

All my aches came back tenfold, and suddenly I
wanted nothing more than to lose myself for a few
hours. We couldn't do anything until daylight anyway.

"Well," Chuch said from the doorway. "I sent an
e-mail to Booke, but it's four in the morning there." He
peered at us. "You guys look like shit."

I wondered how *he'd* look if he'd been in Mexico
City just two days ago, innocently examining Dutch
miniatures. By some miracle I held my tongue, as he
was helping us.

"It's been a long day," Chance said quietly.

If there were a candle I could burn to make me forget
how it felt to touch him, I think I would have lit it. Right
then, I felt empty and broken, missing the way we used
to be. His hand in mine wasn't enough, but then I'd always needed more than he could give. Chance reacted
on me like a drug, and I jonesed for him in ways that
weren't safe or sane. Quietly I withdrew my hand.

Chuch nodded. "How 'bout I get you bedded down?
You still sleepin' together?"

I answered, "No," as Chance said, "Yes." We exchanged a look, and then I added firmly, "He should
have his own bed. I'm afraid I'll hurt his back."

Our host shrugged and set me up on the couch with
plenty of pillows and a sheet to pull over me, as it was a
warm night. "Sorry," he said, looking uncomfortable. "I
turned the third bedroom into a home office."

"It's fine, thanks."

I hoped I wouldn't dream tonight.

Wicked Game

I dreamed of fire.

As on the worst occasions, I woke with the sheets sodden from terror sweat. The sky glimmered with pearly, predawn light, dispelling some of the gloom. I lay there, clammy, my heart thudding like I'd been running. For a moment I couldn't get my breath and the shaking wouldn't stop. Chance used to get up and make me hot chocolate whenever this happened, his eyes half-lidded with sleep. He wouldn't speak, just deliver the drink in a ritual that let me know I wasn't alone. I have no idea why, but cupping the mug between my hands always made me feel better.

You'd think it'd go away for good after so many years, but the nightmare always comes back in times of trouble, like a reminder. Things always get worse when the dream returns; it's a reliable foretelling device in its own way. If I could be sure it was my mother, trying to reach me somehow, I wouldn't mind as much. I don't have much faith there's anything left of her, though, and I've tried several speakers for the dead. They always claim there's interference, a bad connection between this world and the next. I don't try to reach her anymore. Like I said, I have the feeling she gave everything she was to me, and then just floated away in wisps of smoke, not even a ghost.

Still unsteady, I crawled out of my sweaty nest and
headed for the kitchen. I'd make my own cocoa, dammit. If I could find it. Rummaging around in Chuch's
kitchen, I unearthed a box of instant. *That'll work.*

As I filled a cup from the tap, a click made me spin
around, sloshing water on my thighs. A tall, dark-haired
woman stood glaring at me from the doorway that led in
from the garage. "Who the hell are you?"

"Corine," I said, wondering whether lukewarm tap
water and a heavy mug would offer any real defense.
She looked ready to claw my eyes out.

But her wrath went another way. "I'll kill him," she
bit out. "No, I'll cut his thing off. I'm gone four days
and here you are in your underwear. *Pendejo!*" She
stormed down the hall toward Chuch's room.

"It's not underwear," I said, glancing down at my
shorts. She wasn't listening. With a shrug, I popped my
mug into the microwave.

Within thirty seconds—and the microwave timed it—
I heard, "Eva, *corazon*, I—*ow!*" Chuch emerged in a
pair of pajama pants, heading for the kitchen at a dead
run. Eva followed, steely-eyed and ready to castrate.
"Corine, tell her it isn't how it looks."

"What isn't?" Yeah, I played dumb as I mixed the
chocolate powder into the hot water. Stirred, watching
his agitation increase.

"You slept on my couch!"

He'd thank me for this later. "You said she left you.
What business is it of hers?"

"*Dios*, I only went to my mama's house to think
about things. We're still married, Jesus Maria Ortiz
Obregón! You're going to hell!"

Oops. Maybe I wasn't helping. "You never mentioned you were married."

Chuch eyed me with dislike as I brought the spoon to
my mouth, tasting the cocoa. "It wasn't important!
You—"

That was the wrong thing to say. "Wasn't important! Five years and it wasn't important. Just like I don't matter to you as much as your precious cars."

She seemed like she was building up a head of steam so I interjected, "I *did* sleep on the couch and it isn't how it looks. Chuch is helping us out for a day or two."

"Us?" Eva looked oddly crestfallen. Maybe she enjoyed yelling at him, and if what she'd thought was true, she would've had a lifetime supply of ammunition.

"Yeah, us." Sleep rumpled, a red T-shirt hiding the worst of the damage, Chance rubbed his eyes as he came into the kitchen. He looked for me, found me, and offered a half smile. It was an *I'm glad you didn't leave me in the night* sort of look. I didn't blame Eva for checking him out, even with her estranged husband standing right there. My ex just has that effect on women.

"Is there coffee?" Chance asked.

"I'll make some," Eva said, sounding subdued.

I had a residual headache from the dream but at least the shakes were gone. If Eva hadn't turned up, I would have offered to cook breakfast. My scrambled eggs are great. They're also the extent of my kitchen skills, unless you count quesadillas, salsa, or microwaving stuff other people have made.

Over huevos rancheros, we filled her in. On my own, I don't know whether I would have trusted her, but Chuch did, of course, and when you're staying in a woman's home, you owe her some respect. Turned out she came from a long and distinguished line of *curanderas*, but she didn't have the *don*. That's Spanish for gift. We heard all about it, and by the time the meal was over, I felt sorry for Chuch. The woman *was* a talker.

While they spoke, I washed the dishes. It's polite to clean up when someone else cooks for you. I remember that from my mother's upbringing.

"So are you home for good, *mi corazon*? I missed

you." The mood turned a little squishy for my taste and I braced for some canoodling. While I'm all for sex, preferably lots of it, I don't enjoy watching other people have it.

"If you promise to pay some attention to me. No more spending all your time under those cars, okay?"

I could see he wanted to protest that was how he made their living but evidently decided that discussion would keep. Silently I commended his common sense when he simply nodded and changed the subject.

"I'm gonna go see if Booke's gotten back to me. Thanks for breakfast." Chuch kissed his wife on the cheek.

That left the three of us in the kitchen, but I didn't want to hear any more stories about how Eva's *abuela* could cast out evil spirits by rubbing an egg all over someone's naked body. It might well be true but I needed a shower just thinking about it. As I headed for the bathroom, I heard her say, "You're hurt, *pobrecito*. Let me look at your bandages."

My jaw clenched, and my step stuttered. I made myself continue. It didn't matter who changed the dressings as long as someone did. Eva wasn't encroaching on my territory. I didn't *have* territory.

Twenty minutes later, I presented myself in Chuch's office. A designer would call the walls eggshell, but it looked dingy white to me. It was decorated in early garage sale, but damn if he didn't boast the biggest, baddest metal desk I'd ever seen. I was pretty sure all four of us could take shelter under it in case of a tornado. More plaid on a rundown recliner Eva had likely banished from the living room. Among protective knots and clusters of beads, license plates hung on the walls, probably from the first cars he'd restored.

I purely coveted his lamp, though. It would go perfectly in my living room, a naked woman cast in wrought iron for the base and a gloriously overbedizened shade. Black velvet, gold fringe and beads—need I say more? I wanted it, but it wouldn't do to make an offer right away. If I ever got tired of it, I could sell it. Hey, I'm a professional, after all.

He sat clicking away for a minute before acknowledging me. "You got a mean streak, you know that?"

"So I've heard." Most recently, when I wore the frangipani perfume to bed with Chance. "Did your boy get back to you?"

"Sure did. He wants to talk to you two so I'm setting up a VoIP."

I pondered while he worked and eventually put it together, as I'm not what you'd call tech savvy. At this point, I don't have a desktop system, a laptop, or even a BlackBerry. My cell phone suffices for my messaging needs, and I check my e-mail only once every two weeks at the Internet café near my house. Those are all over the place in Mexico since a lot of people see a computer as something you just need to use occasionally rather than a must-have amenity for the home.

"Huh," I murmured, thoughtful. "I draw a picture and this morning, a guy in another time zone is ready to help. I'd never have guessed you could get information about this kind of thing so fast from online contacts."

To be honest, I'd be afraid to broach the subject. I had a hard enough time dealing with people face-to-face who could see my scars as proof and *still* thought I was mental. I dropped down in the Barcalounger with a sigh.

Chuch flashed me a smile. "Hey, that's why they invented the Internet, *hermanita*. To talk about weird shit and download porn."

As the software ran its diagnostic, Chance strolled into the office. There weren't enough chairs so he propped himself on the edge of the monster desk. He looked better today, his wounds bandaged and artfully concealed by a great Boss shirt. Few men could pull off shimmering black and silver stripes with such aplomb. In that same shirt, Chuch would look like a pimp.

Chance arched a brow. "All set?"

A male voice answered in an Oxford accent, albeit a bit tinny from the speakers. "I can hear you. Can you hear me?"

"I can. My name's Chance, and I appreciate your time." As he shifted his weight, I tried not to think about the edge of the desk biting into his butt. That used to be my job, and trust me when I say the man has a truly remarkable ass.

God, I needed to focus.

"Loud and clear," I said. "I'm Corine." I didn't know whether that was correct etiquette but I enjoyed pretending I had some manners, at least in the beginning.

Chuch didn't. "What you got for us?"

There was some urgency, I admit.

"I'm Ian Booke. Let us remember the niceties," the Englishman chided. "As well as the rules of engagement. Beat me in a game of virtual chess and I'll tell you what I know."

Well Played

To his credit, Chuch tried to get around it. "This is important. I'll play you later."

But Booke held firm: no contest, no info.

Chance pushed to his feet and rested his hand on the back of Chuch's chair. "Up. I'll give him a game."

Sighing, the other man got to his feet and moved to the recliner. Well, I didn't intend to sit and watch a virtual chess match, and clearly, Chuch did so I gave him my seat. There were limits to what an ex should expect. Instead I made my way back to the kitchen, where Eva sat in a pool of sunlight, reading the paper. Studying her, I decided she and Chuch were a bit of an odd couple, him short and stocky, her tall and model slim.

She'd been biting on a red pen, so she had a smudge of ink on her upper lip. As I joined her, I saw she'd been circling want ads.

"Job hunting?" Stupid thing to say, but then I never claimed to possess good social skills. Living as I do sort of discourages that.

Eva nodded. "Chuch makes enough money, but I get bored, you know? I want to do something interesting this time, though."

I searched for a suitable reply. "You've held boring jobs?"

In fact, I could relate. Since I can sell just about anything—you might even call it a preternatural gift—I've
worked in retail my whole life. It doesn't get much
worse.

"Yeah. Who knew being a private eye involved so
much sitting around in cars? Really dull."

"You used to be a PI?" Despite myself, I registered
some awe. I always had a weakness for Mickey Spillane
and Dashiell Hammett. I loved diving into a noir detective novel with guys in fedoras and trench coats and with
smart-mouthed dames wearing too much lipstick and
killer shoes.

"Well." Her expression turned mulish. "I didn't actually get the *license*, but what's the big deal? It's just a
piece of paper and I can print one that looks just as good.
I helped my clients just the same and probably charged
them less."

Biting my inner lip against a grin, I processed the information. So Eva specialized in forgery. That was good
to know. Just like you never know when you'll need
your ride tricked out, you never know when you'll need
a passport cooked. In fact, I *could* use one.

"So what's the problem?"

"Chuch says I'm going to end up in jail the first time
a disgruntled client reports me to the license board."

"So make sure they're all gruntled."

Eva grinned at me. "That's what *I* said. But it really is
boring, so I'm looking for a new gig."

"I run a pawnshop in Mexico City."

Don't ask me why I volunteered the information
when I'd done my best to make sure nobody could
find me, but Eva seemed harmless. Chuch would tell
her anyway, I rationalized, if she asked. But truthfully,
I was simply hungry for female company. When I
fled in the middle of the night, I severed all links to
my old life, including my best friend, Sara. If I ever
worked up the nerve, I'd call her. I didn't know whether

she'd be glad to hear from me or want my head on a pike.

"That sounds . . ." She hesitated.

"Boring?"

"Well. Yeah."

We both laughed, and I decided I liked her. "It has its compensations. There's nothing like finding a lost treasure or making a great deal on something."

"So what's your part in all this?" she asked, getting up to pour us some coffee. "I know Chance wouldn't have chased all that way after you unless you can do something for him nobody else can. He's not the sentimental type."

Christ, how right that was, and it stung to hear such a home truth spoken by a relative stranger. If only I'd seen him that clearly at the start of our relationship, I wouldn't be emotionally starved and half-heartbroken over him, even now. To cover how much it still hurt, I sipped my coffee, trying to decide what to tell her.

"I'm a handler," I said at last, unsure whether she even knew what that was.

Immediately she reached for my hands and turned them palms up. *"Dios mio."* Eva crossed herself as she studied scars old and new. "What a curse."

I felt dumbstruck by her perspicacity. I almost never told anyone. People didn't believe my claim, and if they did, it colored their view of me. If they romanticized such powers, they ranked me up there with sugarplum fairies, helpful brownies, and the good witch Glinda. If they demonized them, then I fell somewhere between the Wicked Witch of the West and something you summoned with blood at a crossroads.

To my surprise, she didn't ask about the scars. There are so few handlers out there; maybe she didn't realize I'm unusual. If I'd been born with this ability, it wouldn't work like this. It's more common to petition a practitioner for a divination spell that will permit him or her to read the energies stored in an object, but like all divinations, the information produced can be double-edged and unreliable.

"Yeah," I muttered. "It's not as much fun as it looks."

She regarded me with a soft look in her brown eyes. In a minute, she might call me *pobrecita* and try to tend my wounds. Clearly Chuch had himself a tenderhearted woman, whatever her foibles otherwise.

"He's using you to find his mother," she surmised. "What a shitty thing to do, like you could say no—and you still half in love with him." Tsking, she shook her head.

"I am *not*!"

Instead of arguing, she laughed, and that made it worse somehow. "Lies. You eat him with your eyes, Corine." Then she did say it. "*Pobrecita*. Men can be such assholes."

I didn't. Did I? Unhappy, I clutched my coffee mug, resolving not to permit any more visual binges.

"Anyway. I handled the Buddha statuette his mother left behind and saw a white truck. Something Sanitation or maybe Something Salvation . . ." I trailed off, depressed at how slim a lead that offered.

"Did you check the phone book?" At my blank look, she got up and went to the bureau just outside the kitchen door and returned with a directory in hand. "I guess that's too obvious, huh?" Eva flipped the pages, first looking under sanitation. "Five listings. Would you recognize the truck if you saw it again?"

I nodded. "Pretty sure. White with blue lettering, and I got a good look at the logo."

"So we can eliminate the Salvation Army trucks. Those aren't white." Double-checking the directory, Eva tapped a finger thoughtfully. "I'd rule out salvation altogether, myself. There aren't any other listings."

Wow, she wasn't half-bad at this deductive stuff.

Maybe she should get her license if the forgery thing didn't pan out. "Write down the addresses, and we can do a drive-by so I can check out the trucks." A plan of action cheered me up some. "Let's go tell the guys."

I'd forgotten about the chess game in progress. As Eva trailed me into the office, Chance said, "Check." The pieces on screen meant nothing to me, but I didn't want to interrupt. It didn't take long for Booke to decide he was doomed, though, and after some gentlemanly cursing, he ceded the game, which Chance took with his next move.

"I haven't seen an opening like that since Pavel Blatny played Rasmussen in 'eighty-four," Booke said, openly enthused. "Really unorthodox stuff, but—"

Chuch mouthed a kiss to Eva while reining in his pet Englishmen. "Booke. A deal's a deal, *mano*. Info now; deconstruct the game later."

"Oh. Right." Booke sounded subdued, and I gathered the impression that this sort of thing comprised his primary social outlet. If I were computer girl, I'd message him sometime. Hell, I might do it anyway, provided I could figure it out. "Well, it's clearly a variation on a summoning circle found in the *Lemegeton Clavicula Salomonis*." I wasn't the only one who went blank, but luckily I didn't have to ask.

"The what?" Chance looked at me like I ought to know, but I'm not a witch. I don't use rituals. I don't even look at the old books anymore, though I'd never throw them away. They're all I have left of my mother.

"Sorry," Booke said. "It's a rather famous grimoire. It covers a lot of ground regarding summoning, binding, and making deals with demons. Though I can't be certain from her sketches, I do think the ritual involved the Knights of Hell. Caim, Balam, Murmur, and Foras most closely resembled the symbols, but none of them were a perfect match."

I cleared my throat. "Either my memory or my drawing might have been at fault. In layman's terms, what does that mean, Booke?"

The speakers crackled, and I could practically hear him weighing his response. "I'm not sure," he said at last, "but I believe she used the Knights to enforce a bargain with those four men. Their oath against their souls, sealed in blood."

For a moment, I imagined Knights of Hell coming to collect on a bum deal. Heck of a way to make sure someone kept his word. Never mind how Min knew how to do so. "It must have been important."

"To say the least." Booke sounded amused. "I'll keep investigating the matter if you wish and e-mail Chuch if I find anything."

"That'd be great, *primo*. See what you can turn up on the four Knights she invoked, would you?"

"Absolutely. Talk to you later, Chuch. It was lovely meeting all of you." Booke's teatime manners put a smile on my face even as I turned to face Chance.

You'd think he might be used to bad news by now, but I guess it just never gets easier to hear that your mother knows how to conjure common household demons, never mind the Knights of Hell. Maybe his back hurt, or maybe the huevos rancheros sat wrong, but he looked like he was in serious pain. I wanted to go to him, but remembering what Eva said about eating him with my eyes, I waited for someone else to make a move. Anyone.

"That sucks, huh?" Trust Chuch to reduce it to the simplest terms.

Chance echoed Booke's words with a faintly ironic inflection. "To say the least. But you two looked like you had news when you first came in." He offered a half smile. "I hope it's good."

I let Eva do the honors.

Searching for a Needle

Chance let me drive, a pretty good indicator of his mood.

I caught him looking at me out of the corner of my eye, but I didn't speak, mostly because I couldn't think of what to say. This was new territory for us. Usually I teetered on the verge of falling apart while he appeared cool and removed. Maybe if he'd shown more emotion when we were together—

No. I still would've left. Near death experiences have a way of making you want to change your life.

We had four addresses to check out, and then I'd meet the empathic cop for dinner at Logan's Roadhouse. Given the realities of the job, his abilities must pretty much suck, I decided. Saldana must be exposed to suffering until he felt like one raw nerve ending. I wondered how he could maintain that aura of calm competence.

Ignoring Chance's second look proved harder than the first, and the third made me ask, "What?" in exasperation as we stopped at a red light.

"Do you know what *Lemegeton Clavicula Salomonis* translates to?" He paused in expectation as I hit the gas, maneuvering into the left lane.

"No. Latin isn't one of my skills."

"I looked it up," he said quietly. "It's the Lesser Key of Solomon."

For a moment, it didn't register since I was reading street signs, making sure we didn't miss our turn. Shock streaked through me.

"That has to be a coincidence."

If I didn't consider myself much too young for such behavior, I'd pooh-pooh the notion. Maybe even tsk a little. My lineage does not include ancient kings. My dad, Albie Solomon, was a traveling salesman from Peoria, and he wasn't even Jewish. He left when I was seven, and I haven't heard from him since. The state tried to locate him after my mom died, but nobody could turn him up. Might be dead for all I care. If he didn't love me enough to stay, then I want nothing to do with him.

I turned onto the access road that led to A&B Sanitation. If fortune favored us, their trucks would be outside in plain view so we could tick them off the list. We had four names, and I'd done some calling to narrow it down to that point. Sadly, when Chance read the list, he didn't feel a particular magnetism toward any of the names, which meant we had to visit the four places with white trucks in their fleet.

I've seen him do the trick before—it's a little like dowsing—but that was the first time he ever came up empty. For my sanity's sake, I refused to let myself worry what it meant. But damn, if his luck had left him, we were in *big* trouble.

No need to articulate this fear because it must be eating at Chance as well. He knew my gift alone couldn't carry the day. I needed him to help me find Yi Min-chin, just as he needed me. Was that codependence or symbiosis?

Time would tell.

This street went nowhere except a series of warehouses. Ours was third, set alongside the scenic interstate. To my disgust, all the trucks must be parked inside or were out collecting rubbish. I parked and tried to decide on a good cover story.

Got it.

I glanced over at Chance, one hand on the door handle. "You okay?"

"No," he said. "Not even close. But let's go. We have three more stops after this."

After shouldering my bag, I climbed out of the Toyota and headed for the business office. A small section of the warehouse had been sectioned off, holding a few desks and file cabinets, and a harried blond woman sat tapping her index finger against the phone. I'd guess she was on hold. The brown and gold nameplate on her desk read ANGIE CURRAN.

"May I help you?" Her expression said she'd rather eat cut glass.

So much for job satisfaction at A&B Sanitation.

"May I take a look at one of your trucks?"

"Why?" She sighed and put down the phone.

I tried my best girl-to-girl smile. "Because a garbage truck T-boned my car but I didn't get a clear look at the writing on the side. I just want to see if your trucks are white with blue letters."

"Oh, they're not. Some bastard sideswiped you and drove off?" Angie shook her head as she stood up. "If one of our drivers did that, I'd get his ass fired. But sure, honey, you can take a peek to verify. None of our trucks are damaged. We have a couple in back that are scheduled for repairs, though, so have a look."

"Thanks. I'm visiting every sanitation company until I track the guy down."

We followed her through the "Employees Only" door into the warehouse proper. The space was mostly empty at this time of day, but as she'd said, there were a couple of trucks parked, waiting their turn in the mechanic's bay. White and yellow trucks.

"That's all I needed. Thank you so much for your time."

As we went back the way we came, she whispered, "Your boyfriend's cute but he doesn't say much."

I debated with myself before deciding to let the misapprehension stand. "He has a lot on his mind right now."

"That's too bad. I hope you find the guy who screwed you over. I love that you aren't letting him get away with it, no matter how much trouble you have to go through."

Lady, you don't know the half of it.

Two more stops went more or less like that. Chance worried me with his silence. Usually he handled such situations by turning on the charm and watching resistance to whatever he wanted melt away. I was used to being background scenery, not the star of the show. But I managed.

At the last place on the list, Southern Sanitation, I had no more than parked the car when I saw a white and blue truck pull out of the gated parking area. This legwork stuff worked. I needed to do something nice for Eva.

I followed the vehicle for a moment with my eyes before saying, "That's it. Whoever took your mom has ties to this company. Somehow."

Chance turned his head, and in the sunlight angling through the window, his eyes looked inexpressibly weary. "Thanks."

I tried to smile. "You're welcome."

Jesus, I didn't know what to do with this Chance. He frightened me with his intensity. Once, I'd believed he was all cool calculation, but I was starting to think that maybe he'd hidden a lot of what he felt. I just didn't know why.

"Nothing in the world is like I thought it was." He paused before adding quietly, "Not even you."

I put the car in gear without responding. Just what did

he expect from me? As I saw it, by accompanying him to Laredo, I'd already gone above and beyond the call as an ex. That was for his mother, though, and I suppose he knew it.

Instead of taking the opportunity to rehash our relationship, I said, "We should put Eva on researching Southern Sanitation. Find out who owns it and, if possible, the parent company. The trail has to lead somewhere."

My brisk tone woke a similar response. "Good idea. We'll get on that as soon as we get back to the house. What would you like to do for dinner tonight?"

Uh-oh.

"I already have plans." I made a left onto highway 59, heading away from the city and toward Chuch's house. "In fact I was hoping to borrow the car."

"What plans?"

Here it comes.

"I'm having dinner with Jesse Saldana."

"The cop. You're really going to dinner with the cop who won't let us look at my mom's purse, the purse we'll probably need to bribe someone for you to handle?" His voice sounded tight, but I didn't risk a look at him.

There was a special circle in hell reserved for me. I should tell him the truth; I knew Saldana only wanted to talk about my gift.

"Like I said before, maybe I can change his mind."

"You sure this is a good idea? How do you know we can trust him?"

"I don't." After turning into the driveway, I put the car in park. Angled my body to face Chance. I hated that he looked so good in the late afternoon sunshine. "There is no us. I'm doing this for me."

He flinched as he climbed out of the Camry. I wanted to think it was his back, but I knew better. "You're right. Of course you can borrow the car. Just be careful. I'll talk to Eva about Southern Sanitation so you can get ready."

Why did I wind up feeling like I'd kicked a puppy anytime I tried to put some distance between us? *I am not still half in love with him.*

It didn't help that whenever he got that look in his eyes, I wanted to brush the dark hair away from his forehead. I wanted to press my cheek against his and let him lean on me. Shit, who was I kidding? Even with his back torn up I wanted to take him to bed and make him forget about his troubles for an hour or two.

Instead I went inside and got ready for my "date."

More than One Way
to Skin a Potato

To annoy Chance, I spent more time getting ready than I needed to and headed out smelling of frangipani.

I'd borrowed Chuch's computer long enough to print out a map to Logan's Roadhouse, so I just needed to follow it. All the way back to town, my conscience jabbed me. I could have told Chance why I was going. I didn't know why I hadn't, except I wanted to keep this part of my life separate from him. Disastrous things happened when I let myself get too wrapped up in him.

Typical of its kind, the restaurant possessed lots of heavy wood and neon, metal buckets of peanuts for people to munch on and then throw the shells on the floor. I supposed it added to atmosphere but I wouldn't want to be the one sweeping up at the end of the night. I got a booth near the bar and waited.

The waitress, whose name tag read Betsy, beamed a gigawatt smile at me. I decided she must've had her teeth capped recently. "Evenin'. Are you waiting for more?"

Well, I'd told the hostess somebody would be joining me, so, "Yes."

I hate repeating myself.

"Well, then. I'll get you started and then let you be.

We have loaded baked potato soup and chili tonight, hon. You want a drink? Maybe start with some nachos or some Texas onion petals? Some potato skins?"

"Diet Coke with lime, please." I must admit, it was a little strange to order in English. I didn't know what Saldana would want, but the skins sounded good. "And potato skins to start. We'll order after he gets here."

She made a few notes and wove through the crowd, looking like every other server in her Logan's shirt and jeans. I wished I could have a something with tequila in it but I was my own designated driver, dammit. One plus about such a noisy place: nobody would overhear us. The waitress brought my Diet Coke and, later, the potato skins. Still no cop, though.

"You sure you don't want to order?"

I shook my head. Betsy just *thought* I didn't notice the pitying look she slid my way as she headed back to the kitchen.

Nerves jangling, I fiddled with the pail of peanuts until Saldana arrived, a full half hour after the appointed time. He slid into the booth opposite me, offering a smile. "Sorry I'm late. Work stuff."

"It's all right." But I'd begun to wonder if he would show.

"Jesse," the waitress said with evident delight. "Don't you know it's not nice to keep a lady waiting?" She flirted shamelessly.

If he really was my date, I'd be pissed. Since he wasn't, I sat back with a smirk and let him deal with Betsy. I helped myself to another potato skin while he ordered an iced tea.

Then and there I decided my next boyfriend would be a big, cuddly teddy bear type. No more watching other women devour my men with their eyes. But I enjoyed the kind way he managed to dismiss Betsy without hurting her feelings.

"Sorry," he said again when he'd gotten rid of her.

"It's not a problem." My smirk became a grin.

Saldana arched a brow. "You think this is funny?"

"I do, actually. Serves you right."

"What does?" He took the last potato skin.

"Being both cute and sensitive. You deserve to beat women off with a stick."

"You think I'm cute?" At that Saldana paused, a half smile playing at the corners of his well-made mouth.

I sighed. "Please. You *know* you are. It doesn't matter what I think."

His mama would be so proud of his ability to turn the charm off and on like that. "Of course it does." Saldana gave me a sorghum smile. "You're a woman, aren't you?"

"Yes, but I gave up hot guys for Lent."

He laughed. "It's November, Corine."

"See how well I'm doing?"

"Hmm," he said, eating the potato skin. "Sadly it's not my place to question that decision. We may as well get down to business if you won't flirt back, even a little bit."

I didn't know how much more I could take. "Isn't that against the rules, Obi-Wan?"

"Yes. Gifts tend to run in family lines, so . . ." He made a face, encapsulating his opinion of swimming in your own gene pool. "It's pretty rare for somebody gifted to grow up without a mentor."

My spine stiffened. I didn't want to talk about how I came to be on my own, with no parental figure to explain about special powers, secret societies, and little blue sparks. Then again, if my mother were still around, I probably wouldn't have a gift.

I muttered, "I'm weird. I get it. What's the deal with the underground?"

Before he could reply, Betsy came back with his iced tea and took our orders. We both chose a New York strip, but he got a giant baked potato in addition to the skins. I opted for a salad out of respect for the size of my ass, although if I really cared, I wouldn't eat potato skins.

He waited until she walked away with a last wistful look over one shoulder, but Saldana was all business now. "Like I said, we have a quiet support network. I'll give you the log-in information for the Web site, and I know of a few gathering spots. The closest is a club in San Antonio called Twilight."

"Web site?" I blinked at that.

"Good place to get specialized help. We pretend to be a conspiracy theory group: aliens, men in black, all that. The site's called Area Fifty-one."

"Cute."

"Mostly it makes us feel less alone," he said. "Sometimes it's hard being surrounded by people who have no idea what you can do, and if they do find out, sometimes it's worse. Sometimes it means you have to—"

"Move in the middle of the night?" I offered a wry smile at his startled look.

"Yeah. Well, not me personally. My talent is pretty low-key. But I dated a pyro girl for a while." His mouth twisted. "She was hunted coast-to-coast."

Pyro. Firestarter? I couldn't imagine a positive outlet for that gift, but then I was biased. I shouldn't let myself get distracted.

"What happened?"

To my surprise, he shut down. "We're not here to talk about my romantic history."

Since he didn't want to talk about it, of course I couldn't let it go. That aspect of my psyche explained a great deal about my relationship with Chance.

"White knight complex," I realized aloud. "You go for the bad girl, the one with problems who blows up your car, trashes your house, and steals your wallet. It's not her fault, of course. If she only had someone to love and understand her, that shit wouldn't happen."

"Shit." He regarded me with narrowed eyes as Betsy served two sizzling steaks. "I thought I was the empath."

"You are. That's why this makes perfect sense. You want to save everyone because you know what they're going through. Must make it hell on dating."

"Tell me about it. Try arguing with someone, even if you *know* they're wrong, when you can feel the hurt rolling off them in waves."

"You just want to wrap her up in your arms and tell her everything's going to be okay," I said softly.

Saldana studied me with bitter chocolate eyes, and to my surprise, his gaze dropped first. He attended to cutting his steak with a care that said I'd stepped too close to something private. We'd just met, after all.

For a while we just ate, didn't talk. I thought maybe I'd crossed the line. The white noise of other voices covered the fact that nobody spoke at our table.

Finally he said, "Yeah, well. I can't make everything better, but I *can* put you on the path to meeting more people like us. You already know you can recognize them from the shock. Let's see, what else? Oh, I'll write down the Web site address and log-in." He pulled a pen from his pocket, scrawled something on a napkin, and passed it to me.

"Thanks." I tucked it into my handbag, a gorgeous beaded creation I'd bought at Mundo E.

"On those boards you can find witches, warlocks, psychics, far-seers, pyros, empaths—pretty much the whole gamut of talents, though I don't think I've ever run across another handler on there. I don't vouch for character, though, Corine. Just because they're gifted, it doesn't make them trustworthy. So if you decide to see someone off-line, use the same care you would under normal circumstances."

Was I the only person in the world who didn't get on Match.com for a date? "I've never done that."

"That means don't tell the person where you live.

Meet in a public place. Common sense stuff. But the board is great for finding someone who can help you with specialized research or answer questions about another type of gift. I used it quite a bit to try to understand Heather."

"The pyro girl?"

"Yeah." He didn't elaborate, though, and I didn't press. "If you want, I'll take you to Twilight. We could be there by eleven and they're open until three. We'd need to spend the night in San Antonio, though."

I didn't know how to take that invitation. "Don't you have work tomorrow?"

Saldana shook his head. "Day off. We can hit Twilight tonight, find a place to stay, and then drive back in the morning. There's someone I want you to meet."

I hesitated. "If I go, you get me an unofficial look at the purse."

"Hey, I'm trying to *help* you here, and you're asking for more favors?"

At that I pushed my plate away. I'd eaten maybe half the steak and nibbled at the salad. "Look, I have only your word you want to help me. I'm supposed to accept there's a gifted underground just on your say-so? I'm supposed to drive two hours to a club because you want me to? Sorry, Saldana, but it doesn't work like that. You might be a cop, but you haven't proven yourself to me. Something bad could still happen if I go off with you, so you need to sweeten the deal. Give me a reason to take the risk."

For a minute I thought I'd pushed him too far. His mouth tightened and he threw his napkin on the table like he meant to leave. Well, fine. I had the log-in. I could check things out on my own.

"Deal," he said, throwing down some twenties for the bill. "You come with me tonight, and I get you a look at the purse tomorrow. Let's get going."

Traveling Blues

Talk about surreal.

Before we left, I called Chuch and asked him if he minded picking up the Camry. This served several purposes. The car wouldn't sit all night outside Logan's Roadhouse, Chance would have it if he needed it, and I didn't have to tell him that I was going to San Antonio with a guy I'd just met. I didn't envy Chuch that job.

It also served as personal security. Chuch knew where I was going and with whom. I didn't think Saldana chopped women up and strewed their body parts along the highway to make them harder to identify, but—

Well. I knew too much about killers for my own peace of mind, but last I heard, Kel Ferguson was still in prison. And he'd never chopped up his victims as far as I knew. Quite the contrary, Ferguson had killed with a clean, cold precision that made him seem soulless. Ironic that he'd first been arrested on a kidnapping charge, but once he was in the system, his DNA tied him to a whole string of unsolved crimes.

I preferred to think about the little girl we saved.

With a faint sigh, I climbed into the cop's black Forester. Nice ride, with anthracite cloth interiors, though a little surprising. I'd pegged him as an Avalanche kind of guy.

Saldana played the Dixie Chicks on the way. He didn't say much, and I couldn't blame him. My trepidation probably registered on his radar, so it'd be hard for him not to resent it. I wished I could tell him it wasn't personal.

He slid me a look I found hard to interpret through the intermittent light from oncoming cars. "So tell me, do you ever let down your guard?"

The empathy thing would get old, I decided. Women wished for guys who always knew when something was wrong, even when they didn't tell them, but it was quite another thing to be confronted with the long, tall reality of one.

"Once. It didn't end well."

That was an understatement. I was talking about Chance.

The road from Laredo to San Antonio offered nothing scenic after dark. Still I turned my face toward the window because I didn't want to encourage him. Maybe he even saw in me one of his broken girls, a fixer-upper who needed somebody to understand her.

However, if this underground existed, then I might be able to use it to search for Min. I wasn't sure what use I could make of it, but I knew better than to waste resources. As it stood, we needed every edge to figure out what the hell was going on.

Poor Chance.

Saldana chose the one conversational gambit guaranteed to catch my attention. "You going to tell me what went down at the warehouse?" While I weighed the likelihood of that, he went on, "You have fresh cuts on the backs of your hands, consistent with flying glass. Now, I happen to know something about that, but I don't give you anything until you come clean. Feel like trading info?"

That sounded like a variation on "you show me yours, I'll show you mine," a game that got me into trouble more than once. I narrowed my eyes. "You could be bluffing."

What could he possibly know?

"I could be," he allowed. "But I'm not. Feel free to think it over." With an irritating half smile, he went back to driving.

I did, but the lights of San Antonio spread out before us before I made up my mind. "We went to check out the crime scene," I said finally. "I found a button that showed me what happened there."

"Which was?" To my surprise he accepted my words matter-of-factly. Then again, why wouldn't he? "No, wait. Get to that later. What was the deal with the windows?" He shook his head. "The department can't figure out what caused the pressure change that blew all the windows inward simultaneously. They're throwing around all kinds of ideas."

Reluctantly I explained, though I didn't need to say much. Saldana was familiar with such things, though he couldn't present it as an official explanation. "That's a heavy-duty working." He shook his head as we exited toward San Antonio College.

"Tell me about it. There aren't a lot of people who could bring that much power to bear, and they don't come cheap."

Coplike, he followed my train of thought, though Chuch had already mentioned it. "Which means they're working for somebody who has money. What kind of range are we talking about here? Could it be sent from halfway around the world?"

"I have no idea. Rituals aren't my thing."

No, that'd been my mother's forte, and I hadn't turned my hand to one in a good ten years, not since I gave up all childish dreams altogether.

He thought about it. "I might know somebody we can ask while we're here. Not sure if she'll be in this late, though. We'll see."

"Seriously, why do you care?" The question got loose before I could stop it.

His hands tightened on the steering wheel. "Don't ask me that again. I know some cops don't give a shit, but I'm not one of them."

Wow, I pissed him off, got past the kind, patient persona. For some reason, that delighted me. I cocked a brow at him. "Is that right?"

Oh, I was asking for it.

"I'm your mentor, Corine. That means I'm here to help you." Saldana thumped the dash for emphasis. "Maybe you're not used to this, but I have no hidden agenda. I want to help you figure out how to make the most of being gifted. I know sometimes·it sucks and you feel like you're all by yourself. I'm here to assure you that you're not."

"So you're taking me under your wing out of the goodness of your heart." I sounded so cynical.

"Is that so hard to believe?"

I thought about it. "Pretty much. What's your angle?"

He glared at me before realizing he wasn't going to sell me on the idea of him as a good Samaritan. "By helping you, I help myself, if you turn up something I can use to close the books on this one. I may have to tweak the language in the file, but it's better than an unsolved mystery."

"Got it," I said, satisfied. "You're tying a string to my tail and sending me into the maze. You'll use me to write your report when it's all said and done."

"Christ. You make it sound so sordid."

"I don't mind. People never offer an open hand, and if they do, you should step back to avoid the slap."

Saldana offered me a look that said I'd made the short list of women he'd like to rehabilitate toward a brighter outlook. Too bad. I liked my attitude just fine. We drove through the city in silence for a few minutes.

"Anyway, it's my turn to spill. The security guard

who found the handbag wasn't supposed to be there. He isn't a bright guy and he somehow didn't understand that he'd been let go. Warehouse was closed, no new shipments coming in. So Lenny lets himself into the building and it 'smells funny,' he says."

Blood rituals and demons tend to make a place smell funny, all right.

"Got a last name for me?"

He grinned. "No. I won't tell you that Lenny Marlowe works for Delta Security, the agency that just terminated a contract with IBC, the company that owns the warehouse."

I had a feeling IBC might have ties to Southern Sanitation as well, so I made a mental note. "Thanks for nothing then."

The area where we parked qualified as seedy, a strip on Main full of Goth bars and gay clubs. I don't know what I expected, but I felt vaguely let down by the faded brick building on the corner. Just a small sign in violet neon proclaimed TWILIGHT.

"In the rest of these clubs," he said as we got out, "you'll find wannabes and college kids looking for something different. Occasionally they hit up Twilight as well, but by and large, if you find somebody hanging out there, they're the real deal. Be extra careful—they get the occasional demon as well."

"Doesn't the smell give them away?" Laugh if you must, but I had limited experience with such things.

Saldana laughed as we walked up to the black metal door. "They don't all reek of rotten eggs, Corine. Some can be quite charming, but—and I'm sure I don't need to say this—don't sign anything, no matter how good the deal sounds."

"Got it. No selling my soul to the Dark One. Anything else I should know?"

"Yeah," he said. "You look good in green."

As I followed him into the club, I glanced down at

my cardigan. Chance hated this thing, woven of nubbly yarn in uneven hues. He'd never gotten the appeal of hippie chic, but it went with my long hair at least. Considering I'd bought it at a thrift store for two bucks more than three years ago, I'd gotten my money's worth. I liked how the extra length covered the biggest part of my ass while the belt accentuated my waist. It went over any camisole, and tonight I'd paired it with a pair of embroidered khaki pants and wedge heel sandals with glittery jade beads on the toes.

"Uh. Thanks."

Twilight's interior boasted a faded carpet, red lights in wall sconces, and maroon striped wallpaper. The dark wood timbers gave the place a rough, unfinished look, but the place had a schizophrenic feel—part Texas roadhouse, part dilapidated brothel. Even the music set the mood slightly askew. I didn't know how I felt about entering to the tune of "Devil's Dance Floor." Not my usual thing but toe-tapping nonetheless.

I glanced around, saw half the tables occupied. Nobody looked out of the ordinary, but then again, what did I expect? Horns and tails from folks like me? Disgusted with myself, I turned to Saldana, who took a seat at the bar and waited for the 'tender.

Judging by her freckles, a natural redhead came over after she finished pouring beer for the guys sitting two stools down from us. They could've been construction workers in their dusty hats, plaid shirts, and Wrangler jeans.

With her coppery curls caught up in a pigtail, she radiated country cute. "Hi, Jesse. It's always good to see you."

A place where everybody knows your name . . . and you're always glad you came . . . if you're Jesse Saldana, that is. I wasn't so sure of my own welcome. I've had to move in a hurry too many times to take anything at face value.

"Hey, Jeannie. This is Corine. Make her feel at home, will you?"

"Oh." The bartender's scrutiny gained weight and intensity.

I could feel her searching me as if she could tell by sight alone what my gift might be. Despite my intention to be cool, no matter what the night brought, my fingers curled. I didn't want to *show* my scars any more than I wanted to hide them from squeamish strangers. If I flashed them, I'd bet she would observe that I hadn't been born gifted, as if I'd stolen this ability, and I was tired of hearing it. Salt in the wound, so to speak.

I wasn't a killer, although my mother had warned me of people who shed blood to take other people's magick. Rapt, I'd listened to her stories the same way other girls my age clung to fairy tales. I just hadn't known it was possible to *give* power away.

Not until she died.

The moment passed, but damn if I knew what Jeannie read in me. "What'll you have?" she asked.

"Corona for me, please." Saldana glanced at me. "You?"

"How are your margaritas?" I wasn't the designated driver anymore.

Jeannie grinned. "Cold and strong. Want one?"

I considered for a moment. "Nah, I think I need to shake things up a bit. Can you make a blue diablo?"

Tequila, Blue Curacao, lemon juice, and Rose's lime juice, served over ice. I wasn't a heavy drinker, but I liked my tequila. Well, the good stuff anyway—the cheap variety produced a fast drunk and a wicked hangover. For my money, Patrón was best for sipping, followed by Herradura for mixing, but you couldn't go wrong with Don Julio either.

She cocked her hip and answered with an exaggerated Southern accent. "I can make anything you'd know to order, sweet pea."

"You feeling blue deviled, sugar?" Saldana's voice came low near my ear, limned in sympathy.

"You don't know the half of it." I spoke beneath the music.

Between Chance and his missing mama, it was a wonder I didn't stay right here at the bar until I forgot my own name. I didn't want to talk about it, so I changed the subject. I leaned toward Saldana. "Jeannie. That's not . . . I mean, she doesn't—" To my embarrassment she heard me when she returned with his beer.

Her gray eyes twinkled, crinkling at the edges when she smiled. I revised my estimate of her age to north of forty. "Grant wishes? The whole 'yes, master,' flick my ponytail thing? Nah, that's just my name."

"Right." I hunched my shoulders, feeling out of my depth.

"Thanks, Jeannie. Is Twila around?" Right then I could've kissed Saldana for changing the subject.

The bartender arched a well-plucked brow. "How come you don't come in here just to see me anymore?"

Jesse came back, "Because your husband threatened to tie me up with my own intestines if I didn't stop mooning after his woman."

She beamed. "Twenty years, and Bucky's still a sweetheart." I didn't think that sounded sweet, but I'd already made an ass of myself. "She's in the office, honey. You can take your drinks on back." Her gaze returned to me. "I'll have yours in a minute."

Jesse headed off, but I waited until she delivered my diablo in a chilled, salted glass. "Nice meeting you," I said to her.

"Come on." As he wove through the tables, he beckoned me. "I know she'll want to meet you."

Will she? Why?

The fly-spider feeling came over me but I fought the urge to cut and run. Mustering my courage, I followed him.

Two Truths and a Lie

Twila turned out to be a tall, dark-skinned woman with long braids bound back in a golden snood. She didn't look surprised to see us as she rose and offered a hand to Saldana. Her office offered more faded opulence; the pawnshop owner in me immediately started pricing the furniture.

The heavy cherry desk appeared to be a genuine antique and as such would fetch a hefty price. On a nearby table twin candles burned, filling the room with the smell of incense. The distant throb of bass from the bar shivered into the soles of my feet, rousing the urge to dance, except that'd be socially inappropriate. I fought the urge to tug on my sweater in the face of her penetrating onyx gaze.

"Jesse," she said in the sort of smoky voice that made me think of sex. God only knew what effect it must have on Saldana. Her accent rang faintly with an island flavor. Haiti, perhaps. "It's been too long. Who have you brought me?"

I didn't like her phrasing. Typically, offerings got tied to a rock and left for a hungry dragon. I eyed the door over my shoulder. Dammit, I shouldn't have worn the wedge heels.

"Hello, Twila." To my astonishment, Saldana bent and kissed her knuckles in a courtly gesture.

Should I curtsy? I thought it would be pretty hard to pull that off in cargo pants. *Figures, the one time I don't wear a skirt . . .* I contented myself with a nod.

"Nice to meet you," I murmured.

"Sit down, won't you?" She indicated the leather chairs across from her desk.

Since this was Saldana's show, I sat back while he performed the introductions.

Twila studied me for a moment before turning to him. "I see why you brought her. Fascinating." In her eyes I saw she already knew my secrets, all of them, great and small. But how could she? "You smell of fire. I see it licking at your aura."

I swallowed. Quite uncomfortable to have your secrets laid bare. "Do I?"

"You fear your gift," she went on. "You fear everything you touch will turn to ash."

It always does, sooner or later.

"Such a long shadow, falling on you year after year." I glimpsed distance in her eyes then, as if she saw beyond the office walls. "It shaped what has been and what will be, but you can part your path from it, if you make the right choices."

Color me cynical. "I suppose you're going to tell me what those are."

To my surprise, she shook her head. "Only you can decide your course, child. Seldom have I seen two such divergent futures. One is dark indeed. But this much I can tell you: those who broke your heart so long ago did not act of their own volition. They too were shadow-touched."

I felt raw, exposed, but I had to ask. "You're saying something made them want to hurt my mother?"

"Suspicion and jealousy, mere embers fanned to violent life. Yes. If you want the truth, you must return to Kilmer."

I shuddered. Before, there had remained to me a kernel of doubt. Saldana might have brought me here for some bizarre reason of his own, intending to impress me. There might not be any truth to his claims of a gifted secret society. But my skepticism dissolved. There was no orthodox way she could know about my hometown, and she hadn't gleaned her knowledge via any ritual I recognized. According to my mother's books, a spell like that took time.

"How do you know such things?"

With a faint, feral smile, Twila shook her head. "No. You get nothing more for free. If you expect more of me, you must earn it."

I glanced at Saldana, who sat beside me quiet and impassive. "What do you want?"

She slid a dagger toward me. "Read this and tell me what you see."

So it would be a sacrifice, after all.

Though it meant another scar, I didn't hesitate. I wrapped my fingers around the blade, braced for the pain. It came in long, red waves, worse than usual, and by the time I let go, I felt sick. The knife clattered to the desk.

"You used it to kill a man," I managed. "Stabbed him through the heart."

Her gaze flickered to the cop beside me, as if wondering whether she could be arrested on that basis alone. "Some men need killing."

I couldn't argue with that, as I wrapped my wounded palm around my iced glass. Jesse reached for my hand and I don't know why I let him take it, possibly because he could feel my nausea and pain. For a moment he merely studied the livid burn.

"I'll get you some ice," he said, and left me alone with her.

"You are real." Her tone reflected a peculiar sort of wonder. "People would kill to make use of you." That much I knew. "I've only met one before you. He came from a family of gifted, though, so his talent didn't carry the same price."

"Lucky him," I muttered. "How come it sucks so much for me?" It was mostly a rhetorical question.

I couldn't help but wonder what it would be like to call on this ability effortlessly. No pain. No fire. Sometimes I wanted nothing more than for it to burn itself out, leaving me *normal*.

She seemed to think I really wanted an answer. "Think of it this way. Your power doesn't come natural. When you use it, you're exercising a limb where the transplant didn't quite take. That's why it wounds you."

An unexpected quirk of the spell—I can't imagine my mother meant for me to suffer. I don't think she wanted me to feel her pain every time I touched a charged object, but some things even a good witch can't foresee. I'd probably never know what went wrong in her final moments.

I sighed. "I guess there's no cure for that."

"I'm afraid not."

Saldana returned with a dishcloth full of ice, which I took. He sank down beside me, somehow expectant. Then I realized I should tell her about the sending. Perhaps she could shed some light on things. Quickly I summarized the details.

"Unfortunately, I'm not the one to ask. Like yours, my ability doesn't rely on ritual."

"You have the Sight?"

"That's one word for it. In exchange for certain . . . tribute, the Loa let me see threads of fate. It's not . . . linear, as you know it, and not entirely reliable. I see the larger patterns in play, forces influencing the balance." The light glazed her dusky skin, made of her eyes twin shadows that drank the light. "It hasn't been this bad since the Black Death."

A chill ran over me, dead man's hands. *Dark times.* I've said so myself, even lacking the ability to see as Twila did.

"Do you know what's causing it?"

"I could speculate." She tilted her head, cast a meaningful look at Saldana. "To find your enemy, you should see Maris, but I don't think she's in tonight. She'll know who could manage such a powerful sending."

"I know where she lives," Saldana said quietly.

I caught the undercurrent. *One of his exes?* I knew about Heather, now Maris, and who else? If there were a few more, he rivaled *me* for busted relationships.

A half smile curved her mouth. "I suppose you do. I don't recommend you risk a hotel, though. You'll need protection and there's nowhere safer than right here. You can borrow the guest apartment upstairs."

"Why are you being so nice?" There had to be a catch.

Saldana frowned at me even as she replied, "It often proves helpful to have people in my debt, Corine. You would do well to remember that."

Right. Her kindness concealed a mercenary bent. Oddly that reassured me. Since I didn't want to be awakened by flying glass, I decided to accept her offer.

Before standing, I downed my drink. "I'm pretty tired. Can we go up?"

"Certainly. Jesse knows the way. It was a pleasure meeting you." As I reached the door, following Saldana, she added, "By the way, you've carried the weight of a lie your whole life. Your father didn't leave. He was taken. More patterns than you know bind you and your former lover."

I would have turned, asked more, but Saldana took hold of my arm, leading me along the dark hallway toward some stairs. "That was meant to tempt you," he explained, "but to get more information from her now, you'd need to offer something else. I don't think you're in any shape to do another reading, and anything else would be . . ." He trailed off, letting me interpret the kind of thing Twila might ask.

I shivered. "Thanks."

Between residual nausea and the tequila spiking through my veins, I felt both euphoric and shaky. Saldana kept his hand on me as we climbed to the next landing, where he opened the first door. We stepped through to a flat I could only describe as witchy, full of cut crystal figurines and blue velvet.

Two more steps and I collapsed on the overstuffed couch. Jesse sank down beside me, his hand hovering as though he didn't know what to do but wanted to do something. After a moment I managed a smile but it came from a place that hurt, newly raw.

"I should have warned you. Twila can be . . . intense. And she is assuredly not to be trusted, but she isn't one of your enemies, which makes her an ally, if a dangerous one."

"Enemies. You say that as if you're sure I have loads." I tried to laugh.

His bitter chocolate eyes turned somber. "You're too wary for it to be otherwise, Corine. I've never met anyone more . . ."

Broken? Closed? I waited for the word confirming me as one of his pet projects. I felt a soft sinking inside because that would mean he could never see me as a person, only something in dire need of fixing.

Then he shook his head. His arm came around my shoulders, as if he'd finally made up his mind what he should do. "Lean on me until you feel better. It's all right."

I suspected he'd said that many times over the course of his checkered career, but in that moment, I weakened. His chest felt warm and strong against my head. I closed my eyes, listening to the steady thump of his heart. Bit by bit, the nausea receded, left me with the dull throb of my seared hand.

An empathic cop for a mentor. Who would've ever imagined I'd wind up with such a thing? That suggested an avuncular relationship, but the way he held me didn't feel entirely paternal. I liked his quiet strength and his heat, perhaps a little too much. Too easily I could lose myself in sex. I imagined leading him to the bedroom and lying down on smooth sheets, imagined rough breathing and the sweet tangle of limbs.

Jesse rested his chin on my hair until I sat up. "I'm fine now. We should—"

By the lambent light in his eyes, I could tell he sensed my mood, if not the specific thoughts. He licked his lips and pulled his hands away from me.

"The worst thing about this," he said hoarsely, "is that I don't always know what I want. I feel what other people do . . . and it's hard to separate their desires from my own, particularly when it's raw lust. It's easier when it's a girlish crush since I'm not susceptible to those. But sheer, animal sex . . . yeah. I'm prone to that."

I didn't touch him, but I wanted his mouth, and he knew it. "Then you already know I'm in the mood for a quick, hard fuck. I don't want sweet words or promises. I want a hot body on top of me, and that's all, but I'm not sure it's a good idea."

Jesse exhaled shakily. He swayed toward me. "It's sounding better by the second."

"Would you want me if you weren't echoing my impulses?" That was it, I realized. "Am I your type?"

Soul of Discretion

"I don't know," he said in frustration. "No, I didn't take one look at you and imagine doing you on my desk yesterday. But I don't have a type either. Right now you look fine and you smell *great*." He spoke the last word on a growl.

My heart pounded. Much as I wanted to give over, I couldn't. Part of me felt it was one thing to leave Chance wondering whether I had and quite another to do it. I also couldn't lay down with Jesse without knowing for sure he wanted me back. *Me*, not an echo of my own lust—that seemed too close to masturbation. Not that I object to such, but if I'm going to do that, I might as well get on with it and not catch some poor cop in the backlash.

"It's not a good idea," I repeated. "I'm going to get some sleep."

Saldana dropped his head into his hands and his voice came out muffled. "Second bedroom on the right. I think I'll take a shower."

My knees trembled as I retreated. Any more of him and I wouldn't be responsible for my actions; too bad, because I didn't really want to be. Deep down I'd love it if he took me on the floor like an animal. If nothing else, this proved he intended only my introduction around here, though. He truly meant to be my mentor before I distracted him. I sighed over that as I shut the door behind me.

Fey and winsome, the room matched the rest of the apartment. I coveted the bed with its strange carvings and the matching side table that sported claws on its legs. After stripping to my camisole, I crawled beneath the covers. The things Twila had said worked on me, though, and I found it hard to sleep.

When I finally did, I dreamed of great rushing things made of wind.

I woke early to the first fingers of light stealing across the floor. Nobody had disturbed me that I could recall, and either Twila's wards held, or nothing came looking for me during the night. For the first time I began to feel anxious about Chance. I'd always assumed I was the eye of the storm and that trouble followed because of me, but what if—

Well, I refused to entertain the possibilities when I was two hours away and couldn't see if he was all right.

Saldana sat at the small bistro-style table in the kitchen, nursing a cup of coffee. He looked even rougher than I felt.

"You'll want another shower before we go see your ex," I mumbled. It's hard knowing what to say the morning after you *didn't* sleep with the guy who probably would've been a glorious, mind-blowing mistake. "Then I need to get back."

"I'm not sure all the showers in the world will help," he said dryly. "But noted."

I made myself some toast. Apparently Twila's hospitality only ran so far, as the cupboard offered a box of tea, instant coffee, cornflakes, and some stale bread. It wasn't bad slathered with jam.

When he emerged with his tawny hair slicked back, I decided I could do with some freshening up too. I didn't want to meet someone new looking like I'd been pulled backward through a hedge. By the time we were ready to go, the ornate wall clock in the living room read quarter to eleven.

"Some day off, huh?" I muttered.

He grinned as we made our way downstairs. The sun shone bright for a November morning, and in daylight the area looked even seedier but not actively dangerous. Jesse read my look and said, "Twila is more dangerous than anything you'd find on these streets. Half the community owes her one way or another, so it would take some steel balls to try anything on her home ground."

"Good to know. Maybe some of her scary will rub off."

After deactivating the alarm on the Forester, he opened my door for me. "You're fine the way you are, Corine."

"If you say so." I got in, none too sure of that.

We drove across San Antonio to a neighborhood just off the freeway. Nothing stood out—all the houses were built along the same styles. The only differences came in lawn ornaments or siding choices. Jesse parked the SUV before a pale gold house whose front yard boasted an impressive collection of bearded gnomes in various poses.

Despite the warmth of the sun, a chill crawled down my back the closer we came to the house. It was the middle of a workday, true, so perhaps that explained the unearthly stillness, but there should be birds at least. I heard nothing but silence.

Saldana cut me a sharp look as he rapped on the front door. "Maris should be here. She does palm and tarot readings from home."

"Is she legit?"

"Yes." He sounded distracted. "She's a gifted witch. I've seen her work spells that nobody's managed since they wrote the grimoires. If anyone knows the range on that sending, she does."

Nobody answered.

Wordlessly I circled around to the garage and peered through the side window. Amid shadows thrown by piled junk, a car sat waiting to be driven. He came up beside me with a question in his eyes.

I shrugged. "Well, if she's gone, someone must have picked her up."

"Is it too Han Solo of me to say I have a bad feeling about this?" I loved the way he dropped his Gs, the Texas twang of his voice.

I shook my head. "I don't think so. Do you know where she kept the spare key?"

In my experience, most people hide them somewhere stupid, like taped to the top of the mailbox, under the welcome mat, or inside a fake rock in the flowerbed.

In answer Jesse went straight to a lawn gnome and upended it. "She never changes a thing." His tone held a melancholy fondness. "Let's take a look then."

"Is this questionable legal ground for you, officer?"

"We have a key," he said, which didn't quite answer me, but I let it go.

As soon as we pushed open the door, the place let out a little gasp, like air settling back from an imbalance. The faint breeze carried the scent of rotten eggs. I didn't want to go farther, but I wouldn't let Jesse out of my sight either so I stayed close on his heels.

We found Maris in the bedroom.

"Jesus," Saldana said while I fought to keep my toast down. "It looks like wild dogs got at her."

I couldn't look away from the horror etched into her pallid face or the bloodstained carpet beneath her. The room smelled sickly sweet, faintly of copper and decay. He was right, though. Bits of her flesh were missing, as though something had fed.

"Somebody set a lower demon on her, something hungry and stupid." I could tell he didn't want to believe that by the way he hesitated, so I went on. "These people aren't messing around. They really don't want us to find out what happened to Yi Min-chin."

Saldana froze. "You think we're the reason Maris died?"

"What else could it be? They knew she had something important to say to us, so they made sure she couldn't speak. Somebody at Twilight sold her out."

Jesse shook his head, seeming not to want to believe it. "We're a close-knit community. Nobody would—" He clipped the words, finishing with, "We can't stand here talking. Every second, we contaminate the scene a little more. I have to call this in."

"Is this going to look bad for you?" Seemed to me it would, finding an ex dismembered on her bedroom floor.

"I don't know. Maybe." Saldana ran a hand through his hair and escorted me back to the Forester, where he got on his cell phone.

I wanted to get the hell out of there. If past precedents held true, the San Antonio PD would ask a shitload of awkward questions and then run my prints. If the scars permitted a match, well, that *never* worked out well. They might even charge me with something if they thought they could get away with it and never mind the truth.

Anxiety clawed at me from the inside out, and by the time he hung up, I was a bundle of nerves. "Can I go? I don't know anything, and I really can't be involved in this."

It didn't matter that we were a good two miles from a bus stop. I'd walked in worse weather and worse shoes for that matter.

"Trust me." Jesse brushed the hair away from my face. "I'm not going to let anything happen to you."

Like I hadn't heard *that* before.

Cop promises meant more, I guess, because he was true to his word. He let me sit in the SUV while he dealt with the PD. I didn't hear what they said but they made notes and cut him loose.

By the time we hit the highway, I could breathe again. "Is there anything I need to know? Do we need to synchronize our watches or something?"

He looked pale and tense. I'd never lost anyone but my mom, so I could only imagine how he must be feeling. The woman we found lifeless on her bedroom floor . . . he had once held her in his arms, kissed her blue-tinged mouth, and stroked her hair. He knew the sound of her laughter and her warmth, but she would never be anything but an echo now, coming from six feet down.

"I told them you didn't go in and that I stayed only long enough to see there was a problem, then phoned it in. It made things easier."

"Did you mention the key?"

"The door was unlocked." He spared a glance from the road to impress the importance of that on me.

Interesting. So he wasn't above lying to keep his ass out of the fire. "Noted. Why did we drop by?"

"To get your palm read." At my look he shrugged. "First thing I thought of. They didn't care why. They just wanted to get in there and start checking things out."

"They're not going to find anything. You know that as well as I do."

His brooding expression said he knew that all too well.

The Fiddler Calls the Tune

Saldana let me off in Chuch's driveway. By this time it was late afternoon, the sun sinking beyond the horizon for one of those wild Texas sunsets, a riot of deep color. In Mexico City, the sky looks pale as blue slate even on sunny days. The sunsets don't glow like that either; they're hazy pink and gray. At night the stars give way to city lights.

He hesitated as if he didn't know what to say. Finally he settled on, "I'll keep you posted. Call me tomorrow and we'll set something up for the purse. It has to be unofficial, though. If we get caught, it'll mean my badge."

I'd almost forgotten about that, but I was glad he was a man of his word. I managed a smile. "Thanks, I'll do that. We'll be careful. I'm not looking to hurt you, Jesse."

When he smiled, I realized it was the first time I'd called him by his first name. I didn't know what that meant, but it appeared to please him.

After the Forester drove away, Chuch slid out from underneath a Mustang on a roller board. He shone with grease and seemed cheerful about it. I wondered what Eva would say about the mess on her bathroom tiles.

"Thought for a minute he was gonna kiss you and then Chance would kill us both."

I arched a brow. "Why both of us?"

"'Cause I was out here and didn't stop it." He grinned up at me. "You can say you're not his, but I don't think he buys it. I'm the same way when Eva takes off. Even if she stayed gone ten years instead of ten days I'd still think of her as mine. I'd still be waiting for her to come to her senses."

Yeah, my mood colored the impression, but Chuch's steadfastness struck me as ridiculously sweet. A little misguided, maybe, but sweet. I ignored his less than subtle hint that I should reconcile with Chance. I liked Chuch but he didn't see the big picture. He didn't know I'd spent two weeks in intensive care.

After our last job went so wrong, I'd almost died. I still didn't know who had pulled me out of the building— some nameless rescue worker, no doubt.

I'd been lucky. The people in the squats hadn't gotten off so lightly. If the guy who lit the blaze wasn't serving consecutive life sentences—well. You could say I'd like to see him suffer something worse.

Fire. For me, it was always fire ever since I'd gone running out our back door into the woods. Someday it would catch up with me. But today was not that day. I managed a smile.

"Is Chance okay?" I offered Chuch a hand and tugged. The mechanic was a fireplug, so it took all my strength to get him on his feet, and I suspect he didn't help much.

"Define *okay*. He's stir-crazy and obsessed with whether you're doing the cop. Worried about his mom. Otherwise, yeah, he's great. Booke came up with some more info on the ritual and e-mailed me what he had. Chance is going over the stuff inside."

A fine wire of tension uncoiled. If anything had happened to him while I was with Jesse, I don't think I'd have forgiven myself. I didn't know what I could do to protect him, but some instinct insisted I could safeguard

him somehow. Even if I couldn't *be* with him, the world
would be cold and dark without him in it.

"Good."

Maris's pale face haunted me. A life cut short over
what? What did she *know*? All I had to show for my
night's work was a dead witch and a cop I didn't know
what to do with.

Chuch favored me with a long, narrow-eyed stare.
"You look like shit, but I don't think you got any.
That'll cheer him up some."

"You keep sweet-talking me like this and Eva will get
jealous." That reminded me, though. As we headed inside, I shared part of what I'd learned from Jesse, including Lenny Marlowe, Delta Security, and IBC, who
owned the warehouse where we'd been hit. "So it wasn't
a total loss, and he's getting me in tomorrow to look at
the bag."

I didn't mention the murder scene. Just couldn't, because to speak it aloud would bring back all the mental
images. I'd never seen anyone mauled like that. So much
blood. So much pain. I also didn't mention that the
gifted segment of humanity had organized. If he didn't
know, I probably shouldn't be sharing the info.

Chuch nodded. "Good work, *hermanita*. You must
give a mean hand job."

Naturally Chance emerged from the office on that
note. I fought the impulse to reassure him, but apparently it didn't matter. Wordless, he came over and
wrapped his arms about me. This was what I'd always
wanted from him: some sign he knew what I needed,
even if I didn't come out and beg for it.

Damn him anyway.

I put my arms around his waist, noticing the difference between him and Saldana. Where the cop carried
his muscle lean, Chance crossed the border to thin. I felt
his ribs as he held me.

Oh, he still wore clothing well, still looked impossibly elegant, but he'd lost weight in the year since I'd been gone. I wondered whether I had anything to do with it.

I stepped back and let Chuch do the talking. Right now I needed another shower, wanted to try to wash away the memory of the dead witch's face. It shook me since I'd spent more time in the last few days thinking about my mother than I had in all the years since I'd lost her. Maybe I was making too much of it because it hit so close to home, but gentle women who practiced the art didn't seem to fare well.

Not enough chitin in their armor in a world of tooth and claw.

Perhaps illogically, I felt as though everything connected somehow. If I could just get enough distance, I'd see all the missing links. But that was Twila's gift, not mine, and I couldn't pay her to get involved in this.

The hot water ran over me, and it felt like tears rising in the steam. I sank down in the shower stall and tried to cry. I ached for my simple life: Dutch miniatures and a rooftop garden. Caught between demons and promises, I didn't see how I could survive. Señor Alvarez might get my shop after all.

Though I meant to join them right away, I only managed to put on clean panties and a blue T-shirt before sinking down on the bed. Everything hit me at once and I shook, wrapped my arms around a pillow.

Chance found me like that a few minutes later. His eyes gleamed in the half-light; he raised a hand to the damp fire of my hair, rubbed it between thumb and forefinger. I remembered he'd never made love to me in this incarnation.

"What didn't you tell Chuch?"

It was pointless to protest. He knew me better than anyone alive, and he'd sensed I had something weighing on me from the moment I walked in the door. That was why he held me instead of yelling at me, even though I'd driven him quietly out of his mind by staying out all night and half the next day.

I closed my eyes and yielded, telling him about Maris in a whisper. Before I finished, he drew me to him, but I took care not to touch his back. He would bear scars because of me, as I carried them for him.

What bond did that bespeak? I wasn't sure it was safe or healthy, but I didn't know whether I could resist its pull either. Chance held such dark sorcery in the amber of his eyes, and his scent always made me think of white sheets and writhing bodies.

I wished he'd loved me more.

I wish I understood what drives him.

Then I took the leap and shared the rest.

"So there are others like you," he said. "An organized network, much different than the odd talent we've run across. When did you plan to tell me?"

Sometimes he had a way of making me feel like there were miles between us, as if his mind was ultimately inhuman and unknowable. I sat away from him, frowning.

"I just did. What does that matter, Chance? Or do you want the address of the club so you can look for someone to take my place?"

Pain gathered, pooled between us. I sensed it in the turning of his mood. "Nobody can take your place, Corine. Even if I found a hundred people with your gift."

"You won't." My tone sounded nasty, even to me. I wanted to fight, hoped he'd give me a reason. "It's rare."

He searched my face for some sign. "I already knew that about you."

I bounced from the bed, paced to the window and back. My hair kissed the small of my back, my one vanity. Perhaps I should've found some pants, but he'd already seen every inch of me.

"Please don't. Don't make more of me than I am, or

more of what we had. I think you've romanticized me, and that's why you can't let me go. You have to move on. We're poison together, remember?"

"And *I* think you've forgotten what it was like between us because that's the only way you can stay away. God, Corine . . ." My name fell as a sigh.

"Not now." My anger evaporated, leaving desperation. I didn't know what I would do if he pressed. "Let me finish getting dressed and then we'll talk this thing to death. Eva can whip up some dinner, you can tell me what you learned from Booke. I just . . . don't think it's a good idea to be in a bedroom with you."

Not the way I felt. Not with so much emotion desperate for release and I couldn't seem to weep.

He almost smiled. I saw the quirk of his mouth, or maybe it was a trick of the shadows. "I bet Eva can get us an address for Lenny Marlowe. We'll go see him tomorrow and talk to him about what he saw. Doubt he knows anything, though, or he'd be in the same shape as poor Maris."

I suspected he was right, but it couldn't hurt. "Good idea. Do you know if Delta has assigned him somewhere new? If so, what shift is he working?"

Details. I'd always handled the details that way. Funny that I would be the practical one in our relationship, but it always fell like that. I made sure we had food in the house and that Chance remembered to eat while making deals. He contacted people, talked me up, and for a while, we lived high profile. We made the news when we saved the little girl, but in the end, the publicity caused more harm than good.

To my amusement, that much hadn't changed. He looked blank. "I don't know, but I'll have Eva find out. I imagine she can smooth-talk somebody at the agency."

I'd be surprised if she couldn't.

Legwork

Lenny Marlowe lived in a trailer near an overpass.

Each time a semi went by, the whole thing shook alarmingly. I didn't know how the guard slept at night, which proved a person could get used to anything. The entire place could've fit into the posh suite we'd rented at the hotel in Monterrey, but I had lived in worse places that last year in foster care.

Along with a pink flamingo, two ceramic ducks, and a broken lawn mower, he had a rusty sign in his front yard that read BEWARE OF DOG. It tickled me to find the dog in question was a mouthy Chihuahua with bulging eyes and a spiked red leather collar. Butch sat in the crook of his owner's arm, eyeing us with suspicion.

Lenny himself was a tall, lumpy guy with small, close-set eyes, an overlong nose, and a wide, thin mouth. He seemed delighted to have company, almost conspiratorial, in fact. Chance sat quiet beside me on Lenny's sagging brown couch.

"Well, like I done told the police"—he gave the word a long O—"when I went in, I'd plumb forgot I didn't report there no more. I worked that warehouse six months, and you get into a habit, y'know?" I nodded to show I did and he went on. "But when I got in there, it smelled funny, like bad egg salad. I took a walk through and saw the mess. I'll tell you straight, I got out of there quick."

"I don't blame you. That night, you didn't see the woman who lost the purse?" Chance asked.

"Nope. Best I can figure, they must've had her in there the night before, after I got off work. That was supposed to be my last night on the job, but I forgot and came back. They hadn't changed the locks yet."

"Can you think of any reason they would take a hostage there?" I watched the guard's face, trying to decide if he could possibly be this guileless. It was like interrogating Forrest Gump.

"Well, it's dark and pretty isolated. Most of the businesses have shut down—just that La Quinta Inn left a few blocks away. So I guess if you wanted to beat somebody up, nobody would hear the screams."

Good place for magickal workings then as well.

"Had you noticed anything strange before that night?" Chance looked remarkably impassive, impervious to the idea of someone hurting Yi Min-chin.

I knew better.

Lenny thought that over. "Well, I wouldn't tell this to the cops 'cause they'd think I got a screw loose, but yeah. I work second shift, so it's all dark and spooky, but I swear I heard stuff moving around in there sometimes. Nobody shoulda been there but me."

I exchanged a glance with Chance, and then he asked, "Did you ever see anyone?"

Lenny shook his head. "No. Mostly it was a feeling, and I'd get the willies real bad. I'd turn around and nothing would be there. Sometimes I'd see movement in the shadows but if I shined my light on it, nothing." He hesitated. "I guess I thought maybe birds got in because I heard wings rustling sometimes."

"I bet you're glad to be out of there," I said. Though I tried not to show it, I felt dead man's hands crawling up my back just listening to him.

"No kidding. I work at a desk now. No more creepy warehouses. I monitor stuff on a TV, nice building. I have a phone and everything, but they don't let me order pizza. I'm not supposed to let people in the building at night." If encouraged, he would probably talk about his new job all day, or at least until time for his next shift.

"Thanks for your time," Chance murmured. "We appreciate your assistance."

"So you're trying to find the lady that disappeared, right?" Lenny's voice gained enthusiasm. "I peeked in her purse before I called the cops, but I didn't take anything, I swear. Don't tell, okay? So are you guys private eyes? I bet she was kidnapped. Did you get a ransom demand? I could help, be your bag man or something." His words came out in a single breath, mashed together like a peanut butter and Marshmallow Fluff sandwich.

"No, we're not and we haven't. You already helped plenty." I put down my watery Diet Coke without finishing it and stood. I expected Lenny to produce further useful information like I expected to get milk from a tomcat, but it shouldn't do any harm to leave my cell number. I scrawled it on a page torn from my pocket calendar and handed it to him. "If you think of anything else, give me a call. We'll get out of your way now. Thanks a lot."

"Sure, anytime. I'll keep an ear open for news about that Korean lady. I'll call you if I hear anything." Lenny got to his feet as well. His mama had apparently instilled the rudiments of good manners in him.

Once outside, I asked Chance, "You think they were using the warehouse for rituals at night?"

"Seems like a given," he said grimly. "They probably thought he was too stupid to notice any residual effects."

I climbed in the Camry, considering our next move. "It has to be driving you crazy, wondering how your mom got mixed up in all this."

"Not as much as worrying if she's safe, but yeah. It's

hard realizing I don't know her half as well as I thought I did." He started the car and followed the gravel drive out of the trailer park back to the access road that adjoined the freeway. "She had this whole other life before she moved to Tampa and she didn't talk about it at all. When I think back, she had a way of avoiding questions. If I brought something up, instead of answering, she'd ask if I did my homework or if I'd remembered to take the trash out."

"Maybe she was trying to protect you."

He flicked me a hard look. "I'd rather know what's coming."

Ouch.

"Sometimes it's easier not to deal with things head-on. Sometimes it's better to step aside quietly."

"Better for whom?"

I quit trying to pretend we were still talking about his mother. "Me. You think I could've walked away if I had to look into your eyes and say good-bye?"

"I don't know. Could you?"

"No." The answer came simple and unadorned. "But don't you understand why I had to go?"

The silence built, broken only by the vibration of the engine and the roar of the tires on the road. By the exit he took, we must be heading for the police station.

Chance sounded as if the words were dragged out of him with hooks and wires. "You blamed me for what happened in Tuscaloosa. You thought I didn't love you. You thought your safety didn't matter to me, just the money."

I didn't know what I thought anymore. Certainly I believed those things at the time or I wouldn't have left.

"You took a job that put us up against Clayton Mann," I said deliberately. "Just what did you expect to happen? When you threaten someone who burns down buildings for a living and rapes women for fun—"

His jaw clenched. "I thought I could protect you. Do

you think I don't turn that night over in my head, time and again? Wondering how I could have changed things? You were right behind me, Corine. I went first to make sure it was safe. How the hell could I know the floor would crumble beneath you and leave me standing while you fell?"

Well, that's your luck. Even when he didn't try to use it, good fortune sat on him like a shining, silver crown. Bad things took one look at him and ricocheted to the nearest warm body. So of course *I* fell, not him.

Three stories through burning, rotted timber, old plaster, and asbestos.

Remembering that night, a wave of pain and horror stirred, and I fought it down. His luck was a Sword of Damocles, if ever there was one, a gift I'd come to see as a curse. See, unlike me, he couldn't focus and shut it off, not entirely. It ran through his life in a subsonic hum, striking random notes that called pure chaos. Maybe that doesn't sound like a bad thing . . . at first. It would keep things interesting, right?

Well, try living with him. If we went to a store, it was robbed. If we went to a restaurant, he'd win the millionth customer prize and a free steak dinner or save somebody from choking. Coincidences crawled on him thick as bluebottle flies on a dung heap.

"You couldn't," I said finally, doubt threading my words. "But we were in that situation because of you, and I didn't want to live like that anymore."

"So you left," he said bitterly. "Thinking all I cared about was getting rich off your gift. But it was never the money. Yeah, the guy who hired us to bring Mann down had an ax to grind. The son of a bitch raped and murdered his daughter! In her old pictures, Kelly looked like you, Corine. She *looked* like you. And all I could think about was getting that sick fuck off the streets before he noticed you."

Chance paused, his fingers turned white on the steering wheel. I stared at his profile, dumbstruck. He'd never said a word, not once. I couldn't even remember what Kelly Armitage had looked like before Clayton Mann got through with her. It took him six months inside before he started giving up the bodies. But for a moment, I pictured Chance staring at her pictures and seeing *me*. Was he afraid of losing me, even then?

We'd been living in Tuscaloosa a few months. People knew who we were, but they didn't bother us, except to offer work. Kelly's dad did just that. He had no proof except a father's surety and a gas station clerk's description of a woman who sounded like Kelly getting into Mann's car. But he had a bloody scarf, and that would tell us everything we needed to know.

In the end, that stained scrap of cloth led us right to Mann's lair, a condemned building where he liked to take his girls.

I hadn't wanted the job. Thought it would be too dangerous, based off Mann's lengthy rap sheet. He'd done time before, arson and assault, and if he went down a third time, he might as well forget about parole. But Chance talked me into it.

And that was the beginning of the end.

"I wanted to help people, but not if it meant hurting you, love. Goddamn, I would've done *anything* for you, and you walked away thinking I saw you as nothing but a . . ." He paused. "A show pony. Isn't that what you said?"

How I wished I could believe him. "If that's true, why didn't you come looking for me until you needed me again?"

I hadn't realized until this moment how much that hurt. I spent half my trip across the country looking over my shoulder, expecting Chance to show up demanding an explanation. By the time I reached Mexico City, I realized he never would.

"You almost died because of me. I understood why

you wanted out. What right did I have to keep you if you wanted to go?"

"Is it a question of rights?" I clenched my hands into fists, fighting the urge to yell. "You could've said something. Anything. But communication was never our strong suit."

His voice came as a silver thread of sound, salted with anguish. "Maybe I felt like I deserved to lose you."

I exhaled unsteadily as I realized we'd turned into the parking lot at the station. For a moment I let myself look at him, really look—probably what Eva would term eating him with my eyes. I'd missed everything about him, but time passed and sometimes broken things heal crooked. The pieces didn't fit anymore.

"I don't believe in that, people getting what they deserve. That implies the world is fair and it never has been. You made a choice, Chance, just as I did. You chose to let me go. If you did it to punish yourself, then take off your crown of thorns. What's done is done, and I don't blame you for anything. If we were meant to be together, we still would be." I opened the car door and got out. "Let's go see Officer Saldana."

Expect the Unexpected

Jesse was on the phone when we came into his office. Once again, mess cluttered his partner's desk but the guy was nowhere in sight. I fought the urge to collect the trash and dispose of it on principle. I'm not a neat freak, but there's something wrong about letting food decompose outside of a compost heap. To amuse myself I counted fast food wrappers and dirty cups.

He motioned us to wait a minute by holding up his index finger. "Yes, it's chicken blood in the warehouse." I already knew that. "Did you contact— Oh, right. Yes, sir. I'll try to keep the press from claiming we have a satanic cult operating in town, but I really don't have any— Yes, I agree. The last thing we need is religious zealots picketing the parking lot. I'm sure it was just kids messing around."

I wasn't so sure about that, but I didn't think his captain would appreciate any of my theories. Plus, apart from Jesse, I did my best to avoid law enforcement. Like cats always climb on the one person who's allergic to them, cops always come sniffing around me, sure I've been up to something. Once they stopped me in Cut Shin, Kentucky, for driving too slow.

After hanging up, Saldana sighed. "I have a feeling this is going to get worse before it gets better." As he produced the purse, he added, "Glad you guys are on time. I need to get this back before shift change."

I expected there to be some tension, but both guys seemed focused on my reading. Bracing myself, I picked up the purse, but to my surprise it felt inert. No charge, no searing pain. I opened it, checked inside. When my fingers brushed across a stud holding the strap to the handbag, I received a small shock, not unlike what I got when I touched Saldana.

Somehow inside the current, I heard a breathy whisper that sounded as if it might be Yi Min-chin: "The *zona*."

And that was all.

They regarded me with puzzlement. I guessed the show turned out to be something of a letdown. "You can take it back. I'm done."

Since he'd seen me handle the night before, Jesse looked at my fingers and then the palm of my hand. "It didn't work?"

"Some things just don't hold a charge. Metal has the best resonance for capturing and keeping images. Textiles fade much faster."

This was a synthetic handbag, vinyl disguised as leather. I didn't know whether she'd done this on purpose or if this qualified as a failure on my part. It had never worked like this before.

"Have either of you ever been to the *zona*?" I asked.

Chance looked blank but Saldana arched a brow. "Are you looking for a prostitute?"

I thought of Señor Alvarez, running my shop. How much would he skim, if anything? Would he withhold sales? "I doubt I can afford one."

"What's the *zona*?" Chance asked.

"People in the States usually call it Boys Town. It's a walled compound in Nuevo Laredo where people go looking to party and buy whores. It's legal there," Jesse added, evidently seeing Chance's confusion.

"Yep." I spoke to fill the silence. "They spring up around the border towns."

"I haven't been there since I was eighteen. I guess every guy in Texas checks it out once. If you decide to go for reasons I probably don't want to know, keep a tight hold on your wallets, watch for pickpockets, and stay away from Tranny Alley. The places don't get busy until ten and the party runs till six in the morning. You'll find most people out after dark, if you have questions, but bring bribe money if you expect answers."

Was Chance's mom a former hooker? Why else would she nudge us in this direction? Maybe she got out of the life when she got pregnant with him. Well, the purse seemed to be a dead end otherwise, and I didn't know what to make of this.

"I'll let you get back to work now." I saw about a hundred questions in Jesse's eyes, but I didn't care to answer them. "I'll call you, okay?"

Heading for the door, I didn't see if Chance followed me, but he caught up with me before I left the police station. "Don't keep stuff from me, Corine. What does the *zona* have to do with anything?"

"I'm not sure," I admitted. "I just heard the words when I touched the inside of the purse. It sounded like your mom's voice."

He frowned as we pushed open the door and stepped out into a blindingly bright November afternoon. "But there was no accompanying image?"

"No. It's strange."

Chance knew how backward that was. If an item accepted a charge, it captured whatever its last handler experienced, much like a silent film, but it took a specialized gift in order to unlock it. This sounded like his mother had used the bag to record her words. I didn't know how that was even possible, but if she could do it, why didn't she say more?

Offering a tired smile, he said, "I know you're worried about my feelings, but I don't think anything could surprise me now. My mother knows how to summon demons and she's apparently connected to Boys Town as well. So what's our next move?" He paused outside the Camry, managing to look cool as a Long Island iced tea even as sweat trickled down the small of my back.

I was glad he'd decided to let the relationship stuff go.

"You're asking *me*?" I projected astonishment. "Then I want some lunch."

To my surprise, he didn't argue, just got in the car. "Mexican or Italian?"

Why did I smile because he offered the choice between my two favorites? On his own he'd go Japanese; he loved sushi and I couldn't stand the stuff, except for California rolls. Chance said those didn't count, though.

The hot seat made me hiss as I wiggled around. "Depends. Are we talking about Olive Garden Italian or good Italian?"

"I liked Johnny Carino's when I ate there with my mom, but it *is* a chain, not a dive with red checkered tablecloths."

I happen to harbor a soft spot for dives and the folks who operate them.

"Something more authentic then. Surprise me."

When he pulled up outside a brown brick building on McPherson Avenue, I gaped at the wagon wheels outside the Cotulla Style Pit Bar-B-Q. "Home of the world-famous mariachis, huh? Too bad it's not Saturday night."

"We could come back."

I gave him a look as we pushed into the dim, cool interior. There was a definite cowboy theme going on, a cheerful blend of Western and Mexican decor. The place smelled deliciously of barbeque and most of the tables were full, always a good sign.

A hostess sat us down with two menus, and I decided

on the mixed *parrillada* with *nopales* and beans. He went with chicken chalupas. Chance also ordered us a pitcher of sangria, which earned him points. If he wanted them. Did he? I put that complication aside as the waitress departed.

"We need to figure out the connections here. Once we do that, I think we'll have a good idea where to find your mom." *Easier said than done.* "This may seem like a stupid question, but did you make sure Clayton Mann and Kel Ferguson are still locked up? Even so, they might have someone acting for them on the outside."

Those two topped the list of people who wanted to hurt Chance and me, bad. Ferguson was a stone-cold killer for Jesus. He claimed angels told him that people he hunted would unleash the end times, and God didn't intend to wrap things up yet. He wouldn't say a word about what that had to do with the child he'd stolen, however. Even while he stood in the courtroom facing his sentence, he claimed divine inspiration.

Over and over, he'd said, "God will deliver me. No earthly bars can hold me."

No matter how the prosecution questioned him, he never wavered from his story. Until they took him off the stand in disgust, and there were whispers of an insanity plea.

Sometimes I still dreamed about his eyes, as if he could somehow track my every move. He wasn't easily forgotten. I'd finally managed to shake the feeling that he lurked around every corner, though. Mostly. Except on really dark nights.

In his egocentrism, Clayton Mann didn't see why anyone should get to tell him no. Rape wasn't a crime to him; it was him teaching the woman that she wanted him. And he'd very nearly been the end of me.

As far as I knew, they were *both* in prison.
If they aren't . . .
Chance paled, both hands wrapping around his glass,

and for a minute I thought he might be sick. Then he knocked back his drink as if it were whiskey. "I should've found out first thing. It never occurred to me they might strike at me through my mom. Oh, Christ."

The waitress brought our food and I paused long enough to let her settle the plates. "That doesn't feel right. They're both . . . more direct. And I doubt they know anything about rituals. I just brought it up because we need to cover all angles. How does that go? Eliminate the impossible and whatever remains, however improbable, is the truth?"

I saw the tension ease out of him. "You've been reading Sherlock Holmes again. After you left, Corine . . . I bought a first edition of *The Deep Blue Good-by* because I forgot you weren't coming back. It's still on the bedside table at home."

As a mass market paperback, it wouldn't be valuable. He'd probably found it in a second-hand shop somewhere, but it meant everything that he remembered my passion for Travis McGee, a hero who ranted about the destruction of the Everglades before people practiced environmentalism. I *loved* John D. MacDonald. All those times I rambled about one of his colorfully titled novels, I thought Chance tuned me out. But he'd listened and remembered. If I was wrong about that—

Through the front windows, I watched the Camry explode in the parking lot.

Odds and Ends

"You know"—Saldana eyed the wreckage in the parking lot of Cotulla Style Pit Bar-B-Q—"if you wanted my attention, you could've just called."

"Funny."

He sighed. "When the call came in, I just knew you had something to do with it."

I felt like that was a trifle unjust. I hadn't blown out the windows at the warehouse or killed poor Maris. Chance is the one who attracts trouble like a lightning rod. My life in Mexico City had been pretty quiet. So by my calculations, I needed to stay *away* from him. Adventure followed him like a hound dog after a bone, and I'm not shamed to say I'd enjoyed enough excitement.

"So you came out to see me?" I managed a smile for my mentor. Still didn't know what I was supposed to do with him. "That's so sweet."

"Slow day." Jesse shrugged. "Just the usual gang stuff, so I thought I could spare a few minutes to take a look here."

There wasn't too much to see. The formerly. piss yellow Camry smoldered in half a dozen pieces, and the cars parked on either side weren't in great shape either. If we hadn't stopped for lunch, we'd be dead. Some people might call it coincidence, but we could thank

Chance's luck for that. We definitely had somebody on our tail, though. I suspected they'd planted the bomb when we went into the police station, and that took some stainless steel balls.

Was it possible that our enemies had a guy on the police force? Someone who had a vested interest in making sure nobody ever found out what had become of Min? Well, shit. Jesse had known our every move since I made the mistake of trusting him.

We shouldn't stay with Chuch and Eva anymore. Maybe the mechanic had good wards, but you couldn't charm a house against fire, gas leaks, or Molotov cocktails. It was so wrong that our enemies could aim such a wide variety of threats at us, and we didn't even know whom we were fighting. Or why, for that matter.

I felt numb. Though I've been burned out of my home and seen some scary things in my life, I'd never found a demon-chewed corpse before yesterday, nor had a vehicle blow up before my eyes. These people weren't messing around; they'd kill us if they could.

For the first time I wondered if we should step back and let it go. Maybe uncertainty was better than dying. After all, I'd lived for twenty years without knowing what happened to my dad. My mom and I figured he just left, though Twila tried to sell me a different version of events. Right now I had too many other things to worry about to focus on it, but it weighed on me nonetheless.

Chance finished his interview with Saldana's partner. We finally met the guy, Nathan Moon, and I'd been wrong about him all the way. Not a big, burly type. He was short, bowlegged, and paunchy with a sunburned, sullen face. I still bet he played bad cop.

Shortly he proved it. "So you don't have any idea why somebody would launch your ride?"

I didn't know what Chance had told Officer Moon, but I clammed up, courtesy of cops hassling me over the years. They always thought I was a charlatan, a grifter, or worse. Never mind the fact that Chance and I *helped* people; we didn't talk the elderly out of their pensions. If Saldana wasn't standing here, this would turn ugly. Hell, it might anyway. I didn't know if I could trust him; in fact, things had gone drastically wrong ever since I took him into my confidence.

I lifted one shoulder in a halfhearted shrug and wished I had a long, tall glass of lemonade. "Maybe they thought it belonged to someone else."

"Drug dealing's about the only thing that would get people so riled up around here." Moon pretended to consider. "Maybe if a deal went bad or some money went missing. You think any of them drug dealers drive a Camry?"

"I don't know any," I said sweetly. "So I'm afraid I can't answer that."

Jesse elbowed his partner. "Cut the lady some slack. Remember that talk we had about not treating victims like perps?"

I wasn't sure I liked being classed as a victim, but I didn't protest. The two cops exchanged a look, and then Moon stalked off to harangue one of the uniforms on scene. I imagined their office would be tense for a day or two. Or maybe Nathan Moon just acted like this all the time.

We stood by in the heat while the bomb squad went over the odds and ends. Finally a guy came over, red-faced and sweating. "Here's the timer. Looks like the remains of a digital watch. We'll know more later, but it was definitely a DIY ignition. I reckon they made it out of stuff you can buy at Home Depot."

At that point, Saldana got involved in a discussion that went straight over my head. I swiped my palm across my forehead, ready to collapse somewhere shady and cool, but we didn't have a ride. The rental car agencies would flip over their signs to closed after the busted engine block on the Suburban and now the exploding Camry. Once we established that the police didn't need anything else from us, Chance shepherded me back inside.

As I nursed a Diet Coke in the blessed restaurant air conditioning, he called Chuch. "Hey, is Eva home? Good. I need a favor, and after this we'll call it even. I'm talking about wiping your debt." He paused, listening. "Settle down. I'm not about to ask for a night with your wife. Do I look like Robert Redford?"

I let my gaze wander up and down before answering, "Nope."

Chance scowled and made shushing motions at me. If he'd asked I would've told him he was more Ben Jelen than Robert Redford—better in my book. Even if the actor wasn't almost a hundred, I never went for blond guys, not since a big jerk named Erik had cheated on me. I did like tawny highlights in Jesse Saldana's hair, though. I also liked his sense of humor, his smile, and the way his ass filled out a pair of Levi's.

I *didn't* like the fact that I was beginning to suspect he was dirty and that he'd been assigned to make sure we never learned anything useful about Min. *He could've killed Maris*, I realized. My presence in the apartment didn't constitute an alibi, as I'd been sound asleep in another room. Maybe he hadn't realized it would come to that.

He'd sure as hell looked rough when I got up. I'd assumed he suffered from sheer sexual frustration, but—

When I came out of the nightmare that line of thought evoked, I realized I'd missed the rest of the conversation, and Chance was regarding me expectantly, phone in hand.

I blinked. "Huh?"

"Chuch is giving us the Mustang. We'll have to take better care of it."

"Wow. How much money did you *loan* him?" A fully restored 1972 cherry red classic amounted to a significant gift.

He just shrugged. "Doesn't matter. We're even now."

"Do we need to find somewhere else to stay?"

"I think it's a good idea. I feel bad that we—*I*— dragged them into this. But I didn't realize things would get this bad. Like Lenny, I thought it was a kidnapping at first. Calling in everything I'm owed, I could raise five hundred grand or so if they asked, but at this point I don't think they will."

"They didn't hurt her. I think she knew them, Chance, or perhaps the people they represented." Never mind the ritual. I'd contemplated that first reading a bit, and I got a good look at her face before she dropped the pewter Buddha.

His long fingers drew patterns on the scarred tabletop. Despite my best intentions I remembered a game we used to play, where I lay on my stomach and he wrote Korean characters on my spine. His mother had been teaching me the language and I had a knack for such things, but when Chance put his hands on me, I forgot every English word I knew.

"Pretty sure you're right. If we're going to find the answers, we have to follow her trail. And that seems to lead to Boys Town."

Oh, joy. Was there ever such a twisted relationship? I couldn't imagine another woman agreeing to accompany her ex to hang out with hookers. Sadly I couldn't argue with his logic, as I'd come to the same conclusion myself. Maybe something we learned in the *zona* would bring the other loose threads into the weave, show the larger pattern.

Shit, I sounded like Twila.

After dropping some cash for the waitress, we went back outside to wait. Eva would follow Chuch in the Mustang, we'd take over ownership, and then . . . well. I didn't know.

That was the plan, at least. Chuch turned up by himself about fifteen minutes later. I climbed into the back of his Maverick. Listened to the two of them argue in the front.

"You're loco if you think I'm gonna cut you loose just 'cause it's getting hard, *primo*. You're my friend. I'm not gonna give you a car and say *buena suerte* when you got people trying to blow your shit up. I can help— you know that. I got contacts."

Chuch always said, "If your mechanic doesn't know everything that goes on, then you need a new mechanic." But his willingness to stick didn't mean it was a good idea.

"I know you can." Chance sounded tired. "But I'd never forgive myself if anything happened to you or Eva."

I never heard this tone from Chuch before. "If they look crossways at Eva, I'll hunt them down and cut them open. Stake them out in the desert so they die slow."

"I don't doubt it," Chance said, and I wondered what secrets hid in Chuch's past. What didn't I know about him? "But that won't bring her back. I wish you hadn't left her alone. There was a reason I asked you to have her follow in the Mustang, and not just because I wanted to keep from leading bad things back to your house, if they don't already know we're there."

Silence.

The souped-up Maverick roared as Chuch stepped on the gas.

Second Chances

Once we got there, Chuch ran faster than I would have credited, calling Eva's name.

We found her in the kitchen, chopping carrots and bopping to her iPod. Chuch swept her in his arms, buried his face in her hair. She patted him with a perplexed look and then extricated herself. The sauce simmering on the stove smelled fantastic.

"You guys really wanted this chicken casserole, huh?"

"No, *mi vida*. Chance pointed out that you might not be safe here alone."

At this Eva raised a brow. "I know you're not saying I can't take care of myself, Jesus Maria Ortiz Obregón."

With that knife in her hand, she did look dangerous. Chuch took a step back and raised a hand in a placating gesture. "No, but—"

"What he means to say," Chance put in quietly, "is that you can't defend yourself against random explosions."

"I guess that's true, but I'm fine. Anyway, I've been working on the case, and you were right, IBC owns Southern Sanitation. The funny part is, I can't find any names. It's one of those . . . blind corporations? That seems shady, like they're trying to hide something, you know?"

I nodded, thoughtful. "I'm sure they are."

So IBC was the parent corporation. They owned the warehouse where Min's purse was found, where she'd performed the ritual. They also owned Southern Sanitation, whose truck took her away. That was the link then. If we could burrow beneath the privacy screens and layers of legal crap, the names behind IBC would tell us everything we wanted to know.

"If IBC does business in Texas, they must have a registered agent," Chance said. "You can't work without one. International corporations do it a lot, so people don't know their money is actually going to Okinawa."

Before I could ask, Eva did. "What's a registered agent?"

Chance went into lecture mode. "The person or entity listed as the public point of contact for a blind corporation. This is the address you'll find on all public documents. Having a registered agent offers a layer of protection against legal proceedings too."

"Now, there's a sweet deal," Chuch muttered. "For crooks."

Hm. While I was sure there were legitimate reasons for putting so much padding between a business and the public eye, I suspected IBC did not possess them. Call me psychic. But what kind of operation would benefit from the front of warehouses and a fleet of trucks? Smuggling immediately came to mind. Drugs, maybe?

I glanced at Eva, whose casserole smelled delicious, but I didn't want to derail my train of thought. "What does IBC stand for anyway?"

She knew that off the top of her head. *"Importaciones Bonitas Corporación."*

"Pretty Imports Corporation?" I translated primarily for Chance's benefit since he was the only one who didn't speak some Spanish. "Guess that means the hidden owners come from a Spanish-speaking country."

Which narrowed it down to half the world. I sighed.

"I wonder if we could get something out of visiting whoever fronts for IBC?" Chance turned to Eva with a single brow cocked in the inquisitive expression I'd once found irresistible. "Did you turn up the public address?"

She left her casserole to go get an apple-shaped notepad. "Sure. I wrote it down. When I Google-mapped the place, it looked like it was downtown."

Chance nodded. "We'll check it out."

My stomach growled. Not to change the subject or anything, but, "You need any help with dinner?"

"You can chop up the celery if you want." Eva set the knife on the counter and went to Chuch at last with a knowing grin. Tugged on the bottom of his shirt. "So you were really worried about me, huh?"

"That's not even funny. You know I'd be lost without you, *nena*." Chuch wore a look of absolute devotion that did strange things to my insides.

"Don't worry. I'm not going anywhere."

Chance propped himself against the counter, long and lean. "Forget dinner. We should get our stuff and go. Somebody wants us dead and I don't want you two caught in the cross fire."

With his luck, he did well to worry. Maybe he'd learned something from our time together; people suffered all around him while he walked off without a scratch. Yeah, he had a double-edged "gift" all right.

"Forget it," Eva said.

It amused me that a look from her cowed him more than anything Chuch could say. "You've got to teach me that look," I said to her, smiling.

She grinned back. To give myself something to do, I got the knife and diced up the celery. Eva layered it along with the noodles, carrots, and chicken and then poured the sauce over the top. She popped the casserole dish into the oven, set the timer for thirty minutes, and then washed her hands.

"So are you guys really okay?" she asked. "Did the

car actually leave the ground? I bet it'll be on TV later. Did they interview you?"

"The press hadn't arrived before we left," Chance told her.

Thank God. Having my face on the news would be worse than I cared to contemplate, and it would undo a year and a half of lying low. Anyone who was still looking would know exactly where to find me. I *hated* that idea.

"I have this idea," she went on. "You think this Maris had something important to tell you, which is why they whacked her, right? So why not bring her back to ask?"

"You mean like a séance?" Don't ask me why I raised a brow over that. I guess because they're so easy to fake. Most folks have played at communicating with spirits a time or two; it's a sleepover staple. "Wouldn't we need a medium?"

"Chuch can do it. He won't want to," Eva added, as her husband backed toward the door. "But he can. His *don* deals with the dead. His *tia* Rosario totally possessed him one night after he had too much tequila because she wanted to yell at his cousin Ramon for giving her such a cheap funeral."

I stifled a laugh.

"I'm trying to forget that, woman. You think that was easy to live down?"

Chance appeared to be considering the idea. "We'd need something that belonged to Maris to guide us. It's almost impossible to summon the right spirit otherwise."

I couldn't believe I was about to suggest this. "Jesse used to date her, so he might have something of hers. That would mean bringing him in, though."

It would be a test, I decided. If he was working against us, there was no way he'd agree to help with something that could give us vital information. And I needed to know which side he was on.

"Jesse," Chance repeated. "The cop, you mean?"

"Yeah. Officer Saldana."

If I called him tonight, that would make three times in one day I'd seen or spoken to him. He was going to think I was crazy about him. Or just plain crazy. It didn't matter what he thought, though, just what he said in response to this admittedly bizarre request.

"It's worth a shot." By Eva's expression, she knew Chuch hated the idea, but she enjoyed stirring the pot.

"I'm not doing it," Chuch muttered. "I wouldn't know how to do it on purpose. *Tia* Rosario was just—"

I said, "I bet I know some people who can help us with the ritual aspects of it. Can I borrow your computer?"

The mechanic glared at me. "Not helping." Then he relented, "Yeah, I guess."

Leaving them to bicker, I headed for his home office and sat down at the desk. He didn't have a password, so the screensaver kicked right off. First I dug into my bag for the Area 51 log-in info, and then I brought up the browser.

The site didn't show so much as a picture before I entered the code, and then it took me to a bulletin board of all things, a plain gray bulletin board. As I surfed down some of the subject headings, though, it became obvious this was the real deal.

Need help in Dallas, looking for exorcist.

Have work for clairvoyant.

Fifth down, I saw *medium for hire* and opened that one up. Since I type about four words a minute, it took me a good while to compose and send the private message. I didn't know how soon we'd hear back, though.

As I spun in the office chair, Chance gave me a start, standing silently in the doorway. Just watching me. I couldn't read his expression, but then I never could. In the beginning his beauty had distracted me, but he always possessed a good poker face.

He pushed away from the doorjamb. "You really think it's a good idea, trusting him all the way?"

I didn't confide my private doubts; he'd enjoy it too much. Instead I hedged. "I don't think it's ever a good idea to trust someone all the way."

As he knelt beside me, I saw the gold flecks in his amber eyes. "You never get tired of turning the knife, do you?"

"Maybe you just have a guilty conscience where I'm concerned."

Chance ignored that. "So are you going to call him?"

"Did Chuch agree to give it a try? It's pointless if he's not willing. Though I don't imagine he actually wanted to be possessed by his aunt Rosario, so maybe we just need to ply him with tequila."

"Eva wants him to. Do you think he ever tells her no?"

I thought about it. "Probably not. I need some of what she's got."

"You're great the way you are," he said with some heat. "I was wondering . . ." Chance trailed off, as if deciding now wasn't the time.

"What?"

"Would you ever consider starting over? Us, I mean." At my stunned look, he added quietly, "I'm never going to find anyone like you."

Once I would've been certain he meant my gift. Now I didn't know what to believe or whether I could trust my own judgment.

"I don't know." From the way his face fell, he wanted to hear something else, but I don't make promises if I'm not sure I can keep them. "I need to think and I can't do that right now. There's too much other stuff going on. I don't want to make a mistake."

He reached for my hand. The same sweet thrill went through me as the first night he did that over dinner. "I want you to do something for me," he said quietly.

Another favor? He had some nerve, I decided.

"I already am. You want something else?"

Chance lifted my scarred palm to his mouth and sealed my fingers over the kiss. "Go home, Corine. This is uglier than I knew. I don't think they'll bother you if you back off, so just go. Please."

I yanked my hand away. "One minute you're asking me to be with you, and the next you're telling me to go. Hot and cold, Chance. I *swear* you do it to keep me off balance. Some crazy power game and I—"

His eyes blazed as he flattened a palm over my mouth. By his expression he wanted it to be his lips, which used to be his favorite method of shutting me up.

"You're so clueless it's ridiculous," he growled. "Remember what I said to Chuch? It applies to you. It doesn't matter if I want you with me—and of *course* I do. Christ. You're sunshine to me, Corine." Apparently distracted, he traced the softness of my lips with his fingertips, like a kiss.

I couldn't get my breath, let alone speak.

He went on. "But if something happens to you here, now, there won't be anything I can do to bring you back." By the darkness in his tiger's eyes, I saw that he'd realized what his luck could do to me, what it had *already* done. "No revenge in the world will offer help for that. I need to know you're safe, that's all."

My heart gave a wayward lurch. I tugged his hand away from my mouth before I succumbed to the urge to kiss his palm. "You want to send me away because you're worried about me?"

"Yeah." His voice came out husky. "I should've known better than to drag you into this. I just keep making the same stupid mistakes. I still don't deserve you."

"Nobody deserves me." I half smiled to show I meant something different.

"Come here," he whispered.

I slid from the chair to my knees, let myself lean into

him. His arms came around me but I didn't want to hurt his back. Chance brushed his lips against my temple and I lifted my face, craving the heat of his mouth.

"Aw, man," Chuch said from the doorway. "Don't even think about doing it on my office floor. That's a new rug."

Making Connections

I scrambled to my feet, feeling heat in my cheeks. "So are we doing this?"

Chuch threw himself into his plaid recliner. "Yeah, I guess. How bad could it be?"

Hm, I wish he hadn't put it like that.

"I'll call Jesse then." Though I wasn't exactly eager, I wanted to *do* something. Up until now, it seemed like our unknown enemy had all the advantages. I felt like Jodi Foster in *The Silence of the Lambs*, with a killer watching through night-vision goggles while I fumbled around in the dark.

Chance offered his hand and I hesitated only a second before I took it. He didn't need my support, though, as he eased to his feet with a grace I'd never possess. I didn't know where we stood, but his hand in the small of my back said he had some ideas. I just wasn't sure whether they correlated with mine. That didn't stop me from leaning back against him, however.

With a sigh, I dialed Jesse's cell. He answered on the third ring. "Saldana."

"This is going to sound strange. . . ."

"I expect that of you. What's up?"

"Do you have anything that belonged to Maris?"

"You think I'm a serial killer or something, keeping trophies? Look, I may have a lot of exes but—"

"No, that's not it." How weird that he immediately leaped to that conclusion, though. Just how far did his range stretch? Could he sense my mistrust? "We're going to try to contact her. Just because she's crossed over, it doesn't mean we can't find out what she knew." Put that way, it sounded callous. If he was innocent, he might get mad.

"It doesn't always work," he said, his voice subdued. "And when they come back, sometimes they're . . . not right. You better be sure you know what you're doing."

I ignored that. "Can you help or not?"

He sighed. "Hold on. Let me take a look around."

That must mean he was home. Well, I didn't know what to make of his reaction. He sounded sad and resigned, not angry or unwilling. But maybe he was a consummate actor.

I glanced at the clock. *After six.* No wonder dinner smelled so good. I'd taken only a few bites of my *parrillada* before the Camry blew up. Man, I didn't envy Chance the conversation with the rental company. Customer service people make cops look benign.

When he came back on the line, Saldana sounded odd. "She left something in my medicine cabinet. I never go in there or I'd have sent it back to her."

"Come on over then." I gave him Chuch's address. "We're having chicken noodle casserole and then we're raising the dead. We'd love it if you came."

At this Chance tightened his arms around me and gave me a little squeeze. I didn't know if it was meant to be a warning or what, but I just grinned at him over my shoulder. Even if I let him hold me for a minute, it didn't mean he *had* me.

"Sadly," Saldana said, "that's the most interesting invitation I've received all week. Give me half an hour?"

"Excellent. See you soon." I hit the off button on my

cell and noticed the way Chuch was looking at us. I really hate a man who smirks.

"So I guess you two are—"

"None of your business." I narrowed my eyes on the mechanic.

"Hey, I was just asking if I needed to make up the couch tonight, that's all."

"Does he?" Chance found the sweet spot at the base of my skull and worked his thumb so that a pleasurable chill rippled over me.

"Yeah. He does."

"Oh." I heard the disappointment in his tone as he dropped his hand. Ghostly warmth lingered on my skin where he'd touched me.

"I might hurt you," I said. "Maybe when you heal up some."

We both knew that was just an excuse. More to the point, I still didn't trust him. Between his control issues, his emotional distance, and his luck, I didn't know whether I could survive a second try with Chance.

"Sure. Maybe." As he stepped back, I saw the etched quality to his features.

Why did he have the ability to make me feel like I was breaking his heart? Was I supposed to believe he'd pined for me when he could have anybody he wanted? We weren't soul mates. Back in the day, we didn't have some great, immortal love. Did we?

Then I remembered something my friend Sara said when I was trying to console her after a breakup. I said the usual—"You'll meet somebody else." And she replied: "What does that matter when the one you want is walking away?"

If I got out of this mess, I needed to call her. When I ran, I'd left everything and everyone behind. I'd started a new life in Mexico City, but I hadn't made friends. I existed in a quiet vacuum, interacting but not touching.

"I'm not going anywhere," I told Chance then. "So

we can sort 'us' out after this is done. Worry about me if you want, but I'll see this thing through."

"I hear that's what they said at the Alamo too." Chuch grinned as he pushed to his feet. "I'm gonna go see if dinner's done. Remember, new rug."

Supper sounded like a great idea, not just because I didn't feel up to alone time with Chance. I followed our host back to the kitchen, where Eva was pulling the glass dish out of the oven with giant blue mitts.

"Smells great. Anything I can do?"

The woman loved to organize. "Set the table, and use the good dishes. Glasses are in the cupboard beside the fridge."

"Jesse's joining us. I hope you don't mind."

"That's fantastic! So we're on for tonight then?" Eva got out a big slotted spoon and stabbed it into the middle of the casserole.

I caught the look Chuch and Chance exchanged. They weren't delighted to have a cop sniffing around, probably for different reasons.

"Yeah, it looks like."

We were halfway through the meal when Saldana's Forester pulled into the driveway. I got up to answer the door before he knocked and waved him in. "Everyone's in the kitchen. Come on back. Have you eaten?"

He appeared to take stock of the homey rooms at a glance as we passed through. "No, I came straight over. Will they mind feeding me?"

Of course Eva overheard. "No, we have plenty. Chuch hates leftovers anyway."

The mechanic shrugged. "The noodles get all gluey."

Remembering my manners, I performed the introductions. The guys shook hands and Eva checked out Saldana like she did Chance. Maybe she just liked to look, no matter how much she loved Chuch. I could see her point; sometimes it was nice to enjoy the man candy, no strings attached.

I scraped the last of the casserole onto a plate and warmed it up for Jesse. Tried not to notice the way Chance glanced between us, as if he could somehow sense what happened, or almost happened, in San Antonio. That summoned heat to my cheeks, part anger and part chagrin, considering what I now suspected.

Yeah, this might get awkward. You could stir the testosterone soup with a spoon.

I sat down at the round glass table to finish my own food. Eva either possessed the sensitivity of a tone-deaf airport announcer or she opted to ignore the tension. Either way, she chattered to fill the silence. I could've kissed her for that, but the guys probably would've liked it too much.

By the time we'd cleaned our plates, the mood felt a little lighter. At least I no longer thought Chance was seriously entertaining the idea of killing Saldana and asking Chuch to help him hide the body. I could've taken Chance aside and confided my suspicions, but I didn't. I thought he deserved the uncertainty of wondering about Saldana.

Like a good hostess, Eva started clearing the table. "Dessert, anyone? I have Oreos and Cookies 'n' Cream ice cream."

"I'm seeing a theme here," Jesse said with a killer smile. "I wouldn't say no to cookies. As a kid I loved to open them up and lick the creamy center."

My cheeks burned just hearing that. Surely he knew how it sounded. Somehow I managed to meet his eyes, and oh, yes, he knew exactly what he'd just said, but he didn't intend to flirt with me, or Eva for that matter. Jesse was just provoking Chance.

Chance didn't take the bait, just narrowed his eyes. "No thanks, Eva. We should probably get started."

"I'll have some ice cream," Chuch said, as if oblivious to the nuances.

A glance out the window told me it would be dark

soon. The sky showed the color of bruised plums, stars just twinkling into sight. "Let me go take a look online, see what advice Madame Claudine has to offer."

"Madame Claudine?" Saldana stood when I did, making Chance do the same for fear of looking rude. Chuch just sat rubbing his belly and waiting for his Cookies 'n' Cream. "You picked a good person to ask. She works in Baton Rouge, has a nice little business getting in touch with dead relatives. More authentic than John Edward."

"Who?" I turned with a questioning look.

Jesse shook his head. "Never mind."

Part of me couldn't believe we were actually going to do this. I mean, it would be hypocritical of me to say I don't believe in the afterlife and things that go bump in the night. Shit, some people consider me one of them. But I've never gone out of my way to look for the weird and unusual. Then again, I guess I don't need to because it always seems to find me.

As I headed for the office, Chance fell in behind me. I expected him to make some comment about Jesse, but instead he sat down on the edge of the desk and let me call up Area 51. To my surprise, Madame Claudine had answered, outlining her basic steps on how to go about contacting a dead loved one. I made some notes as I read through.

"Huh," I said. "I wonder if she gives her secrets away to everyone. Or perhaps just those she thinks can succeed at it."

"If what you said about Saldana is true, only the gifted have access to this site." He didn't sound jealous, just quiet and remote.

I've heard that tone more than once over the years, and I used to think it signified indifference. Now I wondered if he withdrew when he anticipated being hurt, distance to avoid vulnerability. Maybe I didn't know him as well as I thought. God, I refused to face the idea that I might've run from him because I was afraid.

We don't have time for this. Min's clock might be winding down.

"Yeah."

I ripped the page off the yellow legal pad and went back to the kitchen. By this time, Chuch and Jesse had finished their dessert and looked like they were just waiting on the fun to begin. Taking stock, I decided the kitchen table would do, even though it had a glass top, not wood, but evidently the round shape was good. We needed six candles and—

"So," I said aloud, "I have good news and bad news. Which do you want first?"

"Bad," Eva said promptly. "The good should smooth it over afterward."

"Fair enough. According to Madame Claudine, we need one more person to do this or two of us should leave. The number of people involved in a séance should always be divisible by three."

"What? Why?" Chuch protested. "That's crazy. There were about fifty people running around when my tia Rosario—"

"You sure it wasn't fifty-one?" I raised a brow.

"No, he's not." Eva frowned at her husband. "Three is a sacred number. Even I know that. The Power of Three is the highest connection to the Creator, the Holy Trinity, all that. You ever look at a Star of David? It's all triangles."

The way Jesse smiled at me as he stood, I knew he meant to start trouble. "I'll take Corine to the movies. Let us know how it goes."

Raising the Dead

"No," Eva said at once. "I'm sure I can get somebody over here. We need another woman to balance us out. What's the good news?"

"Well, otherwise we seem to be set. We have the table"—I rapped on the glass top—"but we need some fresh bread or warm soup as an offering to the recently deceased. Apparently minestrone is best. Do you have any?"

In her message, Madame Claudine went on at length about the best soups. If there was no minestrone, then chicken noodle would do. Under no circumstances should we ever offer a spirit cream of mushroom. I didn't take time to ask why. She also included a list of breads, which must be fresh. Apparently spirits don't take kindly to sourdough either.

"Hm . . ." Eva went to the cupboards, rummaged, and then produced a can of Progresso with a triumphant air. "Will this do? I'm not making homemade for a dead lady. No offense, Officer Saldana. I'm sure she was a lovely person."

"None taken." Jesse eyed me up and down as if wondering whether we were all crazy. We might be. Maybe the movies would've been a better bet, except I wouldn't go off with a guy I suspected might have whacked his ex.

"We'll also need candles." Chance glanced up from perusing the notes from Madame Claudine's list. "Six— one for each of us, since we're using the Power of Three."

"We have some bug repelling ones from the last barbeque," Chuch put in. "They're citronella, though, so they're kind of stinky."

I sighed. "Go get them. Beggars can't be choosers."

"They can," Chuch said, heading for the garage. "They'll just be hungry beggars."

"Hey!" Eva hurried after him, soup still in hand. "What about your cousin Dolores? She used to be into crystals, right?"

"Forget the séance part. Tell her you have ice cream—she'll come."

As she went to look for the woman's phone number, Eva muttered, *"Cabrón."*

I gave Saldana a look.

"What?" Jesse spread his hands, palms up. "I would've shown you a good time."

"That's what I'm afraid of. Did you bring it?" Whatever it was. Damn, it was hard to keep my emotions on an even keel. He'd pick it up if I didn't.

"Sure did." He patted his jeans pocket. "It should do the trick."

"It's not medicine, I hope. I'm not sure a prescription is personal enough."

At that he choked. "Oh, it doesn't get much more personal."

After Eva made her call, we set up. First a warm bowl of soup centered on the table, and then the candles ringed around it. We argued about whether we should light more, as Madame Claudine said spirits crave light and warmth, but I couldn't stand the smell. In fact I had to crack a window just to tolerate the six we had. We scrounged two folding chairs from the garage, and it looked like we were ready.

Dolores arrived within fifteen minutes and came in without knocking.

"Buenas noches!" I expected a big woman, based on Chuch's joke, but she looked like she had a tapeworm, all bones, angles, and jutting nose. She wore ten pounds in bangles and scarves, another ten in jewelry. I'd never seen a woman sporting twelve rings before and tried not to stare.

She made the rounds, kissing all the men soundly. I thought she spent entirely too long hugging Chance, who gave me a half smile over her thin shoulders. Then she smushed Chuch's face between her palms and called him her *primo gordito*.

"It's muscle." Chuch pushed her away and tugged his shirt down over his belly.

"Right, Sancho." His cousin exchanged a glance with Eva and laughed, flashing crooked white teeth. "So we're all set? Let's do this. I haven't been to one of these since we summoned Tio Juan to ask if he meant to leave all his money to that floozy he married."

"Did he?" Sometimes I just had to ask.

"Sí." Dolores sighed. "She was a good floozy."

All business, Eva switched off the overhead light. It was full dark outside, so shadows danced on the far wall and six tiny twin flames flickered on the tabletop, giving it an oddly ethereal air.

Seeing we were ready, I sat on Chuch's left. Chance took a seat on my other side, and Eva dropped down next to him. Jesse and Dolores sat so that we alternated the man-woman pattern.

"According to this"—I squinted at the notes I'd made—"we need to join hands. Who's leading this thing?"

"You." Chuch grinned at me. "You have the instructions."

"Okay, but . . ." I hesitated. "Madame Claudine also said never to have more than one sensitive present. Things can easily get out of hand if the spirits have too much power to feed from. I'm a handler—does that count?"

"I'm an empath," Saldana added.

He gained points for trusting my friends with the information, but maybe he'd done it for exactly that reason? Act like you have nothing to hide—

I snipped that thought before I could reveal my agitation to the cop sitting across from me. Nobody seemed to know whether those combined gifts would overload Maris and turn her into a banshee, however. I didn't want to delay the process by waiting for another message from Madame Claudine.

Finally Dolores said, "Let's just get on with it. Eva said we're having ice cream after we do this."

What the hell.

"Jesse, do you have the focus?"

With a nod, he dug into his pocket and reached across Dolores to drop something in Chuch's hand. "Here you go."

The mechanic peered at it and then flipped it away from him. It hit the table, bounced, and nearly went into the sacred soup. "Are you kidding me, *primo*? I'm not touching that."

"Why, what is it?" I leaned for a closer look and saw everyone else do the same. "Her *diaphragm*? You brought her diaphragm to a séance?"

In the dark it was hard to tell who snickered loudest.

Saldana glared at me. "That's what she left at my place, okay? Do you want my help or not?"

"Fine." A look at Chuch confirmed he did not intend to pick up the latex cap for love or money. "Maybe just having it here will be enough. Jesse, you knew her best, so try to form a mental picture of her. Let's join hands." When we formed the circle, I murmured, "Now that six are one, let none falter until all is said and done. Dear Maris, we offer you gifts from life into death. Commune with us, Maris, and move among us."

The candles flickered the first time I said her name. A cool wind poured through the open kitchen window, and I motioned for them to repeat the chant with me. We spoke it softly seven times and then Chuch twitched violently to the right. His hand almost pulled from mine, but I held on. Madame Claudine had been vehement on that point. The circle must not be broken until the séance ended.

Or it would get ugly.

He opened his mouth and a soft, pretty soprano voice spilled forth. "That's not mine! You bastard!" Chuch glared at Jesse, looked as if he might claw his eyes out. The sight of such purely feminine outrage on the mechanic's rough features sent a chill coursing through me.

"Maris?" Saldana seemed astonished that this had worked. I was too, actually. "What's not yours?"

"That!" The diaphragm did bounce off the table and into the soup then. And then the whole bowl upended into Jesse's lap. "I never used one of those. I was on the pill, you pig! You called me here with something that belonged to one of your other whores?"

I cringed. Maris wasn't in any mood to answer our questions to say the least. Knives on the kitchen counter rattled ominously. Shit. I needed to shut this thing down before she killed him. Leaning forward, I tried to make out my notes. *Why didn't I memorize this?*

"Are you sure?" Only a cop would argue with a deranged and vengeful spirit.

"Of course I'm sure, you ass. Oh, you're going to pay for this. Every one of you is going to pay. They ripped me apart!" Chuch's face contorted as if in memory of the pain.

"Who did?" Chance asked quietly. If anyone could salvage this mess, he could, so I held my tongue for a moment, ready to start the banishment process if things got worse.

"Shadows," Maris said in a little girl voice. "Shadows

with teeth and claws that burned like fire. I'm so cold."
Chuch tried to put his hand over the candles and I
moved with him, but I didn't let go.

"Do you know who sent them?" I hadn't expected
Dolores to contribute anything of note, so I raised my
estimate of her a notch.

"Yes, I—" And then Chuch went rigid, screaming
like a woman. His back arched and he almost flipped his
chair, writhing in unspeakable agony.

"Do something," Eva pleaded. "It looks like she's
killing him."

Terror chilled me and I almost couldn't remember
the words. If anything happened to him, Eva would
murder me.

"Our time is done, we break our bonds, six no longer
one. We bid you go in peace," I said quickly. "Go in
peace, Maris."

The moment we let go of each other, a geyser of
black sludge erupted from the kitchen sink.

Straight on till Morning

The goop rained down on us like black gold, Texas tea.

I swiped it out of my eyes and hurried to see if Chuch was all right. "Should we call an ambulance? Does anyone know CPR?"

"I'm certified." Saldana knelt beside Eva. "Does he need resuscitation?"

As if in answer, Chuch fell out of his chair and hit the floor with a thump, but Eva shooed us away as she felt for a pulse. "I think he's okay. He's just out. What the hell *happened*?"

"An excellent question." I raised a brow at Jesse. He was either unspeakably clever for sabotaging things this way or a careless idiot in this instance. "You brought someone else's diaphragm? How many do you have lying around?"

"Just the one! I really thought it was hers."

Eva glared. "Never mind that. Can you two help me get him in the shower?"

I assumed she was talking to Chance and Saldana, so I got out of the way. Dolores sighed, looking around the filthy kitchen. "No ice cream, huh? I'm going home to take a shower. This was not the most fun I ever had."

"It was nice meeting you." That sounded lame, even to me.

Dolores rinsed her hands and then snagged the carton of Cookies 'n' Cream as she headed out. I didn't blame her. If I wasn't covered head to toe in this gunk, I could use some ice cream therapy myself.

The two guys grunted as they carted Chuch down the hall to the bathroom and dropped him in the tub fully clothed. He came to a few minutes later with the water beating down on him. "What the fuck . . . ?" The mechanic tried to scramble up, slid back against the shower wall. "Shit, that hurt worse than the time the Chevy fell on me."

"Shhh." Eva brushed the wet hair away from his face. "I'm so sorry, *mi vida*. I didn't know it would be like that."

"Something's very wrong," Chance said. "They were still able to hurt her after death, and through her, you."

"It has to be a warlock with a flair for necromancy. Who else could work a sending, summon shadows like Maris described, *and* torture her spirit after death?" Saldana's mouth compressed, and he looked at me. "They did something to her so she couldn't talk, and if we don't free her, she'll go mad. Look, I know you're searching for his mother"—he glanced at me, inclining his head toward Chance—"but I'd consider it a personal favor if you'd help me with Maris along the way. We can't leave her like that."

I agreed, but I hoped it wouldn't come to a choice between sparing a dead woman from an eternity of torment and freeing Min. We had limited time and manpower. Maybe, just maybe, it wasn't him. Maybe Saldana was being straight with us.

Or maybe he'd been ordered to get inside. I wished I didn't like him so much.

"Go see if Booke's still awake." Chuch sounded hoarse from all the screaming.

We filed out of the bathroom, letting Eva take care of her husband. Jesse caught my arm. "I'm heading home. Need anything else tonight, sugar?"

"No," I said first. And then I thought of something. "Could you do me a favor?"

Saldana raised a brow, and I sensed more than saw the sharpening of Chance's attention. "Probably. Maybe," he amended, having some experience now with my requests.

"Run Kel Ferguson and Clayton Mann for me? They're a couple of assholes with a score to settle. I'm not sure they're smart enough to do it through a third party like Min, but make sure they're still in jail, okay? I want to rule out their involvement in this mess."

"Sure." Jesse nodded. "That I can do. I'll call you tomorrow."

"All right. Thanks."

Once Saldana left, Chance murmured, "Good use of him."

After I got a towel from the linen closet, I went to the computer. I found the IM icon without too much trouble and managed to say *Hi* to Booke in the little window. He answered right away, even though it had to be close to two a.m. there, if not later.

Hello, Chuch. How are you? he replied.

It's not Chuch. This is Corine. Can we talk? I don't type very fast. That was an understatement, as it took me about five minutes to get that written.

Absolutely. I'll call. Just click the accept button.

I could handle that, I hoped. As Booke said, it was just that simple. His voice came out of the speakers sitting to either side of the monitor. "Hello, can you hear me? Is everything all right?"

"No, not really." I outlined the evening's events for him as succinctly as I could. "Chuch thought you might be able to help."

"I miss everything," Booke said, sounding disgruntled. "This is what I get for living in Stoke. All we have is pottery."

My geography sucked. I couldn't even imagine where

in Great Britain that was, not that it mattered. "Anyway, what're your thoughts?"

"Well, your friend is right." I heard pages rustling. "There's a spell known to practitioners as spirit wrack. It's quite dangerous as it bonds the life force of the warlock to his undead minions. Very few will risk it, as a sudden termination of the link may result in an excruciating death for the practitioner. It offers control over them, however, even in the afterlife. In this way, the departed can be bound to objects, forced to serve as oracles or—"

I interjected, "Could it be used to torture spirits? Prevent them from telling someone what they know?"

"Yes, I expect it could."

"How do we stop something like that? Assuming we can find the one responsible."

More noise, as he rummaged for answers. I imagined an old-fashioned library spilling over with musty tomes. "He'll have charms to represent each spirit under his control. Sometimes they use figurines, sometimes gems. I've encountered a few who wear them on their person for peace of mind. If they've bound many servants to feed their power, this results in a shocking display of personal adornment."

So we might be looking for a pimped-out warlock.

"Smashing the figurines or gems would do the trick?"

"Yes, if they're breakable. You might have to melt them down if he's used iron or steel for durability."

I sighed. "Great. So to free poor Maris, all we need to do is track down a warlock, steal his charms, and destroy them. Somehow. How do you know all this anyway?"

"I blame my father," he said with a low laugh. "Isn't that cliché? But he specialized in the work of Aleister Crowley, the Golden Dawn, and that sort of thing. He wrote more than one scholarly treatise on the subject. After he died, I took his studies in a more . . . arcane direction."

"Ah, well, thanks for your help. It's been invaluable."

Booke spoke in a warning tone. "This is a serious player we're talking about, Corine. You'll have to get through wards, possibly guardians, and the warlock himself. It'll likely mean killing someone. Are you prepared for that?"

"*I* am." Chance had come into the office in his bare feet. Maybe it was a strange thing to notice, but he had beautiful feet, perfectly arched and elegant.

"Oh, hello. Chance?" Booke sounded almost disappointed that our tête-à-tête had been interrupted.

I was a sucker for voices, so his rich, smooth accent provided me an awful lot of fantasy material. In real life he was probably sixty-seven, had bad teeth and no ass, but not in my head, dammit. In my head he was the suave, sensitive Englishman from black-and-white movies who, for reasons inexplicable to me, lost the girl to Humphrey Bogart.

"Yes. And I know it's going to get rough. It already is, in fact. That's why I want Corine out of here," he added pointedly.

I laughed at the idea of him enlisting a virtual stranger to his cause. My respect for Booke went up a notch when he answered, "She strikes me as a smart, capable woman."

Maybe he had nothing to base it on, but that was nice to hear. I mean, damn, I drove from Shreveport to Mexico City all by myself and managed to get myself a shop on a shoestring budget. So yeah, I felt like I *could* take care of myself, but I understood Chance's concern. This wasn't a typical situation.

That didn't mean I intended to abandon him to it.

"Thanks for the vote of confidence," I said to Booke. "I may be in over my head, but I'll swim."

"Or drown," Chance muttered.

I ignored that because I heard the frustrated concern lacing his words. He carried a lot of guilt about the Mann incident, and I'd made it worse.

"Thanks," I said. "How come you're up at this time of night anyway?"

"Insomnia. Hope I helped a bit. Let me know how it turns out, and . . . thanks for keeping me company a little while." The software chimed as Booke disconnected.

After easing to my feet, I stretched. "We should go clean up the kitchen."

Chance sighed but he didn't argue. "That's the least we can do."

"Agreed."

When I faced him fully, I tried not to laugh. I'd seldom seen him looking less than pristine, and there he stood, spattered in black slime. He swiped a hand across his cheek in a boyish gesture and succeeded in smearing the stuff down his jaw. My expression must have given me away.

"I know, I know. Come on, you." He started for the kitchen.

"Shit."

Chance stopped in the doorway, offering an impatient glance over his shoulder. "What's the matter now?"

"We ruined Chuch's new rug after all."

I hadn't heard him laugh like that in so long.

Before I followed him into the kitchen, I went back to the computer. The idea that Min had ties to Boys Town had been working on me quietly ever since we found the link in Saldana's office. So I hesitated, hands on the keyboard. Did I really want to do this? Yesterday I'd wondered whether she'd been a working girl. Would learning that change how Chance felt about her, about the mystique surrounding his conception?

He wouldn't pursue this angle. I knew that. With a sigh, I typed, "Asian prostitutes Nuevo Laredo Boys Town" into the search field. Google rewarded me with close to two thousand hits, foremost a mention of the infamous donkey shows. But the third hit offered me a picture of an Asian themed brothel that resembled a red pagoda.

I stared for a moment in silence, wondering about the link. Where did the women come from who worked there? How *did* Min get out of Korea?

Well, if we knew that, we might have the answers we needed to find her.

So I simplified my search criteria to "Korean prostitutes in Mexico," hoping for a wider result. That time I got nearly 87,000 hits. My stomach twisted in knots as I read the headlines of various articles:

PROSTITUTION RINGS ON RISE
THIRTEEN CHARGED IN GANG IMPORTING PROSTITUTES
HUMAN TRAFFICKING & MODERN-DAY SLAVERY

I clicked a link on a news Web site and read on:

The Republic of Korea (R.O.K.) is primarily a source country for the trafficking of women and girls internally and to the United States (often through Canada and Mexico), Japan, Hong Kong, Guam, Australia, New Zealand, Canada, and Western Europe for the purpose of commercial sexual exploitation.

By the time I finished, I felt sick. What did this have to do with Min? I fervently hoped she hadn't suffered as I was beginning to fear. Perhaps she'd run from her past only to have to catch it up with her years later.

Her expression as she went with those men reflected no surprise, only resignation. She'd known it was coming; it had just been a question of when.

Now the question was whether we could reach her in time.

Boys Town

First, though, we had a kitchen to clean.

By the time we hauled out the last bag and emptied the bucket of dirty water into the laundry tub in the garage, I wanted to collapse. The garbage disposal had blown itself up and would need to be replaced. Chuch and Eva had gone to bed an hour before, and the fact that she didn't protest told me just how freaked she must be. Chance looked even worse than I felt. His back must be killing him.

"You take the first shower." I tried to be generous.

"We could take one together. . . ." His heart wasn't in the lechery, though, and he trailed off as he ambled toward the bathroom.

I laughed softly. "Baby, I would *hurt* you."

"Promises, promises," he muttered as he shut the door.

Shortly thereafter I heard the water running. With a tired sigh, I sank down onto a kitchen chair. Head in my hands, I wondered how we could handle everything. We seemed singularly ill-equipped.

Chance made it quick, so I took my turn sooner rather than later. The stuff from the disposal was sticky, so I scrubbed hard with Eva's loofah. My skin glowed pink by the time I stepped out onto the fuzzy bath mat. I wrapped up in a towel, wishing I had a robe. As I'd left my bag in the living room, I had no choice but to go out vulnerable and bare.

Hopefully he was already in bed.

To my dismay, I found him sitting on the couch. He hadn't donned a shirt, just a pair of track pants that hung low on his hips, revealing the lovely slope of his abdomen. Oh, Lord, we didn't have on nearly enough clothing to be in the same room.

He glanced up with his heart in his eyes, raw and desperate. A jagged piece shifted to the right inside me. Despite my better judgment, I went to him and perched on the arm of the sofa. Touched his hair lightly. I angled my head to check out his cuts—at least I told myself that, never mind that my pose showed far too much of my thighs.

"Does it hurt?" I touched his bare shoulder, shivered from the heat of his skin.

"More than I knew." By his expression he wasn't talking about his back, but I didn't know if he meant my leaving or his mother's vanishing act.

Since I didn't know what to say, I pretended not to notice the nuances. "Would you like me to do the ointment and new dressings before bed?"

"Please," he said. "But I'm not going to sleep."

I glanced at the clock on the mantel. "Are you kidding?"

"Nope. Boys Town stays open all night, and I've wasted too much time, Corine." He sounded so bleak. "You can go on to bed, but I can't. They're not going to keep her alive forever."

I suspected he knew as well as I did that it might already be too late. Though exhaustion hung on me like barbells, I didn't argue. Just went to find my bag and put on clean clothes. He knew perfectly well I wouldn't let him go out alone. After I dressed, I did his back, tried to ignore the way he tipped his head back with the pleasure of my fingers on his skin. I remembered how to touch him. Wanted to.

But I shouldn't. "There, you're all set. Get dressed."

"Bet you say that to all the guys."

I smiled. "Only the cute ones. You have the keys to the Mustang?"

In answer he plucked a set from the pegboard by the front door.

Driving after dark always makes things look different. I'd have been lost from the second turn, but he drove as if he knew where he was going. I certainly hoped so.

We took the highway out to the International Bridge. They're supposed to ask for passports even at road checkpoints these days, but a twenty here and there solved a lot of problems. The immigration officer took Chance's ID and the bill, considered a moment, and told us to have a good time. They must get a lot of Americans heading over to party in Boys Town, though by his expression I imagine they don't usually bring women along.

The compound lay five kilometers past the bridge. We passed through some bleak areas and he silently locked his door. I did the same. At his instruction I kept my eyes open for the intersection of Anáhuac and Monterrey, and when we first arrived, I was astonished to find a little city within the city. The *zona* even had its own jail, first building on the right.

Chance found a place to park, although I wasn't sure it was safe to leave the Mustang here. He shrugged and took my hand, leading me into the throng. The streets were alive with guys going from club to club. Live music thrummed in the distance, adding a palpable pulse to the night in the form of Spanish guitars and bongo drums. I imagined sunlight would show a different side of the *zona*, but at night, it glowed with vitality.

The unpaved road crunched underfoot as we passed

deeper within. Papagayos, a large club on the right, seemed to be the cornerstone of the district. Everything else looked hopelessly seedy or deserted by comparison.

"If luck will help us here, I suggest you make use of it," I said.

Women in doorways eyed us, and some of them even grabbed Chance with whispered offers. He extricated himself, sometimes forcefully, and stepped to one side. Passersby jostled me as I waited, and I kept a tight hand on my bag.

I hadn't seen him do this in a while, but it was akin to a meditative trance. He closed his eyes and I could feel a shift, hard to describe, but almost like a static charge gathering before a storm. Others seemed to notice it, at least subconsciously, and gave us a wide berth.

When he opened his eyes, he pointed. "That way."

"You're sure?" He'd indicated a small *taverna* a block down from Papagayos.

"As much as I can be. I may need your help with translation, Corine."

I nodded absently, staying close as we wove through the crowd. My stomach felt funny as we entered the faded pink adobe building. It was dim and quiet inside, just a few tables and a man strumming a battered guitar. The 'tender smiled as we came in, showing two dull gold teeth.

The selection of ladies was limited, to say the least. One was so old I couldn't imagine anyone buying her services, but I supposed having no teeth could be considered an advantage in some regards. Her seamed face seemed more suited to modest black dresses and rosary beads than the low cut blouse she wore. We ordered two-dollar beers and I looked to Chance for guidance.

His gaze skimmed the room before settling on a woman of indeterminate years sitting on a stool at the end of the bar. What did his gift feel like? Was it magnetic? Her night-dark hair likely owed something to artifice, but she wore it in a neat knot on top of her head, showing sun-browned shoulders. She was pretty in a shopworn sort of way. When he moved in her direction, I followed him, unsure what to expect.

To my surprise he drew out a relatively recent photo of his mother. I recognized the occasion—heck, I'd even taken the photo when we all went to Disney World. Mother and son stood to either side of Goofy. Seeing the picture made me smile. They both seemed so happy, and Min, as always, looked adorable in a big straw hat and baggy pink shorts. Not the sort of woman I associated with the *zona*.

"Pardon me," Chance said.

He didn't touch her, but she turned with a coolly inquiring look. When she saw us, her expression became calculating. She couldn't be as desperate as the ones who had felt him up outside. "I do both for one hundred American."

If I hadn't been so nervous, I would've laughed at Chance's expression. He's rather straitlaced in some ways. "Ah, that's very kind, but—"

"Ninety, or I return to drinking." Her English came with the heavy accent unique to the border towns.

"*¿Cuánto por hablar?*" I asked, hoping she'd realize we weren't trolling for excitement. *We just want to talk for a few minutes, lady.*

She cocked a brow at me. "You want dirty talk?"

Despite myself I blushed and shook my head. I imagined her being hired to "entertain" a couple while they had sex. "No, just a few questions."

I could see in her eyes that she thought it was a bad idea to answer, but finally she said in English, "Twenty dollars for ten minutes."

Chance paid her and we joined her at the bar. He handed her the photo. "Do you know this woman?"

For several moments, she stared at the picture with a blank expression. "Long time," she said at last. "*Treinta años, más o menos.* But yes, I knew her." Her dark eyes held a warning as she finished her drink. "Better not to question. You get hurt if you ask, but I tell you this: find the old doctor if you want to know. And . . . time is up."

There was no way we'd been sitting with her for ten minutes, but she got up and hurried out, shoulders hunched. Chance radiated frustration as he slapped his palm on the counter. The old woman gazed at us from deep, hopeless eyes, and I wondered how many men she'd serviced in her life, whether she'd loved—or even liked—any of them.

With a sigh I put down my untouched beer. "I bet we're going to see the doc now?"

"You'd win," Chance said.

Secrets

As the clinic adjoined the jail, we backtracked to the guarded entrance. The local police coexisted in uneasy balance with the *federales*. For better or worse, as long as no overt drug deals went down and no important tourists turned up missing, the *zona* operated as a self-governing entity. The army only intervened in extreme situations, like the shoot-out at the corner of Reforma and Paseo Colón, outside Boys Town.

I expected we might have trouble rousing someone, but the *médico* worked nights, just like the ladies. He had a small waiting area with a few chairs, a desk, and an exam room, near the jail. I also didn't think he was the man we sought because he couldn't be more than forty.

"Good evening," the doctor said. "You sick? Maybe you want medicine? For ten dollars, I write a script for Valium. Maybe you suffer from nervous exhaustion?"

His English was better than most, but then it would be, considering he dealt with Americans all the time. I'd noticed that only a small portion of the *zona* catered to locals—the places up near Club New York. Past that lay Tranny Alley, as Jesse had mentioned. I hoped we didn't need to go there next.

After some basic negotiation, he deigned to answer

questions for twenty, same price as the hooker. Chance flashed his mother's picture, and the guy shook his head. "Sorry, no. Never saw her."

"Who worked here before you?" I asked.

"Old Doc Rivera? He has a room two blocks over and he sings sometimes down at the Timpani Club."

Two blocks over. That bordered the area where gringos weren't encouraged to wander, but I didn't imagine Chance could be discouraged.

"*Muchas gracias*," I said to the doc as we headed out.

On the way, we passed any number of small cantinas and pharmacies, where they tried to sell Chance some Viagra to enhance his whoring experience. I snickered.

"I don't want to hear it," he muttered.

"At least they didn't direct you to Tranny Alley. You're awfully pretty."

"I'm so glad I entertain you." But when he glanced my way, I saw the faint hint of a smile in his eyes.

"You always did." That much was true—whatever else our problems, we always had fun together.

Trust and intimacy, on the other hand, give us trouble.

"Good to know you remember some of it fondly." He wrapped an arm about my shoulders to guide me around a passel of noisy Texans congregated outside a bar.

A wave of nostalgia hit me so hard I almost staggered. Once I would have slid my arm around his waist and leaned into him. Once he would've slid his hands into my hair as he kissed me, careless of people passing by around us. When Chance touched me, the world disappeared.

I struggled not to lose sight of why we were here, not to lose myself in him. His step slowed as if he felt that same sweet magic. Much as I tried and as far as I ran, I didn't know whether I'd ever be entirely free of him. He lowered his head as if to kiss me.

"Hey, *roja*! How much?"

Given that I wore a ruffled skirt and a peasant blouse, I could understand the guy's mistake, at least from the back, but Chance growled as he turned, pushing me behind him in the same motion. I'd never seen him wear quite that expression.

"Back the fuck off, redneck."

"Take it easy." The cowboy held up his hands as if to say he didn't want a problem. "I didn't realize she was *your* whore."

I winced. That wouldn't make it better. Impotent as we both felt right now, Chance would be spoiling for a fight.

"You need to find another *chica*," I told him, polite as I could manage.

The guy had two friends with him, who laughed. "What a dumb fuck," one mumbled. "Don't he know to leave the ball and chain at home?"

On the corner the *policía* stirred, glanced our way. Local law enforcement could be swayed with a bribe, but the Texans might have more cash, if it came down to it. Even wounded, Chance could kick their asses, easy, but unless he had a fat wallet too, we'd wind up in jail. I'd noticed there weren't many white women on the street.

"Let it go," I whispered. "This isn't a place to start trouble."

He exhaled slowly. "I know what I'm doing."

Chance lashed out in a lightning strike. The guy who'd called me a whore took a palm to the throat, and the cops started for us at a run. The other two went down in quick succession. By the time the cops reached us, the three lay in a groaning pile. I think they expected to have to break up a fight, not deal with injured idiots.

"They called her a foul name," Chance said humbly. "My mother raised me to respect women." That might sound funny coming from somebody prowling around the *zona*, but the officers simply looked confused. "Perhaps this will help offset the cost of dealing with these idiots?" I didn't see the size of the bill he offered but the police officers jerked the Texans to their feet. They'd spend the night in jail instead of the arms of their favorite ladies.

We walked on. "You just couldn't resist, huh?"

"Nobody talks to you like that," he said quietly.

That sent a shiver of pleasure through me. "You've been practicing. You're faster than you used to be."

He shrugged. "Training helps me deal with excess energy."

Surely he didn't intend to imply he hadn't slept with anyone since I'd been gone. I lacked the courage to ask and wasn't sure I could trust his answer anyway.

Just before the *zona* devolved into rougher territory, I spied a hand lettered sign that read TIMPANI. It didn't look like much, just a dingy white building with an open doorway. Few patronized the club, mostly older men, but pretty young girls sat on each of their laps. An old man played a battered guitar at a table near the door.

I shook my head. "Some retirement."

"That's him." Chance sounded sure, so he started forward, tapped the musician on the shoulder. "Doc Rivera?"

The old man lowered the guitar with a bemused expression. "*Sí*, so I was, once." Most people in Boys Town spoke broken English at least, it seemed.

"May we buy you a drink or a few minutes of your time?"

Rivera laughed. "My time is not as valuable as it used to be, so I will take the drink and thank you for it."

I went to the bar and signaled the bartender for a round, and he delivered them in cleanish glasses. After paying with a five, I waited for my change, which he gave with a scowl. When I returned to the table, Chance was flashing the picture once more. This time, however, we received a much different reaction.

"*Ay, Dios* . . . it has been so many years. How is Min?"

"She went missing in Laredo," I said quietly. "Perhaps you could tell me how you know her?"

God, I hoped Rivera wouldn't say Min was his favorite girl. When Chance reached for me, I laced our fingers together and didn't flinch when he squeezed too tight.

"She worked for me," he answered at length. "Min prepared salves and potions for the ladies who could not afford to go to a *farmacia* for their medicines."

"But she left?"

"Yes . . . maybe thirty years ago? She did not say good-bye. I have worried about her over the years."

"Well," I said. "She was fine up until about a week ago. This is her son."

Doc Rivera shook Chance's hand. "*Mucho gusto. Sí*, I see her in you around the eyes. . . ." He tilted his head. "But I am sorry to hear of your trouble."

Chance downed his beer in one swallow. "Is there anything else you can tell us? Anything that might help point us in the right direction?"

The doctor glanced toward the open door. When I turned, I didn't see anything, but his face changed, became closed and tight. "No. I'm afraid it is very late, and I have stayed too long already. *Buenas noches*." He headed for the back door in an uneven gait.

"You get the feeling there's something they aren't telling us?" Chance said.

I stood, dusted my hands on my skirt. "You think? They're all scared to death."

As we left, he reached for me, tucked me against his side. The gesture warmed me, though I knew he couldn't protect me. In fact, close proximity to Chance could prove dangerous. We'd already proved that.

"Come on, love. Let's get you to bed. You look busted."

Second time he'd used that endearment, and I

couldn't let it go, not this time. Not when it roused such an awful ache. "Please don't call me that."

Chance paused, ignoring calls from ladies in nearby doorways, and cupped my face in his hands. His voice rasped with longing. "You think my feelings for you dried up when you walked away, Corine? You're still my love, even if you don't love me back."

Oh, God.

In Dreams

I hoped he wouldn't ask me whether that was true. Eva claimed I was still half in love with him. At this moment, tired and overwhelmed, I was in no shape to analyze my emotional state. He studied my face for what seemed like a long time and then pressed a soft kiss to my forehead.

"You ready to go?"

This time I didn't protest when we started for the car. To my surprise nobody had messed with it. Considering its purpose, the *zona* seemed peaceable overall, but then there *was* a significant presence from local law enforcement. We climbed into the Mustang and headed for the bridge.

I thought we might have more trouble on the American side, but they just glanced at Chance's ID and waved us through. My blue eyes and long red hair weighed in our favor; I didn't look like an illegal. If Eva could still manage it, I needed to have her cook me a passport, something that would withstand a casual inspection at land crossings anyway.

"Why do you think your mother worked in the *zona*?"

He glanced away from the road briefly. "I don't know. I've been wondering that myself. It would help if I knew how she wound up in Nuevo Laredo in the first place."

I watched him, such a lovely profile. His hair was longer now than when we'd been together and, right now, deliciously tousled. The dishevelment softened his fine, angular features, not that he needed further appeal.

Should I mention it? Yeah, I decided. Chance wouldn't thank me for keeping things from him.

"I did some research earlier."

I decided not to mention why, or what I'd suspected about his mother. Though Rivera had said she worked as a healer in Nuevo Laredo, there was no telling what she did in South Korea. Min had always been reluctant to discuss her past; she'd lived in Seoul once, and that was all we knew. Until now, there had been no reason to pry, no reason to question her secrecy.

"Yeah?" he prompted eventually, sounding tired.

"There's a thriving sex trade between Mexico and the East, including Korea and Japan. I read about a woman who was promised a job in a plastic factory and when she arrived, she was branded with a rose and put to work in a Yakuza-run brothel."

"What do you think that has to do with anything?"

I hesitated and finally just came out with it. "Does Min have any odd scars?"

"You think she might be running from organized crime?" His eyes seared me.

"I don't know. We don't have all the pieces in order to see the big picture. Did she ever say *why* she left Korea?"

Chance sighed as he guided the car onto highway 57. "No. I'm coming to realize I know very little about her."

"Everyone keeps secrets," I said. "It's just a matter of how dangerous they are."

"True." He drove in silence after that. I would have given a lot to know what thoughts occupied his mind.

Shortly thereafter we let ourselves into the house, tiptoeing so as not to wake Chuch and Eva. I knew I should put on my nightgown and curl up on the couch. God help me, tonight I didn't want to.

For once he didn't press. Instead he merely murmured a good night and padded down the hall toward his room, surefooted as a cat. I heard the click of the door with equal measures of chagrin and astonishment. With a sigh I went to sleep by myself.

Usually there's a drifting period, where I don't know whether I'm asleep or awake. This time I shifted immediately into REM sleep—at least, I assumed so, because I had to be dreaming. I certainly hadn't left the sofa, but I found myself standing on a lovely Oriental rug, woven in lush jewel tones.

I gazed around in bewilderment, taking in a room that resembled the old-fashioned library from my fantasy about Ian Booke. From the mahogany shelves to the cream and ivory wingback chairs, it looked exactly as I'd imagined. Even the heavy antique desk sat where I'd pictured it. Oddly I couldn't see past the shadowy doorway, nor did the darkened windows shed any light.

After a night in Boys Town, why would I dream *this*? It made a pleasant change from licking flames and dire portents, however.

"Splendid! I can't believe it worked."

Though I hadn't noticed him before, a man rose from the desk and came toward me. I recognized the voice, if not the face. With rough features, narrow slate eyes, and a shock of nut brown hair, Booke didn't look at all as I'd envisioned him.

"What worked?"

"Oh, I was just messing about with some lucid dreaming and out-of-body experiments. I think *you* must be sleeping."

"I . . . think so." Somewhat disappointed, I tried to be discreet as I inspected him. "Is this how you really look?"

Was that rude?

"No." He shook his head. "I daresay you aren't like *that*, either. I'm afraid I've projected on you. But then, I didn't think this would work. Never has before."

When I glanced down, I restrained a snort. All I needed to complete my Wonder Woman costume was a tiara and a golden lasso. Enjoying the novelty of three feet of shapely legs and a spectacular bosom, I decided not to challenge the fantasy.

"What were you trying to accomplish?"

Could I move around as if this were the real world? I could, though the resulting strut suited Lynda Carter better than Corine Solomon. I sat down in the left-hand wing chair before I tripped on the expensive rug and made a fool of myself.

"Well, I was thinking about you . . . and your problem," he added hastily. His obvious embarrassment struck me as endearing. "Sometimes magick leaves a trail or an astral tell. I can't leave Stoke, or I'd come in person . . . but I wondered if I could help you this way. I focused on you and started trying to home in on where you are—"

"And wound up in my dream? Why are we in your library?"

Booke glanced around, sheepish. "This isn't mine. It's colored by your expectations. I must say, I'm quite flattered. You clearly take me for a man of taste and means."

I realized I'd interrupted him. "Wait, did you learn anything? Did the warlock controlling poor Maris leave a tell?"

"In fact, he did." He lost some of his diffidence and came over, sat beside me in the other chair. "I've never seen anything like it." A side benefit of dreaming, he called pen and paper to hand, began sketching. I leaned close and saw what looked like a stylized U. "Near as I can find, it's akin to an Aztec or Mixtec symbol for the moon."

"And Chuch's house is marked with this?" I wanted to be clear.

"Indeed. It's marked with astral magick. You need

to cleanse the place, top to bottom, or he'll find it increasingly easier to work his spells there, even at distance."

"What about the wards?" To my amusement Booke couldn't tear his eyes away from the breasts that didn't belong to me.

"Summoning Maris, bound like she was, probably undermined them. You're not safe there any longer."

With everything going on, I doubted I was safe anywhere, but we needed to fix things for our friends. "We'll shore them up then. I can't leave Eva and Chuch now, after dragging them into this."

"No, I don't imagine you could." He sounded odd, eyes downcast.

I pushed the hair out of my face, bemused to find such a silky black mane. Oh, I could get such a color from a bottle, but dyed black, no highlights, made me look too Goth. "What're you getting at?"

"You don't seem the kind of person who would leave someone when they needed you most."

Ouch.

"Don't be so sure," I said. "I've done a lot of running in my life. Let things start to heat up, and you'll find me on the way out."

Booke glanced up in apparent surprise, shadows playing over features that didn't belong to him. "I never would have guessed. You have a very steadfast feel."

"I do?"

He nodded. "Unshakeable. Like once you set a course, you don't alter it."

You think my feelings dried up when you walked away, Corine? I didn't even know if mine had.

I managed a smile. "Isn't it interesting, the preconceptions we form from a few minutes in a voice chat?"

"No." Steepling his fingers together, he assumed a professorial demeanor. "By paying an astral call, I've seen your essence, the raw material that shapes your soul. You're stone, Corine. While fire may score you, it won't destroy who you are."

On some basic level I almost understood what he meant, not intellectually but through some underdeveloped sense. If the human spirit could be reckoned in alchemical terms . . . The point I wanted to make slipped from me. Perhaps Chance might grasp it better.

"And you?" I asked. "What about you, Booke?"

"I don't know. We can't see ourselves as we are, can we?"

I wondered about him, this man who seemed to live for broken moments on the computer and perhaps spent the rest of his time lost in esoteric study. Was I actually communicating with him? Or creating the scene out of some subconscious desire? Our predicament meant I couldn't afford to dismiss assistance, but until I checked the information he'd given, I couldn't be sure this wasn't a supervivid dream.

"Does that mean you've never looked?"

"There are a great number of things I've never done," he said quietly.

A moment ago, he'd said: *I can't leave Stoke*. The word *can't* offered a wide variety of perplexing possibilities. In what manner was he bound? And why would *our* problems, half a world away, interest him so?

"There're a lot of things I wish I *hadn't* done," I said.

"Such as?"

"Leaving my mother to die." It slipped out before I could stem the candid response.

Booke regarded me with a somber expression for a moment. "We don't have power over that. We don't get to pick and choose."

"Do you think it's wrong to want revenge on the people who took her from me?"

He gave an odd smile. "What do I know? I'm just a voice, someone who doesn't seem half-real to you."

"You do that on purpose," I accused. "Are you trying to will yourself out of existence?"

The mouth that didn't belong to him twisted. "Perhaps. If it would work."

I reached for him, intending to see if contact cut through the unreality of our dream selves. For just a moment, I wanted to see him as he was.

"No, you mustn't. If we touch, you—"

Wake.

I found myself alone on the couch, still feeling Booke's fingers beneath mine. When I touched him, in that instant, I saw a desolate pebble beach bounded by an endless gray sea. I didn't know what it meant, but the loneliness of it made me ache.

In the silver predawn light I lay reflecting on the ocean between us and the secrets people keep.

A Little Butch

Eventually I managed to go back to sleep for a few hours.

By the time everyone else woke, I wondered if I'd dreamed the whole thing, as in a dream that didn't mean anything, not a lucid dream or an out-of-body experience. Whatever. In the end I decided to share it because the symbol might mean something. We also needed to do something about the wards, if I wasn't crazy.

Over breakfast, I said, "So, I talked to Booke last night. . . ."

"*Dios.*" Chuch looked worse for wear. I didn't think he'd be crawling under cars anytime soon. "Does he ever sleep?"

"Well, I'm not sure on that." I outlined what we'd talked about without mentioning how I knew.

Chance shot me a strange look while I spoke, but he didn't interrupt.

When I was done, Eva cursed, soft and virulent, in two languages. "This is my fault, *my* stupid idea. I'll redo the wards, *mi vida*. You just rest, okay? I'll fix it. I can do this. I've seen you do it a hundred times."

As she went off muttering about sea salt and wormwood, Chuch gave us a grin. "It's not all bad, no? I get to sit on my ass for two or three days until she stops feeling guilty and figures out I'm milking it." He got up from the breakfast table and rubbed his belly. "Time for some quality morning TV. I hope Jerry Springer's on."

The mechanic's expression made me laugh as I went to refill my coffee cup. I hovered at Chance's elbow with the pot. "Want some more?"

"No thanks. I *would* like to know how you spoke to Booke last night, though." He regarded me with brow raised. "I couldn't sleep, so I spent the night researching the sex trade. You never came into the office, Corine. It's not like you to lie, so what's going on?"

Oh. "It wasn't what you'd call a conventional conversation. . . ."

"I'm listening."

I swallowed my ambiguity as I told him the rest. By the time I finished I couldn't interpret his expression; he gave no hint how he felt about my dreaming about some stranger. Maybe I wished for a hint of jealousy, but that was purely selfish. He never indulged in such displays. In fact, the only time I could remember him showing even a flicker of it was when I first met Jesse Saldana.

"But you're sure you spoke to him?" he asked, neutral.

"As positive as I can be. We can call him up to confirm, if you want." Although it would be embarrassing as hell for Booke to learn I'd been having incredibly vivid dreams about him, if I was wrong about the experience. I wasn't eager to talk to the Englishman anytime soon. The whole thing had just been too strange.

Chance shook his head. "I trust you. Let's see what we can dig up on that symbol."

His casual acceptance warmed me. No matter how crazy the stuff I brought him, he always believed me. Smiling, I went back to the living room for my last clean outfit; we'd been away almost a week and I needed to do laundry. From inside my purse, my phone vibrated silently but insistently.

That meant I had a new message.

Huh. I brought it to my ear, input the code, and listened. "Hi, this is Lenny. Lenny Marlowe? You said not to help, but they laid me off at Delta and I got to thinking. You know in them movies how bad guys always return to the scene of the crime? So I got some doughnuts and went over to the warehouse. Sure enough, around two, they came back. They cleared stuff out of there, put crates in a white sanitation truck, but it wasn't no trash they took out. Well, I was real careful and I followed them. They went to 6874 Hal—hey!" An explosive burst assaulted my ear, and then the call devolved into sobs and whimpers.

Oh, shit. The call was time stamped three hours ago. "Chance." He didn't respond right away, so I shouted, "Chance! Come on, we have to go."

"What's the matter?" He came out into the hall half-dressed, but for once I didn't pause to appreciate his bare chest.

"We need to go see Lenny Marlowe."

"Why?"

I understood his confusion but we didn't have time for it. "He might be in trouble."

Understatement. I dressed in record time and sprinted for the Mustang. Chance joined me and put the car in gear. To simplify matters, I gave him my phone and let him listen to the message himself as he drove.

"Shit. Call Saldana and have him meet us there."

That sounded great. It made a nice change to have a cop on our side for once, instead of being in the crappy position of trying to explain the wildly improbable. I still wasn't sure I trusted him, but he was the one who had given us Lenny as a lead. Would he have done that if he intended to watch and kill him for showing a little initiative? Would he really go to that much trouble to confuse us?

I was starting to think . . . No. I hadn't tossed out the

dirty cop idea entirely; maybe somebody in the station was sneaking around his office, listening to his personal conversations? But then again, except for Saldana, I hated cops, so it made me happy to blame one.

Our pet policeman answered on the second ring. "Saldana."

"I may have a problem that requires your assistance," I said in lieu of hello.

He sighed. "You know, Corine, there's a picture of you next to the definition of *high maintenance*. What is it now?"

Because I did need his help, I ignored the insult. "Our mutual friend Lenny Marlowe called me in the middle of the night. I was asleep and I missed it, but the message struck me as alarming, to say the least. We're headed over there to check on him, but I'd appreciate your official presence on scene."

There was a long pause, and background noise increased. Somebody must've come in. I heard him talking and a mumbled reply, maybe from his partner, Nathan Moon. I could go a long while without seeing that fellow and never miss the man. Finally Jesse came back on the line, speaking cautiously.

"Yes, ma'am, I'll take a ride over to check on your nephew. I don't mind a bit, Miss Alice. No, it's no trouble," he added, although I hadn't spoken.

Huh. He didn't want his partner to know he was talking to me? *Interesting.*

"You're good," I said with a snicker. "You should do Vegas."

"I will when you get me thrown off the force," he muttered. "Who knew being a mentor would turn out like this? I'm on my way."

I closed my phone with an audible click and glanced at Chance. "I think I may be wearing out my welcome with Officer Saldana."

A smile pulled at the corners of his mouth. "His loss."

The sky hung over us like a swathe of gauze. Unlike the almost blindingly bright and sunny other days, the air felt heavy this morning, sullen and threatening. In silence we followed the access road leading back to the trailer park where Marlowe lived.

Jesse managed to beat us there. We found him waiting in the tiny excuse for a front yard, beside the BE-WARE OF DOG sign. Chance got out and went toward the porch and knelt as if he were listening to something I couldn't quite make out. I studied Saldana's grim expression and knew we were too late.

"Don't go in," he warned us. "I already called the forensic folks. It's bad in there."

"Pulled-apart-by-demons bad?" I ventured.

Shaking his head, he answered, "Shot-up-with-automatic-weapons bad. What did he say when he called you?"

I played the message for the third time. "I feel like shit. We *told* him to leave it be."

Saldana eyed me with an expression of pure dislike. I didn't expect I'd be fending off his advances anytime soon. "You told him enough to interest him and get him in trouble, the poor dumb bastard."

"You're saying this is *my* fault?" I didn't know if I could argue that. "You gave me his name, so how about we spread the blame around some?"

"You think I'm not aware of that? Christ, *I* told you his name and now he's dead. It's as much my fault as yours. More. I don't deserve to wear this badge." Jesse yanked it off his belt and studied it for a minute, dull silver in the palm of his hand, and then crammed it into his jacket pocket. "I should resign right now."

Oh. So that was it.

"Maybe you bent the letter of the law, but you had good intentions. You wanted to close the case and you thought—"

"Fuck what I wanted. A man is dead. Don't talk to me

about good intentions." Saldana stalked to the end of the drive to wait for the coroner's wagon, now driving down the dusty road toward us.

"We should get out of here. If Moon comes . . ." I trailed off when I realized Chance wasn't listening to me.

With a sigh, I crunched over the gravel to see what had him so enthralled. At last he straightened with a tiny, blood-spattered dog in his arms. Butch had lost some of his attitude but not his red leather collar. Trembling, the Chihuahua curled deeper into Chance's arms, as if he wanted to hide. He regarded us from damp, perplexed eyes, as if wondering how his day could possibly get worse.

"Shit," I said. "We're keeping him, aren't we?"

Chance leveled his best look on me. "What do you think?"

Have Dog, Will Travel

The damn dog fit perfectly in my red spangled sari sling bag.

We left the scene just before the official vehicles arrived, and I had a feeling that was the last favor I could safely ask of Saldana. With guilt weighing on him, he might let his partner lock me up on principle, though it wouldn't bring back Lenny Marlowe.

And Nathan Moon definitely didn't like me. I guessed it was a case of genuine mutual antipathy. Sometimes people just scrape you raw, no logical reason for it.

"Any idea what streets start with 'Hal' around here?" Chance asked.

Butch nudged my hand with his head and I petted him absently. "Wonder if we could Google it."

He eyed me. "You have a laptop hidden in your bag?"

"Smart-ass. I was thinking of going back to the house, but I guess you want to keep moving." I didn't blame him for that. We had targets on our backs, and I'd like to draw the fire away from Chuch if we could.

"Check the glove box. Maybe there's a map."

In my experience people rarely owned a map to the area where they lived, but I looked anyway. I was right. "Stop at the next gas station. We'll buy one."

"What do you suppose he saw that was worth killing him over?"

I could only guess. "The contents of those crates?"

"That seems like a safe bet. How's Butch holding up?"

The dog whined in answer and buried his head in my handbag. "He's stressed. I hope he's not a piddler."

We got off the highway and I went into an Exxon station. Chance filled up the Mustang while he waited, and I bought two Cokes as well as the map. I also picked up a plastic bowl, a bottle of water, and wet wipes for the dog. He didn't much enjoy his makeshift bath, but I couldn't carry him around looking like he belonged in an evidence locker. By the time I finished inside, the leaden sky opened up in an old-fashioned Texas downpour. I ran with my head low; Butch whimpered and disappeared into my purse.

My blouse became transparent when wet, something I hadn't known before. Otherwise the sudden bath didn't feel bad. It made a nice change from the constant heat.

"Got it?" Chance asked.

"Yeah." I unfolded the map and looked for the listing of streets. "Shit, there's a lot of them. It could be any of these."

"Check the address and make a list of the streets that have the right range."

"Good idea."

After rummaging underneath Butch's bony butt, I unearthed a pen and tore a page out of my day planner, not that I ever used it for anything but scrap paper. The dog watched with cautious interest as I jotted down names that potentially fit our criteria. One of them I tapped with a frown.

"What?"

"I don't know. I can't imagine they're doing . . . whatever near a golf course. This looks like an upscale neighborhood. Wouldn't those folks notice strange comings and goings and complain about it to somebody?"

He thought about it. "Depends. There comes a point where every house has such high security walls that the neighbors don't have any idea what goes on inside. In poor areas, nobody gives a shit, and in expensive ones, you pay for privacy. It's middle class neighborhoods where everybody knows each other's business."

"So we're probably not looking for a building in a middle class zone?" I didn't know how I could eliminate those without seeing them.

Butch barked once.

Chance glanced over at me. "What's with him?"

I shrugged. "Who knows? I'm not a dog person."

By the time I finished making my list and checking it twice, I had no idea who'd been naughty or nice. Six streets could potentially be the one we wanted, but I didn't know Laredo well enough to rule any of them out just by looking at the map. I ran a hand through my long hair and decided I wasn't coiffed right for detective work. I found a couple of bands in my purse and started plaiting.

He leaned over to look at my notes. "How did we do?"

"Could be worse. Looks like we have six addresses to check out. Short of spotting a Southern Sanitation truck outside, do you have any idea of how we'll know it's the right place, though?"

Butch barked again, just once.

I raised a brow. "What's that, boy? Timmy fell down the well?"

The dog barked twice. He also looked annoyed at my sense of humor.

A car honked at us, and Chance drove away from the pump. Instead of heading back to the highway, he just pulled alongside the building to park. Maybe he wanted to wait out the rain, but the light in his amber eyes told me he had an idea.

"You think it's possible Lenny trained him to communicate somehow?"

Unlikely, I thought. *Lenny could barely communicate himself.*

"One bark for yes, two barks for no?" I hoped my sarcasm wasn't palpable.

Butch barked once. He glanced between us as if to say, *And you two thought Lenny was stupid.*

"Ask him about the addresses," Chance urged.

I couldn't believe I was about to do this, although it scarcely ranked as weirder than anything else in the last week. "Butch, was it 6874 . . . Halcomb Street?"

The dog barked twice. If we understood correctly, that meant no. Or we were talking to an overly excited Chihuahua to no avail. Part of me thought we'd do just as well to consult a Magic 8-Ball, but we didn't have one handy and Butch was here.

While rain drummed on the Mustang's roof, I went down the list. And when I said, "Halstead Creek Road?" Butch barked once.

"Well, holy shit," Chance breathed. "Looks like we know where to go next. Navigate for me?"

Before I could answer, Butch barked twice. I guessed he couldn't read maps. With a grin, Chance started the car. We'd steamed up the windows, so he turned on the defroster as we pulled out of the parking lot. The wet pavement made a shushing sound beneath the tires.

"It's on the east side," I said. "Are we sure this is the smartest course? They killed Lenny with Uzis or AKs or something."

"Why don't I drop you off at Chuch's place?"

"And then you'll go by yourself? No thanks. I'd suggest calling Saldana if we hadn't already given him a mess to clean up today. He's pretty pissed, you know."

Chance nodded, offering a rather wicked smile. "Yeah, I got that when he started yelling instead of hitting on you. I didn't mind the change."

"That's great, thanks."

"Don't mention it."

We came off the highway into town and followed East Del Mar to our address. It was farther out in the

country than either of us expected, but when I saw the
private landing strip, a feeling of dread boiled up. As if
he sensed it, Butch whined and hid his head. A barricade
with a NO TRESPASSING sign blocked the drive, though
we could move it manually. If we were that dumb.
Lenny probably had been.

"We shouldn't go in."

"No," I agreed. "It's private property. And I guarantee they're up to something shady if they have small
planes coming and going out here."

"So we're being sensible?"

"We have a dog to think about now, after all."

In answer, Chance backed the Mustang onto the road
and reversed. "We need a plan before we go bumbling
around."

"I agree entirely." I thought as we drove, trying to
pinpoint what was bothering me. "Why hasn't the warlock attacked us again?"

"Good question. Storing power for another frontal assault, like at the warehouse?"

"I don't know. And it bothers me." I hesitated and
then added, "But I might know somebody who can help.
Her aid comes with a price, though. Maybe a steep one."

"I'd be suspicious if it didn't. Where to?"

"San Antonio. Butch might need a bathroom break
first, though." The dog poked his head out of my purse
and yapped once. "You heard him—pull over a minute."

"Yes, dear." His amber eyes crinkled as he grinned.

After the Chihuahua did his business and had a drink,
we got on the road. The miles went fast, but I didn't pinpoint why until we were almost there. At some point
over the last few days we'd gotten back on our old foot-
ing, easy and familiar. Most of all, I still *liked* Chance. It
didn't seem the right time to talk about us, though, given
how much I'd discouraged him from getting personal
until we wrapped all this up, one way or another.

As we entered the city limits, I said, "The club's

down near the college." Chance didn't need further directions. I guessed he knew Texas better than me. I remembered Twilight was on Main but I couldn't remember the address, so we cruised a bit before I spotted it. "There we go. Pull over."

Since it was early afternoon, I doubted they'd be open, but I hoped one of the employees might be around tidying up. Sure enough, we found the place locked, but I didn't let that discourage me. I banged on the door with both fists.

Eventually a big guy with a white blond buzz cut came to glare at me. He could be anywhere from thirty-five to sixty. "Can't you read, lady? We don't open until four."

He started to slam the door in my face.

"Wait! I need to locate Twila. Or Jeannie." Maybe the 'tender would know how to find Twila. "Please, can't you help? It's important."

"Are you a friend of Jeannie's?" Suspicion laced his tone.

"Not really. I met her once. Saldana brought me to the club the other night and introduced me around. I met Twila and—"

"*Oh.*" He opened the door and stepped back. "So you're gifted." He said it so casually that I stumbled a bit coming inside. "I'm Bucky, Jeannie's husband. Why don't you come on in, pull up a stool, and tell me about the problem? Close the door behind you, mind. I don't want any college kids in here before we open."

I could see why the guy scared Saldana off even playful flirting. His hands looked as big as frying pans and could probably kill a man with one blow.

"Are you . . . gifted too?" I couldn't get used to referring to it with such nonchalance. I'd spent my whole life pretending to be normal.

"Made, not born," he said, somewhat proudly, I thought. "I participated in the Stargate Project from 1979 to 1981. I'm a fully trained remote viewer."

"That's clairvoyance?" Chance asked.

I was glad I didn't have to.

"Yes, sir, it is. Before they stuck me in the program, I thought that was crazy talk. But there's a lot more 'tween heaven and earth than you dreamed of in your philosophy, Horatio." Hearing Shakespeare paraphrased with such a heavy twang put a smile on my face. "Now go on and tell me why you need to see Twila, and I'll see what I can do."

Chance did the talking. Since I wasn't sure exactly what he wanted to reveal, particularly to an ex-military bartender, I sat quiet while he talked. I guess he trusted the man instinctively because he told the story from start to finish.

That took a while and I nursed a watery Coke. When he finished, Bucky slammed a fist on the countertop. "Now, don't that beat all. A man who'd take his revenge on somebody's mama, well, I don't reckon he's any kind of man at all."

That summed up my feelings too, but I didn't think this was about Chance and me, after all. I felt sure it related to Yi Min-chin and her past that we'd tracked only as far as Nuevo Laredo and the *zona*.

"So anyway," Chance said. "When Corine told me she might know somebody who could help, it sounded like a good idea. We're just not equipped to handle this on our own."

Bucky nodded. "Let me see if I can raise Twila. Just be aware that she'll ask for something in return for her help."

I nodded. "That seems to be the norm around here. We're prepared."

The blond bartender went to the back to use the phone. When he returned, he told us, "She'll see you at five." He handed us an address. "Bring the dog."

Butch whimpered and hid his head.

Desperate Measures

We took the I-35 south and ate lunch at a Carl's Jr. in Von Ormy because we wouldn't leave Butch in the car and I couldn't be persuaded to eat at any other fast food place. What can I say? I love those big juicy burgers. I fed half of mine to the dog, who showed his appreciation by biting my fingers, although not hard enough to hurt.

Then we found a PETCO on the southeast side of San Antonio and bought some basic supplies, such as a tiny stuffed bed, a leash, and a squeaky pizza that I liked more than the dog. We sure enough received some strange looks when we asked Butch what kind of food to buy. He preferred Hill's Science Diet Lamb Meal & Rice Recipe.

At that point we'd wasted enough time and we needed to present ourselves at Twila's place. The address Bucky had given us turned out to be a modest two-story in a reasonably affluent suburb on the fringes of the city. Given her persona, I expected something more Addams Family from her domicile, but she had peonies in the front yard, flower boxes, and a nice rock garden. I liked the glimmering pink stones that lined the flowerbeds too.

The rain had let up finally, leaving everything damp. I strode up the walk with what I hoped approximated confidence. Butch hung out of my bag, taking everything in, and Chance followed a few feet behind us. Gathering my courage, I rang the bell.

To my surprise Twila answered the door herself, though she looked no less exotic on an overcast afternoon than she had in the office at Twilight. Today she wore her braided hair up in a colorful scarf. Whatever she had in mind for poor Butch faded as soon as she saw my ex. Well, I was used to it. For his part, Chance stared at her as if he'd been hit with a hammer. Not so used to that.

She flashed a smile, bright and charming in her dusky face. "Bucky told me of your problem. Come in, let's talk it over."

I performed the introductions, not that either of them appeared aware of me. Twila led us into an immaculate living room furnished in black and white. I sank down onto a black leather armchair with a crunch. There was no way I could live with a carpet this pale. I'd spill sangria on it the first day I bought it, but I did like the lilies in a slim obsidian vase.

"Thanks for seeing us," Chance said.

I suddenly understood what Eva meant when she said I ate him with my eyes, watching Chance do it to Twila. The way he stared, one would think he'd never seen a woman before. Okay, so she was beautiful—tall, shapely, and statuesque with eyes that shimmered like night on the Nile. I fidgeted while they talked softly on the couch, low enough that I might even call it whispering. I couldn't make out the words.

There's a reason people don't hang around their exes, I decided. Butch watched me with moist-eyed sympathy, though to be fair he always looked like that.

Finally, Chance glanced my way and tossed me the keys to the Mustang. "Pick me up in a few hours, Corine? I think we've worked out satisfactory terms."

I clenched my jaw and spoke through my teeth. "Absolutely."

When I let myself out, they didn't even look away from each other. *I do not give a shit.* If he wanted to whore himself out to the queen of San Antonio's gifted, he had a perfect right. So much for his protestations of devotion, though.

I glanced down at Butch. "Looks like it's just you and me, kid. Any ideas?"

He barked twice but looked regretful about it.

I got into the Mustang. I've never been good at a manual transmission, so I ground the gears in getting out of the driveway. Butch put his paws over his head.

"I know, I know," I muttered.

Truthfully I wanted to find the nearest ice cream shop and eat a hot fudge sundae, not that I cared what Chance did. *No, sir.* As I'd had a big lunch, I felt such self-indulgence would set a bad example for the dog. So we drove around until I found a park. He didn't care for the leash and wasn't much of a walker, but I didn't think he needed to spend the rest of his life hiding in my handbag either, no matter how uncertain things seemed.

I needed to touch the life I'd left behind. Maybe it wasn't perfect, but it was mine. So I rang up my shop in Mexico City, and Señor Alvarez answered on the second ring. We passed a few minutes chatting. To be polite, I first inquired about his health before asking about the shop. He assured me everything was fine and we'd turned a good profit, and I told him I'd be gone longer than expected.

"¿Puede trabajar otra semana?" I needed to know if he could work another week, as I didn't look likely to return in a day or two.

"No hay problema," Alvarez said. *"Perdóneme, una cosa más, señorita. Un hombre pasó por aquí hace unos días, buscándola."*

Well, I was glad it wasn't a problem for him to keep manning the shop, but a chill rolled over me at his next words. I'd felt as if we had a shadow, starting that first morning in Mexico City. I shivered and tried to convince myself I was overreacting. A man looking for me didn't necessarily qualify as sinister.

"Looking for me or looking to buy something particular?" I asked in Spanish.

"Looking for *you*." He stressed the last word.

"What did he look like?" The tightness in my stomach must come from the burger.

"I don't know," he said, sounding a trifle impatient. "I was with a customer."

The bell jangled in the background, telling me he had a customer now too, so I let him go. I felt a little better, knowing that I'd have somewhere to return to, provided I survived. However, I couldn't write off my unease as paranoia, as I had good reason for going to ground eighteen months ago.

Just then, Butch saw a cute poodle with a rhinestone studded collar and tugged on his leash, disrupting my thoughts. "All right, I'm coming. First sign of humping, and we're gone," I warned him.

They smelled each other's butts, but then the poodle's owner pulled her away with a sniff and stalked in the opposite direction.

I gave him a sympathetic look. "She wasn't good enough for you anyway."

The park killed an hour, during which time I gave Butch a drink and fed him some Hill's Science Diet, but it was starting to get dark. We walked along the sidewalk, enjoying the sunset despite the stillness in the air. Slowly I registered wrongness. Where was the wind? The birds?

Oh, shit.

I recognized this stillness.

Something bad was about to happen.

Butch barked as if to warn me but I already knew. Quickly I scooped him up and he took cover. Our walk had brought us around downtown and out near the cemetery. It was an old place, full of dead heroes.

The Mustang was a good mile away, so I'd face whatever came without an escape route and without backup.

Dank mist rolled in, more suited to London than San Antonio. The power required to twist the weather like this must be astronomical, and he'd already exerted himself with the sending a few days ago. If anything he, whoever he was, seemed to be getting stronger. I couldn't see to make my way to safety, might even get myself run over if I tried to cross the street. Blind, I tried to retrace my steps, but it felt as if I was being herded.

When I passed between the iron gates into the cemetery proper, I froze. This wasn't a New Orleans–style place with aboveground vaults. Most graves possessed a modest marker, maybe a statue and some flowers. I couldn't make out much between the mist and the dark.

From utter stillness a fetid wind rose. The air stank of death and decay. The prickling sensation of unseen eyes sparked my fight or flight reaction, and God knew I wasn't a warrior on my best day.

I didn't wait to see what might come after me. Hunched low, I dodged between the headstones. There was no rational explanation for the fear spiking through me, the kind of visceral terror a child feels alone in her room when nobody cares enough to check the closet for her and when calling out might invite something worse than whatever lurks in the dark.

Monstrous shapes loomed out: a hunchback that became a gravestone, a towering skeleton that became a statue. The mist felt clammy against my face, ephemeral fingers leaving repulsive residue. My heart pounded in my ears. If I stopped running, something terrible would get me. And I hadn't felt like this since my mother shoved me out our back door with an awful look in her eyes.

In the dead calm I heard only my own breathing. There had to be other people around, people who could help or at least report what became of me. Except I felt trapped, as though I existed in a space separate from the sidewalk surely just a few yards away on the other side of the black iron fence.

Sobbing for breath, I ran until I nearly pitched into an open grave. For what seemed like an eternity I teetered on the edge and finally threw myself backward because I felt the wet soil sliding beneath my feet. I came up on my hands and knees, liberally smeared with mud. No birds. No insects.

Inside this dead zone, there was only me, Butch, and the thing coming for us.

A shudder washed over me like a dead man's kiss. But it was more than a simple chill. All around me, the temperature dropped, so that when I exhaled, I could see my own breath. I literally couldn't move.

Part of my brain recognized the deer-in-headlights feeling, but I couldn't fight it as darkness seeped out of the fog. I'd never seen anything like it, but it felt as though it sapped the life out of everything around it. Dimly I thought of what Maris had said about shadows that ate her up. Heat and light vanished in its proximity, producing a dense blackness that crackled with cold.

I could feel my heartbeat slowing as it approached. The shade didn't seem in any hurry. Inside I screamed with terror and desperation, but I couldn't do a thing in my own defense. Tears froze in my eyes, and I wondered what I'd look like when they found me.

Frozen woman found in cemetery, film at eleven. . . .

Or would my torn flesh look like Maris's?

The shadow drifted closer to me, and I swear I felt the blood freezing in my veins. The strange, unnatural pressure hurt like nothing I ever knew, but I couldn't scream. I wanted to tell the stupid dog to run, but maybe he was frozen too. Resigned, I clenched my jaw, bracing for the worst.

And then a sunbeam split the clouds from above, cut

through the mist like a laser. For a few seconds, the open grave bathed in golden light. But it was enough. With an agonized hiss, the nightmare two feet away from me boiled into dire smelling smoke.

Luck? I'd been saved by a quirk of the sunset? Something like that should only happen to *Chance*.

My muscles ached as if I had literally been frozen. With detachment I wondered whether I should have myself checked for frostbite. I shook as I pushed to my feet. Butch poked his head out of my handbag and gave an uncertain yap.

Well, I didn't have all the answers either.

The fog began to dissipate, at least enough for me to get my bearings. We were closer to the far side of the cemetery, so I made for the gate as fast as my sore legs would carry me. As we ran, I came up behind a fairly tall man in a black hooded sweatshirt. Something about his stride struck me as familiar.

I couldn't place it at first, but as he rounded the fence, I flashed on him slinking into the alley near the warehouse. It couldn't be coincidence that I'd seen him at two attack sites. This might even be the guy we were looking for. Warlocks couldn't go around sporting dark capes or ceremonial robes, after all.

I wouldn't find a better time to confront him either. A display like he'd just put on would leave him ripe to be brained by an old lady with an industrial sized handbag. So I tried for another burst of speed, but my tired body told me I was crazy for attempting a sprint when I don't even take the stairs more than I have to.

A stitch lanced through my side, and lack of oxygen made my vision sparkle. He must've heard me galumphing after him because he began to run. Shit, he was getting away because I was out of shape.

The granite angel seemed to come out of nowhere and I slammed my head into its wings hard enough to see stars in addition to the white sparks. I must've winked out because when I came to, Butch was licking my face, whining in a way that said, *Hey, lady, get up. You're my ride home.*

Blinking slowly, I saw that I lay sprawled on a grave marked Montoya. For a moment I stared at the inscription on the base of the statue. The markings rang a bell somehow, but that might just have been the general ringing in my ears. I touched my forehead and flinched at the red smear on my fingertips.

I found it hard to haul myself upright, even using the statue as support. Maybe I wasn't meant to take out a warlock on my own. I certainly hadn't thought about what I'd do once I caught him, that was for sure.

"We're close to something important," I told the Chihuahua. "They're getting scared or they wouldn't resort to shit like this. You think we can expect big guys with AKs next?" I remembered Lenny. "Oh, right. Sorry. That was insensitive, wasn't it?"

He barked once.

"Let's get out of here, huh? Assuming we can find the Mustang."

Assuming I could drive. Did I even have the keys? I dug in my bag until I found them and then put it down long enough for Butch to hop in. I felt sick and dizzy as I made my way out. Back on the street, the mist had faded, leaving no trace that something very wrong had just taken place.

By the time I reached the car, reaction had set in, leaving me shaking so bad it took me four tries to get the key in the lock. I crawled into the Mustang, put my bag on the seat, and leaned my head against the steering wheel.

I waited a good long time before I trusted myself to drive. Butch watched me with wary eyes. Maybe it wasn't fair but I couldn't help feel this was vintage Chance.

He's having the time of his life while I'm neck deep in

*shit. I should leave his ass here and head back to
Laredo. Hell, maybe I'll go all the way to Mexico City.*
I'd take the Mustang as payment for my trouble. He cer-
tainly didn't need me with Twila on his side.

When I made up my mind, I started the car.

Some Like It Hot

I went back to Laredo without him.

Yeah, I chose the middle ground. As far as I was concerned, Chance could go Greyhound. I promised I'd see this thing through but I didn't say he could dismiss me like a two-dollar whore while he cozied up with someone else. If that sounded like jealousy, well . . . I admitted to some conflicted feelings on the matter. Once I got on the road, I turned off my phone. I didn't want to hear his excuses.

It was late by the time I got back into town. Butch was a perfect gentleman on the way; I guess he understood he needed to be nice to me now, as I was all that stood between him and the pound. Soon as we got out of the car, though, his hackles came up.

There were several cars parked in the drive, but there always were. Lights showed in the office, the kitchen, and the living room—nothing sinister there. I couldn't see any reason not to go on in the house and shook my head over listening to a dog's mood.

"Settle down," I whispered.

Butch glared at me but consented to being pushed down into my bag. I wanted a chance to explain his presence to my hosts, and I didn't know how they felt about pets. Chuch probably wouldn't mind, but I wasn't so sure about Eva.

As I opened the door, I understood Butch's unease. Nathan Moon's gruff, sour voice carried all too well. "So you're saying you have no idea where she is or when she'll be back?"

Mentor, my ass. Saldana sold me out. Men. You can't trust any of them.

Possession of Lenny Marlowe's dog wouldn't look good for me, if the cop recognized Butch. Regardless, I wouldn't let Chuch or Eva take any heat for me.

Summoning a polite smile, I stepped into the living room, conscious that I looked as though I'd been rolling around in the mud and then had let it dry. Which was more or less what had happened. I had a big bump on my forehead and several scratches down my arms, and I was lucky it hadn't been worse.

"Hello, officer. Something I can do for you?"

Three pairs of eyes swung my way, and Eva leaped to her feet. "*Ay, Dios*, what happened? Are you all right?"

Chuch tilted his head to peer out as I closed the door. "Where's Chance?"

My smile felt too tight. "He had business in San Antonio. He'll make his way back when he's ready."

I could tell Chuch wanted to ask about the Mustang, but under the circumstances he restrained himself. Officer Moon looked me up and down, a faint sneer curling his lip. "You look some worse for the wear, Miss Solomon. Maybe you'd like to clean up before I ask you a few questions."

He knew my real name from the police report; that was never good. Still, I pretended to accept his faux politeness as the real thing. I inclined my head. "Thank you. That would be lovely."

I held my purse to me as I went down the hall to Chance's room. "You stay," I whispered to Butch. "I'll be back later." He gave me a supercilious stare and gazed pointedly toward the bed. "Okay, fine."

Hoping I wouldn't get caught with the victim's dog, I

went on down the hall and took the world's fastest
shower. Then I realized I didn't have any clean clothes.
Oh, ugh. I hate when I have to do this. . . .

With a sigh, I went through my bag and smelled my
laundry, found the least offensive outfit, and put it on.
Of course, my skirt and blouse looked wrinkled as hell
from being wadded up at the bottom of my bag, and the
knot on my forehead was turning purple. Peering into
the mirror I counted two other scrapes on my face and
several more elsewhere. I knotted my hair into a quick
braid and gave up.

Well, I was as ready as I ever would be.

I tried to smooth my clothing as I went back into the
living room, where I found the three of them sipping
coffee in uneasy silence. Eva had set out a plate of butter
cookies too, but nobody touched them. Seating myself
on the end of the couch, as far from Nathan Moon as
possible, I tried to look harmless.

With a forced smile, I asked, "What would you like to
discuss?"

"Well," he said with deceptive mildness, "for start-
ers . . . why don't you tell me why Lenny Marlowe's
neighbor described you as one of his recent visitors?"

Damn, I didn't know what Saldana might've told
him. I decided I better stick close to the truth.

"I'm helping a friend investigate his mother's disap-
pearance. We discovered that Lenny Marlowe found her
purse at the warehouse where he worked and went over
to ask him some questions about what he saw. He's in
the book."

All true, as far as it went. *Don't let me start sweating.*
A sour feeling roiled in my stomach as I remembered all
the other times I'd been interrogated, usually in a bile
green room downtown somewhere. Even if they don't
charge you with anything, they can hold you for a
day, and I wouldn't wish those twenty-four hours on
anybody.

"Discovered how? Did you employ a private investigator?"

It'd serve Saldana right if I rat him out after he sicced his asshole partner on me.

If he did.

Maybe Moon was here for his own reasons and had his own agenda.

Somehow I couldn't bring myself to say anything that might get Jesse in trouble. He was my main link to the gifted world, and I didn't want to burn my bridges.

"I wasn't aware I needed a license to ask a few questions, officer. If I was charging for my services, it would be different." After I said that, I sensed Eva's glare, but I didn't meet her eyes. I could stumble off this tightrope any minute and without help. I hoped she wouldn't lose her temper.

"Yeah, interesting you would mention that," Moon said with a tight smile. "According to your record, you did, in fact, run a racket, charging for your 'services.' In our database you show up in four states under three different names. Does that strike you as the behavior of an upstanding citizen?"

That set Chuch off. "Look, unless you're going to charge her with something, I think you've taken advantage of my hospitality long enough."

I held up a hand, not wanting to provoke the guy into hauling me downtown. "No, I'm happy to answer his questions. I'm just sorry I can't be of more help."

The cop smiled, but it wasn't pretty, the way it flattened his pale mouth. "Is that what you told the Arnett family in Madison when you took their money and couldn't find their son?"

I swallowed hard, trying to staunch the tears that stung the back of my throat. That failure still haunted me.

"I refunded the money," I managed to say.

"I don't know what the hell you're doing in my

town," Moon said, getting to his feet. "Or why you're hanging around Saldana, but I do know this. Trouble follows you like stink on shit, and I'll be there when you step in it."

"If you say so." I didn't have the energy for anything clever. "I'm glad Laredo has such a devoted officer looking into Lenny Marlowe's death. He seemed like a good man."

As I got to my feet to see the officer out—courtesy always confused them—headlights beamed through the front windows. I didn't think it could be Chance. The lousy bastard was probably still twined around Twila.

"It's Grand Central around here tonight," Eva muttered.

"No kidding." Chuch pushed himself out of the recliner. "A guy can't even watch TV. I'm gonna go mess around online."

Moon stepped out, and I walked along with him, more to make sure he really went. We met his partner coming up the drive. Jesse raised a brow. "What's going on, Nate?"

The other cop planted his feet. "I might ask you the same question."

"It's none of your business what I do in my off hours."

So I hadn't imagined the tension between them the other day. Maybe Saldana hadn't set this guy on me. *God, I'm glad I didn't say anything about him.* I had a mean streak, like Chance said, but I tried to make sure people deserved what they got.

"Fine," Nate snarled. "But remember I warned you. This girl's bad news, and I'm going to take her down, one way or another."

I watched him stalk down the drive and get into his car. *Damn*, it was nice. I wondered in passing how an investigator could afford a silver BMW convertible. A ride like that would run over a hundred grand, easy, but maybe he squatted at night in a shack. Some people would rather drive their disposable income than live in it.

To be safe, I watched until his taillights receded from view. Moon would be back. His type hated me instinctively. If there was such a thing as reincarnation, he would've been an inquisitor in another life.

Jesse looked at me. "Can we talk a minute?" Honestly I didn't feel up to a conversation with Jesse, not after the way he went off on me earlier. Then, as if it had just registered with him, he murmured, "You're hurt . . . and exhausted. Let me see. How bad is it?"

"I'm okay," I muttered.

Not that my protests made any difference. He dogged my heels back into the house. The living room stood empty, so I guess Eva had gone with Chuch to make sure he didn't download porn or something. Then again, maybe they were doing something else entirely. Muffled thumps and giggles came from behind the closed office door. For all of fifteen seconds I considered the ruined rug. I hoped they'd scrubbed up the black junk.

Jesse cupped my face in his hands, and with careful fingers, he brushed the damp hair from my forehead. "I'll get you some ice."

This morning, Saldana had treated me like his worst enemy, and now he whistled in the kitchen, making me a cold pack for my sore head. Last night, Chance told me he still loved me, and this evening, he was making the beast with two backs with Twila. What with the conflicting signals from men in my life, I was about ready to become a lesbian.

Fucking men. Chuch was the only good one, and he was married. Eva's laughter underscored that point. It would've been nice if they'd asked me if I was okay before disappearing for the slap and tickle, though. I scowled.

I still needed to do laundry, damn it.

I sat there brooding until I heard Butch scratching at
the bedroom door. *Oh, yeah.* As I didn't want him to pee
on the carpet, I hurried to let him out. He went straight
out, did his business, and then came back in. The little
dog leaped into my lap and curled up, as if he knew I
needed a warm body.

When Saldana emerged from the kitchen, he drew
up short, ice pack in hand. "Tell me that's not Lenny's
dog."

Butch growled.

"It's not," I said obediently.

"Is there no end to the trouble you'll get into?" He
sighed and came toward us.

"It hasn't ended yet."

As Jesse sat down, the Chihuahua lifted his head and
snarled low in his throat. Honest to God, he sounded like
a much bigger animal.

"Is that dog for 'touch her and I bite your nuts off'?"

Butch barked once.

Briefly I considered explaining the exchange and then
decided that puzzlement was better than comprehension.
It wouldn't do to share all my secrets. Hell, *half* my secrets typically sent guys running, and this one had something I wanted. I reached for the ice.

"He's a little unsettled," I said instead. "I'm sure he'll
calm down once he gets past his recent bereavement."

Jesse's look said, *It's a dog*, but he didn't speak the
thought aloud. "I came by to apologize. I shouldn't have
said what I did. I was mad at myself and I took it out on
you. There's no excuse. I'm even sorrier I found you
hurt and being hassled by my partner. Guy doesn't know
when to cut somebody a break and he's not much on the
people skills."

"You don't like him." It wasn't a question.

He hesitated a moment and then answered, "No. Not
really. When he makes up his mind about a case, he
doesn't much care about the facts. And I'm sorry he's

got a hard-on for you. I'm also really feeling like shit about this morning."

I put the damp towel on my head and closed my eyes. "Don't worry about it."

"No, I overstepped, and it matters that you forgive me."

"Why?"

His tone gentled. "Because you're just getting to know other gifted, and I'm supposed to make it easier for you, not blame you when things go wrong, sugar."

"It's okay." The apology warmed me. I didn't often hear those words from people who meant them.

"I also came over to tell you something else. I don't want you to be alarmed, but Kel Ferguson slipped his leash in Louisiana."

Shock washed over me in a shivery wave, knotting my insides like a macramé rug. Jesus, Mary, and Joseph, if he was after me, I couldn't run far enough. In the courtroom that day, his eyes said he'd never give up.

"So he might be coming for me." Yes, I stated the obvious.

After what I'd been through this afternoon, however, Ferguson didn't scare me quite as much. That made a nice change.

Butch growled again. Cracking my eyes open, I saw Jesse leaning closer. He lifted the compress to check my forehead, test the edges of the bump with gentle fingertips. "You want to tell me how you got this?"

I thought about it. "Not really."

The shadow thing seemed surreal now. Jesse might even think I was crazy or on drugs. Worse—he might believe I made the story up. I couldn't face that tonight; too many years locked in my room for "lying" about how I came by the scars on my hands.

"Will your guard dog tear out my throat if I put my arm around you? You seem like you could use a hug." I'd almost forgotten he could sense how I felt.

The Chihuahua barked twice.

"Nope," I said, smiling.

Jesse eased closer and drew me against him in a movement so careful it didn't even upset Butch. His palm cupped my shoulder and I felt him drawing tiny circles with his fingertips. With a small sigh I leaned my head against his chest, listened to his heart.

"Better?"

I exhaled slowly. "Some. Maybe."

"You smell so good," he whispered, like he couldn't help it.

His nose brushed my cheek. *Do I?* It was just oatmeal soap and my natural scent. No perfume.

We sat there a while before I confessed, "I had another run-in with the forces of darkness. That takes a lot out of you."

Naturally he couldn't leave it at that, and with a cop's skill, he pried the rest of the story out of me. "He sent you away so he could hook up with Twila?" Jesse shook his head. "The man has brass balls—I'll give him that. She'll chew him up and spit him out."

I didn't trust myself to reply because I might come off jealous, and I didn't want to give that impression when I sat in the circle of Jesse's arm. I liked it too. So I murmured something noncommittal.

As I shifted closer, I caught his deep dark gaze roving my face. It had been such a long time since I kissed someone who knew my real name or anything about me. I hadn't been with anyone who knew more than the sheen of my skin moving under him in the dark in over a year. I wanted a taste.

"Corine," he whispered, soft and husky. "You're giving me that feeling again."

I lifted my chin. "Which one is that?"

"It's warm, honey sweet, and it tells me you want your mouth under mine."

"Maybe I do."

My eyes drifted shut again. Jesse didn't waste any more words, just angled his head down so our lips touched. To my surprise, the dog in my lap didn't even stir. I guessed that meant he approved.

Bliss. His mouth played just so, teased my lower lip until I needed to taste him. My tongue grazed his. Shifting, I sank my hands into his sun-streaked hair, and we kissed for ages in a soft, sensuous give-and-take punctuated by tiny gasps and delicious shivers.

He intuited what I liked from the delicate plucking at my upper lip to the sexy swirls of his tongue against mine. I sucked gently, commanding a moan from him.

When I pulled back to get my breath, he licked his lips. "You're good at that."

Ridiculously I felt my cheeks heat. "You sure?"

Longing licked through me. Without a doubt we'd enjoy ourselves in bed.

Jesse's smile sparked me all the way down to my toes. "Not entirely. Maybe I need to conduct a little more research."

As he kissed me again, I heard Chance snarl, "Well, isn't this fucking great?"

The Little Things

I refused to play further into the scene.

We didn't leap apart guiltily; in fact I rested my head on Jesse's shoulder and smiled. Chance had no claim on me. I just asked, "Finished up in San Antonio, did you?"

Chance looked exhausted. *Guess she rode him hard and put him away wet.* "Yes, no thanks to you. I've been worried sick. Why didn't you answer your phone?"

That almost provoked me. "I wasn't in the mood to talk."

As he came farther into the room, he took in the way Jesse was holding me, and his mouth tightened. "Why'd you leave me stranded?"

"Why did you dismiss me like a bad employee?" I countered.

Jesse frowned at Chance. "Yeah, she could've been seriously hurt today. You should've known better than to leave her unprotected."

That might be pushing it, I thought. I doubted Chance could've done any better than I had, faced with that shade. Still, I didn't mind the support.

"Shit, what happened?" He forgot his grievance as he knelt, peering into my face.

Before I could answer, Jesse did. "She was attacked, you ass."

"It wasn't supposed to work like that." Chance dropped down in Chuch's recliner opposite us.

I raised a brow. "What wasn't?"

"In exchange for my"—Chance hesitated over the word—"help, Twila agreed to call the warlock out. He was supposed to come at us, we waited all evening."

"I'll just bet," I said sourly. "Well, he answered the call and sent something after me. Thanks for that."

"I'm sorry, Corine. I thought I was sending you to safety."

"Yeah, well, we know how your ideas on that tend to work out." The moment the words emerged, I regretted them.

Chance flinched but he didn't argue because he couldn't. "Now will you go back to Mexico City?"

"No!" Leaning forward, I pounded a fist on my knee. "At this point they'd just kill me there. We have to root out whoever snatched Min and take the fight to them. I'm sick and tired of running around like a rat in a maze. I want to blow their shit up." I sat back, astonished at my own vehemence.

Ordinarily I wasn't militant but I'd seen too much casual collateral damage to walk away now. I hadn't known Maris, but Lenny Marlowe had been a kind, gentle soul. They'd exterminated him like a roach, and I wanted payback.

Beside me, Jesse hummed the Rocky theme song. I elbowed him and Butch raised his head with a warning look as if to offer, *You want me to bite him?*

"Well, we may be in a position to do that," Chance said. "I found something for Twila and in exchange she gave me a name. Montoya."

Montoya. That rang a bell. Then I had it.

"The angel that knocked me out," I began excitedly.

Jesse leaned over for a closer look at the lump on my head. "You didn't mention anything about an angel—"

"Never mind that now. I fell down on a Montoya

grave, and on the statue, there was a poem, something about a crescent moon. Damn." Trying to remember hurt my head.

After thinking for a moment, Chance quoted, " 'The Crescent-moon, the Star of Love,/Glories of evening, as ye there are seen/With but a span of sky between—/Speak one of you, my doubts remove,/Which is the attendant Page and which the Queen?' It's Wordsworth."

"That might be it. Anyway, I'm not sure if the poem matters. The symbol etched below it, though . . ." I pushed off the couch and found some scrap paper. "Looked like this, only inverted." I drew the stylized U that Booke had seen on Chuch's house, the Mixtec symbol for the moon.

"So our warlock is a Montoya," Jesse surmised.

Chance nodded. "It looks that way."

"Or he's related to them? It may not be his last name anymore." I turned to Saldana. "If we give you an address, could you get a warrant? I'm sure they're doing something shady. Why else would they need a private landing strip?"

"Too thin for a warrant." Jesse shook his head. "I need more than your gut instinct to do it by the book."

Well, that rankled. No wonder I hated legal garbage. Most of it seemed designed to protect the guilty and persecute the innocent.

Chance asked, "You think Bucky could help?"

I glanced at my ex with grudging approval. "You know, that's not a bad idea. He might be able to tell us what's going on in there."

"Bucky's in bed with Jeannie by now," Jesse said, glancing at his watch. "Since I have to work tomorrow, that's where I need to be too." He flashed me a slow grin as he stood. "Coming, Corine?"

Don't ask me why I hesitated. There was no reason I shouldn't go back to Jesse's place with him. The idea tempted me.

"No." I tempered the refusal with a return smile. "I need to be firing on all cylinders tomorrow and if I go with you, I won't get any sleep."

"That's true." Modesty did not factor as one of his virtues. He dropped a casual kiss on the end of my nose and saw himself out.

That left Chance and me looking at each other. *Awkward.*

"So it's like that now?" he asked. "There's really no chance for us."

"Are you kidding me?"

He honestly didn't seem to know what I meant. "What?"

"You spent all day with another woman and you have the nerve—"

"Whoa, hold up. Just what do you think happened between us?"

I decided to back off. Nothing inspired more pity than a jealous ex. I might even manage to be happy for him someday, but there was no way I'd spell it out. Besides I didn't want to know if he had the nerve to lie to me.

So I shrugged. "Whatever it was, I wasn't allowed to be part of it."

"It was private, Corine." Chance sighed and looked at his hands.

Honestly, he looked tired and worn, not glowing with satisfaction. Although that may have been from riding the bus for a few hours after all the boinking. Served him right, though. At least he hadn't been accosted in a graveyard.

"I just bet," I muttered. *Cool it,* I told myself. *Any more of this and he's going to think you're jealous.* "What did you help her find anyway?" *Her G-spot?*

"Her heart," he said somberly enough that I took a second look at his face.

Whatever that entailed, I suddenly felt sure it'd been bad. "You're okay, though?"

"Mostly. It didn't help that you ditched me. I had to scrounge my own ride back, and then I found you making out with Supercop. I understand why you were mad, though. Regardless of my intentions, I wasn't there when you needed me." He sighed. "I guess I was right to be worried about you."

"How'd you get back?" I wanted to apologize for thinking the worst of him, but the words stuck in my throat.

"Caught a ride with some frat boys making a run to Boys Town. They dropped me off at Chuch's door for beer money." Chance stood, crossed the living room, and sat down beside me, his eyes on my bruised forehead. "Are you hurt anywhere else?"

Butch answered for me with two barks.

"Hey," I managed. "I'm sorry I overreacted."

Thank God he didn't know why. Chance seemed to think I'd left because he sent me off alone, where the warlock targeted me. That was fine with me, better than the truth. I eyed the dog, hoping he wouldn't rat me out.

"I'm just glad you're okay," he said quietly. "No thanks to me. Riding with the guys wasn't a big deal."

I didn't want to talk about it anymore. "Does Chuch have a washer and dryer somewhere? I'm out of clean clothes."

It was stupid late to be washing, but if I knew Chance at all, we'd be planning an assault tomorrow using all our resources. He wouldn't slow down for my delicates.

"Out here. Let me show you."

Butch didn't take kindly to it when I put him down. He trailed after me with a whimper. Poor dog, it had been quite a day for him. We needed to break the news to Chuch and Eva regarding their temporary houseguest and bring his supplies inside.

After hefting my bag, I followed Chance into the shadowy garage. Chuch didn't use it for cars. Instead he stored tools and boxes, carelessly stacked along the walls. I spied what I thought might be a motorcycle, covered by a tarp. Hard to tell in the dark.

We didn't turn on a light. I used the illumination that trickled from the open door. I offered no care to my clothes, didn't separate, just stuffed them all into the washer and washed in cold. He watched me with some amusement.

"It's amazing you've never dyed anything pink."

The cement chilled my bare feet. "Isn't it? Let's go back in," I remembered the untouched plate of sweets. "Maybe have some cookies and then go to bed."

Butch appeared disinclined to cooperate. He sniffed around the edges of the garage and then whined, scratching at the side door that led outside.

"Does he need to go out?"

I shrugged. "Up until today, I never had a dog. How do I know? Let's see."

After we let him out, Butch did indeed pee on a bush, but then he lowered his nose, tail in the air, and snuffled his way around the house. When he got to the foundation in the backyard, he yapped ferociously. If he'd been a person, he would've been yelling, *Hey! Hey! Hey, you! Over here!* He backed away, growling, and implored me with big damp eyes to come see what he'd found.

"Okay, okay."

"Good thing Chuch doesn't have close neighbors," Chance said, following me.

I went over to see what he had—maybe a chipmunk or a rabbit? But as I got closer, I recognized the stench from the graveyard this afternoon. As I knelt, I broke a twig off the nearby hedge and parted the grass.

My stomach rebelled.

While I crawled away to lose my burger in the bushes, Chance took a closer look. "Christ, who the hell would *do* something like that?"

Bending, I picked Butch up and clutched him to my chest. I know, I know. Why does a mangled animal upset me so much? Well, people can be sons of bitches. Animals possess an innocence that humans never do, even in childhood.

Somebody had tortured this poor creature to death, and then bound it to a task that would cause it unspeakable pain. Breaking well-placed wards had shattered this animal until I couldn't tell what it had been in life, just a twitching mound of bloody bone and fur that still tried to creep forward, doing its master's bidding. We needed to put it down, but I shuddered at the thought.

I wiped my mouth and stood. "Better question is why."

"To weaken the wards," Chance realized. His eyes met mine, wide with worry.

"Eva just redid them this afternoon." But as I looked closer, I saw that the poor thing had crawled around and around the house, insidiously violating the sanctity of the lines drawn in sea salt and wormwood.

"He's planning to strike again tonight," he said grimly. "Did she reinforce the wards inside as well? Have you seen Chuch and Eva?"

So much he didn't know, like Moon's ill-timed visit, and no opportunity to tell him. I thought I might be sick again. "Not since they went into the office. We need to see if they're all right."

We went at a dead run, Butch racing at our heels.

Waiting for a Miracle

Chuch and Eva lay slumped up against the wall. It looked as though they'd been heading for the door when . . . whatever, struck them down. They looked pale as death, and my heart clenched.

Please, not them too.

The dog whined out in the hallway, as if pleading with me not to go in there, but I had to know. To my vast annoyance, Chance pushed me behind him and went in first. He knelt and felt for a pulse. "They're alive."

I let out a long breath and tipped my head against the door. "Can you wake them?"

Several minutes passed while he tried to do that. "No. I'm not sure what's wrong."

At that Chuch's eyes snapped open, but it wasn't him. The intelligence staring out at us seethed with malevolence. "You wanted to find me so badly . . . well, here I am. Come get me. You know where. I sensed your presence earlier today, but you lacked the courage to confront me on my home ground. If you want your friends to live long, healthy lives, you won't make me wait." Chuch's eyes closed.

"He's going to kill them anyway," I said numbly. "And us too if we're dumb enough to march in there."

"What do you suggest?" Chance swung Eva's unresponsive body into his arms and carried her down the hall to the master bedroom. With a strength contrasting to his whipcord build, he managed to do the same for Chuch.

"Should we call the paramedics? They're going to need fluids if this goes on long."

He hesitated. "I don't think it will come to that, Corine. If we can't wake them within twenty-four hours, they're dead anyway."

"What does that mean?" God, I was sick of all this metaphysical gobbledygook, sick of magick and cryptic phrases. I missed my shop, missed quesadillas for dinner and a bad Mexican variety show before bed. I liked the one with the fat lady in tight spandex pants.

"There's a silver cord that binds the soul to the body," he explained after a brooding silence. "It's only perceptible in the astral plane. I lived with a girl once who dabbled in out-of-body experiences. One morning, she . . . never woke up."

There was the loss he'd never articulated—the one that made him enforce emotional distance with me. First time I'd heard of her, and it *hurt*. I wondered how much he'd loved her for it to change him so profoundly. Did he wonder whether his luck had tainted her astral explorations? Was she lost *because* of him?

"The cops said her heart just failed," Chance went on. "But afterward, I did some reading . . . and it seems that the longer someone remains in spirit form, the more nebulous the cord becomes. After twenty-four hours, it dissolves entirely. So if we miss that window, we won't be able to bring them back."

Fantastic.

"Let's see. We're completely vulnerable here, and the wards are fucked. Chuch and Eva are helpless if we leave them unguarded, and we have less than a day to take out this warlock." I sighed. "Well, at least we have his address, thanks to Lenny."

Butch barked.

"That's looking on the bright side." Chance tried for a smile and failed. I think we both knew how astronomical the odds were. We needed a miracle.

"And we have to . . . destroy that thing outside." I shuddered, remembering its uncomprehending anguish.

Butch yapped in agreement. It probably bothered *him* even more than me.

In the end, we went after the poor little creature with a set of barbeque tongs and stuffed it into Chuch's grill, where it twisted, squalled, and oozed foul, putrid blood. Chance doused it with lighter fluid, and whatever it used to be, the critter screamed until a column of black smoke boiled forth. Then it disintegrated into ash, inert once more. I hoped to God this bastard necro couldn't animate ashes; this poor mammal had suffered enough.

With a moue of disgust, Chance closed the metal lid. "We owe Chuch a new grill."

"That's the least of what we owe him," I said. "What are we supposed to *do*? If you have hidden resources, this would be a great time to fire up the Bat-Signal."

Chance gave me a weighty look. "Let's get back inside. I don't like the air out here."

No wonder, considering what we just set on fire. I held my tongue, though, and scooped Butch into my arms. The dog refused to let me out of his sight.

For what little good it would do, we locked the windows and doors, and then turned on all the lights in the front of the house, as if they could stave off the dark. Figuring the size of my ass counted as the least of my problems at the moment, I ate half a plate of butter cookies while Chance mulled over our problems.

Butch reminded me with a bark that I still needed to unload his stuff, so I headed out to the Mustang to get his lamb and rice chow, his squeaky toy, and his fuzzy wool bed. The dog watched me through the screen door, barely able to see out while standing on his hind legs.

He must be hungry for dinner. I didn't know that much about dogs. How often should he eat? I should look it up on the Internet and maybe touch base with Booke too. He might have a helpful suggestion about the warlock we faced.

My arms loaded up, I spun and came up hard against a tall, male figure. He smelled oddly of ammonia, as if he scrubbed himself with Lysol each morning. Kel Ferguson had shorn his hair and acquired some bizarre ritual tattoos on his skull that coiled down the nape of his neck. If I didn't fear what it meant, I'd say that was celestial script.

Oh, shit.

"You prevented my doing the Lord's work," he said in his strange, flat voice.

Bad to worse.

"How did you find me?" I fought down panic. If I tried to push past him, he would break my neck one-handed, but surely Butch would sound the alarm soon. I just needed to stay calm.

The maniac regarded me from eyes so pale they shimmered like crushed ice in the faint starlight. "God sent me."

My voice wavered. "Oh, really?"

Anytime, Butch. I'm in trouble, boy. Big trouble. The dog disappeared from sight.

Movement in my peripheral vision drew my eye away from Ferguson. For a moment I thought Chance must be coming to my rescue, stealthily making his way around the garage, until I noticed the shadow had no one attached. Darkness sailed toward me, and it carried the unmistakable aura of the grave.

Ferguson hadn't seen it and I hoped it would veer toward him, seeking the nearest source of warmth. I remembered the thing in the cemetery and knew I couldn't let it get close enough to immobilize me. But it kept coming, slick as oil and darker than night, roiling over the cracked cement with a hiss that was as much felt as heard. Given the choice between waiting for a closer look at that shade and startling the holy killer, well, I threw my armload of dog supplies at Ferguson and bolted.

Just in time too. A frigid burst of air grazed me as I turned, and my whole arm went numb.

Any minute I expected one of them to grab me. If Ferguson did it, my bones would break. If the dark thing did, I imagined it would feel like death, icy cold and full of hunger that nothing could assuage. Shit, this was bad. As if we didn't have enough enemies, this warlock had sprung my worst one. I couldn't imagine how that was possible, but I didn't have time to speculate. My heart thudded in time to each footfall, fear spiking through my veins in an unpleasant rush.

Nothing but dead grass, rocks, and open plain lay between me and the highway. Unfortunately, the road lay two miles off. I couldn't run forever, but I didn't see anywhere to hide. I just knew I had to get away. I thought I heard footfalls behind me, but I couldn't tell if they were gaining on me. I wasn't dumb enough to turn and look.

I ran blind. My foot caught on a rock, and I stumbled, tried to compensate, and still went down, skidding onto my knees. In scrambling back up I saw the shadow looming over me, Ferguson not ten paces behind. My vision blacked as the shade wrapped around me, drawing the heat from my skin and the air from my lungs.

For a moment I felt nothing and then my whole body burned, not with the fire that seared my palm but with a soul-swallowing emptiness. Terror flashed through me as I felt the numbness spread. Soon I would know nothing at all, and—

Oh, shit, I saw the light. *What a rip-off.* My life didn't flash before my eyes or anything. I did want to see my mom again, though.

Except I didn't see a tunnel either, and I *hurt*.

A sharp sting on my left cheek reinforced the notion that maybe I hadn't died. I cracked an eye open. Ferguson stared down at me, pale as corpse flesh, his arm upraised as if to give me another whack. Shit, I'd almost rather have died than find Kel Ferguson straddling me.

"Where did it go?" I croaked.

He lowered his arm slowly. Something trickled from his fingers. "Ashes to ashes, dust to dust."

Great. Crazy Bible talk. I ached all over. Not even the time I got salmonella from some bad chicken felt like this. When he reached into his pocket, I flung my hands over my head. *He must have saved me—though I have no idea how—to finish me off himself.* I had no hope of fighting him, no hope of running.

The thing in his hand squeaked when he squeezed it. I peered through my fingers and saw him offering me Butch's play pizza. "You dropped this."

After some hesitation, I took the toy. He eased off me then, sending a sick rush of relief to my already unsettled stomach. Ferguson extended a hand to help me up. I accepted it instinctively, and then thought about what I'd done.

As we walked—well, he walked; I limped—back toward the house, I squeezed the pizza in a nervous gesture. "How did you get here?" I wondered aloud.

Had he tracked me all the way to Mexico City and back?

"He gave me the means to transcend my earthly prison," he said in a voice that sent shivers down my spine. "Then He guided my steps to your store. I do not understand why a good man like Alvarez chooses to work for you, but following you from there was easy."

"So you're the one who's been hunting me?" A chill rolled over me. Maybe he intended me to lead him to Chance, who certainly shared the culpability for putting Ferguson in prison.

"I'm not hunting you. While I'd never choose to sully

myself with you or your causes, I am the Lord's hand and I work His will. I don't pretend to understand His agenda. He sent me to help you vanquish a great evil, so tell me what you'd have me do."

It took me a moment to process that. "You mean you're not here to kill me?"

His icy eyes didn't even flicker. "I am here to banish the forces of Hell back to the eternal fires from whence they sprung."

"Um . . ." I exhaled slowly. The house came into view, all quiet inside. I picked up the bag of Hill's Science Diet and the fuzzy dog bed. "Maybe you want to come in then?"

"I await your orders," he said.

There's nothing scarier than a fanatic.

"Chance," I called unsteadily as we came into the living room. "We have company. He says God sent him to help us fight a great evil. He also just saved my ass."

"Twice," Ferguson said, "if you count the time in the cemetery."

Squinting, I saw that he was wearing a black sweatshirt. *Shit.* I dropped into a chair, feeling like death warmed over.

Chance crossed the floor in four steps, cast a questioning glance at Ferguson, and knelt beside me. "What happened? Are you all right?"

I told him.

"You're sure you're all right?" Chance shook his head. "Only you could go out for dog food and come back with a man."

"Not just any man. Remember Kel Ferguson?" I braced myself for the reaction.

Maybe we could fight fire with fire, if we used him. A sane person would call the cops as soon as we could get to a phone. Maybe he was toying with us. I couldn't begin to comprehend what went on behind those zealous eyes.

Chance straightened slowly, asking in an undertone,

"Did you bump your head or are you just crazy for bringing him in the house?"

"You wonder why I'm so pale," Kel said with a strange half smile. Chance's expression said he had, in fact, been wondering that. "I've bathed in the Lord's light. God's Hand is not bound by your laws. I see farther. I do not blame you for trying to interfere with what you do not understand, but prison bars will not hold me, nor will they stop my doing His work."

"You're saying God wants you to kill?" Chance kept his hands in plain sight. He probably didn't want to risk setting Ferguson off and having him snap my neck.

"Only those who will perpetrate great crimes against humanity."

I raised a brow. "Even that little girl you stole?"

Over the years, I'd resisted the urge to check on her, figuring she wouldn't want to be reminded of her narrow escape. But I thought of her from time to time and wondered.

"I didn't take her," Kel said quietly. "I killed the man who did. By which, I averted a worse future than you can imagine. If God's Hand had walked on earth at the right time, there would have been no Holocaust."

Chance and I exchanged a look. *How do you argue with crazy?* Well, you don't, if you're smart and you have two friends lying helpless and de-souled in the bedroom. I played along.

"Why didn't you attempt to defend yourself at your trial?"

"There are laws against vigilantes," he answered. "And I *am* a killer. With my DNA at that crime scene . . . and others, they would have incarcerated me, regardless. But such walls cannot hold me. It was an inconvenience, a delay, nothing more."

Given that he stood in Chuch's living room, I couldn't argue that.

"He makes a good point," I said to Chance.

The funny thing was, Butch didn't growl once. He lay curled up on a couch cushion, fast asleep. That reassured me more than anything, which established my state of mind. At this point I trusted a Chihuahua's judgment more than my own.

Chance eyed me as if he wondered whether I'd snapped. "Does he?"

"If you really mean to help, we need some guarantee that you won't hurt us." I didn't think he could be offended by that simple truth.

Ferguson's pale gaze roved the room and then appeared to fix on an ornate wood crucifix hanging down the hall. Wordlessly he took it down and dropped to one knee. "I swear by His grace that I will not harm you or yours while we are united in this fight."

By his expression Chance didn't think too much of Ferguson's promises, but we both knew such things had weight. I decided to give Kel some rope.

"We're planning an assault on a warlock's lair tomorrow. He's likely to have an army of shadows like the two you vanquished today, and maybe worse stuff for us to wade through before we get near him. To be honest, our chances don't look good. We're light on manpower, firepower, and every other kind of power. Is that really what you came for?"

He nodded, as if I hadn't said a single surprising thing. "God sent me."

After exchanging a look with me, Chance shook his head as if we were all crazy. That was when I knew we weren't calling the cops, at least not until everything went down tomorrow. What happened after we stormed the compound on Halstead Creek Road was anyone's guess.

"Well," Chance said. "Welcome aboard. What can you do?"

"This," the maniac said, and the living room lit up like a star gone nova.

Five minutes later, my eyes still stung from the flare. "That'll take care of the shadows. We already know they don't react well to light. But there might be other enemies we haven't even seen yet."

"I have something in mind," Chance said. His smile alarmed me.

In response to his gesture, I followed Chance back out to the garage while keeping a careful eye over my shoulder as well. I didn't like having Kel behind me. But he didn't seem inclined to sit in the living room and watch TV.

Despite seeing his holy smite-light, I couldn't get past the fact that he had killed. Maybe those people would have made a different choice down the road, assuming he was telling the truth. Maybe something would have happened to redeem them. I didn't trust the uncompromising quality of his judgment. I didn't want to believe anything was set in stone.

Because I didn't have much to lose at this point, I asked, "How can you punish someone for something that hasn't happened yet? How is that fair?"

Pausing, Chance shot me a look. "Maybe we could talk philosophy another time?"

I finished the cautionary lecture myself. *Are you crazy? He lit up the living room like the Fourth of July. Don't antagonize him.*

A valid point. If I recollected Booke's crash course in hermetic magick, wizards possessed power over the elements while warlocks worked with demons and death. So if he wasn't a holy warrior, Kel might be an unhinged wizard who killed people who looked at him funny. We didn't need any more enemies, and right now we appeared to be on the same side. I felt dirty for allowing that.

This whole situation was pretty messed up, no other way around it. I wondered if it ever occurred to Chance to walk away. Just leave Min to her fate. But I wasn't sure that would get this crazy son of a bitch off our backs at this point. We'd come too far and poked around too much. People who wielded this kind of power, no matter its origin, didn't take kindly to being thwarted.

Nothing in my life had prepared me for this. Even knowing there were bad things didn't measure up. Holy shit, I was a lobster, neck deep in boiling water, and reflecting that the bacon bits in the trap really hadn't been worth it.

The washer buzzed. What a funny, ordinary sound.

"Your laundry's done," Kel said mildly.

Smothering a nervous laugh, I crossed to the washer, popped the top, and loaded my wet stuff into the dryer. Chance crossed the shadowed garage and uncovered a stack of boxes. Inside we found an astonishing array of weapons. I could've started a small war with what Chuch had stored casually out here. Rummaging, I found a flamethrower, a crate of grenades, several AKs, and assorted ammunition. I might be able to make use of the grenades; I used to pitch a pretty mean game of softball.

"Just what the hell did Chuch do before he became a mechanic?" I asked.

"Arms dealer," said Ferguson, as if he read from an invisible scroll of our secret sins. "Mostly to Nicaragua. He retired when he met Eva."

I glanced at Chance for confirmation, and his expression revealed a shocked horror that told me our nutty new ally must've been right on the money. Shit. We might really have God's Hand on our side. *That* scared me more than a simple maniac.

Heaven help us.

Oh, crap, it already had.

Close but No Cigar

None of us slept that night.

Hey, I defy anyone to sleep with the likes of Kel in close proximity. Even if I didn't suspect he stabbed ice picks through people's eyes, I would've found his intensity disturbing. And his eyes . . . well, on the surface, they glittered like frost, but if I gazed at them too long, the ice began to look like fire. Maybe I was as crazy as him, but I started to feel he actually might *not* be human.

Before we left, Chance redid the wards after a consultation with Booke. The Englishman gave us his phone number and promised to stand ready if we had questions for him. Despite the grimness of the situation, the idea of having a hermetic scholar on call amused me. Last thing, I fed Chuch and Eva some crushed ice, hoping that would tide them over until we returned. If we did.

"If you don't hear from us within four hours," I said to Booke, "call the authorities. Have them send paramedics to the house. Maybe modern medicine can save them where we fail. You have Chuch's address?"

"Just a moment; let me fetch a pen." Pause. "Very well, go on. I hope it won't come to that," he added, sounded worried.

"Me too. Wish us luck."

"You have it," Booke said. "He's there by your side."

True enough. We didn't say good-bye. That might be a bad omen. I hung up and set the cordless handset back on its cradle to charge.

"Will you keep watch over them?" I asked Butch.

He barked twice.

"Oh, no. You can't come with me." The Chihuahua didn't look convinced. In the end, I fed him, took him out to do his business, and then left him to play guard dog, whether he liked it or not. "If you hear anything suspicious, dial 911."

Butch cocked his head at me. Sometimes I felt like he understood me completely, word for word. I needed to go home. Clearly the stress was making me nuts.

I got in the back of the Mustang because neither of us wanted Ferguson, or God's Hand, or whatever he was, out of our line of sight. Part of me still couldn't believe we hadn't called the cops already. Talk about strange bedfellows. I listened to the men loading up the trunk; we'd cleaned out Chuch's souvenirs from his former life. I hoped the weapons would be enough.

As we drove into the dawn, I heard a low litany in what sounded like Latin. Shifting sideways, I saw Kel's mouth moving. His eyes were closed, his face uplifted.

"Is he praying?" I whispered.

Chance shrugged. "I guess. We can use all the help we can get."

Ferguson said, "We shall prevail. Our mission is blessed."

There didn't seem to be a lot to say after that. I wouldn't argue with a killer touched either by divinity or madness, but his certainty didn't ease my jitters.

When Chance pulled into the drive on Halstead Creek Road, Ferguson climbed out. Though the gate was solid metal and should have required a remote, he powered it open with his bare hands. I listened to the groaning steel and shivered.

"It will be easier since it's daylight," Chance said

quietly. "But it still won't be a cakewalk. I don't know what all this son of a bitch can bring to bear on us, so stay together and keep a sharp eye out."

I nodded and then realized he probably couldn't see me. "Understood."

We followed the gravel path around to the barn that doubled as a hangar. There were several outbuildings nearby, and I could only guess at the purpose. The house itself had probably been built about ten or so years ago. The two-story structure looked well kept but not pristine, as blowing winds full of Texas dust took their toll on the stone. Oddly, it didn't look as I imagined a warlock's evil lair would. There were no brooding granite gargoyles, no creepy Victorian architecture. Maybe I'd seen too many movies.

The men climbed out and Ferguson pulled the seat forward for me. His expression made me want to piss myself in fear. I'd never seen that combination of ecstasy and acceptance before, like he knew he might die here and that excited him. *I guess if you believe you're God's Hand, you're eager to be reunited with him so he can reward you for all your good work.* I shuddered as I crawled out from behind the seat.

"First objective," Chance said. "We need to find the warlock's focus charms and destroy them. He might not realize we know that's the root of his power."

"Since he's expecting us, wouldn't he keep them on him?" I asked.

Kel closed his eerie eyes as if listening and then informed us, "There's a great evil in the upper stories. If we can reach them, it will hamper his ability to combat us."

Big if.

I didn't ask how he got that information because I just knew he would say God told him so or maybe one of the angels. *What does it say about us that we're taking him at his word?* We passed through pearly streaks of predawn light while heading for the house.

"He's sure to have them protected somehow," I said.

They nodded in agreement, but we couldn't change course; Chance and I because Chuch and Eva were counting on us. For Ferguson it was a different story, one I didn't dwell on long.

The irony lay in the fact that we were about to commit any number of crimes to get at this bastard, the least of which would be breaking and entering. Not surprisingly the doors were locked. Kel circled the building checking for a mundane security system, and then turned up silently beside us, shaking his head.

"He has a different kind of alarm in place."

We crouched near the front windows, undecided. The prospect of untold magickal consequences didn't appear to disturb Ferguson, but then what did? I'd never seen any real emotion on the man's face other than divine purpose and conviction. Maybe he believed God would protect him, but I wasn't so sure about Chance and me.

"Let's call Booke," I whispered. "He's been practicing the astral thing—that's how he was able to identify the warlock's tell. Maybe he can do something for us here. We won't be able to see him or contact him once he joins us in spirit form, but I think it'd be smart to take all the help we can get."

"You think he'd do that for us?" Chance bit his lip, undecided, and I wanted to brush the tumbled hair away from his face. I didn't. "It could be dangerous, even for an astral body. We don't know what guardians lurk around this place."

That possibility made me twitch, as if unseen eyes watched us and reported our every move. Booke could make up his own mind, I thought. I would outline the dangers, and he could choose whether to help. None of us knew enough about magick to deconstruct an alarm, though, so when we went in, we'd set it off, if Booke didn't come through.

I dialed the international calling code and then the rest

of his number. He picked up on the first ring, sounding hushed but anxious. "Corine? Is everything all right?"

Since he already knew what had happened to Chuch and Eva, I thought that was a remarkably British question. "Well, no worse than it was anyway. We have a proposition to offer you. If you help out using that astral thing and do what you can with the magickal traps, we'll parcel up any artifacts that you see and want. Ship them to you in Stoke for your collection. Then again, you'd have to be crazy to say yes. I mean, it's pretty risky. And not everybody is into stuff the way I am. I could be bought for a really nice lamp—"

"You want me to come *now*? I'm just a scholar, you know. I've only studied these things in the abstract." I'd surprised him. I heard it in his voice.

"It's all right," I said. "It's dangerous. I understand. Can you offer any advice then? We don't know anything about magickal alarms."

"Typically, they summon a guardian or the master himself," Booke told me. "I . . . yes. I do have some advice. Don't move from where you are until I ring you back. I'll see what I can do."

Ridiculous. I wished we'd thought of this before we left home. My knees throbbed from kneeling, so I sat down behind the hedge. I checked to make sure I'd set the phone to vibrate. That would be perfect, if my J.Lo ringtone alerted the whole compound.

Perhaps ten minutes later, the phone gave me a tingle in my right pocket. I answered with a whispered, "Booke? Are you all right?"

"I did it," he said. "You're clear. Break a window quietly and he'll be none the wiser. I also found the room where he keeps his foci. It's in the attic, up the stairs and behind a false wall. It was such a rush to apply something I've only read about—"

I hated to interrupt him, but the clock was running. "We'll talk more about it later, okay? Thanks so much."

"Corine, wait—"

"I'm sorry, what?"

"I took the liberty of scouting for you as well. In the far building, the hangar, he's keeping prisoners. They appear to be young women, stored in crates like animals. All their auras looked weak. This fight could turn into an abattoir if you aren't careful."

Shit.

"Thank you. We needed to know that."

After disconnecting, I relayed the information to Chance and Ferguson, although I wasn't sure he cared if innocent bystanders died for God's glory.

"It just keeps getting better," Chance muttered.

I rubbed the bridge of my nose. My whole body ached from lack of sleep and last night's attack, and a headache whispered at my temples. If I didn't rest soon, it would flare into a full migraine. "Do we go after his charms and risk his killing those people to feed his power? Or free the people and risk his unleashing his full strength on us?"

"Neither," Ferguson said. "You two go after the hostages. I'll destroy his foci. Get them out of here, though. They can't be close enough for him to strike when we hit him."

"Why hasn't he sensed us?" That had been gnawing at me. "If he did yesterday—"

"I've fixed my luck on it," Chance said quietly. "That's all I can do. We need to be quick, though. I can't concentrate like this forever. It . . . hurts." As he said that, a single drop of blood trickled from his nose.

"That's it then. Go, Ferguson. We'll take care of the prisoners. You do your part."

Without a word, Kel produced a cutting tool and went to work on the window. We turned and headed for the far building. Set at the end of the landing strip, the hangar looked as though it had been built to house a small plane, perhaps a little storage as well.

"What're we going to do?" I whispered. "This is a crappy rescue."

"Maybe there's a truck. We'll just drive them out of here and set them free."

His words sparked me. I'd been struggling with the separate pieces for ages, and it finally clicked. Before, I'd wondered what kind of operation would use a fleet of trucks, warehouses, and a landing strip. I'd guessed smuggling of some kind, drugs being the obvious choice, but between our trip to the *zona*, what I'd learned about the flesh pipeline on the Internet, and what Booke had said about the prisoners, the truth coalesced for me.

"That's it."

"What is?" Chance crept toward the corrugated steel structure, only half listening to me.

"The connection. Southern Sanitation is a front for IBC, right? *Importaciones Bonitas Corporación?*" I shook my head in disgust. "Pretty Imports Corporation. What's prettier than young women?"

Chance's gaze kindled with realization. "They're trafficking women. According to what I read about the sex trade, Mexico is often the first point of entry from the East. Sometimes the victims remain there, where they're put to work in an Asian themed brothel."

I nodded, remembering the red pagoda in Boys Town. "Then they ship the women in from Nuevo Laredo, if they're intended for local use." Saying it aloud sent a cold shiver of horror through me. "That's where the fleet of trucks comes in. And if they're meant for other ports of call, they use this hangar—"

"And the landing strip," Chance finished.

"I'd guess the warlock procures for them and offers another valuable service." When he regarded me blankly, I added, "The girls are drugged and shipped in crates like animals. *He* takes care of the ones who don't make it. That's how he conjures those shadows at will. How else could he kill so many people and go undetected?"

I wasn't positive I had the whole picture yet, but that was most of it, I thought.

"You're right," he said. "You must be. Maybe my mother stumbled onto it? Maybe one of the women she used to treat in the *zona* came to her with information?"

I didn't know about that, but my gut instinct said no. It was something more, something else. That might play a part, but the story didn't end there. Why else would Min have gone with her captors willingly? But I couldn't even guess.

"Do you have a bolt cutter?" I asked as we came up to the padlocked door.

Chance had packed a messenger bag full of God knew what. He'd spent hours in the garage last night, going through the remnants of Chuch's former life. I definitely liked his current dishevelment more than the coifed perfection he had sported when we were together. Between the black leather bag and the weapons on his back, he made for a pretty vigilante killer. Was I irredeemable because that sent a tiny thrill through me? Maybe.

He might *be* that, soon enough.

"I think so."

Chance cut the lock and we stepped inside, paused on the threshold to let our eyes adjust to the dim interior. I thought I heard something banging around near the back. Someone who needed help? Instinctively I started that way.

As we sprinted for the far corner, a scream echoed off the walls. Forty souls keened their anguish and then fell silent. I didn't know whether we'd set off a fail-safe that executed the prisoners in the event of an unauthorized entry or if Ferguson had triggered a trap somewhere.

Either way, it didn't matter.

"We're too late," I whispered.

The shadows rose.

Out, Out, of This Damned Spot

The hangar pulsed with a pale, unwholesome light.

The space looked large enough to house a plane, but right now it contained only row after row of crates containing the bodies of dead women. It was our fault. We hadn't been fast enough, careful enough.

But I couldn't let myself think along those lines. We hadn't kidnapped them.

Later I could drown myself in guilt, drink Irish whiskey, and brood over my role in this mess. Right now I had to focus on surviving. If I didn't, then the people ultimately responsible for this would get off scot-free.

I should be manning a cash register, damn it. Instead I hefted a grenade that wouldn't do shit against these things. Southern chicks who couldn't remember their natural hair color weren't meant to fight monsters. But I'd stand for those who couldn't fight back. Like these poor women, like Maris, like Lenny. Maybe I hadn't been born to the task or even chosen for it by Powers That Be, but I wouldn't back down. A need for justice drove me on.

That was the reason I'd accepted Chance's terms, left my quiet life, and climbed on this roller coaster in the first place. Back then I just wanted the people who killed my mother to account for their crimes. Now I

wanted the sick bastards who'd stolen these girls to pay
as well.

Smoke writhed all around us, coalescing into spectral
forms. I actually saw it when they recognized their al-
tered states, ruby red eyes fixing on us with the hungry,
envious rage only dead things feel for the living. Guns
and grenades wouldn't work against creatures of pure
will and darkness.

And we'd sent God's Flashlight off to break some
statues.

If we could do it over, I might go another way. As
they closed on us, I backed off. Their proximity chilled
the air, so that I saw my breath when I exhaled in a demon sigh. Tendrils snaked toward us, tasting us. I could
almost hear them keening in anticipation.

They flowed between us and the door, circling with
slow but inexorable intent. Shit. I wished I could call
Booke, but it was down to Chance and me. We'd live or
die together.

"Ideas?"

Chance shook his head. "I'm fresh out of holy water.
We shouldn't have split up."

"How thick are the walls?"

We were too far from the door, and the shades were
trying to encircle us. If I could blow a hole in the wall,
we might get out of here.

"Good question. What do you have in mind?"

"Just trust me and get down."

Rather than waste time we didn't have in explanations, I pulled the pin on the grenade in my hand and
hurled it. Chance hit the deck and rolled as debris showered down on us. The entire hangar groaned and shuddered, but when the smoke cleared I saw I'd blown a
small hole, maybe big enough to crawl through.

I could feel the cold of the shadows closing in on us.
Any closer and we'd start to freeze up. I remembered the
agony from the cemetery.

"Hurry up!" Fear made my voice sharp.

He caught my urgency. On hands and knees, we scrambled for the makeshift exit. Ragged metal sliced my palms and my knees as I pulled myself past just in time. Dust ground into the open wounds, and I couldn't restrain a moan of pain.

As we fell back into the grass, the spirits slowed. Maybe they couldn't tolerate the sun? I guess I'd seen too many vampire films. They didn't disintegrate or catch on fire, but they hesitated before boiling out of the ragged hole in the wall.

The light wasn't enough.

Ragged arms reached for us, smoky and nebulous things that contrasted unnaturally with the chill in the air. The light hurt them as they pursued us even into the sunshine. Oddly, they seemed to be holding back, as if waiting for confirmation of their desire to suck the life out of us.

I stumbled to my feet and tried to decide what to do. Chance didn't look sure. His nose bled, no longer a single drop but a steady stream.

"Ease up," I begged. "He already knows we're here."

Grimly he shook his head. "That's not what I'm concentrating on anymore."

Before I could ask, things got worse.

A lightning bolt split the sky, and thunder clouds boiled up from nowhere. Eerie and unnatural, the sky beyond showed pearly gray that would ripen into blue as the day went on. We stood in the heart of unnatural night, carrion winds rising around us, and still couldn't see our enemy.

From everywhere and nowhere, a voice boomed out. "Finish them."

Unbound by the close confines of the hangar, the specters spread into a writhing wall before us. Through their shifting mass we saw movement—the stiff, pale forms of dead women lumbered toward us. Not even the twilight of the rising storm could hide their pallor and wounds, the charged shimmering air making the scene even more surreal.

Jesus, that wasn't even fair. With the murder of one human being, the warlock could create two enemies: their transformed spirits and their dead flesh. I slanted a quick look at Chance, who had taken a position at my back.

Somehow I managed to smile as I said, "Seems like overkill, doesn't it?"

"I guess we pissed him off with our persistence. Lion, thorn in paw."

Chance and I had been backed into more than a few tight spots, but this qualified as the worst. I recognized the chill creeping over me as the wave of shadows crept closer. Overhead, the sky boiled with unnatural clouds. We needed light, but I didn't think I could count on a stray sunbeam, especially when Kel had called the one in the cemetery.

Where the hell was he anyway?

Then the entire upper story of the house exploded, smoking splinters and glass glittering through the darkened air as fire burst the windows. The impact sent me face-first into the dirt.

The shadows hesitated, no longer bound to their purpose. Beyond them, the corpses showed the same undirected confusion, shambling steps taking them away from us. Some drifted toward the back of the house, now licking with flame. I heard the screams of Kel's combat with the warlock, but I couldn't think about him. Other shadows stalked us still: dead things affronted by the heat and vitality of the living.

Screw it. I wouldn't go out quietly.

I'd practiced last night. *Press down with my thumb and slide the pin out, then let fly.* I'd done it once already, against the hangar wall. With fingers gone numb, I pulled the pin on a grenade and pitched it at the advancing shades. The explosion roared in my ears, threw dirt, and did nothing to the shadows. Except make them recoil.

"Heat," I called to Chance. "They're afraid of fire. We should head for the house!"

His look said I'd gone insane. But I'd lived through conflagrations that killed other people, and these things couldn't take heat or light. When Clayton Mann lit his own lair on fire and I fell three stories, I'd proved I could survive my worst fear. I could do it again.

I spun and staggered toward the burning building. I wasn't sure how I felt when he followed me without another word. It did something crazy to my insides.

I could hardly make myself move, already chilled and sluggish. Deadly frost whispered at my heels as I made for the porch. At this point I felt like I might be seeking the least objectionable way to die.

All around us, the storm roared with insane fury. The warlock wouldn't be able to keep it up for long with so many factors draining his strength. That was assuming Kel didn't slaughter him outright, incinerate him in holy fire.

Pure heat roared over me as I coiled myself under the windowsill. Chance tried to wrap himself around me, but the closest shadow snatched at my arm instead. A wave of blackness washed over me like an oil spill.

It wanted me. Maybe they recognized my taste now. And I couldn't fight back this time. Nowhere to run. The fire wasn't enough. Too slow, not quite hot enough.

And I'm so cold. . . .

Funny, I thought as I began to fade. *I always figured I'd burn.*

"No!" Chance shouted, but his voice sounded as if it came through a long tunnel or maybe out through a pipe organ.

As I blacked out, I dreamed I saw Kel locked in terrible battle with a dark figure wreathed in unholy tendrils of smoke. God's Hand carried a slim silver knife, the blade flashing too bright in the heavy air. Kel muttered, "Go with God," as the warlock raised both arms. I wanted to flinch, fearing the outcome.

But I was so very cold. . . .

The next thing I knew, the whole world lit up with blue-white fire. A terrible crack split the porch overhead, and Chance shielded me as charred wood fell. The air smelled charged, different than the smoky plume rising from the ruined house.

Thunder boomed, shook the very ground we crouched upon. Lightning. Only Chance could've made that happen. A thousand and one probabilities . . . He spins the coin a hundred times and comes up tails every time.

"Oh, God, Corine . . . your lips are blue."

Three times now, I'd nearly been taken by shadows. And three was a weighty number. Fire had saved me, just as it claimed my mother's life. I didn't understand, but the meanings would come later.

"I'm all right," I managed to say through chattering teeth. "We should see how bad it is out there."

The sounds of fighting had either ceased or were overwhelmed by the burning house and the raging tempest. Chaos raged around us, energies snapping like broken electrical wires. Chance reached for me, the back of his hands crisscrossed with new scratches and ash, and I let him tug me to my feet.

Huge raindrops spattered us, rousing a hiss from the burning house behind us. The black storm gathered power as if fueled by its master's fury. Howling wind lashed us, made it difficult for me to keep my balance. Chance put an arm around me as hail pelted us.

Together, we rounded the house, staying well out of back draft range. The open plain assumed a nightmare hue, stinking of death and decay. His flesh golems staggered toward us, no longer lacking direction.

Which meant God's Hand had failed.

The Threshing Floor

I could hardly wrap my mind around it. We'd survived only by virtue of Chance's luck and my strange relationship with fire. Flames had stolen my mother and nearly slain me in Tuscaloosa, and I suffered its kiss anytime I used my gift. Maybe that meant something, but I didn't possess the leisure for self-analysis.

Behind the house, we found him.

Kel lay still as death, covered in more blood than I had ever seen. Once I would have screamed like a maniac, but we still had to deal with the master's meat puppets.

And when the dark one showed himself, it wouldn't be good.

Animated corpses closed in from all sides of the smoldering farmhouse. With his power depleted, doubtless the warlock hoped to wear us down. If only we could find the bastard, end this once and for all—but his mindless children would rend Kel limb from limb if we left him where he'd fallen.

We stood back-to-back once more, ready to make our last stand. Chance slung the automatic rifle from his back, removed the safety. His gun sparked as he fired into oozing zombie flesh. A young girl, beautiful in life, jerked as pieces of her shoulder and arm went flying. Still they came.

Their unseeing eyes never moved, whitened with a grotesque film that spoke of the veil between this life and the next. No matter what we did, what damage we inflicted, their expressions never changed. Like inexorable automatons they came, robbed of everything but their master's will. Their clothes hung in bloody tatters.

Adrenaline sang in my veins. These things were slow, so it worked to our advantage. My grenade landed in the path of a half dozen figures, and being brain-dead, they didn't detour around it. The subsequent explosion churned dirt all around them as the flash of fire and metal tore them apart. The air stank of burnt meat, and still they crawled toward us, if they had limbs left to drag themselves forward.

"Damn," I muttered, swaying to my feet and falling back. "We need some napalm."

Chance flashed me a grin. "Chuch would've needed to special order it."

I realized that the zombies behind us were guarding something. The wounded warlock must be hiding, taking shelter behind his remaining minions. Booke had said destroying his foci might kill the bastard, so this warlock must know something Booke didn't. Well, it didn't matter what tricks he had up his sleeve.

Righteous anger rose up in me. "This is for Lenny!"

I primed another grenade, sent it skimming along the ground toward the nearest group, and then dove for cover. When it detonated, the earth churned up, bodies flew to pieces, and the stupid things fell, stumbling over their own severed limbs. Chance unloaded a full clip into them as they twitched and split wide open beneath the barrage of automatic fire. The creatures sounded like splitting melons when he hit them in the torso. The stench of bodily effluvia joined the bitterness of smoke and charred flesh.

Bile rose up in my throat. Even though I hadn't taken their lives, I despised being forced to decimate the remains of girls who had surely suffered enough. It would take a field team days to figure out who was who and notify their families. Grief warred with outrage. There'd better be a special circle in hell reserved for this son of a bitch.

And why? To keep us from finding out what happened to Chance's mother? The cold rain felt like tears spattering my cheeks. Who the hell did this guy work for?

Reaching back, I came up empty-handed, and the last wave swept over us. I went down in a foul-smelling pile of rending hands and severed limbs. I struggled and screamed as teeth sank into my shoulder. They had no appetite, but they would consume me.

I kicked out, feeling my knee lodge itself in someone's open abdomen. I couldn't tell how much blood belonged to me. Above me, I heard Chance swearing, fighting to reach me. All around I heard the sickening snap of bone.

For one shining moment I saw his face, livid with rage and resolve. Chance raised his rifle and smashed it into a dead woman's face. I tried to scramble to my feet, sobbing. His hands slid against mine, wet and sticky as he pulled me up.

"Jesus," Chance breathed.

He bled from a hundred shallow cuts. And I was worse off. Our fury and determination wouldn't be enough, could never be. The stream of bodies never seemed to end. As soon as Chance knocked them down, they struggled to their feet again.

And we were only human.

As if in answer to a prayer I hadn't thought to offer, Kel struggled to his feet nearby. His silver knife gleamed as he waded through the putrid corpses like a threshing machine. His pale skin ran with blood and black ooze. His tattoos glowed with a faint blue light through gore and mud.

Claws sank into his flesh; misshapen arms and legs tried to drag him down. Their teeth tore whole chunks from his torso while he snapped necks and broke jaws. I didn't know how he kept going; Christ, I'd thought he was *dead*. His blood ran but he didn't seem to feel it; each new wound appeared to drive him to greater ferocity. Kel wouldn't stop until he reached his target, not for death or the devil himself.

Kel carved the last of them into pieces so fine they lay in writhing chunks on the ground. Like the tormented animal the warlock had sent to break the wards, these poor things had no choice but to answer his command, even through the failings of fragile flesh. I'd never seen anything so macabre.

Half buried in bodies and dripping with gore, God's Hand swayed on his feet. A few wounds on his back showed the pale glint of bone. For a minute I thought he might die on his feet like a gladiator of old. A chill went through me, made of equal measures awe and alarm. I thought about steadying him but I couldn't make myself reach out.

"We have to find him," Kel said in a voice as weary as the grim reaper itself.

Chance nodded. "If he gets away here, now, it's over. We have no hope if he has a chance to rest up for the next round."

To say nothing of Chuch and Eva, whose lives depended on us. Since I could barely walk unassisted, that didn't bode well for them. But I wouldn't give up. Not when we'd come this far.

"Can you home in on him?" I asked Chance hopefully.

He shook his head. "I'm burnt, nothing left. I'm sorry."

I remembered how he'd bled out the nose. "Don't be."

"If he tries to run, we'll have him," Kel said.

I frowned. "He won't run. Not when he knows this area better than we do. He'll lay low, hoping we limp away. But he doesn't know us very well if he thinks we'll accept a standoff. I guess you didn't see where he went after—"

Kel fixed me with eerie eyes. "No."

"The hangar," I realized out loud. "The house is destroyed. Maybe he's got a car or a panic room."

The guys exchanged a look, and then Chance said, "Let's go."

All of us limping, we slid into the shadows of the hangar. The storm had begun to abate, tapering to an almost natural rainfall. It drummed on the metal roof, giving the space an oddly tympanic sound.

So many empty crates, from which the bodies of stolen women had risen up. I found myself jumping at each creak, each scuff of a shoe against the cement floor. I couldn't see shit, and I hurt all over. More than anything, I wanted this to be finished.

And then I got my wish.

"Move, and she dies," came a raspy voice.

Arms came around me from behind. I couldn't see him, but Chance could because the nose of his rifle came up. Kel hesitated, knife in hand. I could see him weighing the likelihood of making the kill.

"I'm nearly spent," the warlock continued. "But I have enough power left to take her with me when I go."

Since he stole souls, I'd wind up bound to him in whatever hellish afterlife awaited. I tried not to whimper; I really did. I'm not altogether sure I succeeded. At that point I just focused on not pissing.

"Okay," Chance said soothingly. "Let's talk terms. What do you want?"

"Oh, it's too late to parlay," he rasped. "But I'll take her with me as insurance."

Like hell you will. I couldn't feel a weapon; nothing pressed into my ribs or against my throat. He wasn't terribly tall either because I could feel his breath on my hair.

In one motion I slammed my head back against his nose and stomped down hard on the top of his foot just as Chance muttered, "Just like Tuscaloosa, Corine."

I dropped onto my face, hoping my ex was fast enough to save my soul.

The rifle report echoed like mad inside the hangar, but it did the job. A warlock who's shot his wad dies just like anybody else. More blood spattered me.

Arcane energies crackled around us as the madman fell, reflected in the rumbling thunder. The earth shuddered as if it would split wide open beneath our feet. But as the warlock gasped his last, I thought I heard the rustle of leathery wings.

Kel reached me first, tugged me to my feet. I didn't know what it meant when I accepted his help without hesitation. Christ. I stared at the dead guy on the ground. Chance had blown his face clean off.

"What do you suppose he meant when he said it was too late to parlay?" Chance swiped a hand across his forehead, smearing his face with blood and less identifiable fluids. He slowly sank to the ground, the rifle still gripped in his hand.

He must be thinking about his mother.

"I don't know. I hope Chuch and Eva are okay. Was killing him enough?"

I didn't necessarily expect an answer. As I knelt next to Chance, adrenaline trickled away and left me feeling empty. I felt every scratch and bruise, felt nauseated with shock and the increasing reek of the women's remains.

But Kel replied, "It should be."

God's Hand stepped over the warlock's body, dark with gore and bright with satisfaction. If he felt the pain of his wounds, he ignored them; he showed none of the deep weariness weighing down on Chance and me.

"Let's find out." I wiped my hands on my ruined khakis and whipped out my cell phone. No point in worrying all the way there.

The phone rang six times before someone picked up. *"Bueno."*

"Chuch," I breathed. "Thank God. Is Eva all right?"

"Yeah, she's right here. What the fuck is going on? I had some really loco dreams, like I was trapped in this statue, right? So I wake up . . . and I think we been robbed." He hesitated. "Expensive shit too. The garage is trashed and now there's this weird Chihuahua watching my every move. Did I do peyote last night?"

I found myself grinning despite all my aches and pains. "It's a long story. We'll be back soon. I hope." With that, I hung up.

"We should get out of here," Chance said. "That smoke is going to attract attention and I don't think we want to be here when—"

Sirens interrupted him. A car with flashing lights sped down the drive, and a familiar voice ordered us to stand down. I finally thought to check the dead warlock for ID, hoping we'd then be able to figure out who he worked for.

Oh, Christ.

We'd killed Nathan Moon.

Eye of the Storm

On the hangar floor we had a dead cop.

By my side stood a convicted killer with a knife in his hand. Shit, this did not look good. We came out, hands in the air.

The siren cut off with a yelp and Jesse Saldana slid out of his car. "Drop your weapons! Get down!"

While he trained his gun on the three of us, I flattened myself on the ground, as instructed. Chance hesitated only a moment before discarding his rifle. I didn't think Kel would comply, though. Bullets might not even stop him.

To my surprise, he lay down beside me. Maybe God would get him out of this too. Saldana looked ill as he approached us, both hands on his weapon. He took in the destruction and the smoldering house.

"Stay down. No sudden moves. I called for backup and two more cars are on the way." His eyes said, *How could you?* "Moon called me, Corine. He said you were here trying to kill him. I told him he was full of shit, but then I heard gunfire."

"Jesse, give me a chance to explain—"

"You have the right to remain silent," he cut in. "Anything you say can and will be used against you in a court of law. You have the right to an attorney. If you cannot afford an attorney, one will be provided for you. Do you understand the rights I have just read to you? With these rights in mind, do you wish to speak to me?"

I dropped my forehead onto the backs of my hands, feeling older than my twenty-seven years. The men on either side of me possessed the sense to keep quiet, at least. Jesse radiated steely purpose. *This can't be the same man I kissed last night.* His eyes looked cold as he gazed down at us. The fact that Moon was nowhere to be seen didn't matter. Saldana knew deep down how this battle had played out, and maybe he hadn't even liked the guy but cops didn't let people get away with killing their own.

How could he not *know*, though? The air stank with foul magick, and we were surrounded by corpses. Before, I'd suspected a dirty cop must be behind our trouble in town, but I'd suspected Jesse. I just hadn't turned my eyes in the right direction.

It might not be too late for Min if we could get moving, put the rest of the pieces together. Of course, a lot depended on the next five minutes. I had to convince Jesse to let us go. Once the other officers arrived on the scene, we were done.

"Moon lured us out here," I said desperately. "He's the one who did Maris. Enslaved her. Don't you get it? The reason he came by last night was to see if he'd successfully breached the wards." I paused and took a breath, gauging his response.

He looked unsure; he was listening. So I went on, "After he went for me in the cemetery, he didn't have power to burn, so he needed to make sure his strike would get through. Hassling me was just a bonus. Afterward, he attacked Chuch and Eva in their own home and tried to add them to his collection. He didn't try anything on their turf and in person for mundane reasons— DNA and forensic evidence could tie him to the scene. Out here, he thought he could control the outcome and then clean up, nobody the wiser."

"Lies." But he didn't sound sure. Maybe empathy helped him discern my sincerity.

"Believe her," a feminine voice whispered. A cool white mist rolled in, but it felt peaceful, gentle. *Maris.* "I came to thank you. And now I have."

In a blink I might have missed it or imagined it, but by Jesse's expression he'd shared the delusion with me. His hands shook.

"See?" I pushed the advantage. "We helped you, just like you asked. You wanted us to set her free."

Jesse regarded me for a moment longer. The shadows I'd noticed beneath his eyes the other night seemed twice as dark. I wondered whether he would throw us to the lions, even having heard the truth from Maris.

"Get up," he bit out. "All of you. It looks like a war went down here. Maybe I can blame it on rival drug cartels. What's in the outbuildings?"

"Nothing now," Chance said gravely. "Moon killed the women who comprised his next shipment. I'm sorry we couldn't save them. We tried."

Kel spoke for the first time, and I thanked my lucky stars he sounded relatively normal. He shouldn't have been able to move, bearing those wounds, but Jesse was in no state of mind to notice details. Good thing too or he might ID Ferguson from his mug shot. "We should check inside to see if anybody survived."

I glanced at Jesse. "Do we have time? You said backup was on the way. I don't want you to get in trouble for letting us go."

After checking his watch, Saldana said, "You have about five minutes I'd say. Let's take a look inside."

I felt dizzy and sick as we passed by the human detritus, so many corpses, pretty and still. My heart hurt. So many futures cut short and for what? We continued into the warehouse, where Saldana paused at his former partner's body. He stared down at Nathan Moon with a sick anguish. I didn't know what to say, so I stood silent. Chance and Kel had split off from us to roll the place.

"I should have sensed it," Jesse said, low. "I should have, but I didn't. All I ever got from him was self-satisfaction, annoyance, or impatience. Nothing sinister."

He was a happy little sociopath. Not your fault. But I didn't say it aloud; Saldana probably wouldn't hear me anyway.

Toward the back, behind a partition, we found a woman with a pulse. I didn't know why she'd been culled from the herd, but it had saved her life. Jesse swung her up in his arms. She seemed delicate as a flower against the tanned warmth of his skin. When he carried her into the sunlight, she opened her eyes and whimpered, shrinking away from us wild-eyed.

"It's okay. We're not going to hurt you," I assured her. "Jesse is a policeman. He'll get you some help."

"You're not taking me to Diego Montoya?"

Montoya. Twila had given Chance that name, Montoya, in exchange for his help, and I'd already guessed we were looking for a Montoya, based on the symbol that linked the grave I'd found in San Antonio and the astral tell Booke saw on Chuch's house. Well, now we had a first name, which would make it easier to find him.

The girl grasped at Saldana with thin fingers. Her whole body shook, and her eyes rolled in her head as if she were a spooked horse. Her English was awkward. "If take me, they will—" Her voice broke. I heard her teeth chattering. "They told me they get me good job, then I send money to my family. Instead, put me in box, they make me do bed-work. If I don't, they kill me." She sobbed out, "Home. I want go home. Take me home."

He murmured to her in quiet reassurance. Far in the distance, I heard sirens. That was our cue. "We need to go. If you learn anything from her, give me a call."

Saldana regarded me from dull eyes. I'd broken

something in him, or maybe it was simple disillusionment. "All right. I'll see what I can turn up on this Montoya too."

Once we patched up a bit and checked in with Chuch, we'd start looking for Diego Montoya. I didn't care how many guards we had to wade through, or if he had a dozen more pet warlocks. *We're coming, Min. Just hold on.*

Nobody said a word as we jogged to the Mustang. We all piled in and pulled onto Halstead Creek Road with a squeal of tires. Maybe a quarter mile down the road, we passed two cop cars, lights blazing. They buzzed past us and continued on to the scene, where once again we'd left Jesse a hell of a mess to clean up.

I didn't know how he'd explain all the body parts and the disgusting smell, let alone a field full of dismembered women. Maybe the poor girl we saved would add credence to his story. But any cop who walked away from a fight that killed his partner would be in for a rough ride, let alone under these circumstances.

Even if said partner had been a corrupt son of a bitch.

I supposed the outcome depended on who actually owned the property. Christ, I hoped we hadn't gotten Saldana fired. On the whole I had bigger worries, however. My whole body ached, I hadn't slept in two days, hadn't eaten since the cookies last night, and we had a war to wage.

"Are you two okay?" My voice sounded hoarse.

"I'll live," Chance answered. "If my head doesn't explode."

God's Hand made no reply.

Putting aside my own aches, I leaned forward, anxious. "Is he . . . ?"

Wouldn't that be just what we needed? Another dead body. My own head throbbed like a sore tooth.

Chance couldn't take his eyes off the road long enough to check for a pulse but said, "Doubt it. If he was going to kick off, he'd have done it already."

I couldn't help but agree. "Did you find anything in the hangar?"

"I'm not sure. Could be something, could be nothing. We found what looks like a cargo manifest, detailing their 'pottery' shipment and where it was supposed to go. It might be a dummy sheet and worthless, but at this point, it's all we have."

A few minutes later, we arrived at Chuch's place. I felt bemused to see Butch standing on his hind legs, peering out the front door. God, I was glad that stupid dog was okay. I slid over and climbed out the driver's side. Butch barked as I went around the car to check on Kel.

When I bent toward him, his eyes snapped open. Despite myself I stumbled back a step, out of his reach. His eyes just weren't right.

"We're here," I said stupidly.

"Thanks. I'll be all right in a few minutes." He made no move to get out of the car, though, so I just left him there. I had enough to worry about.

Chuch met us at the front door, evidently alerted by Butch's impressive watchdog performance. "*Dios*," he said. "Look at you two. I guess you found my stash, huh?" He took in the rifle dangling from Chance's hand. "Let me put that away for you, *primo*." His eyebrows almost shot off his forehead. "Man, this is going to be some story. Why don't you guys rinse off some of the blood and then tell me what the hell's been going on?"

That sounded like a great idea. I took a five-minute shower and Chance took his turn next. We all met up in the kitchen, where Eva simmered some bean soup that smelled like heaven. She greeted me with a great big squeeze that hurt my ribs. "You okay, *cariño*?"

Tears filled my eyes as I hugged her back. I hadn't realized just how much I cared about her until this moment. "Yeah. I'll be sore in the morning, but I'm all right."

Her love hurt, though. Whatever I said, I had about a dozen wounds that needed tending. The bite on my shoulder might fester if it wasn't treated.

Chuch took a seat at the kitchen table and drummed his fingers on top. "You want to fill me in? Why is there a tattooed dude asleep in the Mustang? Why did you need all that hardware? And where did the creepy Chihuahua come from?"

After pouring us both tall glasses of iced tea, Chance sat down and let me tell the story. Butch whined until I picked him up, and he sat with his chin on the table, overseeing the proceedings. The tale took the better part of an hour, and by the time I finished, both Chuch and Eva regarded us with astonishment.

"You mean those loco dreams were true?" the mechanic asked finally.

With a nod, Chance answered, "More or less. When we destroyed the foci that held you, your souls were free to follow the silver cord back to your physical bodies."

Chuch ran a hand through his long, dark hair, looking grim. "What about the guy outside? What's his deal? Did you hire a merc?"

Damn. I'd hoped to avoid discussing Kel.

"Not exactly. He, ah, showed up last night, claiming God sent him to help us rid the world of a great evil."

Eva gave me a long look. "And you didn't think he was crazy? Your first impulse was to arm him?"

"Well, it wasn't my *first* impulse. . . ." I tried a smile. God knew what she'd say if she found out who he was.

"Wow." She shook her head. "So you went off with a nut job and you took out the warlock. You didn't even have Chuch's good stuff. He has a *real* cache of weapons hidden better than that. You know, just in case."

"When you find Montoya, I'm going with you to rescue your mama and take him out," Chuch said quietly. "You'll need the extra firepower . . . and he crossed the line when he let his goon mess with my wife."

I expected Chance to protest but he simply stared at Chuch for a minute. As if making a judgment based on something he saw that I couldn't interpret, he simply nodded. "We need some rest. It's been a tough twenty-four."

To say the least.

"Eva, can you put your mad investigative skills to tracking down something about this Diego Montoya?" I asked.

She nodded. "I'll start with the Internet and work from there."

"Let me make some calls," Chuch said. "I know some people who might be able to tell us something." He glanced at Chance. "It may take some bribe money, though, *primo*. They won't cross these people for nothing. We got to make it worth their while."

"How much? I can get my hands on ten grand, maybe. It would take longer to—"

Chuch laughed. "Relax. You could get these guys to kill their own grandmothers for a thousand dollars, let alone talk some shit."

The clearing of a throat drew our eyes toward the kitchen doorway. Kel stood there under his own power, blood soaked but ambulatory. "May I use the shower?"

I exchanged a glance with Chance. *Should we tell them the whole story?* He slowly shook his head.

Eva recovered first. "Sure. It's just down the hall. Towels are in the closet to the right."

"Let me show you." Bone tired, I pushed away from the table and led the way to the bathroom after getting him a clean blue towel from the linen closet. "Do you need some help? I can bind up your wounds afterward if you want."

In answer he pulled his filthy shirt off and presented me a back crisscrossed with scars. Some must be old and puckered the pale skin, but the wounds he'd taken today, just hours ago, showed livid purple. Already healed.

Seeking proof, I reached out and almost touched my fingertips to his skin before remembering who and what he was. I pulled back. "How is this possible?"

"God takes cares of His own," he told me, and shut the door in my face.

As the water hissed on, I returned to the kitchen in time to hear Eva say, "Well, he's a weird one. You know he has angel names tattooed all over his head?"

"Yeah, it's kind of hard to miss," I said.

Eva fussed over me and then Chance, daubing at us with various medical supplies and antibiotics. My jaw practically cracked on a yawn. The bean soup wouldn't be done for hours, and I wanted sleep.

"Get some rest," Chuch ordered. "We'll do some of the legwork this afternoon. I hope we'll be ready to pay some personal calls tonight."

That reminded me: I needed to get in touch with Booke. It was a testament to his self-control that the phone wasn't ringing off the hook.

"Thanks." As he stood, Chance swayed and had to catch himself on the back of his chair. "Come on, Corine. Let's take a nap."

Well, he looked too busted to try anything, not that I felt inclined to argue over sharing a bed with *anyone* right now. I remembered how he had taxed his luck, blood pouring out his nose.

"In a minute," I said, heading for the office.

Chance followed me, looking puzzled. He got it when I sat down at the computer and went looking for Chuch's IM icon. "Glad you remembered, much as he helped us."

I nodded as I typed with my awesome hunt-and-peck skill. *Booke? This is Corine. We're fine. We got the warlock.*

His immediate response made me think he'd been sitting by the computer all this time. *Did you save the prisoners?*

The question hit me like a fist in the chest, and I had

to take a minute before I could answer. God, it hurt to think of girls we didn't save.

No. I think the hangar was booby-trapped somehow.

After reading over my shoulder, Chance curled his palm around the nape of my neck, soothing me. I remembered how he used to do that, first delving beneath my hair with an impossibly delicate touch. Shivers stole over me.

Long pause on Booke's end as he processed our failure. *I'm sorry. But thank you for letting me know you're all right.*

No problem, I typed. *The place burned down, so we don't have anything to send for your collection. I'm sorry.*

We were a sorry lot, weren't we?

I didn't say yes for the possible reward, he returned eventually. *This is the first time anyone's ever asked for my help, the first time I didn't feel like an incompetent, ineffectual fool. Thank you for that.*

Wow. I had no idea what to say. So Chance leaned forward and keyed, *Welcome. We'll keep you posted, but now I need sleep.*

It was less personal than what I might've said if Chance hadn't been there, given that I'd shared dream space with Booke. There was such an aching loneliness about him. The Englishman took it as a farewell, however, and signed off. I let it go, standing with a tired sigh.

"What's his deal?" I wondered aloud as we headed for the spare room.

Chance shrugged. "One problem at a time, Corine."

There would never be a better time to indulge my curiosity about something else. As we stepped into the bedroom together, I asked softly, "What were you focused on, back at the compound?"

Silence answered me, so I lay down, too tired to pursue the matter. Just before I drifted off, I wondered whether I imagined his whisper:

"You making it out of there, no matter what."

Enemy of My Enemy

Eva woke me at dusk.

My eyes felt gummy as I peered up at her. She gave me a shit-eating grin, and I realized Chance and I had twined together in our sleep. He always wrapped around me like a second skin. I used to sleep so well that way, and I had again this afternoon.

I crawled out from under him and slid off the bed. "Did you find something out?"

She led the way to the living room, where I encountered the unlikely sight of Chuch watching TV Azteca with Kel. Butch lay curled up on Kel's lap. I'd been too tired to fret about whether he'd keep his promise about not harming us or ours, but the last kernel of worry dissolved.

"Well," Eva began. "We found a place to start, at least."

"You're amazing!" I sat down on the edge of the couch. Butch leaped into my lap, and I stroked him absently. Before she could go on, Chance padded out and joined us, dark hair standing on end.

"Don't let me interrupt," he said with a sleepy smile.

She clearly wanted to share the minutiae of her search, so we let her. Truthfully Eva's thoroughness impressed me—she'd make a hell of a private eye—but I

wanted her to get to the meat of the matter. I restrained
my impatience.

"So," she concluded, "we need to hit La Rosa Negra.
According to Chuch's contacts, it's a hangout for—"
Eva dropped her voice so low, I didn't catch the name.

Chuch filled in the blanks. "Mercs, ex–Army Special
Forces. They used to work for the cartel, but word on the
street is they're independent now. They don't like people
poking around in their business, but they *might* be interested in selling information on Montoya, if we catch
someone at the right time."

"Sounds dangerous," I said.

By Chuch's expression, I'd earned a promotion from
Captain to Colonel Obvious. "No shit. They won't even
talk to you and Chance if I'm not there. People still remember me from Nicaragua." His dark gaze went to Kel
watching TV with Butch on his lap. "Cue ball should
probably stay here with Eva."

"You think I need a guard dog?" His wife bristled.

I grinned despite myself. "Butch or Kel?"

"Shhh," Chuch said. "You know I don't want you
coming with us because you're too beautiful, *nena*.
Some *pendejo* would hit on you, and then I'd have to
hurt him. Pretty soon the place'd be busted up and
crawling with uniforms before we learned anything."

"You're full of shit, you know that, right?" But I saw
he'd talked her out of going with us by her soft little
smile.

I probably could've taken offense that nobody thought
I was so hot I'd distract the mercs from conversation, but
I decided to let it go. I did okay, after all. Some guys dug
the long hair and hippie chic.

Eva's bean soup had been simmering for hours, so we
ate supper before getting ready to go out. I had a feeling
La Rosa Negra would be a dive, so I dressed accordingly:
worn jeans, peasant blouse, sweater in my bag just in
case. I was glad I'd managed to squeeze in some laundry.

"We set?" Chuch asked when we'd dropped the last bowl in the sink. I felt a little bad about sticking Eva with the dishes, but not enough to put off our errand.

"Yeah." I answered for Chance and me.

The mechanic fixed a narrow stare on Kel, who'd gone back to watching TV Azteca after the meal. "Anything happens to her, I hold you personally responsible, *primo*."

"I'll guard her with my life." Funny, when Kel said such things they carried the weight of a vow writ in blood on the pages of some holy book.

Butch yapped, but I shook my head. "No way," I told him as we went out the door.

Because he knew where we were going, it made sense for Chuch to drive. The Mustang was parked behind the Maverick, so Chance tossed him the keys. Like any conscientious short person, I crawled in back.

"How far are we going?" Chance wanted to know.

Chuch got us on the highway before he answered. "Near downtown. 'Bout twenty minutes, I guess."

I leaned forward. "Anything we should know?"

"It's best if you let me do the talking. Chance is here for obvious reasons." Yeah, I knew why—to make it more likely we'd run across someone willing to part with information on Montoya and to pay the bribe when we found the guy. "I think maybe we should've left *you* at home with Eva."

I snorted. Like I'd have gone along with that. I had too big a stake in this to permit them to form a boys' club at this juncture. Plus, you never knew when my gift might come in handy.

Before I could bitch, Chance shifted, elbow on the back of the seat, and put in, "Yeah. Those jeans are a felony."

"That bad, huh?" I glanced down at the worn denim. Chance never appreciated my sense of style.

A slow smile curved his beautiful mouth. "That *good*.

Do you know there's a rip on the back of your left thigh?"

"Ah, no." Great. Now I'd worry all night whether my ass was hanging out.

"Sexy," he told me. "Shows just a hint of skin."

I quirked a brow. "I thought you wanted me in suits from Lord and Taylor."

"Once I did. Now I just want you." Beneath the rumble of the motor and the rush of the tires against the pavement, his words crushed me with their candor. Need laced his tone, shot straight into my nervous system.

God, I hated that he could move me like this. My chest hurt, so I rubbed it, and then cursed silently when I saw his gaze tracking the movement like he'd kill to touch me again. For Christ's sake, why *me*?

My pained bewilderment must've shown because Chance turned around without another word. I stifled a sigh. Like too many dark chocolate truffles, he was rich, sinfully delicious, and bad for me. . . . His gift might *kill* me. I knew that, but I couldn't quell my longing altogether.

"We're almost there." Cutting in when he did, Chuch did me a favor.

I sat quiet as we drove the last few blocks and found a place to park. Even in the dark, La Rosa Negra didn't look promising. It appeared to be a crumbling stucco building painted an unlikely shade of green. To my surprise, shiny new cars lined the curb outside.

This wasn't just any seedy little corner bar stashed beyond a warren of one-way streets and seemingly pointless construction. The men who congregated inside had money to burn; they just didn't want to do it conspicuously. Our cherry Mustang looked right at home alongside the other sports and muscle cars.

I could guess what it was like inside. I'd been inside a dozen cantinas like this in Mexico City. Sometimes, on nights when dreams kept me awake, I wandered out into the neighborhood to nurse a beer, letting the susurration of other people's lives wash over me.

"Let's do this." Chance climbed out of the car and offered his hand, which I took.

He pulled me from the back seat easily. Whipcord built as he was, I didn't doubt he could carry me off like a Sabine woman, should he take a mind. I exhaled and took a long look at the Corona neon sign flickering in the window before calling myself ready.

Chuch was already headed for the door, paying us no attention. This appeared to be familiar ground for him. Maybe he even hung out here on his own when Eva let him.

To my surprise, the strains of Reik's *"Invierno"* greeted me when we walked through the door, a more soulful song than I expected to hear in such a place. Three couples danced to it in the small space before the bar. *Not* a boys' club.

As my eyes adjusted to the light, I took stock of my surroundings. Low ceilings were hung with amber paper lanterns, giving the room a warm glow. Scarred tables had clearly seen better days, and countless high heels had left their marks on the wood floor. None of the chairs matched, and the decor consisted of various neon signs. Apart from the painting of the maiden holding a black rose between her teeth, La Rosa Negra could've been transplanted to any border town.

Chuch was calling the play, so we followed him to a table. He signaled the waitress for a round while the regulars studied us. Guys dressed in black sat in groups of three or four; they didn't look likely to strike up a conversation.

"Do your thing," he murmured to Chance.

I had no idea what I should be doing, if anything, so I took my beer with a nod of thanks and waited for some sign from Chuch. He merely sat there, quiet, drinking, and looking watchful. I guessed you couldn't hurry something like this. Chance, on the other hand, fairly crackled with purpose. What must it be like to be able to focus your will and shake whatever you needed from the cosmos?

I listened to the music purring from the vintage-style Crosley CD player. As we waited, a mellow Franco De Vita ballad melted into Shakira singing "*Ojos Así.*" I'd never been able to resist its rhythm, but I tried to keep my butt-shaking to a minimum. The dancers broke apart and started gyrations that suited the tympanic melody.

Chance touched me on the arm. "I can do this and dance at the same time," he whispered. "You want to?" I must've looked astounded because he added, "I *can*, you know. I just never did. Not with you."

From his expression, he regretted it, but back then, he didn't want to lose control. After his lover died, he probably hadn't wanted to yield me that much, as if hiding emotion prevented it from being true. "You really think we should?" I asked.

It seemed a little unprofessional somehow. But maybe it would make us seem innocuous, as if we'd heard this place was a quiet place to dance, nothing more.

"Taking out the warlock gave us some breathing room. It will take his boss a good long while to find someone to replace Nathan Moon. We're better off now than we've been since I first picked you up. So, yeah, if you want to dance, we should."

Given this opportunity to see another side of him, I couldn't resist, not when the lyrics could've been written about Chance. I took his hand—five steps to the dance floor, and the world went away. There was just the rhythm and desperate longing in the singer's voice. To my surprise, he matched me with feline grace, moving in sensual lockstep. His hands framed my hips as our shoulders worked, our bodies a breath away from full contact.

Back and forth, eyes on mine, he showed me he *could*

cut loose. How fitting he'd chosen this song since I'd never in my life seen eyes like his. Tiger eyes, tawny, striated, and—right now—burning with heat, even though I wasn't wearing a tailored suit or expensive shoes. I was still Corine Solomon in ratty jeans, but have mercy, his look—

Ah, action. A guy who had been drinking alone shoved away from his table and made his way toward ours, where Chuch sat. This guy was small and thin, but I didn't make the mistake of judging him harmless. The man radiated coiled readiness.

Chance spun me out and back toward him. His arms came around me and I wound mine about his neck, undulating in tight metric shifts. I forgot why we were there. When he leaned down to kiss me, I forgot my own name.

Thankfully I did remember kissing him was a bad idea, so I danced away, shoulders rolling. I twirled in his arms and writhed with my back to him. That seemed safer for about thirty seconds—until he drew me to him and ran his hands down my sides. His hips cradling mine, he left me in no doubt how much he wanted me.

Jesus, who could've ever guessed Chance had this level of exhibitionism in him? He'd always been so tightly wound. By the time the song ended, I needed a cold shower.

I didn't ask for an encore, practically staggered back to my seat. We'd probably melted the polar ice caps. My ex followed, looking insufferably pleased with himself.

"I know you," the guy was saying to Chuch. "Managua, wasn't it? Been a long time, and I wasn't sure when you first came in, but . . . we did business."

And there it was—the fruit of Chance's luck. I supposed it made sense not to go poking around; Chuch had said these guys didn't like that. Instead, we'd get our information in a subtle way.

"*Sí.*" The arms dealer–turned-mechanic jerked his

head at the vacant seat. "Esteban, right? You brokered a deal for me, I think." I had no way of knowing whether Chuch remembered him, or if he was making an educated guess. "I'm out of the business now, but I don't mind buying you a drink for old time's sake."

The merc grinned as he sat, showing a gap between his front teeth. "If you're buying, I'll take a shot of Gran Patrón."

Nice. Esteban's taste in tequila impressed me. Since she was eavesdropping, the waitress went to get it without being asked. The rest of the patrons seemed to relax, losing interest when they realized we were a known quantity. I let out a slow breath.

"So what you doing now?" Chuch made the question casual.

The guy shrugged. "Whatever, you know? Mostly private security."

I could fill in the blanks.

The waitress delivered the tequila, Chance bought another round of beer for the rest of us, and the two across the table from us renewed their acquaintance. Casual stuff, guy talk, but I saw how Chuch was maneuvering the conversation. *Damn clever.*

"You know," the mechanic said at last, "I'm retired. But if a personal situation came up, if somebody crossed the line and messed with your family, what would you do, *mano*?"

A sharklike smile twisted Esteban's mouth. "First, I'd kill the guy who did it. Then I'd find the one who gave the order and make *him* scream."

Into the Breach

The CD ended, and the dancers went to order drinks.

Into the relative silence, Chuch muttered, "That sounds about right. I already got the hired gun. Now I'm looking for his boss."

"If I had a name, I might be able to help you." Esteban's sudden tension said we were on thin ice. If he worked for Montoya, we might find ourselves in the middle of a firefight, outnumbered and outgunned. Guys like these hired on with whoever paid best.

I sensed Chance's increased focus. We needed luck now more than ever, but would Chuch gamble on it?

"Montoya," he said finally.

"No shit." Esteban appeared relieved and took a sip of his Patrón to cover that. "Looks like we can do some business. See, I work for Escobar . . . well, way down the food chain, but I hear he's always happy about anything that fucks up a Montoya."

That seemed to imply there was more than one, but we were only interested in Diego, whose name we'd gotten from that poor girl. Otherwise, I didn't follow; nor did Chance by his expression. So we both sat and waited for Chuch to respond.

"Rivals, huh?" he grunted.

Esteban nodded. "I-35, among other things."

That was enough for me to piece things together. Escobar and Montoya headed up rival cartels, and that was *great* news for us. If this guy didn't know where we could find the son of a bitch who had Min, he might tell us who did.

I was impressed, but not surprised, that Chance sat quiet all this time, letting Chuch do his thing. Handsome as my ex was, you'd think he suffered from a surfeit of ego, but nope, not so much.

Chuch looked thoughtful. "This is a good deal for you, *mano*. If we mess him up, you tell your boss you played a part in it. If we get our cards punched, you know nothing about it. Should we talk terms?"

For the first time, Esteban asked about us. No introductions had been made until that point, but he was too smart to go forward without knowing all the factors in play. "Slow your roll, cuz. Who're your silent partners?"

"Friends," Chuch said without hesitation. "They got my back in this."

Chance didn't leave it there. "Montoya took my mother," he added quietly. "I don't stop coming for him until I'm dead, or he is."

You'd think a guy who worked for the highest bidder wouldn't give a shit about that. Not so. Esteban narrowed his eyes and slammed his fist on the table, drawing looks from the other patrons. He crossed himself and then spat as if to ward off a curse.

"*Mierda*," he swore. "Only sons of bitches go after women or children to get to us."

I decided not to counter his assumption that Montoya had a grudge against anyone other than Min. It seemed better to exploit his righteous indignation. If he found out Chance's mother knew dark rituals and how to summon the Knights of Hell, he might lose sympathy.

"True." Chuch finished his beer, and I noticed he'd been nursing the same one all night, probably to keep himself sharp. "How much will it cost to get you to send a question up the food chain for us?"

"One K for my time," Esteban said. "I'd do it for free, but . . . you know."

"No problem. A man has to know what he's worth." Chuch gave a half smile and peeled off ten bills from a roll he brought out of his pocket. "I'll leave you my cell number. Call me when you know something."

"It'll take time," Esteban warned us. "But we should be able to get you a list of their compounds. You'll have to figure out where he's taken her."

"Can do," Chance said.

He'd dowse the list for us. And if that didn't work, Booke might be able to scout them. Surely he could tell us where she was. For the first time, I didn't feel hopeless. With Montoya's pet warlock blown to shit, we had a real shot, assuming he hadn't killed Min days ago. If we couldn't manage salvation for Min, then we'd wreak vengeance, closure for Chance. I preferred the former, but I'd take the latter.

Esteban was still staring at Chance with an odd, haunted look in his dark eyes. "It happened to me too. My sister, Rosita." He brought a rosary from his pocket. "This is all I have left. They never found a body, just . . . this." By the pain I saw graven on his face, she never would've left it behind if she had a choice. It looked like a family heirloom.

I gazed at the antique silver necklace with a mixture of horror and resignation, knowing I might be able to touch it and give him an answer. Chuch offered a nearly imperceptible nod. Men who worked for the cartels would have seen many things over the years, most of them weirder or more horrific than what I did.

"May I see it?" I held out a hand, bracing myself. I knew it would be bad.

Beside me, Chance tensed, but Chuch checked him. Esteban seemed surprised but he passed it over nonetheless. A deep breath prepared me as best I could, and then I dropped the natural focus that prevented me from reading an object.

Pain seared me in black, licking waves. My vision flickered and spiraled inward, dumping me into Rosita's last moments. I felt her confusion and anguish as the man reared above her. I sensed her desperate desire to live while the agony of live wires sizzled in my palm. I bore it all—Rosita's pain and the anguish of my mother's death simultaneously. When I came to myself, I was weeping, the rosary on the table.

"What the . . . ?" Esteban took the necklace like it was a snake, staring at it in bewilderment. "Is she okay? Should I call a doctor?"

Chance was already getting some ice for my palm. He knew the drill. I hoped he had the balm somewhere in his pocket, as this had been a bad one.

For at least five minutes, my teeth chattered too badly for me to speak. Chance rubbed my back and tended my palm while Chuch asked me with his eyes what I'd seen. I didn't want to *do* this; Christ, I didn't want to tell Esteban. But maybe knowing would be better than uncertainty.

Through raw waves of nausea, I managed to say, "It was someone she knew. She wasn't afraid of him at first. He came to the door, they spoke, and she agreed to go with him. I can never hear what they're saying, but I recognized your name on the man's lips. I think he knew you too."

It would kill me to tell him the rest. My uninjured hand curled into a fist as I watched the merc's eyes close. His throat worked, but he didn't question what I knew or the manner in which I'd acquired the knowledge. His eyes opened. "Tell me the rest."

Chance rubbed my back. I drew in another steadying breath. "They got in his car. It was an old metallic green El Camino; she didn't notice the plates. He took her to . . . a lake. I think it was a lake."

"Lake Casa Blanca," Chuch offered, low. "It's the only one nearby, so it must've been, if it happened here."

Esteban sat as if he'd turned into a pillar of steel. "*Mierda*! I know someone who drives a green El Camino. I used to work with him. But go on."

I just couldn't go into detail, not aloud. It's bad enough I'll see this again and again in my dreams.

"He tried to kiss her. She slapped him. He . . . raped her. Hit her. Choked her."

He punched her in the face as he penetrated her, came just before she died. Poor Rosita hadn't even been spared that, clutching her rosary in bloody hands. It must have spilled onto the shore when he dragged her body into the water, and the bastard didn't notice in the dark.

"Tell me what he looked like," Esteban demanded. "I think I know who it was, but I want to be sure before I kill him."

"He stood a head taller than her," I said slowly, visualizing him in my mind's eye. "He wore a black jacket, jeans, white shirt. He had a heavy mustache, acne scars on his cheeks. And he had tattoos on his fingers. Letters. They spelled something."

"D-E-A-T-H," the merc said quietly. "He thinks he's a real badass, the right hand of death."

"If they search the lake, I bet they find her," Chuch put in. "I'm sorry, *mano*."

In answer, Esteban gave Chuch back the thousand bucks. "I would've paid a lot more to find out what happened to her." To my surprise, the small man hugged me around the shoulders, a short, hard embrace that almost hurt. "It's been years, but I know where to find the *hijo de la chingada*."

The bastard deserved to be called worse than that. I felt vaguely astonished at how readily he'd accepted my gift. Yet there was no other way I could've picked up on those details, especially the car and the man's description. Perhaps he'd seen other gifted at work.

"Good luck," I murmured as Chuch stood.

That didn't begin to encapsulate my feelings, but Esteban just studied me, as if he knew. "I'll be in touch." He folded to his feet as I did—a gentleman, oddly enough.

When we quit the bar, relief rushed through me. Who knew what might've happened if Chance hadn't been there, or Chuch?

We drove back to the house in silence, me nursing my sore palm, the guys lost in thought. A man would die as a result of tonight's work—no trial, no jury, just an execution. I had no doubt of it, but I didn't doubt he deserved it either, not after what I'd seen him do to Rosita—and probably others after her.

Before we went inside, Chuch checked the wards. Though the warlock was dead, we couldn't be too careful. As we came into the living room, we found Kel still watching TV. That made me smile despite the pain. He didn't glance away from the moving images on the screen. The light glazed his skin, cast his tattoos into sharp relief. Butch bounced around my ankles until I picked him up and scratched him between the ears.

Eva was in the office, doing more research on the Net. "I never knew it was so bad," she said as we came in. "It's crazy. Last September, gunmen burst into a club and threw five severed heads inside as a warning. The people who took Min are not fucking around."

I thought we'd established that. Then again, Eva hadn't *seen* some of the things I had. That made a difference.

"They've joined forces with malevolent powers." Kel spoke from the hallway. "Using demons and dark magick where simple force fails. If we do not stem the tide, they *will* consolidate their control over the country, and drugs will be the least of their crimes."

Was he thinking about the girls, stuffed into crates like so much produce? God knew they would haunt me.

Chance reached for me as if he sensed my thoughts. He hugged me around the shoulders and I leaned into him for just a moment. "Montoya owns IBC, doesn't he? Selling girls into slavery pays a whole lot better than waste management."

"I'm pretty sure he does," I answered. "That's the only connection that makes sense. But proving it would be harder."

Kel turned then and his smile chilled me. "We don't need proof. We need to know where he lives."

"I got that covered too, *primo*." Chuch grinned. "If I can't find out about it, it ain't worth knowing. Now I'm just waiting for Esteban to get back to me."

"You weren't the only ones who found something," Eva said with a smirk. "I called your cousin Ramón and asked him to go check out the address for the registered agent that fronts for IBC."

"Good thinking." Chuch took a seat in the recliner, leaving Chance and me leaning up against the wall, Butch nestled against my shoulder, and Kel listening from the hall.

"The place was totally ransacked." She clicked a few times on the computer and brought up a folder. "I downloaded some snaps from his cell phone before he left."

We all leaned over to take a look. Blood spattered walls, paper shredded all over the floor.

"Christ," I said. "It looks like somebody died in there."

"Probably the agent," Chuch said with a shrug. "With the warlock in charge of the operation gone, Montoya is cutting his losses and tying up loose ends."

Shit. Good thing we had another avenue open for finding Montoya. I hoped like hell Esteban would come through.

War Council

We sat around waiting for Chuch's phone to ring. I fed Butch, let him out, and then held him in my lap while others did the talking. I wondered if he missed Lenny.

Arguing passed the time best, and Eva was all over that.

"When we hit, I'm going too." She folded her arms and dared anyone to disagree. "I know how to handle myself." I expected Chuch might have something to say about that, but she went on. "And it would be stupid to leave me here by myself where anything could happen to me. At least if I'm with you, you can protect me, right?"

Oh, well played, Eva.

That silenced the rising protest from her beleaguered husband. I glanced out the window, saw the wide open sky fading to dawn—mauve, pink, and pearl streaks along the horizon. Like a nocturnal monster, I yawned. Man, my sleep schedule was all screwed up.

Still, we needed to lay our plans. Yesterday morning, we hadn't done such a stellar job of that, and only Chance's luck combined with Kel's berserker battle prowess carried us through. We couldn't count on that again.

Apparently Chance shared that opinion because he

said to Eva, "Get a pen and paper, will you? We need to talk strategy."

"Good idea!" She bounced to her feet, hurried to the kitchen, and returned, ready to take notes. I laughed softly at the idea of having an assault secretary.

"Here's what I have in mind." Because Chance thought better on his feet, he slid off the couch and paced the length of the living room. "Once I find the location, we send Booke in first to check for magickal traps."

"You should ask him," I pointed out.

He nodded in agreement. While Chance went to look for Booke online and Chuch checked his weapons cache, I ate a bowl of bean soup for breakfast. No one came to see about me. I sighed and took my bowl to the sink. I had a wounded palm and a festering zombie bite on my shoulder that needed tending.

Was it unreasonable of me to want Chance to put me first? The way he blew hot and cold comprised my chief objection to resuming our relationship. With that dance, I thought maybe he'd changed, but now I stood in the kitchen with a burned hand and no help. I knew he was worried about Min and wanted to be ready to move on a moment's notice. I got that, but I hated he hadn't asked if I was okay after all we'd been through in the last twenty-four.

Shit. Maybe I was just high maintenance.

Since everyone else was busy, I went around checking wounds. Chance waved me away; he was talking to Booke on IM. Well, fine, let him get gangrene. No help for it, I'd have to do for myself, so I headed to the bathroom. The bite on my shoulder looked puffy. It hurt when I poked it, but all I could think to do was slice it open and pour peroxide on it. I probably needed a tetanus shot.

Hesitating, I gazed at myself in the mirror. Didn't recognize the woman with the bruised eyes and cuts on her face. Only the long red hair looked familiar.

"You want me to?" Kel asked from behind me.

I froze, fixated on the knife in his hand. Maybe I had a death wish because I heard myself say, "Yeah, please. I don't think I can cut myself."

If he'd said, *My pleasure*, I'm sure I would've run screaming. Instead he set about sterilizing the blade. Then, with the precision of a surgeon, he made a small incision, opening up the inflamed skin. I tried not to think of the dead woman's teeth that had made those marks.

Not for the first time, I wished I had some kind of healing ability instead of the "gift" of being able to read objects. Part of me wished I couldn't do that either, but ambivalence crept in when I considered being without it. Good or bad, the touch defined me every bit as much as my blue eyes.

Could I actually *live* a normal life? And would it feel like giving up the last link to my mother if I did figure out some way to burn out this gift I never wanted?

It shook me, how ably Kel treated my wound. Such a fine line between killing and healing. One small slip of the scalpel and the doctor becomes the murderer. By the time he finished bandaging my shoulder, I could feel myself trembling.

"Thank you," I muttered, and ran for the kitchen, where I stood gazing out the window above the sink.

"You okay?" Eva asked.

I started and tried to pretend I wasn't edgy as a cat in a guitar shop. "I don't know," I said. "I feel like shit. I'm tired, and I want to go home, but I don't know if I've got one."

The shop might not feel the same when I got back to it. *If* I did. That seemed less and less likely as the days wore on.

"You'll always have a place here with me and Chuch."

Her offer surprised a sniff out of me. Kel and Chance

filed in just as we hugged. Chuch was still out in the garage, taking inventory.

Eva fetched her notes. "What did Booke say?"

A knock at the front door forestalled whatever Chance might have said. Though it was a warm morning, we had the curtains and storm door tightly shut, for obvious reasons. I unhooked the chain, turned the bolt, and peered out the screen door cautiously.

Jesse stood there looking like he'd lost his best friend. Dark smudges cradled his eyes, and he'd gone way past five o'clock shadow. The stubble on his chin had probably taken two days to accumulate. Since he didn't wear his badge clipped to his belt, I concluded his visit must be unofficial.

I didn't know where we stood. We'd kissed on the couch. Yesterday morning he had my face in the dirt, shouting at me not to make any sudden moves.

"Come on in." I stepped back.

What the hell would we do if he recognized Kel? The tattoos and the bald head were new, though. Maybe Jesse wouldn't recognize him without the mop of dirty blond hair.

Jesse paused just inside the doorway, took in the activity, and managed a smile. "Throwing a party and I'm not invited?"

I hesitated. "Not exactly."

"Look, is there someplace we can talk in private?" Saldana obviously lacked the mental energy to pretend he wasn't on his last legs.

Chuch called from the garage, "You can use the computer room."

As we went down the hall, I ignored the looks Chance and Eva gave me. Kel seemed to miss the undertones, or maybe he just didn't care. I went into the office, shut the door behind us, and dropped down into Chuch's plaid recliner.

Instead of sitting, Saldana propped himself against the wall and stared up at the ceiling.

"How bad was it?" I laced my fingers in my lap to combat the urge to touch him.

"Bad," he said heavily. "I'm on suspension, pending an investigation. I came out here because I did a little digging. Took me all night and a handful of favors, but . . . Moon was made, Corine. He started out in life as a Montoya, changed his name back in 'eighty-two. They got him on the force, and he'd been working for the cartels from the inside ever since."

Weird. It apparently bothered Saldana more that his partner had been dirty than the fact that he'd also been a warlock who bound people's souls to feed his own power. I nodded, listening.

"Anyway," Jesse went on. "I know you're planning a strike. I recognize a tactical meeting when I see one. My partner did a hell of a lot of damage, and I may lose my badge over it. If you're going over the border, I want in."

I thought long and hard about my reply. "You can't go as a cop. This is vigilante territory, Jesse. I don't know if it's a good idea."

He shrugged. "I don't care. I'm on leave, so this is for me and for Maris, who died because I couldn't see what was right in front of me. What's that they say? There are none so blind as those who will not see."

"You can't blame yourself for this. I'm just sorry it turned out like it did." My head started to throb.

A slow breath escaped him, like a balloon deflating. "You and me both, sugar."

"I bet you wish you never set eyes on me," I said quietly.

Jesse shoved away from the wall then, came toward me. I didn't know what to make of that until he knelt, took my hands in his where they rested on my knee. He bent his head and rested his brow on our joined fingers, oddly like an obeisance.

"No," came his muffled reply. "That's not what I wish."

I wanted to stroke his hair, but I'd put ointment on my palm not long ago. He probably wouldn't want that on his head, so I held still, listening to him breathe. This man would never hesitate to give me what I needed emotionally; to do otherwise would go against his very gift. I think he wanted me to ask what he wished. He was waiting for it.

When I didn't, Jesse pushed to his feet with a faint sigh. I held firm, though. This just wasn't the time to talk about personal affairs. With a faint flicker of regret, I followed him to join the others.

The day went slowly, but we had no way to motivate Esteban beyond what the information I'd given him should have already done. Since I'd been up all night again, I crashed on the couch with the others all around me, talking strategy. I woke in late afternoon to the sound of Chuch holding forth on why it was best to burn Montoya's compound to the ground once we found it.

After rubbing my gummy eyes, I pushed to a sitting position and took stock. Kel was the only one in the room, but the TV was off. Apparently he'd been watching *me* instead. That should have sent a cold chill through me, but he didn't terrify me anymore.

I must have a transparent face because he said, "They're in the kitchen. Esteban called five minutes ago. They faxed him the cargo manifest and he passed it along to someone in his organization who could make sense of it."

"Thanks."

"How's your shoulder?"

I wished he, of all people, hadn't shown concern. That softness humanized him in ways I didn't care to entertain. Since it was a good question, I slid the shirt from my shoulder, craned my neck, and examined the bite.

"Seems to be healing," I answered after a moment. "Is there anything I should know about an undead bite? I won't turn into a zombie by the next full moon?"

He actually gave a half smile. "Not as far as I know, but human bites *are* more likely to become infected."

"Noted. I'll keep an eye on it."

I felt like I should say something more, but damned if I knew what, so I just nodded at him in thanks and made my way into the kitchen. Chuch, Eva, Chance, and Jesse sat around the table, like when we'd held the séance, except Chance was staring at a list. The top seven things on it had been crossed off, with eight more to go.

As I knew better than to interrupt, I stood quiet and let him work. Energy tingled in the air all around him, like a localized static electricity storm. Touching him at this moment would render a shock on the wrong side of painful.

The Ortizes acknowledged me with eye contact, but they too found themselves rapt in the face of Chance's gift. Jesse simply gazed at me in silence, unsmiling. I suppose he had wanted to talk about things this morning, but if I wouldn't with Chance, it didn't seem fair to change the rules for Saldana.

I leaned in for a better look and found what looked like a roster of properties owned by Montoya. *Go, Esteban!* Chance went down the list, striking off five more locations with the pen in his left hand. The thirteenth, however—

"This is it," he said, tapping the page. "He's taken her there. I'm sure of it."

We finally had a location. With his pet warlock dead, Montoya would have lost all ability to block Chance's talent.

"I need to make some calls," Chuch said. "Lay hands on stuff I don't have in stock. I should be set within a few hours, though."

Saldana didn't say a word. He'd either silenced the

cop part of himself, or he no longer cared about the law that had let him down so profoundly with his partner. I couldn't worry about anyone but Min right now.

As part of my preparation, I wet my hair, braided it tightly, and then pinned the braids up. I couldn't do anything about the color on such short notice, not that I wanted to. I liked being a redhead. With a sigh, I peered into my jumbled laundry and decided on black: black jeans, black hoodie, sturdy black shoes. It was the best I could do.

By midnight we had all the cards in play. Chuch had rounded up the last of his supplies and Booke agreed to scout for us. It was time.

I freshened Butch's water, let him out in the yard, and then pushed him inside the front door. He stared at me with big, mournful eyes, but I didn't think he'd be an asset to the mission. Then again, I might not be either.

"Sorry, bud," I said. "Not this time. Wish us luck?"

He yapped once.

Good thing—we'd need it.

Montoya's Mountain

We crossed the border in Jesse's Forester. It made sense since we numbered six, plus all the gear. I huddled down in the back since I didn't have a passport. If I lived through this, I'd have Eva cook me one. Luckily, Jesse being a cop meant they didn't look too hard at any of us. Once we passed the second checkpoint, I sat up, uncovered my head, and leaned up against a duffel bag.

Nobody spoke much on the ride in, and I didn't blame them. So many things could go wrong out here. Montoya might burn our bodies in a giant pile and nobody would ever know the difference. My nerves vibrated like violin strings.

The dashboard clock showed nearly two a.m. by the time we neared our destination. Early morning in Great Britain. I rang Booke.

The man really didn't sleep. He sounded alert and eager when he answered. "I've had a chance to check out the location. I neutralized a few minor wards for you, but the man appears to rely on strength of arms and manpower for protection. I'm afraid you'll have quite a fight on your hands when you get in there. There's only one way up or down the mountain, unless you fly out."

"What else can you tell me about the way up?"

"Five kilometers on, there's a plateau where you'll have to leave the vehicle and proceed on foot."

That did it. When I got back to Mexico City, I was joining a gym.

Booke paused. "You *will* be careful, won't you, Corine?"

"As much as I can," I hedged.

"That's all I could ask then."

"Anything else you can tell me about the place?"

"Yes, actually."

Dutifully I relayed Booke's summary: gated entry, two sentries, more in the courtyard. Montoya's hideaway resembled a Spanish-style hacienda with breezeways and open courtyards. Regular patrols in the corridors.

When I'd finished, he murmured, "Call me when it's over?"

That too depended on the outcome, but it didn't hurt to accede. I disconnected and put my phone away, rose up on my knees to peer out the back window. Out here there were no lights, just an endlessly dark sky and the shadow of the mountains in the distance.

The Forester shuddered as we left the highway and took the dirt road. We slowed because it was rough, and we didn't want to break an axle. Hiking would take us all night. Jesse drove with both hands on the wheel, his expression grim. I caught myself studying him. What was he to me? Mentor? Friend?

"Glad we did some recon," Chuch muttered.

"We will be fine," Kel said calmly. "This is a holy cause."

What do you say to that, really? Everyone sat in silence until Eva pointed to a slight widening in the mountain road. "That must be it."

Well, it wasn't what I'd call a plateau, but we climbed out of the Forester and divvied up the gear. We hiked upward in single file, careful not to speak above a whisper. The air felt thin and cold.

By the time the gate came into view, I breathed shallowly so as not to give away how much I wanted to huff and puff. Since I was the only panda among long, lean wolves, I didn't want them knowing how out of shape I was.

To my surprise Chuch took charge. His hair bound back with a navy bandana, he seemed utterly at home. Maybe he'd led forces in Nicaragua too. At this point nothing could surprise me. "We need to get somebody inside quietly, someone who can kill in silence and open the gate for us without setting off any alarms."

"That would be Kel," I said at once.

God's Hand drew his slender silver knife. "Watch the doors."

The shadows took him. That's the only way I can describe it, because one moment he stood there with us, and one moment he was gone. Eva shivered. "I think maybe el Señor did send him, but *Dios*, does he have to be so creepy?"

No more than five minutes passed before the huge iron doors swung open. We didn't see Kel anywhere but that had to be our cue. Staying low, we clung to the walls and slunk inside, where we found him manning the sentry station. Kel pushed a button and the gate closed behind us while he wiped his knife clean against his pant leg.

"Good," Jesse said. "No point in alerting them."

Booke had said there were more guards in the courtyard but I didn't see any. Chuch followed my gaze around the tiled square. Only the fountain broke the silence. "Did you kill them all, *primo*?"

Expressionless, Kel asked, "Would you like me to?"

Before Chuch could answer, a shout went up from a man on one of the balconies. Shit, we'd been spotted. As he dove wide, pulling me with him, Saldana called, "Get down!"

Bullets bit into the ground where we'd been standing. With a wide smile, Chuch took cover behind a marble statue and returned fire in short, controlled bursts. One of the guys fell, striking the tiles with a heavy sound. Eva crawled to her husband's side and produced a slender, short-barreled weapon like she knew what to do with it. When she shot the next guy cleanly between the eyes, she proved she did.

"No joke, you can handle yourself," I muttered.

I couldn't hit the broad side of a barn. The best I could do with an automatic weapon was lay down cover, and after watching me fire at some cans in the field behind Chuch's house, they'd decided I shouldn't have a gun because I might hit our people with friendly fire.

The last of the guards fell with a gurgling cry. "We go room to room," Chance shouted. "Kill anything that fires on you. Use the radio only if you find Min."

He loped off in a crouching run. Though it shouldn't have hurt for him to leave me behind, it did, perhaps because it seemed so symbolic. I knew better than anyone that his luck might get me killed in a situation like this. Ironic— he could best safeguard me by staying *away* from me.

Eva and Chuch reloaded and made their way more carefully in another direction. Kel was already gone again in search of more sinners to punish. Jesse grabbed my hand and hauled me toward the east doors that led from the courtyard to the first floor of the house.

"You're with me. I'm supposed to be watching out for you." Saldana managed a smile. "That whole mentor thing."

Between gunfire and sparking lights, I couldn't tell where everyone else had gone anymore. I wasn't sure splitting up was the best idea, but we weren't fighting an army on a unified front. My heart beat like a kettledrum as I followed Jesse around the corner.

He'd traded his police-issue weapon for a heavy Colt .45. The gun shone in Jesse's hand, big and heavy enough to kill someone if he coldcocked him. I'd tucked an emergency grenade into my gear, which consisted of a Maglite and some bottled water. They didn't think highly of my martial skills, and rightfully so. I wouldn't chuck my grenade unless we needed something blown up, though. Like zombies. Or a wall.

The moment we slipped into the house, we came across two more guards heading for the courtyard at a run. I guessed they didn't know we were already inside. I dove behind an ornate, expensive sofa, and Saldana fired twice, the weapon thundering in the enclosed space. They both went down before they had fully registered our presence.

"Holy shit," I said, clambering to my feet.

His smile came a little easier that time. "Top of my class, marksmanship. Usually it's a paper guy that I shoot through the head, but same principle."

From other corners of the house I heard screams of pain, Chuch shouting in Spanish, and the staccato report of automatic weapons. Pausing by a window while Jesse scouted ahead, I caught a glimpse of Chance slipping through an open doorway across the courtyard, gun blazing. Then I remembered it was stupid to stand in front of a window at a time like this and dove around the corner.

"We should move along, see if we can find Min," I said. "Sounds like the others are cleaning house."

"You've got some scary friends, Corine."

If I hadn't been so nervous I would have laughed. He didn't know the half of it. Inside the house, someone screamed in pain.

Jesse shot three more guys and nearly took a bullet himself as we fought our way up the stairs. I tried to stay out of the way, but I did whack one with my flashlight as he stumbled past Saldana. He staggered and Jesse lashed out with a neat kick that sent him spinning over the railing. At the halfway point up the stairway, the lights showered sparks and gave out entirely. Finally, there was something I could do.

I turned my Maglite on. "Better?"

"Much."

The house had a strange, spooky air, the dark split only by my yellow beam. I heard staccato gunfire in the distance and screams that were often cut off abruptly. Around each turn I never knew what we'd find: bad guys, our crew, or nothing at all.

"Booke said the only other way off this mountain was to fly," Jesse whispered. "So he'll have a chopper somewhere on grounds and maybe a panic room. We should be looking for both."

That lit a fire under me. We searched room to room, looking for any sign of more kidnapped girls or Yi Min-chin. We found evidence of Kel's or Chance's passage in several corridors, strewn bodies and pools of blood where they had swept through and cleared the way for us. Jesse and I had covered almost the whole second story when we entered a lavish bedroom. It looked like a woman would sleep here, and as I stepped inside, I smelled Min's perfume, White Linen.

"She was here," I said. "I'm sure of it."

Saldana held the light for me while I searched. I went through the room like a blind person, touching everything. When we opened up the desk drawer, my fingers grazed a metal object that threw a spark.

"Something?"

Chance and Eva stood in the doorway. I hadn't noticed their arrival. Kel and Chuch crouched behind them, keeping watch for more of Montoya's men. The mechanic muttered beneath his breath about the need to hurry. "Yeah. Something," I replied.

Drawing a deep breath, I curled my hand around the pen, accepted the pain as the price of my gift. Agony sizzled through me, echoes of fire, and then I saw a simple image. Min sat at this desk, writing a note. I watched her, and then she rose, folded the thin paper into a tiny square, and slipped it into the frame of the painting that hung beside the window.

The pen slipped from my fingers, struck the floor. Wordlessly I beckoned to Jesse, who aimed the flashlight for me. My hands shook as I delved for what she'd left behind.

Yes, here.

In the circle of light I read her words with him. *The shepherdess.*

"What the . . . ?" I took the Maglite from Jesse and shone it around the room until I found a white and blue statuette on a high shelf.

"What did it say?" Chance asked.

I sensed his tension as he came toward me. I passed him the note as I moved toward the far wall. And the corridor exploded.

"Incoming!" Chuch shouted.

Oh, Christ, not fire. Not. Fire. Despite my near-prayer, the hall blazed, flames licking up the wall. Shit, they were trying to burn us out. Smoke filled the room in a deadly haze. Chuch fired at Montoya's men, who were running away. They'd turn this building into our pyre, which meant Montoya was safe somewhere.

Jesse had mentioned something about a panic room. Well, I needed to be there because I could feel terror rising in my brain, threatening my ability to think and reason. A scream caught in my throat, choking me.

I staggered toward the shepherdess. Min had found it important enough to mention, so I'd take a look at it if it was the last thing I did. And it might be.

Eyes watering, I reached up to the shelf and touched it. Tried to pick it up, but it wouldn't budge. The room swam, and the heat threatened to blister my skin. I could hear the others coughing. I pitched forward and the statue slid forward as in a groove. Through distance roaring in my ears, I heard a click.

Then someone said, "Corine found a door. Let's go."

If These Shadows
Have Offended

I did what now?

I felt dimly aware of an arm wrapping around my shoulders to guide me down some stairs, but I'd inhaled too much smoke to see anything but a bizarre whorl of messy colors. My flashlight spun around the walls until someone took it from me.

"Close the door!" I thought Saldana said that. "It's reinforced steel behind the plaster; it'll provide a fire break for us."

"Everyone okay?" I tried to ask.

One foot after the other. I could do this. We'd reached the bottom of the staircase before I had all my wits about me again.

"Chuch got burned." I heard Eva's voice, but I couldn't see her until the Maglite shone on her face, now covered with blood and soot. Her eyes glistened with tears, rage, or both. "I don't know how bad."

"Molotov cocktails are a bitch," Chuch grunted. "But I'm okay. Just need some aloe. Don't worry about me, *nena*. I'm tough."

If Chuch got burned, Kel probably did too. But nobody gave a shit about him. In a weird way, that saddened me.

She sniffed. "That's exactly why I worry about you. You're too 'tough' to admit how bad you're hurt."

Kel rejoined us then. I hadn't even realized he'd slipped off to scout. "It's like a vault down here," he reported. "There's another reinforced door down at the end of this corridor, and it's locked. Nothing else. There might be another exit from inside the room."

"Panic room. He probably dug himself an escape tunnel to where they keep the chopper," Saldana said. "I know I would."

"The *hijo de la chingada* better be in there," Chuch growled. "He owes me some skin and blood."

Chance had been oddly silent. I sensed his tamped fear and anguish, but we could only move forward. We'd find Min here, one way or another.

"I have a grenade," I said then. "Any way that'll get us through the door?"

"Not without a little luck," Chance said.

Saldana had the flashlight, so he shone it on my ex, and in the beam of light, I saw Chance smile.

So be it.

"Take cover in the staircase," Saldana ordered.

The others complied. I pulled the pin, took aim, tossed, and then dove around the corner. The subsequent boom certainly alerted Montoya that we'd found his hidey-hole, if he hadn't already fled, but we couldn't help that. Time to finish this: for Maris, for Lenny, for those unknown girls, and, not least of all, for Min.

When debris stopped raining down, other than a dusty trickle of plaster, Chuch led the way down the hall. To my disappointment, the metal door stood intact, charred but solid. Then Jesse ran the light along the edges where it joined the cement.

"I never would've believed it," Chuch said, jubilant. "The wall's starting to crack."

Thanks, Chance.

Eva took up his train of thought in the seamless way

married couples sometimes had. "If we put our backs into it—" She trailed off, probably thinking it was better we just got to it.

After a good minute of solid shoving, the plaster and cement crumbled away and the heavy door toppled inward. I shouted in warning, hoping Min would stand clear. As one, we rushed into the room.

Whatever I'd expected to find, it wasn't this.

Min stood in the center of a ritual circle, much as she'd done in the warehouse. The room swam with candles guttering like a host of mad fireflies. Bizarre runes adorned the simple concrete floor. Four men surrounded her, but none of them held weapons, and it looked very much like *she* was in charge.

"Thank the spirits," she said, as though she'd been expecting us. "Kill these sons of bitches, will you? I'm sick of their faces."

With that, she dropped the candle in her hands and dove wide.

Everything seemed to happen at once. As weapons sparked, lending the room a bizarre staccato flash, I dropped to the floor. I couldn't tell who was shooting whom, so I stayed down, listening to cries of pain and muffled thumps.

When Saldana swung the Maglite around the room, I found our people shooting at an empty tunnel. A trail of blood indicated we'd hit at least one of the men, but I didn't know where they'd gone. And then we heard the distant sound of a chopper powering up. Jesse had been right, it seemed.

Chance hugged Min hard without saying a word. Now wasn't the time for explanations. In the yellow beam of light, she looked exhausted and worn. We needed to get her out of here.

"We can't go back up," Saldana said. "We'll have to leave the way they did and hope for the best."

Dug from solid rock, the tunnel led deep into the

mountain and emerged some distance from the house, which smoldered behind us like a symbol of divine judgment. Chuch hissed through his teeth as we moved, and I guessed he hurt more than he'd let on. At some point, Chance had been shot in the upper arm, a flesh wound that would hurt like a bitch. If it had been any one of the rest of us, that person would probably be dead.

Min hadn't spoken, other than to thank us. She had a lot of explaining to do, but we were content to let her do so once we were safe, relatively speaking. As for me, I didn't have the breath to speak as we hiked back down the mountain. I felt numb.

By the time we reached Jesse's ride, Chuch looked greenish pale. Eva helped him into the back, where he leaned his head on her shoulder. The rest of them clambered into the vehicle, but Kel stood apart.

Our eyes met for a moment, and he inclined his head. His face bore faint burn scars now, but they looked ancient. He might heal, but he still suffered. And nobody cared.

Without a word, God's Hand turned and walked into the night. Our alliance had ended for the moment, but I suspected I hadn't seen the last of him. He'd spoken of a great evil, and we hadn't vanquished it, just sent it scurrying for cover. This felt like the first skirmish in a coming war, one I wasn't sure I wanted to fight.

I wanted what I'd always wanted—a normal life, my pawnshop, the freedom to drink too much tequila and dance like there was no tomorrow. Maybe I'd never possess the peace most people took for granted. That sounded like self-pity, so I quashed the thought in time to hear Chance ask:

"You're sure you're all right?"

"No permanent harm," Min assured him, but she would tell us nothing more until we were safe behind Chuch's wards.

Strange, after what we'd done, to have them wave us through at the U.S. border. Something like that should write its story on a person's face, but Jesse had a good, trustworthy mug, it seemed. He'd cleaned up with some bottled water, and they didn't look at the rest of us.

When we got to Chuch's place, Eva took him to their bedroom and bustled around gathering medical supplies while Jesse, Chance, and I sat in the living room with Min. Butch looked quite relieved to find me home. Well, he wasn't the only one. I checked his food, refilled his water dish, and let him out to do his business. *Nothing like a dog to ground you.*

I felt quite impatient by the time we all reconvened in the living room, where Min had insisted we wait. Even dirty and worn, she radiated the command of a small, implacable queen. Disbelief and love warred within me; I couldn't believe we'd saved her. I acknowledged then, as I hadn't before, that I hadn't thought I'd see her alive again.

"You have all earned my trust with your courage and your ingenuity," she said at last, "and so you have earned my secrets."

"It's about time." Chance smiled to show he was joking. Mostly.

Being uninjured, I took a seat on the floor and listened.

"Long ago, a lifetime ago, I practiced the art in Seoul. I made potions and charms, removed curses. To some I am a witch, a sorceress, a healer, a shaman." She lifted her shoulders to show that the name made no difference to her. "But I did *too* well, and I gained renown. A local crime boss noticed me and wanted me to work only for him, only against his enemies and on his orders. He took me, kept me against my will." Her nose wrinkled, as though the memory held an unpleasant smell, even now. "I did not like living as a slave."

"What happened then?" I prompted, hardly aware I'd done so.

Min flashed me a smile, one warm enough to melt the ice caps. "He was part of an operation that smuggled girls to other countries. Mexico. I managed to hide myself with them, and that was how I ended up in Nuevo Laredo, where I slipped away from the guards one night. But I had no money, and I could not hope to survive without a nest egg, so I begged work from Dr. Rivera."

All the pieces started to click. Chuch and Eva did not speak, nor did Saldana. I expect they thought this tale belonged primarily to Chance and me.

My ex ran a gentle hand over his mother's hair and murmured, "Yes, I know."

She continued as if he hadn't interrupted. "At first I simply lay low and brewed potions and tinctures in the back room of his clinic. I rented a room above one of the brothels and thought only of hiding. But slowly I came to care about the girls for whom I made the medicines." Min exhaled shakily, staring at her hands.

"Of course you did." I knew better than anyone what a loving heart she had.

"When one of them came to me, weeping, I did what she asked. She said her lover had got her with child, but once she had the baby, her patron would steal her son and leave her to starve. She'd claimed a *bruja* had seen it in some bones. I did as she asked."

Eva spoke for the first time, murmuring, "You made a potion to abort the child."

"I did." Min lifted her chin. "She had no money for a doctor. It was her choice."

"Montoya's son," I guessed aloud. It was the only thing that made sense.

"Yes. He has been seeking me all these years." Her shoulders lifted in a helpless shrug. "If I had known the extent of his tenacity, I would never have returned to Texas. I thought he would've given up long before now. It has been so many years."

"There's got to be more to it," Saldana said.

"He murdered the prostitute who refused to bear his child," Min replied. "But as she lay dying, she told him she had hired a *bruja* to hex him—he would never sire a living heir, and the empire he had carved from his countrymen's bones would crumble to dust. He is an old man now, and still he has no sons."

"He thought you worked the curse." Chance's tone left no room for doubt. "That's why he wouldn't kill you until you removed it."

"It wasn't me," she said, spreading her hands. "There is no curse, unless you count the magick of a dying woman's promise. But he believes. The power of the mind is a strange and wondrous thing."

"What were you doing in the warehouse?" I asked, diffident.

"Before I agreed to 'remove the hex,' I forced them to take part in a ritual that prevented them from striking at Chance, my only son. I thought it wise since they would eventually discover I have no power to impact Montoya's inability to sire children, and Diego can kill me only once." Her dark gaze hardened. "No matter. The spell is binding. Hell itself will come for them, should they renege."

Eva smiled at Min. "Then you stalled. You needed rare ingredients, or the moon wasn't right, or Montoya must have a cleansing fast and a purifying bath of goat's milk—"

"You are a smart woman," Min said in an approving tone. "But the time came when it worked no longer. I was faking it when you finally arrived." She managed another smile for Chance. "You had me worried."

A witch was only as good as her ingredients, after all. And they wouldn't have permitted her anything they didn't control.

"Sorry about that," he murmured, low. "We got there as fast as we could."

Min hugged him. "I know. I'm glad you went to get Corine. You had brooded long enough."

There wasn't a lot to say to that, and I was exhausted. My jaw practically unhinged on a yawn. That seemed to be the cue everyone had been waiting for.

Jesse asked me to walk him to the door, where he kissed me. Not a lover's kiss, but not an innocent one either. I touched a fingertip to my lips and watched his taillights trail away into the glimmering, predawn air.

As though she'd spoken enough, Min quietly claimed the bed Chance had slept in, which left the two of us on the couch. We sat, too sore to move. His wound needed cleaning, but I couldn't bring myself to do it, not when he'd forgotten mine the day before.

I remembered I needed to call Booke. It would be early afternoon there. I dialed.

He picked up on the first ring. "Corine? What happened?"

"We saved her," I whispered, delighted to be able to say it. "We weren't too late. And we're all more or less in one piece."

"Thank God." What a lovely, plummy voice he had. "And thank *you* for calling me. I've been entirely on pins and needles since you rang off."

I felt like I was going to pass out, so I hung up shortly thereafter. There would be consequences from tonight's work—and Montoya's retribution—but I was too tired to worry about them right now. I put my head back and closed my eyes.

"You kept your promise," Chance said softly. "Now it's time for me to keep mine. And I will, whatever the cost. But I need to know, Corine. Will you come back to me?"

My gut response was *Hell no*, but my heart said, *Oh yes*. Aloud I said nothing at all.

ACKNOWLEDGMENTS

First, I'll thank everyone who contributed to this book: my husband, Andres, who read the first draft; my agent, Laura Bradford, who didn't think she'd like it (then she did); and of course, the wonderful Ivette, who gently corrected my Spanish. I also can't forget the talented staff at Roc. Once again, Anne Sowards has turned my coal into a diamond.

Next, I should mention the people of Mexico, who charmed and informed me. I did my best to capture the magic of living as an expatriate in Mexico City. Many of Corine's observations come filtered through my eyes. There's a rich tapestry of belief in the supernatural running in an odd lockstep alongside Catholicism, and people are generally more accepting of the mystical and/or inexplicable there. There is a whole town of witches and warlocks in Catemaco. In fact, there's a precendent for the cartels hiring *brujos* to work hexes as they would hit men to kill. I tried to be true to the many stories I heard from friends and relatives. Any mistakes or liberties are my own.

Finally, I must thank my readers. I'd be nothing without all of you. I welcome your letters and appreciate your support more than I can say. I hope you enjoy the world I've created.

Turn the page for a sneak peak at the second novel
in the Corine Solomon series, *Hell Fire*

Home Again

I'm still a redhead.

Before we left Texas, I touched up the roots, and then I had some tawny apricot highlights put in. I guess that meant I intended to keep this color for a while. Symbolic—I'd made a commitment, at least to my hair.

Too bad I couldn't do the same with Chance. I didn't trust him entirely, and what was more, he didn't trust me, either. He secretly thought I'd leave, which I had done; die, which I'd *nearly* done; or break his heart. I just hoped I wouldn't combine the three.

Until we resolved the conflict between us—such as his luck, which might kill me, and the former lover he wouldn't talk about—I couldn't be more than a friend to him. He knew it too. I think he'd known as much even when he pressed the point back in Laredo.

The Mustang purred along, emphasizing Chance's silence. He wasn't happy about this trip to Kilmer, Georgia, but he'd promised, and I wanted answers. He owed me.

When he'd shown up at my pawnshop in Mexico City, asking for my help after our breakup eighteen months before, I agreed because he swore to turn his luck toward helping me find out what happened the night my mother died. This point was nonnegotiable. I needed to

understand why it happened, and who was responsible.
I wanted justice for her death. Now that I'd fulfilled
my end of the bargain in Laredo, he was keeping his
promise.

We passed the woods that encircled the town.
Sometimes, when I was a kid, it had seemed to me that
someone simply burnt a patch out of the forbidding
forest, and there, Kilmer had been built. Over long
years, the trees grew back in around it, overhanging the
rutted road.

With the windows open, I smelled dank vegetation
heavy in the air, and pallid sunlight filtering through the
canopy overhead threw a sickly green glow over the car
as Chance drove. McIntosh County didn't get snow or
earthquakes, and the median temperature was sixty-six
degrees. It was also deeply historical, containing forty-
two markers. I knew all about local history: how old
Fort King George was built nearby in 1721; how the
Highlanders voted against slavery in 1739, not that it
did them any good in the long run; and how the War of
Jenkins' Ear motivated early settlers to attack Spanish
forts. There were still ruins on Sapelo Island.

Just a piece up the road, there lived the only known
band of Shouters, a Gullah music group. I'd seen them
perform the ring shout once at Mount Calvary Baptist
Church. I couldn't remember which foster parent had
taken me; there had been so many, and most of them had
thought I could benefit from religion in some form or
another. On paper, this seemed the perfect place to live,
steeped in cultural heritage and tradition.

On paper.

In Kilmer, the rules of the Deep South lasted long after
laws and social expectations changed in the wider world.
White men did as they pleased, and everyone else kept
their mouths shut. I couldn't rightly say I'd missed it.

"This place has a weird feel," Chance said, breaking
the silence at last.

"You're getting it too?" I'd always thought it was the trees, but we'd passed beyond them. Now only scrubby grass lay between us and the weathered buildings of town. Overhead, the sky glowed blue and white; it was a pretty, partly sunny day that should've warmed me a lot more than it did.

"Yeah." Before he could say more, a dark shape darted in front of the cherry red Mustang. Chance slammed on the brakes, and only the seat belt kept my head from kissing the dash. The car fishtailed to a stop.

Butch whined and popped his head out of my handbag. He was a blond Chihuahua we'd picked up along the way; I'd resigned myself to keeping him, but I hoped we hadn't scared the shit out of him. I had important stuff in my purse. I soothed him with an absent touch on his head, my heart still going like a jackhammer.

"What the—"

Chance motioned me to silence as he got out of the car. Hands shaking, I needed two tries to do the same. I checked the back, staring into the dead air beneath the tunnel of trees. Black skid marks smeared the pavement behind us.

He knelt and peered under the Mustang. Despite my better judgment, I joined him. Butch hopped down and backed up three steps, yapping ferociously. A low animal growl answered him.

Near the tires, a big black dog lay dying—a Doberman. We hadn't hit him, but all the blood oozing out of his ragged wounds told me he wasn't long for this world. He'd come from the tall grass that lined the road, or maybe from the trees beyond the field. A hard shudder rocked through me, and the air turned as cold as a northern winter night.

"Something got at him," Chance said finally. "Are there bears here? Wolves?"

I had no idea. I wasn't a wildlife expert in any location, and I hadn't been back to Kilmer in nine years. Things changed; habitats evolved. But times must be tough if wild animals had been forced to resort to hunting dogs.

I couldn't seem to look away from the shadow-dark flesh. The animal gave one final whine, as if he understood we couldn't help, and then he died. I saw the moment his eyes went liquid still, living tissue reverting to dead meat. There was a blood trail we could follow, but I didn't think that was a good idea. *Sizable claws created those wounds; nothing we need to mess with just before nightfall.*

I glanced down at the Chihuahua as he sniffed around next to my feet. "What do you think? Do you smell anything you recognize?"

He yapped twice. *Hm, so it probably wasn't a regular wild animal.* I shivered, wanting nothing more than to get off this road.

We'd acquired Butch after his prior owner was killed, and we were astonished to learn he could communicate on a basic level. There was something special about him for sure, but I had lacked the opportunity to investigate what his other talents might be. This certainly wasn't the time.

Never one to miss an opportunity, Butch scampered into the weeds and did his business. I exhaled a long, unsteady breath, and then pulled myself to my feet using the Mustang's hood. If I believed in omens, we were off to a hell of a start.

Chance went to the trunk and wrapped his hands in rags used to wipe off the oil dipstick. Before we left Laredo, Chuch—our mechanic friend—had taught him how and threatened to beat him if he didn't look after this car properly. So far Chance was doing fine.

Wordlessly, he reached under the chassis and towed the carcass to the side of the road. Without a shovel, that was really all we could do, but I appreciated the kindness. Otherwise, that poor dog would be splattered all over the road when the next car came, and he had suffered enough.

Even if we did have digging tools in the car for some unlikely reason, I wouldn't have been interested in hanging around. My intestines coiled into knots over the idea of losing the light out there, within a stone's throw of those dark trees. The whorls on the bark resembled demonic sigils in the wicked half-light, and the long, skeletal limbs stirred in the breeze in a way I simply couldn't like.

There was a reason I hated these trees. I'd hid among them while my mother died.

While Chance took care of the dead dog, I gave Butch a drink and tried to reassure him that he wasn't doomed to suffer the same fate. His bulging brown eyes glistened with what I'd call a skeptical light as I hopped back in the Mustang. Chance joined us shortly, working the manual transmission with a dexterity I couldn't help but admire.

"What a welcome." He shook his head.

"Tell me about it." As I said that, we passed a faded white sign that I knew read WELCOME TO KILMER, HOME OF THE RED DEVILS AND THE WORLD'S BEST PEACH PIE.

"Think anyone will recognize you?"

I shook my head absently, taking in the familiar sights. It was bizarre. The road into town hadn't changed at all. Ma's Kitchen, an old white clapboard restaurant, still sat just outside the city limits. The shopping plaza on the left had been given a face-lift—fresh paint and new lines in the tiny parking lot—but the general store, the dry cleaner's, the Kilmer bank, and a coffee shop still occupied it. The names on the dry cleaner's and coffee shop had changed, but otherwise, the town seemed just as I'd left it.

If we stayed on this street, we'd wind up in the town square, where the old courthouse reigned like an aging duchess who refused to admit her day had passed.

The clock on the tower hadn't worked since before I moved away, and I couldn't imagine, given the faded air, that they'd come into the money to fix it since. The "historical" district simply contained the oldest houses; most hadn't been restored.

But Kilmer retained a certain turn-of-the-century charm, if you didn't know what lurked beneath its exterior. I recognized Federal-inspired houses with their rectangular structure and slim, delicate iron railings; those stately old dames mingled freely with Georgian homes with hipped roofs and quoins.

Most of those neighborhoods exuded a genteel aura of decay. The streets hadn't been paved in a long time; they were faded to the pale gray of rotting teeth from years of neglect, and Chance had to turn smartly to avoid the deep potholes.

"It seems sadder," I said at last. "Smaller."

"Well, you're older now." To his credit, he didn't say I was bigger. That would've earned him a slap upside the head.

Anyway, I *wasn't* bigger. I still needed to lose a few pounds, but I'd been pretty chunky at eighteen when I climbed on that Greyhound bus. At the gas station–cum–video store, I'd begged a lift from a farmer headed into Brunswick. I'd known buses ran from there, so I'd used my school ID to get a discount ticket and I rode all night. The next morning, I got off in Atlanta with just a backpack and a few dollars in my pocket.

My chest felt tight, remembering. I'd gotten work at a used bookstore the following day. The owner had felt sorry for me, I think, but I loved that job. I rented a room in a boardinghouse, and I was happier than I'd ever been in Kilmer. I had been sadder than Roy to see the bookstore go under. With no friends and little money in the bank, my life took a turn for the worse. I'd left Atlanta with only enough money for a bus ticket, and things went south from there.

But I didn't want to think about that.

By the time Chance met me, I'd put myself back together somewhat. But I'd held eight different jobs in half as many years, and I seldom stayed in one place for long. There was nothing like running from your memories while trying to fit in, though I never made it. People always seemed to suss out that I wasn't quite like them.

It was more than the scars on my palms that came from a gift I didn't want. My mother's death stayed with me in the form of the pain that subsumed me each time I read a charged object. There was a name for what I did. Most people called it psychometry; *I* called it a curse.

For years, I tried to forget.

When Chance came into my life, he changed everything. But I wouldn't think about that, either. Sometimes the past needed to stay buried; it was the only way you could move on. And sometimes you had to dig it up, because that too was the only way.

For my mother's sake, I had to deal with what'd happened in Kilmer. I'd find answers about the men who came by night to our house and burnt the place with her trapped inside. I'd discover why. Maybe then the dreams would stop. Maybe then she could rest. In the twilight, the town looked so quiet, almost peaceful, but to me, it hid a fetid air. Corruption fed in the stillness, like a pretty corpse that, when split open, spilled out a host of maggots.

I'd be the knife that cut this place wide and the fire that burnt it clean.

In her life, Ann Aguirre has been a clown, a clerk, a voice actress, and a savior of stray kittens, not necessarily in that order. She grew up in a yellow house across from a cornfield, but now lives in sunny Mexico with her husband and two adorable children, who sometimes do as they are told. You can visit her on the web at www.annaguirre.com.